You Do Not Have to Say Anything

You Do Not Have to Say Anything

Nick Wilson

Matador
Unit E2 Airfield Business Park,
Harrison Road, Market Harborough,
Leicestershire. LE16 7UL
Tel: 0116 2792299
Email: books@troubador.co.uk
Web: www.troubador.co.uk/matador
Twitter: @matadorbooks

ISBN 978 1803130 026

British Library Cataloguing in Publication Data.
A catalogue record for this book is available from the British Library.

Printed and bound in the UK by TJ Books Limited, Padstow, Cornwall
Typeset in 11pt Minion Pro by Troubador Publishing Ltd, Leicester, UK

Matador is an imprint of Troubador Publishing Ltd

In memory of Deborah Ann Riley

PART ONE

1

'So. What's your evidence?'

I have this silly smile. It won't stay down. It's like a thick, new mattress. You could jump up and down on my mouth today, wearing your heavy boots; it'd still spring back up. It's making it hard to apply my lipstick.

'I mean,' he says, and leans forward in his chair to be earnest. 'Marriage is quite a serious offence. You can't just go around accusing a man of inciting marriage. You need proof.'

Rashid, ambitious learner detective and tired and cash-strapped parent, believes he married too young. I squidge my lips and face him.

'Is it "incitement"? If my fella writes in the sky with a plane, "Marry me, Ruby!"? Or if, in front of a tropical sunset, he carves it in the sand as I look down from my cliff-edge balcony? Is it "incitement" if he bribes the cast of my favourite soap to turn to the camera, at the moment I'm most agog, and say it on his behalf?' I've been reading quite a lot about

3

marriage proposals and I know these have all taken place somewhere in the world. 'Or is that "soliciting" marriage?'

It's only been two months since we passed our detective's exam. Already the knowledge is fading.

Rashid reclines in his chair to consider. 'Abet. Counsel. Procure… Or "attempt"?' He perches on the edge of his seat. 'If Jools has bought a ring but hasn't yet offered it to you, is that "more than merely preparatory" to committing the choate offence?' He nods at the cupboard under my desk where he knows I've hidden this month's *Berkshire Brides*. 'Before he makes his move you should consult your manual and decide how you're going to react. If you accept him, then you may be involving yourself in a conspiracy.'

'Why are you still here?' I ask him. 'You've been doing this for free since 5.30.'

He sighs. 'Because if I go home now there'll still be time to take my mother-in-law to the Thames Frockley Flower Show. It's the grand opening at seven. One of her favourite royals has come to cut the ribbon. Besides,' he says, and turns to look at the door, 'I'm waiting for the files to arrive. Wanna prepare for the coming week.'

There's a loud garrotting sound behind us. *Eye-ah!* We glance towards the DI's little glass office where DS Teague is standing in the doorway, her head held at a tilt to one side. She's grinning at him coyly, like she wants to show that she's picked up on his double entendre. But she's mistaken. The DI isn't like that. *Eye-ah!* So that was the sound of her laugh. A relief. Sounded like she'd accidentally looped her lanyard round the door handle and someone had shut the door.

My eyes meet Rashid's. He whispers. 'Why would anyone transfer from the Met to Cattlegreen? Nothing ever happens here.' He takes another look at her. 'I think she's harbouring a secret.'

I have a notification. Jools.

On my way. Pick you up in fifteen. :)
Love you so much. xxxxxxx

I have a flashback to something we did last weekend in bed. Before I met Jools I'd never have guessed that such an activity could be enjoyable. Now I can't get it out of my mind. These flashbacks are becoming a problem. I had one yesterday, when I was in someone's home, supposedly taking their statement. I ended up… *Oh, please, God, I didn't.* I don't want to think about it. *Oh, I must be losing my…* But tonight I can't be embarrassed. I'm too happy. My wince loosens. I feel like I'm floating at the top of a very long thread, like my chest's crammed full of balloons, and if I say anything it'll come out all squeaky, like I'm a character in some TV programme aimed at the under-fives.

'Oh God.' Rashid sees my skipping-rope smile hanging once again, gormlessly, between my ears. 'Jools, bruv. This is a lifetime commitment. Consider!'

I laugh and tap my phone. 'This is my evidence. He's coming to "pick me up"!'

Rashid frowns. 'So?'

'He's coming to meet me at the nick. He never does that!'

'And…' he slides his eyes to the side, 'this means you're going to get engaged?'

'He's not even letting me go home to get changed. It's going to be tonight, I know.'

'Right.'

I read an article last week which I found comforting. *Will My Man* Ever *Pop the Question?* It said that sometimes it's the guy who needs you most who takes the longest time to propose. His heart is set and his mind is certain, he's just too afraid you'll say no. Or it might be that his *method* of proposal – which, although it needn't 'necessarily' cost the earth, should be in public and at least bold enough to excite well-wishes from strangers for it to rank as a true love-event in a woman's life – takes a lot of time to plan or save up for. Practical advice was offered on how to remain stable mentally during the wait, and there was a list of the telltale signs that your man is working up to something. Among these were 'breaking with routine behaviour', 'more than usual hand-holding' and 'demonstrating a high regard for the institution of marriage'.

'We saw *Bridesmaids* the other night and, during the wedding scene, he, like, *really* squeezed my hand? Like, y'know, significantly? And he got quite stroppy when my mum led the three cheers at Aunty Rita's divorce party. "The way your mum and her sister carry on,"' I impersonate his considered, courtroom way of speaking, '"anyone would think that marriage is the family curse." And, well, yeah, basically, he's a really epic guy.'

Rashid stares at his computer and nods. 'Does Jools actually speak like that?'

'What? Yeah. He's proper. And prim.'

'"Prim and proper", I believe, is the idiom.'

'Yeah, that.'

He nods again. 'That's your case?'

'Well… yeah.'

'Mmm. I wouldn't take it to CPS just yet. Ah!' The porter

appears, pushing a trolley of files. Rashid sits up and rubs his hands. 'What have we here?'

He goes to the trolley and bends to examine the bags. Focused, intent, he reminds me of my lurcher snuffling a tree stump. I've started to tidy up my nails, now that my lips are sorted, and to try to piece together what's going on behind me in the DI's office. I gather DS Teague has spotted the photos of his grandchildren.

'Awww. Look a'da liddoo faces! Aren't they bwoodifoo at that age? Mine are nine and ten. Little people in their own right. All as it should be, only now I just don't want to bite their bums.'

I pause my filing. Did she just say her kids are nine and ten?

'Usual suburban rubbish.' Rashid tuts and reads from an MG5. '"Three-nines call was placed at 01.40. Complainant reported she had received a text from her husband: 'The secrets end tonight.' The call handler could hear smashing glass, and the complainant relayed that her husband was trying to climb through the window. Upon police attendance at 12 Smithy Forge, Fountainford, Adrian Carmichael, thirty-seven, was found hiding in a bush in what was discovered to be his wife's lover's garden. At his feet was a golf club. Parked nearby was his car, in which arresting officers found a kitchen knife wrapped in a tea towel."'

I pout. 'What did he have to say for himself?'

'"In interview the suspect made no comment regarding the offences but submitted a prepared statement: 'I met my wife on the balcony of our council block in Bermondsey. We were sixteen years old. On our first date she told me that she'd like one day to live in a big house in suburbia. I left school the very next day and set to work to make it happen. I learned a trade and built a firm, and on the 12th September 2000 we got married at St Mary the Virgin in Rotherhithe. We said that day that we'd stay true to each other. I now live with my wife and children in our home in Cattlegreen. For twelve years I've worked fifteen hours a day, six days a week so that we can afford it. I was informed yesterday that my wife has been having an affair for two years…'" Hmm.' Rashid strokes his chin. 'He's got no previous convictions. Bit of an overreaction, though, don't you think? Knife? Golf club?'

I look over my shoulder. DS Teague is putting on her coat. Need to be careful here.

I was brought up in a part of town where the customs and practices predate the latest Home Office policies and the up-to-the-minute thinking of the West Thames Police. Where I come from, most of the grown-ups still believe that a relationship is the most valuable asset you can have. In terms of what is important in life, nothing else comes close. Your better half's a basket in which to hold all your eggs. That other, more reliable, potentially more lasting brands of happiness are available nowadays seems to have quite passed some of them by. So that, if a Mrs Carmichael were to play away on my estate, a Mr Carmichael might think she and her lover were tinkering with what he stood for, playing fast and loose, perhaps, with his point of being alive. Kitchen-knife-and-golf-club-grade response proportionate, some might say in my manor. Did what any man would.

Not saying I agree. Wouldn't say so if I did. What we're dealing with here is domestic violence, or something connected to it. And at Cattlegreen Police Station you don't expend resources seeing things from a suspect's point of view;

not where DV's concerned. Certainly not before DS Teague has left the building.

'Well,' she says, passing our bench, 'starving mouths to feed.'

She does this, I notice. The shift is over but she can't just say goodnight and go. She has to give an explanation as to why she's not doing more work. Like the only reason she's leaving the office before me and Rashid is her other pressing responsibilities. I'm not even pretending to work. In five minutes Jools will be picking me up. And he's deliberately not said where we're going!

'Sarge?' Rashid calls out. He gets away with 'Sarge'. A couple of weeks ago – you'll start to think I've got it in for the DS, but I promise I shan't go on – a couple of weeks ago, on the day she transferred here from London, I greeted her with, 'Hi, Katie!' She stared at me and said, 'It's DS Teague.' When I reminded her we'd been together at police training college she tutted at her forgetfulness and gave me a watery smile. But she's never said, 'Call me "Sarge".'

'Why's this come to us? Carmichael?'

She comes a bit too close to him, colliding with his personal space like it's something solid parked in between them, with the effect that it shunts his head back half a foot.

'I mean, where's the investigation? We've got the texts, we've got the weapons, we found him at the scene. What more are we looking for?'

'It's not Mr Carmichael we're after.' She picks up the file that was underneath the one that Rashid has. 'It's Mrs Carmichael we've got.' She touches his hand as she points. 'That's just background. Mister's made cross-allegations. Appears she's been fleecing his company in order to keep her lover in the manner to which she's made him accustomed.' As it glides from Rashid's face to mine, her feverish man-smile transitions, loses heat, and lands with ice-tipped wings. 'You just can't trust some women.'

My nail file grates to a halt. *You just can't trust some women.* My mouth opens. I'm about to ask her to repeat what she said but she's on her way to the door, profiling her smile as she goes. *Flipping heck.* She's jumped on the first passing bandwagon. She's only been in Cattlegreen five minutes.

Rashid tries to make eye contact.

'Interesting, Mr Carmichael's prepared statement,' I say, swerving my colleague's sympathy. 'Giving the date he got married, naming the church. Is he asking us to check up? It's like he thinks he has authority to act this way; that he's got the law on his side.'

'Unfortunately for him, not the kind of law you get in police stations.'

'No,' I say. 'The law they made with their vows.'

Married. Church. Vows. The words stack up like a little heap of winnings. Once again, my lips bend back into shape. DS Teague is out of my mind, and in her place is the thought of a sunny day in a big dress. The peal of bells, raining confetti, relatives weeping with joy. All soon to be mine. Marriage. For which all else has been training. A wedding. The day my life goes live. Can't wait any longer. I'm off to be with my man.

I'm gathering my stuff when the phone rings. Rashid and I share the telephone; it stands midway between us on our desk. I wait to see if he'll answer it but he's engrossed in the Carmichael file.

'Hello.'

It's Zuzanna at the front counter. 'Ah, zere's a lady here... Vould like to report a crime.'

Zuzanna's not been with us for long.

'Are you going to take down the details?'

'Ah...'

'Then they'll allocate the job in the morning and—'

'She vould like to speak to a detective.'

'There's only me and Rashid left here and we're both on our way out. Besides—'

I want to ask her to get a uniformed officer but she's not listening.

'It is a serious crime?' I hear her ask the member of the public, or 'MOP' as she'll be known to us. 'It's a serious crime,' she relays to me. 'And you've committed it?'

Uh...?

'She says she's ze von who committed it.'

I've now got Rashid's attention. One of us will have to go down and speak with the MOP. He knows I'm meeting Jools. All I have to do is pull a face and he'll deal with the woman himself. We're new to the department and both of us want to make our mark. But I'm supposed to be getting engaged in a minute. I dither. 'I'll be right down.'

'*Ruby's not getting married in the morning...*' sings Rashid as I reach for some clean sheets of paper. '*Ding-dong, the sun's not gonna...*'

I flash him the full thirty-two-teeth Teague smile.

The walk to the door leads past the DI's office. He's still there, as ever, head down, files spread, snapping at the heels of his latest criminal quarry. I consider knocking on his door. This might turn out to be a big job, so maybe I should keep him in the loop. I decide against it. I've taken a lot of DI

McQuade's time already today. Want him to think I've got *some* initiative. And what's he going to say, anyway? *Go and see what she wants.*

Out in the corridor there's a guy waiting for the lift. I've seen him around; I think he's in witness care. Twenty years old, I'd say. So fat he wheezes, and too lazy to walk down a single flight of stairs. He's face to face with one of the anti-DV posters DS Teague got me to Blu-Tack around the nick the other day when she saw me talking. A stressed-looking lady stares out of a window. 'Are You in an Abusive Relationship?' I can barely meet her eye. *No*, I murmur mentally. *Sorry. Mine's brill.*

On the ground floor I stand with my pass poised. Through the glass strip in the door I see a woman sitting upright in the waiting area, fiddling with her necklace, staring into the air. Jools sits next but one. Like the woman, he's not distracting himself with his phone. Legs crossed, chin high, he's relaxing with his prim and proper thoughts. Not the sort of guy you'd find hiding in bushes. A knife-and-golf-club man all the same, I have no doubt about it. He'd reach for them as soon as you touched a hair on my head. I love him. Love, love, love, love, love him. Talking of hairs, one of Grande's is sticking to my skirt. I brush it off and swipe open the door.

Zuzanna nods me towards the woman. Making my way over, I catch Jools's eye and make a 'five minutes' sign with my fingers.

'Hello,' I say. 'I'm Learner Detective Ru Marocco. You want to speak with a detective?'

She flicks me a glance, then nods and looks away.

'Can I ask what's it about?'

Her lips twitch. 'A murder.' The word jumps about like an insect.

'Are you sure?' My next remark, I'm aware as it escapes from my lips, is that of an actual idiot. 'You look much too nice to do that.'

She looks down into her lap. I snatch a look at Jools. He's observing us.

'Would you like to come this way? There's an interview room free—'

'You've got to arrest her,' Jools says. He's got his tablet out and has begun to take notes. He looks up. 'You can't ask her any more questions. You'll have to book her in.' He pulls out a card from his wallet and gives it to the woman. 'Jools Main. Defence solicitor. Sorry, I couldn't help but overhear.'

The woman studies the card. 'Do I need a solicitor?'

'Yes, it sounds like you do. Come on.' He stands and looks at me expectantly. If he ever does ask me to marry him – and it won't be today – I really hope he won't look so much in command of the situation as he does right now.

'What's your name?' I ask.

'Freya Maskell.'

Hesitantly, I place my palm on her shoulder. 'Freya Maskell, I'm arresting you on suspicion of murder. You do not have to say anything but it may harm your defence…'

If I finish the sentence I'm unaware of it. Anyway, the woman's stopped listening. No one listens beyond the first seven words of the caution. They just think, *How long am I gonna be here?* and, *Who'll look after the kids?*

'Murder' is not a word that's often spoken in the custody suite at Cattlegreen Police Station. The two cells are mostly occupied by sobering drivers, calling through the hatch for another breath test and, hopefully, the return of their keys. Custody Sergeant Jenner has been here for years and makes out he's seen it all. But, as he operates the computer – thoughtfully, like he's losing against it at chess – I bet he's wriggling with excitement inside. Freya Maskell and I wait at the counter as he considers his next move. I feel like a first-time entrant at an angling competition who, by a fluke, has bagged a whopper and now is having her catch weighed. A killer whale, lost up the Thames and stranded here in the Home Counties, looking very out of place.

'Where do you live, Freya?'

'21C Ruthin Gardens.'

I know it. There's not really what you'd call a wrong side of the tracks in this part of suburbia. Cattlegreen's all a bit well-to-do. Ruthin Gardens isn't the best part, though.

'Date of birth?'

She's twenty-eight. Two years older than me.

'Occupation?'

'Unemployed.'

'Any issues with your physical/mental health?'

She looks like she's not getting enough to eat. Very nervous. Biting her lip and scratching with her thumbnail against the pulp of her finger. She shakes her head, but then stumbles.

'You all right?' I ask her.

'Yeah,' she says. 'I think the blood's just gone down to my feet.'

Everyone shows concern, like she's some star. She is, in a way. Announce you're a murderer and, goodness, you light up the room.

'I see you've brought your solicitor,' Sergeant Jenner says.

Neither she nor Jools denies it.

'You have certain rights whilst you're in custody…'

He tells her what they are. She nods to show she understands. He asks if there is anyone she wishes to have informed of her detention; she shakes her head. She places her belongings on the countertop so that Sergeant Jenner can make a record of them. It sounds a bit funny when he says, 'One library card.'

She gives up her phone.

'Have you got the PIN for this?' I ask, hoping to catch her off guard.

'I'd advise you not to disclose that,' Jools says. 'Not at the present time.'

In the usual order of things, at this stage I'd tell him, as my suspect's legal representative, what our evidence is. With that information he'd then advise his client whether to give an account when we come to interview her or else to make no comment. We call it 'disclosure'. Tonight there's no disclosure. Jools knows as much about this investigation as I do. He takes Freya Maskell off to a room for a private consultation, and I go back upstairs.

'What is it?' Rashid asks, following me as I walk through the office. He's not going home until he knows all about it. 'What's she done?'

'Oh, she's only murdered someone.' I look over my shoulder at him and mime *Eek!*

The door to DI McQuade's office is open. He looks up as I stand at the threshold. I tell him what's happening.

'Jools is with her,' I explain.

'Jools? Your boyfriend?'

I nod. It occurs to me there may be a perceived conflict of interest; that he might take me off the case. He's looking at me like he's thinking about it.

'Let's run her through PNC.'

I give him the details.

'Caution last year for possession, Class A drugs. Caution in 2008 for shoplifting. No convictions… D'you think she's nuts?'

'Not picked up on any signs. She looks after herself. Well, she's gaunt, but she's very well turned out. Doesn't seem to be seeking attention. Focused. Follows instructions, answers questions in a normal way.'

My phone vibrates. Sergeant Jenner has texted.

She's ready for interview.

The 4th August 2012. The greatest day in the history of British athletics. It was also the other time that Jools and I sat on either side of this table in Interview Room 1 at Cattlegreen Police Station. I try to catch his eye. I want to share the significance. But if he's aware of it, he's not letting on. He's in business mode and is lost to me.

Things have turned dreamlike. An hour ago Rashid and I were working on our reflective pieces about *Policing a Diverse Community*. Now I'm with Jools, back in Interview Room 1, with my DI sitting beside me, watching as I prepare to interview a murder suspect. I can't believe DI McQuade's letting me deal with this, that he's letting me ask the questions. I'm doing everything deliberately. Breaking the seals on the interview cassettes seems to take an hour. Writing out the labels, I worry that the DI is looking, seeing if I can spell. All eyes are on me. The silence lasts too long. Soon people will sigh and drum with their fingers on the table edge. Meanwhile, Freya Maskell's husband lies rotting under the patio, or her bedridden mother cools, whilst the pillow that bore the imprint of her face slowly regains its shape.

'This interview is being held at Cattlegreen Police Station. The date is the 13th June 2014. The time by my watch is… 19.25 hours. Also present in the room are…' I look at Jools, expecting him to announce himself. It crosses my mind that he might take advantage here. His only concern is for his client. He's not going to help me. Now that I've invited him to speak he might just stare me out and, in six months' time when this tape is played to the jury, there'll be silence and – to repeat a phrase they sometimes used in the van – I'll sound like a tit.

Everyone introduces themselves. I draw a deep breath.

'Is it all right if I call you Freya?'

I want her to look at me but she won't meet my eye. She's still wearing her coat. I've seen it in Karen Millen. The likes of me can only dream of wearing stuff that price. Just her top would cost my week's wages. Did she nod at the mirror, I wonder, this afternoon as she prepared to confess to her crime? *Yes, I think I'll go with the turtleneck.* Did it occur to her that the next time anyone in Cattlegreen sees her in it she's going to be middle-aged? She turns her head to Jools. From her angora jumper, her neck sticks up like a stalk. The skin of her throat shines dully, like the silver of her necklace. Jools nods. She turns her gaze back to the paper cup of water on the table, so slowly that I have time to think of a sunflower keeping its face to the sun. She takes a slow sip.

'Yeah,' she says.

'Whilst you're at the police station, Freya, you have certain entitlements…' Here we go again. 'And I'll remind you that you're under caution. That you do not have to say anything…'

Jools waits for me to finish, then speaks. 'For the benefit of the tape, I'm advising my client to make no comment to all your questions. This is because I have not had disclosure of any evidence that you may have that could form a case against her.'

'Thank you for that,' I say, and have a flash of fantasy that he will bring out a ring from his pocket and declare the whole thing a joke, and that Freya and the DI will clap and shout as I tearfully accept his proposal. But then it all goes exactly as he says.

'Who did you murder?' I feel the DI's stare upon me. 'Sorry, I should say, "kill". When did it happen? Why did you do it? What was his name? Or was it a woman? Or was it your baby?'

If she'd just make eye contact, I'm sure we might start to get somewhere. But she only stares at her cup.

'Have you had a baby, Freya? Does the father know what you've done?'

'No comment. No comment.'

The DI has a go. 'Freya, you came here to confess to a crime. Do you not want to do that now? Do you not want to clear your conscience?'

'No comment.'

No comment. That's all she's going to say. She and my boyfriend have put their heads together and this is going to be her strategy.

In the meantime, Rashid's phoned home to make his excuses regarding the Thames Frockley Flower Show and has been hard at work on our database. He's determined not to be sidelined. I'm back in the office and he's practically jostling the DI and me with what he's found. Not that it amounts to much. No one's been reported missing within a five-mile radius. The morgue have no bodies that they can't account for. The electoral roll suggests that Freya lives alone.

'What do we do now?' I ask the DI.

'Go to her home, have a look round. I mean...' He reminds himself that Rashid and I are newbies. 'Don't go ripping up floorboards. Just see, y'know, if anyone might be noticeable by their absence.'

We put on our coats and go down to custody, where Sergeant Jenner dangles Freya's keys above my palm. 'Lose them, you pay for the locksmith.'

'Sarge.'

In the pound, I make my usual joke. 'Do you want to drive?' For all his top university education and his flying colours in the detective's exam, Rashid's not yet been approved as a police driver. 'Oh, I forgot.' I pat him on the shoulder. 'I'll have to.'

We belt up and switch on. 'Go, go, go!' I shout, and do a wheelspin. Rashid looks like he's going to be sick.

The gate slowly opens, we emerge into the real world, and I pull myself together. This might actually be serious. 'Do you think I'll get to run with this?' I muse, as we drive along the high street. It's not that warm; still, there are quite a few people eating outside at the front of San Gimignano's. That's where I thought I might be proposed to. Seems silly, now.

'Sure. If Freya Maskell's a fantasist, which she probably is, and it's a case of wasting police time. If there really is a dead body then forget it. The major crime team take over, don't they?'

For all that, I can tell Rashid's kicking himself for not picking up the phone when Zuzanna called. He doesn't think Freya's making this up any more than I or the DI do. We look at each other. Two months on the job and we're out alone on a homicide. We stare at each other and gape.

It's getting darker. Clouds that were white a few minutes ago, as I looked out of the DI's window, now look like smears on the sky. A breeze bends the trees that line the road. The smell of sap enters the car. Even at this hour, commuters emerge from the station gates. For all who keep normal office hours, I imagine, a pleasant sense of Friday is in the air.

'What I don't understand,' says Rashid, 'is why she took the trouble to come to the station to make her confession? If she was going to do that, why did she change her mind?'

I haven't explained this. I lower my chin and tell him it was because of my boyfriend.

'What? Jools happened to be there waiting for you and…?'

'Yeah,' I almost snap. 'He butted in, appointed himself her solicitor even though she hadn't asked for one, then advised her not to admit to it after all.'

Rashid has some 'delicacy', as I believe the word is, and doesn't pass comment on this.

There aren't many flowers in the garden at 21 Ruthin Gardens, but someone's mown the grass and there's no junk strewn about. I push the communal door and we advance into the smell of paint. The foyer has been swept and the post gathered. Freya's flat is on the ground floor. At the front door, I stand with the key in my hand. I take a deep breath. Something I heard myself say in the interview is haunting me. I'm scared I might find Freya's baby.

But behind the door there's no sign that she might be a mother. No toys or buggies jam the hallway; no house rules or classroom efforts hang from the walls. Nor is there any mail that might tell us if anyone else lives here. The kitchen is spotless and tidy. There are two rooms that could be bedrooms, but only one has a bed. The spare one she uses as an office.

'Only one toothbrush,' Rashid observes in the bathroom.

'No shaving cream,' I say.

'Maybe her husband had a beard.'

'Maybe that's why she murdered him.'

Freya's secrets, if she has them, are as safe in the lounge as they are in the kitchen and the bathroom. No family photos, nothing amongst the CDs and DVDs to hint at what she's about. What's the difference, I find myself wondering, between minimalist, as Jools would probably describe this place, and what I would just call bare?

We declare at least three of the rooms corpse-free. Finally, we go to her bedroom. There's a smell of good perfume and she has a king-size bed. I'd say those sheets are silk, or else a very soft cotton. On them lies a red Gucci bag. I've seen it in the shops. It'll have cost her, or someone, a grand.

'She lives alone,' says Rashid, from the window side of the bed.

'You think?' I doubt this for the simple reason that there's no team of teddy bears propped up against her pillows. I've never lived alone myself, so wouldn't really know. But if I did I'm sure that's how I'd console myself.

Rashid speaks again but I don't catch it. I'm staring into the drawer where she keeps her underwear.

'Ru.'

It's more like a filing cabinet. No ball-shaped scrumples here. Her knickers, which look new or perhaps even pressed, spread flat and seem to be ordered. I filter them with my fingers, like banknotes. There must be fifty pairs.

'*Ru.*'

Freya Maskell is the sort of woman who matches underwear to occasion, even when no one will see. This pair feels like baby skin. This pair… Where do you get clothes *like* this?

'Definitely she lives alone.'

'Eh?'

He stands with his arm outstretched, his face braced for a nasty smell. I move round the bed and see he's pointing at a vibrator in a bedside drawer. Rashid thinks sex toys are substitutes, designed for the lonely.

'Wonder what's in the wardrobe?' I say, swiftly moving on.

We open it up. There's a lot more here that's not for the likes of me. Jaeger. Harrods. Some of it borders on being fancy dress. Ball gowns, wigs, spangled shoes with six-inch heels.

'She said she's unemployed,' Rashid says. 'Looks to me like she's running some sort of clothes business.'

Hands on hips, I strain for intelligent thought. If I don't come up with something, he'll think I'm not rising to this miraculous occasion. 'It's so tidy.' I sigh and arrange a thoughtful frown. 'It's almost like she's cleaned the place with her trip to the police station in mind.'

'What? Destroyed the evidence?'

'Possibly.'

'Mmm. One potential flaw in that theory.' Finger to chin, Rashid savours a long, sarcastic moment. 'People who want to hide evidence generally don't come to the police and say, "I've committed murder."'

I point at him. 'Good thinking.'

He blows out his cheeks. 'No sign of a struggle.'

And now we laugh silently, to the point that he staggers and I grip my knees. Pent-up excitement. Like me, Rashid would like to make his assessment of the scene by drawing upon years of detective experience. But he hasn't got those years, and instead he's having to draw from TV cop dramas in which 'no sign of a struggle' is a staple. We are *so* far out of our depth.

We leave the flat to commence our house-to-house enquiries. Opposite, no one's in. Upstairs, directly above Freya's home, a young mother opens the door. The family only moved in a week ago and she doesn't know anyone yet. The block's other inhabitant is an old man. He's been here since the place was built.

'Yeah, she's been here a couple of years. No problem. Keeps herself to herself.'

'Does she live alone?' I ask.

'Think so. She has a friend. Bloke in a wheelchair. You sometimes see her pushing him in and out.'

'You don't have much to do with her?'

'No. Spoke to her a few months ago. I left my car lights on. She knocked on my door and let me know.'

We go down the stairs and I phone DI McQuade. Rashid thinks we should seize Freya's computer but I don't think we've got the power.

'No, don't worry about that,' the DI says. 'Just come back. We'll give her another interview and if she doesn't say anything we'll have to let her go.'

They've given Jools a seat in the custody suite. He looks up from his tablet. 'Any progress?'

I ignore him and ask the detention officer to bring Freya from her cell. We assemble once more in the interview room. This time the DI takes over the questioning.

'Freya, you have the benefit of a legal adviser and, so far, you've taken his advice to make no comment to our questions. And that is your legal right. But it seems to me that you came here tonight with a purpose that wasn't really concerned with your legal rights. You came here to do the right thing. Am I correct? Is that what you were going to do?'

Again, a drugged sunflower-turn of Freya's head towards Jools. The light catches her complexion. It's like ivory.

Jools says his lines. 'For the benefit of the tape, I'm advising my client to make no comment to all your questions. This is because I have not had disclosure of any evidence that you may have that could form a case against her.'

The DI gives him a courteous nod, then addresses himself to the suspect. 'Did you come here to be honest? To own up to something you did? Because if that was your intention, that is what you should do. You know that, don't you? You told Learner Detective Marocco that you killed someone. She's recorded it. I've read it in her pocket notebook. If it is true, you should say so. It's better all round. Think of the deceased…'

I'd forgotten about the deceased. All I can think about is the knickers she's sitting in. Which did she choose for the occasion? Is she wearing a bra to match?

'…Doesn't he or she deserve justice? I don't know. Maybe you don't think they do. But what about their loved ones? Won't they need peace? And what about your conscience? Will you be able to sleep at nights, knowing what you've done? Maybe you can. In which case, do you want to live out the rest of your days looking over your shoulder, waiting for someone to get their revenge? Hopefully, we'll get to you first. That would be better, wouldn't it? Safer. But then it'll be too late to say you're sorry. Because this is the time to do that. If you've killed someone, we'll get the evidence. We always get the evidence. And then it won't mean anything that you're sorry, because all the time you're waiting for us to prove what you've done, you're not being sorry at all. Now, Mr Main here is a well-respected solicitor, and I'm sure your legal rights are safe in his hands. But you may think that it's not your legal rights that are the most important thing at this stage in your life. Do you think? Say what you came here tonight to tell us, Freya.'

'No comment... No comment... No comment.'

And that is that. Freya Maskell is bailed and everyone goes home.

2

I'm staring at the laundry basket. The wicker is starting to unravel. I've never woken up facing this direction and I hadn't noticed it before. It's usually Jools who's turned away. I'll open my eyes and there's his head, and for the first minutes of my day I'll watch his ears and his hair. My phone is charging on the bedside table. It's just too far away for me to get without propping myself up on an elbow. I want to see if anything's been posted about last night's shenanigans in town, but if I make a dip in the mattress, it might rouse him.

It's not as though we've fallen out – not officially, at least. If anything, when we drove away from the nick on Friday night it was like we were on a first date. Doing everything deliberately, thinking about what we said. The way you act when you don't know someone. He wasn't going to make love to me that night; he just wanted a cuddle instead. I couldn't stand the weirdness of that. I pushed back against him and stirred around with my hips until, well, really, he had no choice.

Yesterday he was on duty at the Saturday court in London and I didn't see him. By the time he was home I was with Lorna on our long-overdue mission to paint Thames Frockley red. Never again.

We'd been having quite a good laugh in the pub. Some of Lorna's mates mind their Ps and Qs when I'm around, knowing I'm The Law, but these ones made me feel part of the gang. The trouble started in Tangos when someone marched onto the dance floor, holding her phone out for Lorna. (It turns out my sister has spies planted in every pub and club in town.) Live footage from Wetherspoons down the road, where Lee was in public view, laughing with an unidentified girl. Well, everything ended with that. Jaws were set, handbags were clasped and off they all trooped, leaving me on my own, like a lemon. They returned ten minutes later, corralling Lee, their prisoner of war, and gloating about how 'the situation' had been 'resolved' out of CCTV view in the Wetherspoons toilets. 'But we shouldn't be telling you, should we?' cackled one girl, who hadn't been with us in the first pub. 'You might lock us up!' Another one – sullen, whose face I think I might have seen in work emails – seemed to be rubbing her knuckles. Lorna spent the rest of the night smooching with other boys and peeping at Lee over their shoulders, as he stood at the bar and got drunk. And she wonders why I've been putting off our girls' night out for so long.

He's getting up. I close my eyes. I hear the kettle warming in the kitchen and I reach out quickly to check my phone. No updates. The kettle clicks. I hunker back down. A mug is placed on my bedside drawers and I feel him stroking my hair.

'Hello, stranger.'

My eyes closed, I smile tightly. We've never been like this before and I don't know how to play it.

'You have a good night?'

'Did I wake you when I got in?' I open my eyes and, staring at the unravelling laundry basket, give him the briefest of facts. I'm not trying to make a point here, and I'd hate him to think I'm sulking, but that first-date-falseness thing we did on Friday night was horrid and I don't want to fall back into that. But he's wearing me down. With every stroke of his fingers, a new skin of resentment rubs away. I sit up, take a slurp of tea, and begin to fill him in on the details. Suddenly, everything feels natural again and I chatter on, eager to share all that I know.

'I'm sorry, Rube.'

'What for?'

He bends forward and kisses my cheek. 'For Friday night.'

I break off our gaze. 'What? Don't be silly. You were doing your job.'

'And hobbling your investigation. It's just… I couldn't sit there and do nothing.'

'Honest, Jools. It's okay.'

'She was about to sign away the next twenty years of her life…' He frowns and dabs something from my cheek. A stray eyelash. He rearranges strands of my hair and smooths my eyebrows with his thumb. To my slight embarrassment, his touch makes me let out a sound, a bit like a squeaky toy. 'Can I have a snog?'

'One condition,' I say, and turn to face him full on. 'You'll have to tell me what Freya Maskell said to you when you were in consultation.'

His face falls. 'Ah, I can't.' He puts on a whine. '*Client confidentialit-ee.*'

'I'm joking. Come here.'

My kiss is assertive and takes him by surprise. He splashes tea on the duvet.

'Hang on,' he says.

'Leave it.'

My mouth makes noise on his face. I sound like Grande devouring his bowl of food. I can't help it. Normal service has been resumed. Me and Jools are back. The next half-hour is what my life is all about. Making love, being in love. Everything else that happens in my week is just gaps and waiting, whatever I might pretend at the time. Afterwards, I doze off.

I wake up to cold tea and a dizzy feeling that Friday never happened; that the sense of our being separate was nothing but a nasty dream. 'What are you doing?' I ask.

Jools is propped up and tapping on his tablet. More legal stuff. He never stops. 'Solicitors' forum. Adding my two pennyworth.'

I draw close and read the screen. 'Who's Mark Wells?'

'An upright, hard-working and much-maligned businessman, according to Ridealgh & Co, his solicitors. Your Met colleagues say he's a gangster.'

'A gangster, then.'

'I couldn't possibly comment.'

'Why's he in the news?'

'He's in the Old Bailey. His murder trial starts tomorrow.'

That word again. It's beginning to sound familiar.

A new thread appears.

I imagine that Mr Wells is a somewhat demanding client. Well, with uplift and a lot of chargeable hours in store, the drinks are on Steve Ridealgh!

Someone else writes:

> *You may as well just hand him the keys to the Legal*
> *Aid Agency.*

Fascinated, I watch as Jools types:

> *Good things come to those who wait. I've known*
> *Steve for ten years and I can honestly say this*
> *brief could not have come to a more diligent and*
> *committed lawyer. Congratulations, Steve, on*
> *handling such a high-profile case.*

'Who did he murder?'

'Er, let's see… Femi Yar'Adua… Accidentally scraped the bumper of Mr Wells' BMW.'

'BMW?' I say. 'Phwah. New Audi A6, I could understand it.'

Murders, rare in these parts, are an everyday occurrence where Jools works.

I reach over and scroll up. 'Cor. Steve Ridealgh's boat really has come in, hasn't it?' About a dozen solicitors have posted to say so. None of them mentions Femi Yar'Adua.

Grande trots into the bedroom. He rattles his ears and sneezes, lands on the bed like a bomb. Jools puts down his tablet and seizes him. 'What's the smell?' He puts his nose to the dog's head. 'Leather and biscuits. Aaah. The household's lowest life form. And that's with a police officer living here.'

Grande's solemn look reproaches him. *You shouldn't abuse us so, master!* This dog has no sense of humour. But he does have a strong sense of fun. He pulls his head free of

Jools's grasp and, using his snout as a mallet, butts us both gratuitously in the nose. *Bat-and-bite time!* The game goes like this. To show that he's sorry for having assaulted us, he bats himself in the face with his tail. This hurts and makes him angry, so he retaliates by biting his tail. This also hurts. He bats himself. He bites himself. Wagging and growling, he grinds through little circles on the bed until teeth and tail call a sudden truce and he falls fast asleep on his spine.

I was a bit of a pushover when Jools asked me out. Put up no resistance, caved in straight away. When he asked me to move in, on the other hand, I drove a hard bargain. 'I come with the lurcher,' I told him. 'Access all areas, sofas and bedroom – the lot.' Jools just blinked. Now he can't get enough of him.

'Fancy the Surrey Hills?' he asks over the breakfast table.

'Brill.' I don't care what we do. In fact, I have a theory that, with the sun out, and all made up with my fella, the day couldn't be less than wonderful even if it tried. Then my phone goes and I see the word 'Mum' on the screen, and my theory is put to the test.

'Do you know anyone who might want a whippet?'

'I can ask around. Is it a puppy?'

'Yeah. There's a litter been brought to the Centre. We're going up there this afternoon to have a look at them. Ian's driving my car.'

'Ian's driving your car?' I say it so slowly she chuckles.

'Yeah. He's having lessons. He's feeling really well at the moment. I'm thinking of getting him some wheels for his birthday. That's something else you could look into, if you know anyone who's got a little runabout they want to sell.'

'Or swap for a whippet.'

'Yeah. Second-hand whippet, one not-very-careful previous owner. By the way, what the hell was going on in town last night?'

'Why? What have you heard?'

'The phone's not stopped. I had a call from some girl's mum, demanding to know who Lorna was with at Wetherspoons; "the one who hit her daughter". I had Lee's mum on the phone an hour ago asking where Lee is. Told her I dunno. Now I've just been up to the spare room and there he is, snoring his head off.'

Outside the sky is blue and the trees are a brilliant green. Grande hops into his cage in the Škoda, I bagsy the wheel and we're off. Soon we're driving past the nick. It has a completely different meaning for me outside the working week.

'It's where it all started.' I grin at Jools. *The Story of Our Love.* I say it with the capitals and in a kiddie's voice. It's the only way I can get away with saying it at all. 'How's Sonny Bryant?'

His client's name makes Jools beam. 'Not seen him for some time. Back on the straight and narrow, maybe.'

That's the thing about our jobs. We're like doctors who only get to see you when you're sick. With coppers and defence lawyers, you only cross our radar when you're up to no good.

Saturday 4th August 2012, as well as being the greatest day in the history of British athletics, was also the day when Sonny Bryant travelled from London to Cattlegreen. When professional shoplifters have made themselves too well known locally to be guaranteed a safe and productive work environment, they get on their bikes, or in their hired cars, and seek out new opportunities. An *away day.*

That summer I'd been patrolling the anti-fracking demonstrations with Connor and the rest of the special patrol force wallahs. The Vanguard, we called ourselves. Owing to a wrist injury, though, I'd been subbed, and by this time I was on light duties, interviewing suspects at the nick. I didn't really like it. Too much time waiting around for interpreters and appropriate adults and, above all, defence solicitors who, when they did finally materialise, rarely brightened my day. But on Saturday 4th August, which they wouldn't allow me to have as annual leave, the nick was where I wanted to be, and when detained person Sonny Bryant said he wanted his brief 'from London', that was just fine, so far as I was concerned. My mind wasn't on the job anyway. It was on the Olympics, and, for as long as Sonny languished in his cell, I was happy to watch as much as I could on the custody suite television. But it turned out to be not much at all.

'Of all the days to get nicked, Sonny chooses this one.' The first words Jools ever said to me.

'I thought you were coming from London?'

'That's where my office is. I live round the corner from here.' He smiled. 'You been watching the Games?'

'Trying to.'

He looked at the custody record. I disclosed to him the evidence we had.

'Your client was stopped by officers whilst driving on the Frockley road. Approximately £2,000 worth of clothing was found in the boot and on the back seat of his vehicle. Many of the items were still in cellophane covers with the tags still on. When asked to account for them—'

Jools looked up from his notetaking. '"I borrowed the car

from my mate, whose name I can't recall. That stuff was there when I took it."'

'How did you know that?'

'Every day is Groundhog Day in Sonny Bryant's life.' He frowned and stared at the air. 'If we box clever d'you think we can wind things up in time for the eight hundred metres?'

'We've got the interview to do.'

'It shouldn't take too long. He always goes no comment. Doesn't matter what I say.'

'Well, the thing is, we haven't traced all the losers. Debenhams and House of Fraser have identified what's theirs, but there're two other sets of clothes we can't account for. We need to hang on. There's still a chance the losers might report their loss.'

'Hmm.' Jools rubbed his chin. 'Shall I have a word with him?'

The DDO went to fetch Sonny whilst I asked at the charging desk about an interview room. Sergeant Jenner said there weren't any free and I was going to have to wait.

'Can I get you a coffee?' I asked the friendly solicitor, his client once again back in his cell. He said I could. When word got round I was making it, Sergeant Jenner raised his eyebrows and the DDO gave a tut. Hospitality isn't usually extended to defence solicitors at Cattlegreen.

'What did you do to your hand?' Jools asked as I passed his plastic cup.

'Punched a protester in the mouth.'

He stared at me to see if I was telling the truth. 'You did that to *stop* him protesting?'

I was close enough to him to notice that the corners of his eyes crinkled when he smiled. He seemed like someone you could have a laugh with.

'You think Ennis is in with a chance?' he asked.

''S looking good.'

'I've been watching her since Melbourne in 2006. It's that focus… almost frightening.'

I hadn't come across a defence solicitor like this one. Normally, when they weren't taking their clients' instructions, they would shut themselves off in rooms, where they'd yawn and prod about on their phones, or else they'd be brisk and cross and stalk about with clipboards, enforcing their clients' rights and acting like *we* were the ones threatening to stand in the way of justice. I made up my mind that, because he was obviously a genuine athletics fan, and it seemed the right occasion, it wouldn't be boastful of me to tell him that I knew Jessica Ennis a little. I was figuring out how to word it when he said, 'New Look and French Connection.'

'Sorry?'

'They're your losers. Sonny's unidentified goods?'

'Ah.' I turned to go and investigate the new lead.

'Oh, you won't have to get statements. He says he'll admit everything.'

'I thought you said—'

'I know. Usually he makes no comment. The thing is… It's a bit awkward… There's one condition – no, not a condition. Sonny… has a concern. He planned his day's activities so he could be home in time for this evening's track and field events. Says that if he coughs he'd like to be allowed to watch Ennis and Farah. Here. He'll miss it otherwise.'

It took a moment for me to take this in. When I discussed it with Sergeant Jenner he thought I was out of my mind.

'What? So he pleads not guilty in court and says he was

induced by your promise of special treatment to make a false confession?'

'I'm not making him a promise. Just want to know if it's doable.'

He's a grump, is Sergeant Jenner, but he's a patriot. 'Third in the world!' He'd been whispering it all day as the medals jingled in. He kept telling the DDO to update the prisoners, assuming they would care. 'Britain ranks third in *the world!*'

'Well,' he said, 'we'll wait to see what he says. If we… decide we like him… I suppose he could be our guest for a short while.'

An interview room became free and, once more, Sonny was produced from his cell. He started off all front. 'I'd give 'er one,' he said, scowling and nodding in my direction as he was led through the door. 'Fit as.'

'Sit down and behave yourself,' Jools said to him.

Sonny gave him a warning look but did as he was told. 'Right. You're aware of the deal, yeah? My brief's told you, innit? I get my motor back tonight, I get to watch the eight hundred—'

'Sonny,' Jools said. 'Get one thing clear in your head. There's no deal. If you want me to read out your statement I will. If you want to answer the officer's questions, then do it. If you want to make no comment, no one's going to force you. It's no skin off PC Marocco's nose, and whatever you do will make no difference to what happens after this.'

Sonny and Jools eyeballed each other until, with a sigh, Sonny blinked first and relaxed. This solicitor was so different. Often, I'd seen them show off to their clients. Speaking to me, they'd use words like 'to whom' and 'acquired' and 'best interests' to prove their superior education. With their clients, they'd drop Ts and Hs and end sentences with 'yanartamean?', trying to make it sound like they'd never even been to school. But Jools wasn't like that. He didn't put on airs. He definitely wasn't trying to make Sonny his friend. Sometimes they do that. They bring their clients presents, which the custody sergeant has to remind them to leave at the charging desk.

I switched on the tape. 'The time by my watch…' Six minutes before Jessica might start to win the heptathlon. It didn't look like we'd make it. 'You do not have to say anything…'

Jools waited for me to finish cautioning, then read from a prepared script. 'My client instructs me to tell you that he stole clothing this afternoon from four shops in Thames Frockley: House of Fraser, New Look, Debenhams, and French Connection. On each occasion he entered the store alone and with the intention to steal. All that he stole was placed in a rented vehicle and was recovered at the scene by officers. Everything that has been recovered, he stole. He asks me to tell you that he is sorry for his actions and extends his apologies to the police and the staff at the stores in question. He has no other criminal investigations or proceedings outstanding, nor does he take Class A drugs. He has fixed accommodation with his mother and is eminently suitable for bail.'

I closed my eyes and ran the points to prove through my head. It was all there in the confession. I had nothing further to ask. 'Great,' I said, and switched off the tape.

As we took our seats behind the custody counter, the girls were shuffling in the blocks.

'Come on, Jessic-ar!' Sonny called out to the screen. He turned to Sergeant Jenner. 'You see Greg Rutherford jumpin'?'

Sergeant Jenner nodded.

'Eight metres,' said Sonny. 'Eight metres an' more. How far is eight metres?'

Sergeant Jenner regarded him for a moment, then told him to stand up. 'See down the corridor? From where we are now to the door of your cell? Move your feet here. That's eight metres exactly. I measured it this afternoon.'

'*Waah*,' said Sonny, and smiled at the world at large. ''S far, man.'

The gun fired. The girls ran.

'Come on, Jessica!'

This time it was Jools calling out. Then it was the sergeant. Then me. The 128.65 seconds that followed rattled out like machine-gun spray. I gasped, I remember, at the sight of her. Bashful, smiley Jess, whose faded jeans and hoodie used to hang and straddle mine in stinking changing rooms around the country. *Look at her now!* I thought. Those thighs. That midriff. That shining skin, flowing over muscle like a stream. That locked-in, keep-out race face, focused on her feet, on putting one in front of the other, as far and as often as she could. This was what you looked like, then, as the seconds passed and the best in the world couldn't catch you, on the day when disappointment stayed away.

'*Yaaaaaaahhhh!*'

'Seven,' said Sergeant Jenner to Sonny, both back in their seats, tears brushed away on their sleeves. 'Seven golds since lunchtime.'

'This country is so good at sport! Hey, Officer,' Sonny turned to me, 'is it true you know Jessic-ar Ennis?'

'Jess – eh?' I impersonate. 'Jess – air?' By now I'd told

Jools about the English Schools AAA meetings. 'I've met her. A few times.'

Sonny looked at me like there was something there that he hadn't noticed before. Maybe on top of the uniform there was an actual human face. 'Wow, man. Knowin' Jessic-ar. Wha' a honour.'

The whites of Mo Farah's eyes were still minutes off. But I don't think it crossed Sergeant Jenner's mind that anyone should move from our little hideaway behind the custody counter. On the other side, an officer, leading a prisoner by the handcuffs, waited for his attention. Mo did his thing and the four of us jumped up and down. Then Sergeant Jenner gave Sonny the keys to his car and let him off with a caution.

It was as I was seeing Jools out of the door into the pound that he began to say something. Then he hesitated.

'I didn't know you could do that,' I said. Normally, I can't flirt to save my life, but things were different that day.

'What?'

'Appear to be out of your depth.'

His smile was sheepish. 'I hope you don't think I'm being out of order. But—'

'"Please can I have your number?"'

Two years on, I'm still working on my impersonation. Just can't quite capture the clumsiness. He smiles and gives me a steer.

'"*Pleeease*, can I have your number?"' Exiting the M25, I take my hand off the gearstick and give his knee a squeeze.

The roads branch and narrow, rise and fall, until the hum of the motorway is trapped in a valley behind us. We park up in the woods past Friday Street.

'I went to the office after court yesterday,' Jools says as the three of us set out on our ramble. 'Lester was the only one there.' Lester Legarde is top man at Legarde & Co. 'He said, "Glad to see I've got someone on the payroll who's not afraid to show some commitment."' I'd like to meet Lester one day and determine whether Jools's impression is accurate and he really does talk like a cockney kazoo. 'Ten minutes later he called me into his office. "I've been keeping an eye on your time sheets. Impressive. Your efforts aren't going unnoticed."'

'Daddy's going places, Grande!' I tell the dog whilst unclipping his lead. We're in the woods now. Instantly, he sprints twenty metres and brakes hard. *A leaf!* His ribs quiver as he snuffles each serration of the one he has selected from the trillions around.

'Salary review next month,' Jools says. We emojify our faces. If there is one to signify a gleeful greed for the future, that's the one we've got on.

I'm a townie through and through, although I like being in the outdoors as well. Just don't know enough about the countryside to say what's nice about it. I suppose it's exciting that I might see animals. Also, I like the smells. This cool, musty one, for instance, of toadstools or bark, or whatever it is. And the trees, too, though I couldn't name a single kind in this wood. You never hear a bad word said about trees; it seems they only ever do good. Walking amongst them makes me feel that I'm mixing with the right company.

We turn onto a track that runs along the edge of an open field. A guy on a mountain bike appears. 'Have you got a white greyhound?' He's noticed Grande's lead, which is swaying in my hand.

'Yeah. Well, a lurcher,' I say, and notice that he's gone off. 'Where is he?'

The cyclist points behind him. 'There's a dog running rampant in a field behind those trees. He's chasing the sheep.'

The guide said, 'Dogs can roam free in the woods.' I hadn't even noticed that we'd left them. Instantly, I want to be sick.

Jools beats a path through the brambles to where the man is pointing. We can't see anything to begin with. Then, in the distance, a pale swirl. A drift of sheep, driven in arcs by a white, barking dot. I can't believe it. A minute ago I was feeding him a treat.

'Come on,' Jools says.

We climb over a barbed-wire fence and sprint down the field. Then we hear a shot.

'It's the farmer.'

We stand panting.

'He's got a gun.'

I've been lingering courteously. Now I leave Jools behind and run to where I can see a man in cap and wellingtons, striding towards the commotion, preparing to fire again. Dog and flock wheel in his direction. Very soon, the gap between them will come into his view and his target will be clear.

'Stop shooting!'

There's a metal gate. I vault over and charge towards the farmer. He closes his eye and hunches against the handle of his rifle.

'That's my dog. Stop shooting!'

Jools appears behind me and calls out, 'Put the gun down.'

For the first time the farmer registers our presence. He turns and his gun points at us. I should stick my warrant card in his face and tell him I'm a police officer. Instead, I hide behind Jools.

'Put it down,' Jools says again.

The gun is lowered. 'That dog is endangering my livestock.' The farmer turns and reloads. He aims and fires again. I cry out.

'*Nooooooo!*'

Jools marches up close to him. 'My business card. It's got my contact details.' He holds it up for him. 'If any of your sheep are injured, you know how to get me. I shall pay the whole of your loss. We shall have the dog under control as soon as you put down the gun. Please…' He smiles and catches his breath. 'Put the gun down now.'

The farmer looks at the card but doesn't take it. He cocks the gun to reload.

'No!' Jools says to him and goes to grab the gun. The guy turns the barrel back towards him. He curls his finger round the trigger.

'*Aaagghhh!*' I hear myself screaming.

Jools takes a step back, but then puts himself in the farmer's personal space again. Calmly, pleasantly, he says his piece once more. 'We're going to take the dog from your field. Put the gun down and we'll do that right away.'

They stare at each other until the determination drains from the farmer's face and the barrel droops to the ground. Then the air is pierced by a screaming bleat and up it bobs again. The farmer tries to train his sights back on Grande but Jools won't get out of the way. I walk backwards, then break into a run.

'Grande!' I shout. 'Grande!'

'Ruby, no!' Jools shouts back. 'Don't go onto the field!'

The sheep are squealing with terror. The dog is biting

their heels and their ears. I'm so frightened that my dog will be shot, or that I might be, or Jools. Over my shoulder I see him dancing in front of the farmer like a striker harassing a goalie as he tries to drop and kick. Every time the farmer moves and aims his gun, Jools stands in front of the muzzle. I find a stony patch and pick up a handful of pebbles. I throw and they go everywhere. One hits Grande's snout. It's not hard enough to hurt him but he loses some ground. I sprint to the sheep he's closest to and try to head him off. I've never run as fast as this. It ends with a dive and a catch of his collar, and a yelp as he slams to the grass. I look over to the farmer. He is watching but not moving, no longer aiming his gun.

Jools runs across the field and crouches by my side. 'You okay?' He's never seen me cry. Not outside the Odeon multiplex at least.

I clear my throat and take a breath. 'Yeah.'

He shakes his head. 'What a dick.' Now he puts his hand to my cheek. 'Let's get out of here.'

He clips the lead to Grande's collar and helps me to my feet. The three of us shuffle off. In the distance, the farmer follows us with his eyes until he becomes a scarecrow, a silhouette, and finally, as we lose him to sight, a murky thing of the past.

'Shouldn't we report him?'

'Dunno,' says Jools. 'He's got the right to protect his sheep, I suppose.'

'Firing a gun when there's people around?!'

We climb an embankment and look down on the field.

'Do we owe him money?'

'Can't see that there's been any casualties.' Jools shrugs. 'Should have taken my card when I offered it.' He considers a moment longer. 'Oh, he's taken up enough of our day. Let's forget him.'

But I can't walk any more. Shaking, I double over. 'Please can we go home?'

Jools takes me in his arms and holds me.

'I was rubbish. I let the dog free where there was livestock. I should have taken control of the situation. But I panicked and—'

'Shhh.'

He squeezes me so I can feel our hearts beat together, like they're boxing. I shan't know for sure unless he tells me but I think he saw that I hid behind him for a moment back there. I was about to admit it but he's pressed my mouth to his shoulder so I can't. Maybe it's his lawyer instincts. Or maybe he knows how to be lovely, just when I want him to be. He leads me to a low wall and we sit and look at the view. Grande, panting happily, scans about for more fun.

'No way I'm a copper.' I shake my head. 'That wasn't how a copper behaves.'

Jools ponders this whilst taking in the scenery. 'Okay. Let's go through what happened.' His tone is gentle. 'When the cyclist told you what was happening, what did you do? Did you dither? No. You acted straight away. When the gunfire started, did you move towards the danger or away from it? You got right in there, didn't you? And then I told you to stay off the field. I shouted; I was firm about it. But you thought for yourself. You ran after the dog. Very dangerous, but the guy wasn't going to put the gun down until his sheep were safe. That occurs to me only now; you saw it straight away. You had the better idea. And you caught him. It was amazing. Who else could have done that? We worked as a team. We played to our strengths. I talked; you acted. It's what we do. Yes, it was horrible, but no harm done, we sorted it. And that's because you're a good copper, not a bad one.'

'I suppose… when you put it that way.' I was almost in tears a minute ago, but now I've an ear-to-ear grin. He's given me a self-esteem transfusion, just as I was bleeding out. It has taken him less than sixty seconds to talk me round. Either he's a genius or I'm a *very* simple soul. 'Is this what you do in court?' I sniff and give a little chuckle. 'Make your clients' crimes seem like acts of public service?'

'Just another chapter in *The Story of Our Love*.'

This is the cue, normally, for the other to repeat the title in a silly voice. But I don't. I like his sentence just as it is.

'Do you mind if we don't go home?' he asks. 'There's something I've still got to do.'

Up and down hills, in and out of woods, the air warms and freshens. Jools puffs and pants and pretends not to welcome the rests as Grande, now on a very short lead, stops to investigate smells. We talk again of the salary review and take our minds off guns and gradients with thoughts of nice things to come; of cars and clothes and weekends away. At the top of Leith Hill, by the tower, we sit and count the counties and wonder if, wobbling in the haze that rises from the South Downs, the straight line of the horizon could really be the sea.

'Something's wrong with his tag,' Jools says, ruffling the dog's throat. 'The name plate's fallen out of the casing.'

I worry that the farmer will find it and somehow use it to work out where we live. But then, with a thumb, Jools raises Grande's collar for me to see, and I begin to laugh.

'Must have happened at the farm.'

Now I'm laughing quite hard. He's hidden the name tag. What hangs from Grande's collar is my engagement ring.

'Sorry,' he mutters. He looks away and busies himself, twisting some blades of grass. 'Not very romantic. Just thought… just wanted to include Grande in the moment.'

I study the ring and watch how it glints in the sun.

'Actually,' he says, gathering back some of his confidence, 'I was going to ask you before.'

'Really? When were you going to ask me before?' Friday night. San Gimignano's. Any money.

'The 4th August. 2012.'

I look at him.

'Seriously. That was when the fog lifted and I saw the way ahead. I walked out of Cattlegreen Police Station knowing why I'd been born.'

'You having a laugh?'

'No. It's true. I was at the point of asking you but I bottled it.'

'And asked for my number instead?'

'Yeah.'

I tilt the ring in the sunlight. The gleam pours down the side to the bottom, like liquid in a flask. 'And now, two years later, you got the urge again?'

He smiles and turns courtroom-prim. 'In the end I thought it'd be wise to take a moment or two to reflect.'

'Do you think Grande would mind if I keep it?'

He puts his ear to the dog's mouth. 'He says yeah. But only if you'll be my wife.'

'All right, Grande. I'll do it, just for you.'

Again, my fiancé's face falls. 'They're not… real diamonds.'

'I don't care.'

'You like?'

I nod but I can't talk. 'I like,' I say at last.

We lie down and begin to kiss. There's no one around. I can see that he's looking to check. He'll do it here and now if I let him. But I'm dirty and sweaty and worry that people might come. What I really want is to go to the pub.

We find The Jolly Thatcher. It's old and dark and, with only two other customers, the bustling, boisterous pub Sunday I hoped for hasn't quite got off the ground. Not a place to have a spare champagne bottle in the chiller, I would have thought. But it's my day of magic and, of course, one's there.

Jools looks around and nods whilst he counts the heads. 'And five glasses.'

'What are we celebrating?' asks the landlord, who is the sort who welcomes both strangers and their dogs. From my limited knowledge of rural hostelries, I'd say his type doesn't come automatically.

'Take your pick. First we didn't get murdered and now we're getting married. Whoa!' Jools recoils as the cork pops and ricochets off one of the low wooden beams. 'Sorry, that brought back an unpleasant memory.'

The two of them talk about the farmer. I turn to the couple sitting at the nearby table and strike a pose with my ring.

'Ah!' says the lady as she clasps my fingers. 'That's beautiful.'

Her name is Jen. The gentleman with her is Graham. They are married. Thirty-two years in his case. Twenty-eight in hers. They are neighbours, and their other halves are on the way. Happiness is making me extroverted, almost manic, and in no time these complete strangers know that I'm here because of a certain shoplifter, that it's him they should thank for their free glass of fizz.

'Well, it's very generous,' says Graham, shaking his head at the onslaught of sudden detail. He raises one of the glasses that Jools has placed on the table. 'Here's to you.'

'Did you know that, Graham?' the landlord calls over. 'Harry Lowe's got his gun back. Near enough shot these folk dead.'

'Makes me shudder to hear the name,' says Graham truthfully.

'Barred for life, that one,' says the landlord.

All parties' spouses arrive at once. I stand up and shake hands, then sit them down next to me. Before Harry Lowe's name can further darken the conversation, I tell them about falling in love. 'It just hits you out of the blue!' I say as I distribute more champagne.

'It does,' says Eve, the landlord's wife, who has come out from behind the bar to join us. 'It's like a strike of lightning.'

'Lightning, yeah!' I stab my finger in her direction. The alcohol has gone straight to my head. 'I was happy in a relationship when I first set eyes on Jools. Thought I was. And then I realised in a moment that I'd never known what love is at all.'

'Oof!' Barbara exclaims. 'When it hits you, you know it.' She turns to look at her Graham, who is twiddling Grande's ear.

'You know it,' agrees Graham, giving me a humorous look that says, *Can't really* not *say that, can I?*

Another bottle of champagne is delivered to the table. Jools stands at the bar, offering his debit card. Eamon the landlord waves it away.

'I'm thrilled for you, dear,' Eve says. 'Doesn't seem fashionable, nowadays, to make commitment. But being married is the key to real and lasting joy – in my book, anyway.'

She regards her companions in turn, making her observation into a question. Few return her gaze. No one wants to be the first to answer. Maybe this isn't a matter to discuss in mixed company. Or maybe they feel they're being challenged to mark their partner's exam paper under the public gaze. Glances are exchanged. Eyebrows are raised. Grins are stifled.

'Definitely,' says Graham at last, and he gives me another of his looks.

'Can't imagine life without him,' says Jen, looking dreamily at Al, causing him to blush and look at the floor.

'That's it!' I confirm it like I'm the one with twenty-eight years' experience of marriage. 'That's what you've got to ask yourself. Not if you can live with 'em. It's can you live without 'em?!'

When we write our CID essays, we're always told to acknowledge our sources, so I should tell everyone where I got that. But *Berkshire Brides* sounds a bit of a silly place to stumble across something so profound.

9.30pm

At school, when I was seven or eight, we went on a trip to the biscuit factory in Thames Frockley. A guide explained the process as we crocodiled from the sacks of flour at one side of the factory to the lorries loading up at the other. In between there were the machines, groaning and grinding, rocking and squeezing, the parts sliding in and out to a rhythm. I stared until I was hypnotised; I got left behind and the teacher had to come back to find me. It was wonderful that sacks could be turned into biscuits. They called this 'making things'.

We're at home and in bed. It's mid evening. The window and curtains are open and there's still some light in the sky. I press with my palms on Jools's chest. Raising myself, I look underneath me at where we join, and I think of my day at the biscuit factory and my long stare into the machines. Did I know something then, even at that young age? Did I sense, in some vague way, a future role for myself as part of a whirring machine? It seems to me that this bed is Jools's and my little factory, and we, too, are in the process of making. Making biscuits; making love. We are the machine the raw materials of our day must pass through. The shared thoughts, the secret glances, the plans, the surprises, the laughter. All these are now being processed so that the finished love-product can exist.

'If I tell you something, will you promise to keep it a secret?'

He gives me a sleepy grin.

I stop moving. 'I'm being serious.'

'I promise. I promise.'

I bring my eyes close to his, checking that the promise will be remembered. 'Because if this gets out I'll lose my job. It's something I did at work.'

'Tell me. It won't go any further.'

Already, I wish I hadn't felt the need to start this. He'll adore what I have to tell him, whilst I shall feel ashamed. It seems a completely one-sided transaction.

'I was in someone's flat, taking a statement. Thursday, I think it was.' I close my eyes to think. Was it Thursday? Or Wednesday?

I feel his hands slide underneath me. He's trying to raise me. He wants me to carry on with what I was doing. But the day it happened matters. I want to tell him the exact truth.

'It was filthy. It stank. There was dog mess on the carpet. The guy I was talking to, he was reporting being burgled by his neighbour. Said he'd had his Xbox stolen and his wife's tablet had gone.' I don't want Jools to lose his firmness. Mentally, I press the switch on the biscuit machine. The pistons slowly move. 'But I didn't believe what he was saying. There's a feud going on with the neighbour and this guy's made false reports before. I should have questioned his account.' The years on the athletics track have made the muscles in my pelvis quite strong. I give Jools a squeeze. 'But I didn't care. I wasn't even thinking about it. I was thinking about you. About this.'

He gasps. 'What did you do?'

In the pleasure of the canter, my mind goes blank. He has to ask his question again.

'I put my pen down and I asked if I could use the toilet.'

'What happened next?'

'He said yes.'

'What happened after that?'

Oh, God. What have I got myself into here? Do I really have to tell him this? *All* of it? Does he have to know *everything* about me, about how weird he makes me feel? Is there *nothing* I want to hold back from him?

'I went into the toilet and I flushed it. Because the person who'd been in before hadn't done that. Then I tore off pieces of toilet paper and I arranged them in a horseshoe so that they covered the seat. Then I sat on it.'

'Is this true?' he asks, though he knows he doesn't need to. 'What happened next?'

I stare at him hard and decide that I'm going to say it. He has to know what a feeble, slutty girl he's turned me into. He needs to face up to his responsibility. But I have to find the right words. I don't normally use crude vocabulary. Obviously, I know it. I'm a copper. But I don't store it up for use on appropriate occasions. Those occasions, anyway, I find are few and far between. Even when I'm taken by surprise or come across something horrific, nothing rude gets dislodged and suddenly coughed out. So I don't have any instinct for this and it's hard to know what to say next.

'What did you do, babe?'

There is a word I know. It's on the tip of my tongue. Thinking it is making me pant. But I don't want him to hear me say it. It's coarse. It's a word they use in the van. It was low, what I did on Thursday, but I don't want him to think I'm usually like that.

'Please, my love,' he whispers. 'Please. Tell me what you did there.'

'Touch' would carry my meaning. A nice and acceptable word and clear enough. But I need to be braver. I do want to be thrilling, even though I don't want to be coarse. I want him to know the truth: that I'm dirty and I want him to be dirty with me. Another word comes. It makes me sigh as the sound of it rolls in my head. It's the right one. From close up, it photographs the thing that I did. The thought is enough. I'm starting to wail. I think of the neighbours and the open window. There's nothing I can do.

'I fingered myself.'

'What?' He hasn't heard me.

My throat is glued and it comes out just as breath. 'I fingered myself.'

A witness, alerted by the cries, breaking open the door onto our scene of violent shaking, would probably think I'm strangling him. His eyes show only the whites. My grip on him is so tight, there must be a snarl on my face. But in my mind's eye I see busy hands in latex gloves shuffling over a conveyor belt. Love, cut into biscuits, taken and put into boxes and loaded onto vans or sent to subscribers online.

Very soon he's asleep. I lie on my back and look at the fading summer light. I'm engaged. Somehow it doesn't seem real. Under the duvet, I twist the ring round my finger. Yes, today Jools and I took our first step towards the altar. The holy place of gowns and veils, where men and women give voice to the most serious intentions they'll ever have. The place that has obsessed me since Aunty Rita gave me her video of the wedding of Charles and Di, that I watched and rewound for months. I'm to be married. This sleeping man is going to be my husband. And, for the rest of my life, these are the only snores I'll hear. In the twilight, I smile. I don't want to miss a single one.

The way he proposed wasn't exactly what I'd been expecting. I mean, he's not the flamboyant sort, so there was never going to be skywriting, or opera sung up to my bedroom window from the street. But I've not heard of the task being delegated to a dog before. I liked it, though. It was original. And the weather and setting were perfect. The party at The Jolly Thatcher just happened, and we soon scrapped any plans of spoiling it for the sake of a sober drive home. The taxi fare included an uplift for carriage of a dirty lurcher and came to £110. We've got to go back tomorrow and fetch the car. Who cares? Some days you've just got to go with the flow.

But it's not the happiness of the day that I'm feeling. The sound of the shots from Harry Lowe's gun keeps playing in my head and every time it makes me realise that Jools and I could be heading for the church right now for quite a different reason than to be married. Plus, I very nearly lost Grande this afternoon, and, if I had, it would all have been my fault. It's also nagging at me that, when the shooting started, I hid behind Jools. Maybe, on my special day, off duty and strictly as a one-off occasion, I'm allowed to be cowardly and to use my fiancé, my 'gentleman of the very highest quality', as my shield?

There's something else, though, that bothers me, as I close my eyes and twirl the ring on my finger, like it's the dial of an old-fashioned wireless and I just can't find the frequency of Radio Bliss. There's a face in my mind. Not Jools's. It's the woman I spoke to on Friday, who came to the station to report a serious crime. A murder. I see Freya Maskell. Really, I've been thinking about her all weekend and what it is that she's done. About all the time that Jools spent with her in private, about what she told him and what he said that made her change her plan to tell the truth.

I open my eyes and turn my head to watch him. Only his hard skull separates me from Ms Maskell's secrets. He sleeps soundly, knowing they are safe. This is the man I have pledged my life to, the one I can keep nothing from. This is the guy I felt ill at ease opposing last week on the badminton court in a match of mixed doubles. It just didn't seem right not to be on the same side, not to be pulling together and working for the same ends.

At least, that's how it seemed to me.

3

Breathless, I halt on the pavement and pretend to browse a window display. With luck, the woman in the Russian hat won't notice and will pass me by. Against the bustle of the street I hear the tap of stiletto heels approaching. The sound, if my plan succeeds, will rise and peak and die away. It stops. I turn my head slowly and there she is, standing, waiting. She is tall, graceful and cold. I fluster on, but always in the direction of where I know she wants me to be. I jostle the crowd, desperate to blend in, to avoid, to make ground, but the big grey building where she will have me is starting to loom. I should run. I should sprint down this alley and shake her off. Instead I do what I always do in this dream: I cross the busy road to the foot of a flight of stone stairs. Here, I raise my eyes and look to where the steps lead: to the revolving doors of the department store or town hall or office block – whatever it is that the fateful place is masquerading as. I turn again, this time with a moment's relief. The Russian hat is nowhere in sight. But then it is – there, bobbing in the press of people. The crowd clears and, on the far side of the pelican crossing, she faces me. She wills me to walk up the stairs. If I do, I know she will follow me and something bad will happen. She clasps her fur coat around her. Underneath, I believe her to be naked.

And now the alarm goes and it's Monday. I get out of bed and get dressed. Jools hasn't got to be up until seven. I look at him sleeping and feel guilty. I should have been dreaming of him. I text him a note, reminding him he's without a car. I kiss his forehead and pray to myself that he'll be safe. What a ninny I am. All he has to do is take the train to London.

6.50am

First day of earlies and, before anyone here does any work, I'm owed a *lot* of attention. Newly engaged female officer's prerogative. I'll have to announce it, of course. No point waiting for any of the blokes to notice I'm wearing a ring. Where's that Rashid? I want a word with you, my lad. Still pooh-pooh my engagement theory? Still think I've no case? Well, check out Exhibit A here. You *sure* Jools doesn't want me for his wife?

But there's an atmosphere in the office. I can tell that now's not the time. No one's yawning. The usual questions aren't humming in the air. *You got that tenner you owe me? What did you make of* Game of Thrones? *Anyone seen my mug?* Everyone's wide awake and focused, scurrying about or sitting bolt upright at their screens. Something's afoot.

DS Teague has her coat on. She catches my eye. 'Have you got a moment, Ruby?' Dangling between the tweezer-tips of her thumb and forefinger is a statement with my handwriting on it. She leads me into a conference room and closes the door. 'This VPS for Raj Hussein. Not quite sure that we've got enough in it. Can you pay him a quick visit? Flesh the statement out a bit?'

The clock behind her says 7.07am. 'This minute?'

'Yeah, bit of a dawn raid, I know.' She presents her troop of teeth for inspection; all present and correct. 'Trouble with Raj, he's hard to pin down, and it's Evans' first hearing this week.'

Last month, Messrs Evans and Hussein had a full and frank exchange of kicks and punches over something one had posted on social media, the gist being that the other was a see-you-next-Tuesday. 'One man's tweet was the other man's poison,' was how Rashid summed it up. Raj, to the satisfaction of many on the Borden Estate who borrow his money and buy his drugs, all at an exorbitant rate, came off much the worse. And he started it, too, according to witnesses. Not that any of them was willing to make a statement. Evans and Hussein were, though. Both wanted police involvement, for some reason. Anyway, Raj phoned 999 first, so we charged the other guy.

'"The whole thing has left me severely traumatised" I think is a given,' says DS Teague. 'Not being neg but, of course, a racist assault is traumatic.'

'Raj isn't alleging it was racist.'

My observation elicits no spoken response. She merely smiles at my greenness.

'What I think the court needs from a victim personal statement is an exploration of *why* gratuitous racial abuse so aggravates the offence. What you need to give is an insight into the violation of self-esteem and the undermining of a victim's sense of inclusion; an account of…'

Why does she want me to call at Raj's now? I truly don't understand. Something is so going on here. DI McQuade, who is passing, sees us through the glass.

'So,' DS Teague says, and buttons up her coat. 'If you could interrupt his cornflakes and—'

The DI knocks and enters. 'There you are. Has Katie told you the news?'

Their smiles are like the ends of a see-saw. His shoots up whilst hers comes crashing to the ground.

'We have a body.'

'A dead…?'

'Dead and vaguely suspicious. Katie, d'you mind if Ruby stands in for you on this one? There may be a link with something we worked on on Friday.'

Walking into the pound, the DI gives me the keys to the car. We get in and I take a long time adjusting my seat. I'm an advanced driver, trained in tactical pursuit and containment, and here I am, alone with the DI, awed by the status gap, mentally chanting *Mirror-signal-manoeuvre* like I'm seventeen years old.

'Off on a new adventure,' he announces as I steer us onto the road. 'Been doing this job for thirty-one years; loved every minute. So, so proud of the service.' I've never seen him this excited. He looks like he's truanting. 'We're not glamorous, we're not always popular and few of us are heroes.' He beams at me. 'But we're unbeatable.'

I have no idea why he has said this, but I'd pay to have a recording. I'd play it on a loop at the start of every week.

It's made me lift my chin and stare through the windscreen a little more sternly at the world.

'Ever miss the special patrol force? The excitement? All this sitting around in an office, I bet sometimes you'd love…'

He remembers that I'm the one who joined CID partly for 'personal reasons'.

'Worked in the van myself,' he says, and smiles again. 'Used to quite like the rough and tumble. The team spirit. All for one and one for all.'

We leave the town and follow the road to the river, which is where the body's been found. My mouth's getting dry. I've been doing this job for nearly six years and in that time I've seen… what – five, six dead bodies? Average one corpse a year? Like murderers, they have a charisma they probably don't deserve. At least they do, maybe, in the eyes of those of us who are drawn to life's extremes. I suppose this is what the DI was driving at. Police officers are the sort who'd just rather spend their Monday morning dealing with someone's dead body than reading about it in the *Metro* on the way to work.

'How are you getting on with the new DS?'

'Yeah,' I say. 'Good.' I can't think of anything else to say so I give a firm nod instead.

'You trained with her, didn't you?'

I nod again. 'She seems to be doing really well.'

He pauses to choose his words. 'Not sure if I heard right, but did she say… something unkind to you on Friday night?'

'What? Yeah, no. Like. I mean…' I missed out 'totally'. Spoiled the perfect bimbo sentence.

'"You can't trust some women"? Something like that? Was she referring to…?'

I owned up to all this at my CID interview; was candid about why I wanted a new start. It's all coming back to him. I'm the one who lived with Connor Sines. Connor, the copper's copper, who they'd follow to the end of the earth. And I dumped him for a defence solicitor. No one wants to be in a van with someone who'd do that. But DI McQuade recruited me all the same.

'I don't think she meant anything by it. I just think—'

'The van's a world of its own,' he interrupts, putting my non-existent 'just think' thought out of its misery. 'There you all are, cooped up for weeks on end, only yourselves to rely on. It knits you tight. The downside is, you've got to conform. As soon as you look outside the group… Still, I don't see what it's got to do with Katie Teague. And I shan't put up with bullying in CID.'

'Oh, I've never thought that anyone's been bullying—'

'"Banter", as they call it, is one thing,' he says. 'But I'm not letting it go beyond that. I'm not having anyone in my team being bullied.'

As chance would have it, among the first officers on the scene is my one-time Vanguard colleague Tom Barnard, one of Connor's best friends. He 'Sir's the DI and leads us across a field, all the while pretending I'm not here. This is all the bullying amounts to. A shun-until-further-notice. When the DI has his back turned I smirk and splay my fingers, forcing Tom to be the first to see my ring. Shan't tell Jools about this. It's the sort of behaviour he'd be likely to think of as common.

A guy from the river police meets us. He's covered in mud. He says the body's been in the water for days and probably didn't enter it anywhere round here. In fact, it may have drifted down from Frockley. The deceased had been staying there in a hotel. His wife reported him missing on Saturday. It took four of them to haul him onto the bank. Now they're standing well clear. He's on a stretcher, bulging in a blue rubber bag.

'Anthony Gibson,' says the pathologist. 'Still had his wallet.'

She draws down the zip. A plump middle-aged man wearing a loud checked jacket. One of Mr Gibson's eyes is staring. Heedless of the pathologist, the DI closes the lid. Then he closes his own eyes and it looks like he's thinking a prayer.

'Well?' he asks the pathologist.

The pathologist shakes her head. 'We'll have to take him for a proper examination.' She points to a dark reddish patch on the side of the man's head. 'But you see here? I'm not sure but I think that happened before he hit the water.'

Back at the nick, the DI goes into his office and closes the door behind him. DS Teague is with Rashid, perched on the edge of our desk. She glances at me and continues with what she is saying.

'Any link to Freya?' Rashid asks, interrupting her. *Freya.* We've been texting our theories all weekend about Friday's mystery woman. Now she seems nearly tamed.

'Dunno,' I say. 'Someone may have hit him. But it'd take someone bigger than her, I reckon. He's pretty chunky.'

'You hear about Friday?' Rashid asks the DS. 'The woman who told Ruby she'd murdered someone?'

DS Teague chuckles. 'Hollywood-bes. That's what we called 'em in the Met. Not being neg.'

'How do you mean?' Rashid asks.

'Attention-seekers. They make up a story, act out a part. They use us 'cause they know we've got to take 'em seriously. 'S just a need some people have to star in their own soap opera. Now...' She stands, breathes deep and draws back the veils of her cheeks. Revealed is a May Day parade of her duckwalking full dental might. 'Raj Hussein. Victim personal statement...'

3.50pm

Raj wasn't picking up and, when I went round, his partner said she hadn't seen him for days. So now, with no crime that we know about taking place here in the leafy suburbs, and the deadline for our reflective pieces drawing near, the DS is making us do our coursework.

Policing a Diverse Community. That's what it says on my screen. On Rashid's, too, although it's *all* that I've written on mine. I think about gossipy Gurbux, owner of Singhsbury's on the high street, where I buy my *Berkshire Brides*. I remember the *You're so welcome I could eat you!* smile I did yesterday that even DS Teague would have wrenched her mouth on as I signalled my approval to two passing, scowling boys holding hands. Maybe that's what policing a diverse community is all about. Making sure no one's left out. Six words. Only 994 to go.

My mind strays onto my own diverse episode and the return in the night of the woman in the Russian hat. I used to dream about her a lot but, now I think about it, it's been years since the last time. Never did find out what was beyond those revolving doors. She's based partly on someone I met. Someone's mum, who came into the changing room after an event. I was lounging in my underwear and, I remember, she looked at me. That's all. Not in any significant way, but in a way I knew I'd remember. The fur-coat-no-knickers thing, I stole from Princess Di. What brought that on, I wonder…

'If my mother heard that there may be cultural reasons why she wouldn't report crime,' Rashid mutters, 'she'd probably say,' he impersonates her accent, '"You think I pay council tax for you coppers *not* to do some bloody work?!"'

I tilt back on my chair to see what he's written.

'Stop copying.'

'I wasn't, I was—'

The phone goes and, before I can finish lying, he's slapped his hand on the receiver. I'm beginning to feel I know Rashid. He'll have beaten himself up all weekend for not taking Zuzanna's call the other night.

'It's for you,' he mumbles. 'It's the DI.' He hands me over.

'Can you come to my office?' the DI asks. 'There's something I want to show you.'

Instantly I'm up on my feet. 'There's three Fs in "fluffy".'

'What?'

I put my face by Rashid's and together we look at his screen.

'There. Where you've put, "Let me be your fluffy hamster, Katie, so you can stroke my furry tummy."'

It comes out solemnly and quietly and our colleagues at the desk don't realise it's intended for them. For a moment, the idea dances in the air that what I've said might be true.

I knock on the DI's door and enter.

'Sit down here,' he says, rising from his chair to give the desk over to me. 'Watch this.'

'What is it?'

'Watch it.'

He presses a button on his laptop. Grainy CCTV coverage of a barroom appears on the screen. At the bottom, a time reference: 'Thu 12.06.2014, 21.11 hrs'. Above it, a man in a loud checked jacket sits alone at a table.

'Anthony Gibson.'

'Now. Watch this.'

The DI fast-forwards three minutes. Mr Gibson has started to read a newspaper. A woman appears, back turned to the camera. She walks past his table and something happens that alerts him. The quality of the footage is poor but I can see that, at the same time as he turns his attention from the newspaper, the woman looks over her shoulder. I gasp.

'It's her.'

The DI springs from his chair beside me and taps the pause button. 'Who?'

'Freya Maskell.'

'How can you tell?'

Helplessly, I nod at the screen. 'You can see. It's her.'

He starts the action again. Now I see Mr Gibson reaching down to the floor. Freya must have dropped something. Whatever it is, he picks it up and offers it. She turns so that her face is towards the camera, but the footage is so unclear it's hard to see her expression. It doesn't help that she's wearing a hat. They talk for a minute, Mr Gibson gesturing more than once to a seat at his table. Her necklace gleams as she dithers. Finally, she takes the seat and is lost to view.

'Damn,' I say.

'Just off camera,' says the DI. 'All you see now is this...' he forwards to where Mr Gibson goes to the bar and returns with two drinks, 'and this.' After twelve minutes' acquaintance the pair leave together in the direction from which Freya Maskell came. The DI switches off the recording and stares at me. 'How can you tell it's her?'

I don't know what to say. I can't understand why he needs to ask. 'It's her neck,' I say after a long pause. 'Don't you remember the interview? When she turned to consult... her solicitor. The long, slow neck. Like... a sunflower.'

'A sunflower?'

Normally, a lapse into poetry when my boss has asked for hard facts would embarrass both of us. But I'm angry. If this weren't DI McQuade, I'd want to shake him and tell him to open his eyes.

'Which bar is it?' I ask, trying to think round the problem.

'The Thames Frockley Travelodge. The deceased was staying there.'

'There must be more CCTV. We can—'

'The hotel security guy who can access it is on a long weekend. He's being urged to hurry back but it seems he's not exactly going to bust a gut over it. The only camera that anyone could get into was this one in the bar.'

I can't help but look into his eyes. This is fantastic; he must see that.

He smiles. 'I thought it was her, but the quality...' He shakes his head. 'I'm just not sure it's good enough.' He holds my gaze. 'I don't think I could swear in a court of law that that is Freya Maskell. Could you?'

A thrill of relief pumps around my veins. I give out a hoot of a laugh. 'That,' I nod at the screen, 'is Freya Maskell.'

Tuesday 17th June, 11.50am

The head of security at the Thames Frockley Travelodge has been neglecting his duties. Apart from in the bar, not a single CCTV camera was functioning at the end of last week; not one in the whole hotel. As a result, instead of following Friday's comings and goings in the foyer and in lifts and along corridors, I'm spending my morning watching an absorbing game of cricket.

So far, the CCTV trawl from outside the hotel has thrown up just two views. One is of the barbed-wire-topped boundary wall of a scrap-metal yard next door to the Travelodge. The accidental glimpse of the river is so partial, and the chances of discovering anything from it are so small, I've been told I don't need to look at this yet. The other footage is of the car park which the guests use, situated a hundred metres along the towpath from the hotel. This is where Mr Gibson's Vauxhall Vectra was before we seized it yesterday. In between the hotel and the car park are school playing fields. I've found I can keep an eye on the Vectra and at the same time critique the mixed-ability cricketers bashing it out in the background. A bowler has got his run-up all wrong. I'm counting the paces and studying his angle when the DI comes into the room.

'Anything?' he asks, and stands to look over my shoulder at the screen.

'He parked it at 16.38 on Thursday and walked along the towpath in the direction of the hotel. It's now 11.15 on Friday and he hasn't come back.'

'Hmm. Getting nowhere fast with this one.'

'Have forensics come up with anything?'

'No. Well, all they've got to work on is his hotel room and that's been reoccupied since he was in it. Completely contaminated. We've no phone and, even if we had, Mr Gibson's wife says he always went pay-as-you-go for some reason, so we can't even ask round for call logs. There were two rooms near enough to his that were likely to have accommodated potential witnesses and only one of those was being used. There was a man in the room next to his but he's playing hard to get.'

'Have they done the post-mortem?'

'Yes. Mr Gibson didn't inhale any water. Confirms he was dead before he went in the drink. Didn't drown, at least. And he was struck on the temple by something man-made. All as the first pathologist suspected. It's something. Oh, and it definitely is Mr Gibson. His son confirmed it last night.'

'What happens now?'

'The super's got to decide if there's enough evidence of foul play for this to be referred to the major crime team. I need to brief him soon as.'

'Shall I… carry on with this?'

'No. Do me a couple of statements. First, describe what happened on Friday. What Maskell said in reception, go over that blow by blow. Second, do an ID statement, spelling out why you're sure it's her on the hotel bar CCTV. You'll have to do that one really well. The super's seen the footage. Says it's impossible to make anything out. He's going to take some persuading.'

2.30pm

I've been summoned to the duty superintendent's office. Cattlegreen's too small to have its own designated superintendent. They all work out of Thames Frockley and take turns to come up here. At the door I take a deep breath before I knock.

'Enter!'

I do as the lunched-languid voice commands. Inside – Well, I never did. Look who's come from Wiltshire on promotion! – a man called Oliver Bartlett relaxes nearly horizontally behind a heavy, shiny desk that smells of polish. He's so low down in his chair he looks like he's trying to limbo underneath it. This is not exclusively his office, and yet displayed behind him on the shelves are what I recognise to be his medals and trophies gained on track and field. Stretched out so that he's almost parallel with the carpet, his fingers knitted into a little pillow behind his head, he looks like he's never fully recovered from the exhausting effort of winning them.

'Learner Detective Marocco, sir.'

He unlocks his fingers and points straight at me. 'PAA two hundred metres gold. 2011? 2012?'

Fame at last! Almost. '2011. Four hundred metres.'

'Of course.'

'And eight hundred metres.'

'Yes, I remember. You swept the board.'

I steal a look at DI McQuade, who stands by the super's desk. There are two chairs free. It appears he hasn't been invited to take either one.

'You still competing?'

'No, sir.'

'You look like you still work out.'

'Yes, sir.'

So much at his ease it seems he's been squirted onto the chair from a bottle of blue ketchup, Superintendent Bartlett strokes his chin. 'What do you think, DI McQuade?' He continues to stare at me as he talks to the man by his side. 'Is Learner Detective Marocco's judgement sound enough to rely on?'

The DI is startled. 'Er, yes. I'm sure. She's very able.'

One of the medals the super's displaying is the 2011 Winning Force. I can tell by the blue-and-green ribbon. Personally, I think that if I had acquired an item of property by deception, I'd have the foresight to hide it before inviting fellow police officers into my room.

The superintendent's face turns very grave. 'Because we don't refer every blunt trauma death to the major crime team. If you don't plan your pole vault correctly and you end up landing on your bonce, that's a major misfortune, not foul play, and it would be a scandalous waste of resources, and a matter of personal embarrassment for me, if I were to bring the major crime team in only to have them remind me of the fact.'

'Yes, sir.'

More silence, more staring. It's like he's alone watching the telly.

'Len, thank you for your help with this. I shan't take up any more of your time.'

The superintendent reads my statements and the DI utters, 'Oh,' as he realises he's being told to leave the room. The door closes softly behind him.

'I've not seen Freya Maskell, of course,' the superintendent says, still appearing to read my statements. 'But I've watched the CCTV several times and, to be frank, I don't think that even a member of her own family could be certain who's in it.' He looks at me.

'It's Freya Maskell, sir.'

'You're sure of that? After, what, less than an hour in her actual presence?'

'Yes, sir.'

He reads aloud from my ID statement. '"From the slight sway of her hips, the turn of her neck, her gait, height and body shape, together with a silver necklace that I recognised from our meeting less than twenty-four hours later, I have no hesitation in confirming that Female 1 in the exhibited footage is Freya Maskell." Super recogniser, eh? And yet, I notice, you appear to have no recollection of when you and I have met.' He raises his eyebrows and waits. 'I mean, I don't claim elephant status, but I knew you instantly. You're a memorably attractive woman, admittedly, so maybe that gives me the advantage. All the same, you and I spent a good deal longer than an hour in view of each other.'

I thought I was being polite pretending I don't remember him from Sports Day 2011. The superintendent's confidence that I won't mention all the reasons why I do remember him surprises me. 'You won gold at the high jump. One metre seventy-three. You captained the South Central mixed tug o' war team in the wind-down session and we almost beat the Met.'

'Ah, much better.'

'And you refereed our soccer match against Hampshire, and if we'd won it, we'd have had more points than any other force.'

'Ve-ery good. I did. Oh, now I'm impressed. Yes, that still rankles with me, that tug o' war. If only that idiot in the silly trainers hadn't lost her footing and slipped onto her fat... well, never mind. No time for sport now, with the great and the good watching my every move, wondering when I'm going to throw my hat in the ring and go for an ACC job. 'S a shame… Anyway, to business. Possible unlawful killing. What have we got? A body, a confession to an unspecified murder, and an ID which seems to connect the two. Yes?'

'Yes.'

'I seem to remember from chatting with you before that your real love is athletics. I had the distinct impression you wished you'd pursued that as a career instead.'

'Not at all, sir. So far as I'm concerned, that's behind me. I'm a police officer now and I want to be the best one I can be.'

'Hmm.' He nods and settles his gaze on the desk. 'How long have you been with CID?'

'Two months.'

'You ambitious?'

'Yes, sir.'

'Not afraid of hard work?'

'No, sir.'

'Like to do a stint with the MCT?'

I breathe in sharply and let slip one of my squeaky toy noises. 'Would that be possible?'

'Don't see why not. I mean, it's not necessarily within my gift. MCT pick their own, and they only pick the very best.' He looks frank. 'I wasn't the best there, not by a long chalk. Certainly not during my first operation…' He shrugs. 'Might hold some sway, I suppose. A recommendation from one of their old boys.' He pouts. 'From the youngest and most decorated superintendent in the Southern Counties. I just think… if that focus, that grit I saw on the sports ground can be applied to some serious police work…'

He allows me to do some swallowing and bowel-waggling whilst he makes up his mind.

'I'm going to refer this case to the MCT,' he decides at last. 'Not only that, I'm going to recommend that they take you on board to assist. Happy with that, Learner Detective Marocco?'

'Yes, sir.'

'I'm sure I've made it sufficiently clear that I make my decision at some risk to my reputation and standing within the service. I expect you not to let me down. You won't let me down, will you?'

'No, sir.'

He gives me the look that Grande gives me when we both know it's way past the time for his walk. 'Very good. On your way.'

4

Just got a text from Rashid:

The Face of Modern Policing.

I press the link to the *Thames Frockley Gazette* and there he is at my old sixth-form college, grinning his award-winning brown face amongst the black, the white and the yellow. Community engagement. His CV must be groaning at the seams. One more commendation, prize or distinction and it'll explode like a feather pillow. Meanwhile, I'm at HQ, waiting to be debriefed in the incident room. The *incident room.* I'm sitting next to a plaque which bears the magic words. I angle my phone for a selfie.

Has the Face of Modern Policing ever been in one of these?

That's my caption. I ping it off and the door opens.

'DC Marocco?' He's neat and short and very young; my age or less. Young enough to use my first name, I'd have thought. Swinging from the lanyard around his neck, his pass bears the letters 'MCT'.

'Well, Learner Det—'

'DS Bibby. D'you want to come through?'

He stifles a yawn and waves his pass at the sensor. The door swings and we make way for workmen delivering tubs of water and rolled-up camp beds. We follow them into an open-plan office. A woman in overalls is drilling into a wall. Elsewhere, computers are being installed. Plain-clothed officers peck away at keyboards or hold phones to their ears, drumming on the desk with free fingers as they wait for someone to pick up. 'When did they book her in?' someone asks. 'Mark it up on the board.'

'Is Freya Maskell back in custody?'

The DS nods and stifles another yawn. 'Sorry. Didn't quite make it to bed.'

We take seats in a quiet corner. He found time to shave, if not to sleep. The sunlight shines on the crust of polish on the toe of his shoe. I notice an emblem on his tie: 'QC'. He is opening his laptop when his phone buzzes.

'Do you mind if I take this? It's my wife.'

I stand up to leave. He waves me back into my seat.

'Kim's coming round for the little one… plumber'll be there at ten… wants to be paid in cash… I already hung out the washing…'

There's been a pipe burst. Mrs Bibby sounds frantic.

'…Mum's taken care of the shopping… you just rest. Love you, honey. Everything's gonna be all right.' Hanging up, he smiles apologetically. 'Not very well, I'm afraid. Touch of postnatal depression.'

I expect that someone else will have to debrief me as it's clear that DS Bibby is needed at home.

'This confession,' he says, obviously reading the situation differently. 'On Friday night.' He places his fingers over the keyboard. 'Take me through what happened. As much detail as you can.'

He could read my existing statements. One of them is on his screen. But mine is not to reason why. Flexing his neck from time to time against the collar of his pressed white shirt, he listens with complete attention as I tell my story once more.

'So the guy in reception turned out to be a solicitor?'

'Yeah.' It'll probably come out at some stage but, in the meantime, I don't want to let on about my relationship with Jools. But I'm making a hash of pretending. Twice I've caught myself too late and called him 'Joo'. 'My... the solicitor sort of appointed himself. They had a private consultation.'

This detail seems to interest the DS. 'How long did that go on for?'

'Forty-three minutes.' I've checked the custody record. A long time to talk about the weather. Enough time, probably, for Freya to tell her hired new BFF why, when and how she killed Anthony Gibson, and who helped her do it and where those people might be. The things I believe she'd come to confess, and if he'd only let her, we wouldn't be sitting here now. It's for Jools's sake that I'm trying not to say his name. I don't want DS Bibby to have a low opinion of him.

I have a horrible thought. Jools worked late last night and was gone this morning before I got up. 'Is she...' I stammer. 'Is she having the same brief today?'

'She's got a woman,' DS Bibby says. 'Asian? About forty?'

'Ah,' I mutter. Thank God. There's no one of that description who works in Jools's firm.

The DS asks about our search of Freya's flat. 'Can I see your pocketbook?'

I give it to him. He studies it for quite a long time.

'A red bag, by any chance?'

'Er…'

'You've written here, "Gucci handbag". Was it red? There was no bag in her home this morning.'

'Yes, it was. Red. I'm sorry, I should have—'

He hands me my book back. 'Thanks for this. If anything else comes to mind, here's my card.' He gives me it. 'Actually, you'd better store my number in your contacts. The brass seem to want you and me to be colleagues for the time being.' He frowns. It's as though there's a cursor on my face that's stopped blinking and he realises that he's going to have to switch me off and reboot me. 'You'll be part of the investigation. You're working with the MCT.'

I try to say thank you. It comes out as 'Th…', followed by a little squirt of noise from my nose.

'Nothing that will tax your grey matter today. But there is a practical problem you can help with.'

He takes me to the exit and directs me to the refectory on the third floor where, he tells me, I should wait for further instructions. In The Coppers' Kitchen I sit with an Americano until a well-dressed woman appears, smiling and waving a bandaged wrist.

'Are you my driver?'

'What?'

'Are you Ruby?'

'Yeah.'

'Claire Luthwood. Family liaison officer in the Anthony Gibson case.' She nods at her bandage. 'Can't believe how stupid I've been. Did this last night playing squash. Totally preventable; I should have… Anyway, I need to be in Hereford, meet the bereaved. You drive, don't you?'

'Totally,' I say, and stand up – too quickly, so that I cough on the dregs of my drink.

'Don't kill yourself over it. Even I can be nice to only so many relatives in one day.'

In the lift Claire re-enacts her squash court fail. 'Say this is the line.' She points to a spot on the floor. 'So, I bend like this and then suddenly, *aaaghhh*! Stupid of me even to think of going to the gym at a time like this. Three-hour wait in A&E. Lucky I had my laptop. They didn't email today's briefing pack until midnight and it took me the whole time just to read that.'

Down in the pound I'm disappointed to see that my designated car is a homely old Vauxhall Astra. I thought MCT would swagger around in Cosworths at least. I set the satnav and ease us out of the basement car park into the Frockley sunlight.

'How did you get on with Paul Bibby?' Claire asks as she waits for her laptop to power up.

'Yeah, he was nice. Made me feel a bit underdressed.'

'Sets very high standards, rather to some people's annoyance. Nearly got to the stage of fisticuffs between him and your superintendent yesterday evening.'

'Pardon?'

'It was "I *ree-eally* don't want to have to pull rank" on one side and "With the *vvv-ery* greatest of respect, sir" on the other. They were stood toe to toe. It was almost funny. The super must be a foot taller than the DS. There he was, bearing down on him, the DS not moving an inch.'

'What was it about?'

'You! The SIO always has Paul pick the team. Ollie was rooting for you, and he wasn't being very subtle about it. Paul said, "This isn't stray dogs and point duty. We don't work with any old plod."'

'Omigod, I hope that's not how he sees me.'

'Seems not. MCT wouldn't have you even doing this if they didn't trust you. You'd be making the tea and stapling the exhibit folders. If that.'

She settles down to her reading. Stop-starting through the city traffic, I have a chance to check her screen. Emails. Statements. Codes of practice. ACPO manuals of guidance. Home Office directives. There's a beautiful day on the other side of the window, but not once does she take a look. Claire is probably one of those people who have nightmares about going to work unprepared. And, for all that she's smiley and full of life, I suspect she's competitive. She's got me worrying that, with the MCT, I may be out of my depth, and I think she may have done it on purpose. Then again, maybe not. I'm being too guarded. I need to lighten up. My time with these guys will be brief; I should enjoy it whilst I can.

Bit by bit, my optimism restores until, as I accelerate down the ramp onto the M4, wow! Pure exhilaration. DS Teague wanted me in the office today to finish *Policing a Diverse Community*. Instead, I'm out on a murder. There's so much I'd like to ask Claire. On the motorway I steal glances at her every so often to see if she might be up for a chat. But her concentration on her work is cast iron. If I were to say anything I'd feel like I was butting in. Also, I'm not at all sure of my status, despite having been appointed to the team. I'm afraid she might stonewall my questions; that, in her eyes, I'm to be treated as need-to-know. So the next ninety minutes pass in a silence that it falls, finally, to the satnav to break.

'We've had the heads-up from West Mercia,' Claire says, roused by the change of speed as I take the exit. 'We might find Mrs Gibson a challenge.'

I'm pleased to hear the word 'we'. I wondered if I was going to have to wait in the car.

'She doesn't believe her husband is dead. Even though her son's identified the body. Hereford officers say she's not in the least bit upset. Her only concern was that they might get into trouble over their mistake.'

Suddenly 'we' doesn't sound so great. Vanguard cops don't really do feelings. In fact, I'm still getting used to police work that doesn't start with '*Chaaaaa-rge!*' and end with a scrote dangling and kicking from my outstretched fist and a celebratory '*Owzaaaat?!*', with maybe a thigh strike and a headlock in between. Today's mission seems a bit sophisticated for the likes of me.

'What role will I have?'

She looks at me over the gearstick. Again, she raises her poorly paw. 'Write?'

We enter the street where Mrs Gibson lives. Here, people clean their cars and cut their hedges. It's the sort of neighbourhood where everyone owns their own home. The house is detached, a bit like my mum's. Even bigger. Claire knocks on the door. A man, aged about thirty, opens it and lets us in.

'Mum, the family liaison officers are here.'

Mrs Gibson hurries to us. She has her coat on. 'Oh, more police officers.' She smiles. 'We had police officers here yesterday, too. Have you finished with his computer? He's going to need that back.'

'I'm Claire, Mrs Gibson,' says Claire. 'This is Ruby. We've come from Thames Frockley?'

'What a long way! Come in. And call me Hannah. I'm very sorry, I won't be able to stay with you for long. I volunteer at the British Heart Foundation Wednesday afternoons.'

A younger woman, presumably her daughter, comes through from the lounge. 'They're not expecting you today, Mum. I phoned them.'

'Don't be silly, Phoebe. I can't let them down.' Hannah leads us into her home. 'But you must have a cup of tea. Or a glass of lemonade? Did you come by the motorway?'

Her children, who have introduced themselves as Phoebe and Ryan, share a look. In the kitchen, drinks are passed round and Claire asks that we take seats at the table. Her voice is calm and certain. She looks each family member in the eye.

'We're not counsellors. Our priority is to assist the investigation, and that always comes first. But you're in strange territory and, doesn't matter what you think at the moment, you need a guide. I don't want you ever to feel you're being kept in the dark.' She hands them each a business card. 'Day or night, please call me. Whatever you need to know about the post-mortem, about the funeral, about the courts. Or if there's anything you remember which you think might help us find the person responsible, don't think it's probably not important. Always let me know. It's going to help the investigation if you trust me.'

My biro is poised; my notebook open on my lap.

'What sort of man was Tony?'

They look at each other for clues.

'Describe him. Five words.'

The instruction sparks the beginnings of a debate.

'Funny,' says Phoebe.

'There for you,' says Ryan.

'That's three words,' corrects his mother. 'That only leaves us with one left.'

'It's okay,' says Claire. 'As many words as you need.'

'Lovely,' says Hannah. 'He's adorable.'

'Honest,' says Ryan. 'Great dad.'

'Brilliant grandad,' says Phoebe, who, I can see from the many family photos, has a child.

I glance at Claire. I'm not sure when to start writing.

'Was he from round here?'

Hannah nods. 'Yeah.'

'When did you meet?'

Like soothing shade screening her from a harsh sun, a dream casts itself across the widow's face. I click the end of my pen.

'When we were seventeen. I was working at the boiled sweets factory. One day I was coming home on the bus. Didn't have enough for my ticket, for some reason. He just appeared. "I'll pay the rest," he said. Never had anyone show interest in me before. Very respectful. Dated six times before he even kissed me, and then he asked my permission. He was always, always talking. It took some getting used to. I was from such a quiet home. He said he was going to be a salesman. "I could sell snow to the Eskimos." He was famous for saying that. He was born to it. He made me laugh. I didn't really know what laughing was before I went out with Tony. But he was gentle. That's what I really liked about him. We waited until we were married before we had our children. That was Tony's idea. He's quite religious and a bit old-fashioned in some ways. His job really took off and we moved here. That was in 1984. I packed in my job at the factory to be a stay-at-home mum.'

Hannah loses herself in thought whilst her children stare at patterns in the lino. The silence becomes uncomfortable and I will Claire to speak. Instead, she waits.

'Phenomenal work ethic,' says Ryan, raising his head with a jerk. 'I'll tell you the sort of man we're talking about. I went off the rails when I was fourteen—'

'You don't have to tell them about that,' interjects Hannah.

'No, Mum. We've got to be honest.'

'Yes,' says Claire. 'This is what I need. For you to be as honest and frank as you can.'

'So, yeah,' continues Ryan. 'Anyway, long and short of it was, I got arrested over something and I almost had to go to court. The teachers said I was mixing with the wrong crowd. Someone recommended a boarding school. I ended up going there. Best thing that could have happened. It made me. I don't like to think what would have become of me if I hadn't had the break. Thing was – and Dad never mentioned it or made me feel like I owed him anything – the fees were, like, massive. It meant he had to be on the road even more than ever.'

'I didn't hardly see him for two years,' says Hannah.

Now I'm scribbling like an invigilator's said that there's five minutes left on the clock.

'Same with me,' says Phoebe. 'I'm not all that good with money. Well, I'm better now. But a few years ago I ran up quite a lot of debt on credit cards. I wanted to declare myself bankrupt. Dad, though, didn't want me to have the stigma. So he worked even harder. Paid the whole lot off for me.'

'Deserved better than us,' Ryan says.

'He did,' agrees Phoebe.

'Don't ever think that,' Hannah warns them with sudden assertiveness. 'Your father cannot be more proud of you. Both of you. He's always telling me.'

'Did Tony have any hobbies?'

I want to open the window. Pressure seems to be building in the air. With Claire's every 'did' instead of 'does' and every 'was' instead of 'is' it feels like the walls won't stand the strain.

'He goes to church,' says Hannah.

'Yeah, church. Bit of DIY…'

This starts them laughing.

'Mr Bodge-It,' says Hannah. 'That's what we call him.'

'Family was his hobby,' Ryan says. 'Family and work. Nothing else really counted with him. We were pretty… tight-knit.'

'Did he have any enemies?'

The thought seems to them bizarre. They shake their heads.

'No. You couldn't make an enemy out of Dad.'

'Doesn't have a mean nerve in his body.'

'He'd do anything for you. He was the most patient, friendly, giving man.'

There is a loud sniff, followed quickly by another. One by one, the voices in the kitchen fall quiet.

'Are you okay?' someone asks me.

'Yeah, I'm…' A tear falls onto my notebook. 'I'm sorry…'

'*He-ey.*' Hannah stands me up and leads me into the

daylight by the sink. She holds me close, pats my hair. 'There, there.'

'I'm sorry. That's so unprofessional.' I'm sobbing uncontrollably. 'He sounds like such a nice man.'

'He'll be back soon,' whispers Hannah. 'Don't worry. Then you can meet him yourself.'

Over her shoulder, the fridge magnets stare me in the face. One bears Tony's motto: 'Selling Snow to the Eskimos'. Next to it is a photo of the man himself. Relaxed and humorous, a man in love with what he has. Convulsing, I press myself into his widow's shoulder. As I try to speak, tears and strings of slime fasten me to her coat.

'I lost my father, too.'

Thursday 19th June 2014, 6.50am

DS Bibby can't believe it. 'Your resilience and emotional detachment are cited repeatedly in your service record. Superintendent Bartlett vouched for your focus and mental strength.' He addresses the windowpane quietly whilst scratching his neatly combed head. '"Cool as a cucumber" is how Len McQuade put it. "Soaks up the pressure."'

'Sarge—'

'And yet you cried. Not in sight of the bereaved. Actually *on* her.'

He's untangling the facts, primping and straightening them, trying to match them up, as though they were socks from a washing machine. It's embarrassing but nothing worse than that. It's himself he's bollocking, not me. His error of judgement has frightened him. Even with all his strains – the sleep deprivation, the press speculation, the difficulties he has at home, the ticking custody clock – he's asking himself, *How could I have got her so wrong?*

'In my defence—'

'You're not in trouble,' the DS interrupts. Startled, he realises I might be alarmed. 'No, I'm not having a go. I just needed to be clear on the details. No.' He tries to shake from his head the notion that I, not he, am to blame. 'Family liaison is a specialism. You've not been trained for it and you didn't ask to do it. You did your best and, from all accounts, you did it well…'

He sees my frown.

'I phoned the Gibsons to make sure they were still onside. They are. They liked you. Phoebe said her mum appreciated your empathy. And Claire said you were a very useful ally. Obviously, she had to report back… that you got upset.'

I see that my sense of what's 'obvious' in MCT is going to need some work.

'All I'd say is, keep detached.' He draws a hand to the left. 'Keep what you feel here…' He draws a hand to the right. 'Keep what you think here. That way you can keep methodical. Apart from that…' He brightens. 'What did you make of Mrs Gibson?'

'I emailed you my report.' I was up until two writing it.

'Yeah, haven't had time to read it yet. Claire said she's in denial.'

'It's really sad. She's still expecting him to come home.'

He raises his eyebrows and takes a breath. 'When she finds out what we've found out she might not mind so much that he won't. Come on.' He stands. 'Today you'll be working with the techies.'

I follow him to the opposite end of the incident room,

where fellow auxiliaries are in a huddle by a computer. I hear a familiar *Eye-ah!*

'Not being neg. Ha, ha. I mean, whatever floats your boat.' Katie Teague shrugs and pouts, miming her struggle to relate to what she has read on the screen. 'Interesting that this sort of thing's come to the provinces,' she observes, sobering upon DS Bibby's approach. 'It's already a thing in the Met.'

'Morning, morning,' greets DS Bibby.

The group disperses and I glance in Katie's direction, meaning to say hi. She avoids eye contact and wanders off with the others. That's my line manager. The two of us, fifteen miles from our usual workplace, here together by chance and she won't even acknowledge my presence. As for my point of contact among the techies, DS Bibby needs make no introduction.

'Well, I never did,' says Russ Rogers, rising from his seat.

'It's the Vulgarian,' I say.

DS Bibby is bewildered.

'We worked together in SPF,' I explain.

'St Joan of Arc,' says Russ.

'It's a long time since I heard that.'

'Tough as old boots. Pure as the driven snow.'

I laugh. *Aw boats.* He's even more Berkshire than me.

DS Bibby nods at the computer on his desk. 'You've got love letters to trawl through.' He leaves us to it.

'I saw your statement,' says Russ. He chuckles. 'Anticlimax, eh?' He acts out some chirpy banter between Freya and me. '"Hi. I just murdered someone!" "Yeah? Who ya murdered?"' At which point, as Russ imagines it, Freya turns thoughtful. '"Er, actually, I'm not gonna tell you. You might send me to jail."'

'A tease, eh? So what you doing here?'

His happiness wilts. 'It wasn't the same after, y'know, the thing with you and Connor. The atmosphere changed in the van.' He shrugs. 'Made a new start in high-tech crime. Now I'm on loan to these guys.'

It's good to see him. Russ 'Raise You' Rogers. I lost more money playing poker with Russ than I made in all my years of overtime. The Vulgarian. A demonstrator once shouted that word in our direction. We looked it up in the online dictionary and decided the guy must have been talking to Russ, who, in a very competitive field, was by a head the biggest yobbo in the van. But when the rest of them turned against me he refused to take a side. He said, 'It's no one's business but theirs.'

'What's Katie Teague doing here?'

'Who?'

'She was just standing here.'

'The one with the teeth? Dunno. She's been milling about since I got here. Cor, what a gob. Didn't know if she was making space for the massive laugh I was about to make her do or if she meant to swallow me whole.' He nods over my shoulder to the next desk, where she's laughing so hard with someone else she's just met that she's having to press her fingers on his shoulder to keep her balance.

'So,' I say, turning my attention to the computer. 'What had the deceased been up to that might so distress Mrs G?'

Russ swivels round in his seat and taps the keyboard. A website homepage appears on the monitor. The words 'Guilty Secrets' stand out in swirling font.

'Escort agency?' I ask.

'Sort of.' He enlarges a portion of text so that I can see it. 'But read that.'

The introduction announces:

*Guilty Secrets is a fantasy workshop where,
uniquely, our actresses, who are all trained
therapists, prepare with our clients online before
any face-to-face meeting takes place. Typically
over a period of weeks or even months, actress
and client correspond by email, imagining roles,
inventing scenarios and exploring dialogue, really
digging deep to isolate the particular passionate
itch that needs to be scratched. Client/actress
rendezvous, which takes place in a safe and secure
environment, is carefully scripted and executed
at the highest professional level and, because it is
both long-anticipated and exactly tailored to the
client's core desires, provides a depth of release
that is generally unavailable in mainstream sexual
activity.*

Russ scrolls up to a gallery of who I presume are the actress/
therapists. 'Recognise this person?'

There's Freya Maskell. My palm wipes slowly down my
face.

'Didn't you even suspect that Tony Gibson was her client?'
He bursts out laughing. 'Check your mug!'

I'm blushing, I know. Of course. The Gucci bag. The
expensive clothes. The supposed unemployment. Why else
would Freya be patrolling hotel bars?

Russ screws up his features. '*Classic* Marocco.'

'I'm sorry, Russ.' I'm laughing myself, now. 'The thought
just never entered my head.'

He touches my arm. 'Dear old Ru. Promise me you'll never change. Er, yes. The suspect and the deceased were enjoying a game of GSS.'

'Of what?'

'Grunty, Shouty, Squirty.'

'What?'

'They were sharing willies.'

'Sharing…? Have we got a witness?'

He shakes his head and taps again on his keyboard. 'It's on here. This is their… correspondence. Clients of Guilty Secrets actually script their sex.'

'This is what Freya Maskell does for a living?' I am simply stunned. 'So…'

He completes my question for me. '…what did she get up to with Tony Gibson?' He straightens up in his chair. 'That's what you're going to help me find out. We're doing the downloading. I'll show you what to do. The early indications are that it wasn't very savoury. You've seen the CCTV from the hotel bar?'

'Yeah.'

'What happens there is all role play. The bit where she drops her hanky?'

'I thought it was a glove.'

'It says "handkerchief" in the script. Planned. He knew she'd do it.'

'She…' This is going to be a blurt, I know. But there's only so much thinking you can do before opening your mouth, otherwise the conversation just stops. 'So, she dropped her hanky on purpose?'

Russ frowns at me. 'That's right, Ru,' he says, very slowly, matching the pace of my thoughts.

'And… what? So they've both learned their lines? They're acting?'

'There's actual dialogue. You know, like in plays? His first words are something like, "Excuse me, you dropped this." She thanks him. Then they talk about the hotel and how long they're staying. That sort of stuff.'

'Do we know Tony's fantasy?'

'We're starting to get the gist. They'd been writing emails for weeks. See here…' He opens another window, on which I read a greeting:

Hiya, Vixen…

'Who's Vixen?'

'You make up a name. That's hers. He calls himself Logan.'

I read on.

Great to hear from you. It's a real pity elf 'n' safety won't let you carry an actual knife. A big yes to the rope, though. I hope you remember your knots from Girl Guide days! Still not sure of location. Advantages of bedroom, as I see it, are a) comfy, b) good for bondage, c) privacy, although, TBH, not sure I want privacy. If weather forecast good, maybe outside? Genuine drag-into-a-bush scenario? Main thing is I REALLY want to hear 'You're going to do exactly what I say.' You can whisper it into my ear, or just say it like you're teaching a fact. Making me wild now to think about it.

Freya's reply is below.

> *Hey, Logan,*
> *Yeah, no knife, no Rohypnol, I'm afraid. Important*
> *we stay on the right side of the law in what we do.*
> *That definitely does NOT mean that we're not gonna*
> *reach down right to the heart of your fantasy. I*
> *think you're wise to concentrate on the words. We*
> *need dialogue that'll really underline the power*
> *imbalance. All I'd say is, from my experience, a*
> *bit of flexibility in the timing can be good. If I say*
> *the things you want, but maybe not when you're*
> *expecting to hear them, then the element of surprise*
> *can be a real turn-on...*

I look at Russ. 'What's going on?'

He looks uneasy, like he has bad news to break. 'From what we've been able to piece together, really he wanted to be faithful to his wife. He told "Vixen" he couldn't be aroused by any scenario that involved cheating on her. Trouble was, Mrs Gibson wasn't putting out.'

I think I know the term. 'She wasn't... sharing willies?'

He shakes his head. 'No GSS.'

'How did he hope to square that circle?' I ask, borrowing a phrase from Jools.

'He wanted Vixen to... force him.'

9.50am

My first MCT team briefing. In the conference room they're jostling for seats. Russ has gone outside for a smoke and has asked me to save him a place. I hope he hurries up. It feels babyish, sticking my hand in the way as colleagues move to occupy the chair next to me.

Morale in the team is high. There's a rumour going around that the guy in Room 311 has been run to earth. That's the room next to Tony's at the Travelodge. His statement is supposed to be dynamite. What Russ and I are unearthing is pretty explosive, too. We're having a very good morning. Banging.

'Is this free?' The guy who's asking is a regular. He's got the QC tie and the MCT stare. They all look at you the same way here, with a naturalist's frown, like you're a specimen in a cage. *Sorry, Russ*, I think, and gather my lanyard off the chair. Copying my new companion, I mute my phone.

Russ complains the MCT are too serious, that working here isn't like being in the van. Between our retches and splutters, as we've undeleted such emails as the one in which Freya asks tactfully to scale down the levels of violence Tony asks of her, or the one where Tony records the very phrases he wants to use to beg for Freya's mercy (I am older and *so* much wiser than I was two hours ago), we've been chuckling about the demos and the street fights and the pitch invasions we survived and which now seem like good times. 'Laughter was the fuel that powered that van,' he's been saying, adding with a mutter, 'Not like here.' And during today's performance review with Paul Bibby, at ten to flipping seven in the morning, I admit I'd have been inclined to agree.

But I've changed since then, I can feel it. I know it's me he's referring to, partly. I know I'm letting Russ down, as we mine the comedy gold that is the deceased's transgressions and I pass up on chances to match his smirks, better his quips. But, unlike me, he's not met the bereaved, and that's why we see this job differently. The penny hasn't dropped with Russ yet. It has with me. It happened this morning as I found myself reading the emails not through my eyes, but those of Hannah Gibson. And I guess the penny has dropped at one time or another with everyone here who wears the QC tie or brooch. At some point when you work in the MCT the reality dawns that what we're dealing with is murder; the fact that one person has caused another person to stop. It's the worst thing you can do. And what is starting to drive me on, as it drives DS Bibby when he abandons poor Mrs Bibby to deal with a burst pipe by herself, and drives Claire Luthwood as she swots one-handed in the hospital and reports on my failings to the brass, isn't dull or vindictive, or losing one's work-life balance; it's the knowing that, unless we take this seriously, put it at the top of our priorities, ahead of our families if necessary, even our chance of a laugh, someone may get away with what they've done.

'What does "QC" stand for?'

My neighbour turns his face to me. Elite thought-concentrate pipes like icing through the nozzles of his pupils. '"Quietly, ceaselessly." It's the MCT motto.'

I'm glad Russ isn't here. He'd have laughed at that. Myself, I'm more inspired than at any time since I hung up my running shoes.

Apart from a single seat further along the row, it's standing room only. A CSI guy kicks and sways among our ankles, trying to get it. No one moves to accommodate him. There are mutterings that CSI have underperformed on this case. They've spent four days in Room 310 and, contaminated or not, there's a feeling they should have found *something*.

The senior investigating officer is DCI Trigg. He enters the room at ten o'clock on the dot. With him is DS Teague.

'Morning, morning. Not going to keep you long. Quick update on progress, then DS Teague,' he smiles as, picking the stepping stones with care, he crosses from one end of her job title to the other, 'senior... domestic abuse... stalking and... harassment... liaison officer—'

'Nailed it!' she says, and winks at him. 'DASH.'

'—is going to say a few words about the important role she has in this investigation. First of all, good news from Northumbria. Our Sunderland witness has finally broken cover, made a statement. This is the gentleman who had the room next to the deceased on Thursday night.' He refers to his tablet. '"I don't know what time it was but I was woken by sounds from the room next door. A woman was shouting. It was something like 'Get on your knees' or 'Get on the floor'. It sounded like there was a man with her. He was groaning and sounded in pain. I thought it was the television so I put my earplugs in again and went back to sleep."'

From the line of standing stragglers by the wall, I hear Russ snort. He looks around for a face to share the joke with. I turn away before his eyes catch mine.

'Is Ruby here?' the SIO asks.

I jab my finger about two inches up from shoulder height.

'There she is. Yeah, well done, Ruby. It's down to Ruby's confident ID that we took in the suspect and seized her laptop. And what a treasure trove that was. So now we have a body, a meeting between the suspect and the deceased that's captured on CCTV, evidence of a joint violent sexual fantasy, and, less than twenty-four hours after we know they were together, a clear confession of murder by the suspect. Still no motive, still no weapon, still no crime scene, still no idea how the deceased came to be in the Thames. Lots more to do. Any questions?'

The woman in front of me puts her hand up. 'Is the hotel security guy of interest? I mean, not to load one camera might seem unfortunate, but an entire hotel full of non-functioning CCTV?'

The SIO shakes his head. 'His failings are all down to his own honest incompetence. We have no reason to think he had any involvement with what happened to Mr Gibson.'

Someone else speaks up. 'Are there any marks on the body that may have come from the scripted sexual activity?'

'No. The reddish blunt trauma injury to the right temple is the only sign of human agency in Mr Gibson's death. That, by the way, is dye, of a kind commonly used on leather.'

My neighbour raises his hand. 'It has to be a theory of the case that this was a role play gone wrong. It also now seems the role play took place in the hotel bedroom, in which case presumably the suspect had help from somewhere to get the deceased out of the room?'

'And why would she move him anyway?' another person enquires.

The SIO nods. 'Dunno. As I say, we've still got a way to go. Okay, I'm going to hand you over to Katie.'

Katie rises thoughtfully to her feet. 'Don't wanna hold you guys up; know you've got urgent stuff to clear. Hi – DS Katie Teague, senior DASH liaison officer. Completed two years' work with the Met's High-Risk DV Advisory Group; now working closely with Superintendent Bartlett on the area-based DV thematic at Cattlegreen. Ollie has asked me to support and advise the team over the course of the investigation.

'You don't need me to tell you, DV has very much become an officer's hot potato. For good or for ill, careers are rising and stalling under the glare of the DV spotlight, the spotlight that is always beaming down on us from the offices of the great and the good. Let me remind you of the government's definition of a DV crime, as it was redrafted last year: "Any incident or pattern of incidents of controlling, coercive or threatening behaviour, violence or abuse between those aged sixteen or over who are or have been intimate partners or family members, regardless of gender or sexuality."

'Now, I know what you're thinking: *What has this to do with our suspect and the deceased, Tony Gibson?* Well, it's not the classic DV scenario, I grant you. And that, I would suggest, is precisely why this investigation is potentially a minefield. Can I ask, is there anyone here who, during this investigation, has thought to fill out a DASH questionnaire? Anyone flagged this up on the system as DV? Considered enhanced witness service for others apart from the bereaved? No one? To be honest, I'd worry about you slightly if you had. But let's look again at that definition. "Any incident… of… violence or abuse… between those aged sixteen or over who are or have been intimate partners." Intimate partners. Those who have engaged in a sexual relationship. What are we looking at here? What do we believe Ms Maskell and Mr Gibson had been doing?'

Now there's a hubbub. Katie raises her voice to talk over it.

'Not here to alarm you guys, but there's always forms to fill and boxes to tick. Ignore them at your peril. My job is to help you conduct your enquires in accordance with force DV protocol. Dot i's and cross t's. Basically, you can see me as someone who's just here to watch your backs. Unsure of the victim's charter, don't know what services to offer your witness – come and see me. You'll find me during office hours at the desk by the photocopiers. My door is open any time.'

Everyone gets up to go.

'Is she for real?' says the woman in front of me as we file out.

'What?' the guy next to me wonders. 'So the deceased plays away from home and *he's* a victim of domestic abuse?'

I realise that no one who is murdered here on Katie's patch is going to die unsung. She'll see to it personally that all are buried with full honours in her career plan and marked with a headstone in her CV. Once Russ has finally dropped that penny, I wonder if he might pass it on to her.

Friday 20th June 2014, 2.15pm

This time yesterday our tails were up. The investigation was going somewhere and the office was buzzing. That now seems a long time ago. Since then we've come no further forward. The mood is turning tense. We have until 9pm to charge the suspect or release her. There's a feeling the CPS won't buy it.

Russ and I have been asked to observe a final interview. Much of what they're asking Freya Maskell is about the stuff we've found on her and the deceased's computers. We're sitting in the next room by a monitor, watching four very tired people slug it out.

'How did you get to know Mr Gibson? Do you work as an actor/therapist for Guilty Secrets? Is this an online escort agency? How long have you been working in this capacity? Do you work under the name of "Vixen"?'

Freya has been shuttled between this room and her cell for almost four days. She looks anxious and drawn. It feels like I've known her forever but it occurs to me that, in an hour or two, it'll be exactly one week. She turns to her lawyer from time to time as first DCI Trigg then DS Bibby put the questions to her. Am I imagining it or is the pride beginning to drain from her face? Is it me or is the sunflower starting to wilt?

'On the 26th May this year, did you email Mr Gibson in the following terms? "I will abuse you. I will tell you in detail what I shall do to you, then I shall do it." What abuse did you subject Mr Gibson to? How many times did you and Mr Gibson meet? Did you abuse him on every occasion? Where did you generally meet?'

When I phoned DI McQuade yesterday to update him and told him that Freya Maskell's a sex worker he wasn't surprised at all. Or surprised only in the way that Russ had been: that I hadn't known all along.

'No comment. No comment. No comment.'

'This has all got to count against her,' I whisper to Russ as Freya breathes her trademark refrain. 'If she's got an innocent explanation her brief will have told her to give it.'

Through the screen I stare at her solicitor, the latest random confidante she shares the truth with; the truth which the rest of us here have been racking our brains and wrecking our home lives the whole working week to find out. I don't like her. Sitting there like a clucking hen, brooding on Freya's secrets, serenely keeping her counsel whilst a major crime goes unsolved. I feel jealous. *Why did you tell her, Freya?* I want to know. *What's she got that I haven't?*

'On the 1st June Mr Gibson wrote to you in the following terms: "I want to be punished for betraying my wife." Is that what you did to him? Did you punish Mr Gibson? Did you take it too far? Where did you kill Mr Gibson, Freya?'

Freya opens her mouth. I hold my breath. All of a sudden

I don't want her to speak. If she owns up they'll send her to prison and I'll never see her again, at least not while she looks as she does now. She alters the shape of her lips. Different words poke heads from their burrow, lose heart and withdraw. She closes her mouth. And now I change my mind entirely and will her to tell all she knows.

'We've checked Mr Gibson's bank account. He had paid you; what more did you want off him? Or was it a mistake? Did it all happen by accident? We believe that you own a Gucci handbag made of red leather. Was there anything heavy inside that bag?'

'No comment. No comment. No comment.'

I'm so sick of hearing the phrase. All the psychobabble I've had to read these last two days on Guilty Secrets. All the stern stuff about the need to find the words. 'The keys that will unlock you.' Say it out loud, get it off your chest, heal your festering conscience. Words are 'the breeze that airs your poisoned mind'. After ninety hours of solitary contemplation, 'no comment' is all their actress comes up with.

7.50pm

I don't know if, on the night of the 4th August 2012, Greg Rutherford, Jessica Ennis, Mo Farah and their people went to the pub to celebrate. If they did I imagine their faces might have looked like the ones around me here at The Grapes. Serenely exhausted. Blissfully disbelieving. Pride-stamped with the knowledge of a job well done.

'There were moments when I'd have bet my pension the CPS was gonna NFA it,' says DS Bibby in front of me in the queue at the bar.

'What did they say?' asks the guy beside him.

'"She murdered him one way or another. What other conclusion can one draw?"' The DS departs from his business hours no-banter policy to do his impression of someone who's been educated in everything except how to speak like a normal human being.

Katie Teague lurches into him, almost splashing him with Prosecco. 'Whoops,' she says. 'Who put that policeman there?'

I buy my wine and Russ his pint and Claire her lime and soda. Behind me, as I wait for my change, I hear someone say, 'Ru Marocco thinks…' I don't catch the rest. I turn with my tray and, subtly as I can, cast about to see who's citing my opinions. It's one of a group of QCs. A product of my brain is now available in stock in the minds of the MCT. Just when I thought life couldn't get any better.

My gang are squeezed on a bench in the corner. Katie Teague has placed herself next to Claire.

'Had a call from Ryan Gibson,' Claire tells me as she takes her drink. 'Hannah's tried to throw herself out of a window.'

I stop moving.

'Not high. But upstairs. At the house.'

'"Tried to"?'

'The children caught her as she was stepping out. They've taken her to A&E, had her sedated.'

Katie speaks into the rim of her glass. It sounds like she's saying her stocking is itching. 'Sorry,' she says as she sees our blank expressions. 'Stockholm syndrome.'

'What?' I ask.

'After years of abuse she's rid of her tormentor and now she can't handle the freedom. Held a conference on it in the Met. Classic reaction.'

'Oh, I don't think he was abusive,' Claire says.

Katie looks coy. 'There are always two DV realities. The "I was hit by a cupboard door" one you actually believe in when you're talking to police officers. The "Please don't take my kids away; he's really a lovely fella" reality. And there's the reality reality which only you and your guy know about.' She belches and looks into her drink. 'Believe me. I've been there.'

Claire looks at me and then at Russ, who's making good the levity deficit by telling a joke to a non-job fella on his other side. She brings her face close to Katie's. 'You're a victim of domestic abuse?'

''S why I transferred.'

'But I thought you and your partner were… still together.'

Katie nods. 'Still love the guy. In a way. And there's the children.' She looks like she's about to cry. 'We wanted to make a new start; thought maybe a slower pace of life would be a good idea.'

Claire gives me another glance. With all her experience, even she's unsure where to go with this. 'Is it working out?'

'So far. I mean, there's been no repetition of… the physical aspect. But he'll question me tonight when I get home. Where have I been, who have I been with.' She looks up from her glass and, just as suddenly as they tumbled, her spirits take to the air. 'Sir! Sir!'

Superintendent Bartlett has appeared at the bar. He's bought drinks for DCI Trigg and DS Bibby, who smile and shake his hand. All's well that ends well. Katie is up off the bench and jostling in his direction. Russ, with us in mind and body once more, nods in her direction as she goes.

'I kept an eye on her "DV desk". It was directly opposite ours. Didn't see a single copper go to seek her advice.' He takes a sip of his pint. 'In fact, have you noticed, even here, she always goes to people; no one ever comes to her? Actually feel a bit sorry for her, for all her "Look at me!"'

We tell Claire how we know each other and Russ describes his two days working alongside 'Joan of Arc'. '"Good grief! Oh my goodness! Do people actually do that?!"' He's lucky he didn't get squeamish Rashid.

Claire says, 'Bless,' and pats my arm. Then, as Russ excuses himself and goes to speak with someone else, she draws a little closer. 'So what did you make of your family liaison experience?'

'I found it quite traumatic. Well, you saw.'

'You do at first. I still do on occasion. But you'd be good at it. You've got the human touch; it's all you need. It's important work and a great way to get into MCT, if that's where your real interest lies. I'd be happy to recommend you, if you want to get trained up.'

I wasn't expecting this. This is fantastic. 'Well, so, yeah, I suppose. That'd be great.'

'I'll speak to DCI Trigg.'

I make my way to the ladies'. Good news, together with four sips of wine on top of three hours' sleep, has made me pleasantly drunk. Superintendent Bartlett is coming the other way along the corridor.

'Profitable week?' he asks, standing very near and looking very tall.

'Ah, sir, it was amazing. Yeah, it was a really good experience.'

He nods. 'Time you had something serious to cut your teeth on. Ordinary plain-clothes work can be a tad dry for those of us… with a bit of oomph.'

'Yes, thanks so-o much for giving me the opportunity.'

We used to have kit inspection on the parade square at training school. From the angle of the tilt of your hat right down to the millimetre-deep shine on your shoes, the brass would look you up and down. That's the way Superintendent Bartlett is looking at me now.

'Done with talking shop,' he says, up close like it's a secret. 'How about we splinter off from the crowd and get ourselves a decent glass of wine somewhere?'

'Ah, sir, I'd love that—'

'Better leave separately. I'll make my excuses now. See you downstairs at The White Cellar in quarter of an hour.'

'—but it's my turn to make the tea.'

'You live with someone?'

'Yeah, we're getting married.'

'Oh. Right. Well, I'm sure your fiancé won't object to a short delay. Not when it's time spent with a person of some influence who's interested in developing your career.'

'Yes, but I've got to walk the dog, too.'

'You're putting your dog before your superintendent?'

'He's not been out since the walker took him at lunchtime.'

Superintendent Bartlett is confused. He shakes his head and clears away the fog. 'I understand totally. You have commitments. Some other time, Learner Detective Marocco. I hope your dog enjoys his walk.'

He leaves me with a big, warm smile. That's so nice. I'm relieved. It'd have worried me all weekend if I thought I'd upset him.

5

'I don't understand,' Lorna says, staying the shortbread oblong by her mouth. 'So "Tommy" is… female?'

'Yes,' I say, and rearrange the shopping bags around my feet underneath the table. 'Thomasina. I didn't know myself until the other day.'

'I thought it'd be, like, you and three blokes. Beer and jeans and, you know, *Match of the Day*.'

I blow on my coffee and shake my head. 'Tommy texted Jools last week. Said she'd be flying into Heathrow and would call by. Then yesterday his boss said he needed to see him over the weekend; something important's cropped up. So, yeah. The plan sort of formed itself. Proper dinner party.'

My sister pouts and surveys the Saturday-morning Costa queue. 'Thomasina?' She screws her face up. 'What, is she an old girlfriend?'

'Dunno. They knew each other at university. She's a journalist or something.'

Lorna puts down her latte and, two minutes having passed since she last did it, checks her phone. 'Odd that she should pitch up out of the blue. You'd have thought she'd know to butt out now that Jools is engaged.'

'He's still allowed to see his old friends.'

'Even his exes?' She looks at me. 'Bit weird that he's never let on that she's a woman.'

I begin to wonder if it is a bit weird. I snap myself out of it.

'Have you asked to see his Facebook account? They may be in touch more than he lets on.'

'Lorna!'

'Or give him a dick-sniff.'

'What's that?'

'You know. Check where they've been. It's what Jadey Dancer does when Curly May-Clutton comes home from the pub.'

She meets my stare with a smile. She knows better than to think we'll ever agree on what men are for or why it can be a good thing to have one.

'Maybe I should open the front door to her holding a golf club and a knife.'

'Mmm, you could.' Lorna sucks up some latte and suddenly turns all sophisticated. 'Although if you do that Jools might think you've not hosted a dinner party before.'

'I told him that this morning. He said he'd cook when he saw how scared I was. Wish I'd let him now.' The thought of the evening ahead makes me want to crouch behind my old van riot shield.

'Why didn't you?'

I stare at the wall and shrug. 'Wanted the guests to see him looking like a proper husband and me like a proper wife.'

7.15pm

Lester Legarde *does* talk like a kazoo. Jools has got him to a T. And his laugh is straight out of my grandad's collection of old comics. *Yuk-yuk-yuk.* Bristly, leering characters did it when they thought they'd the upper hand. I didn't know it happened in real life. *Yuk-yuk-yuk.* It's coming from Jools's study. They've been holed up in there two hours.

Meanwhile I'm in the kitchen, doing a Lorna, checking my phone non-stop.

Red wine – breathing.
White wine – in the fridge.
Serviettes – ironed and rolled into the wooden rings Jools asked me to drive all the way to Frockley to buy.

I've got a new list app. The bullet points are copied from a *Berkshire Brides* article I'd kept titled *Are You the Perfect Hostess?* I'm ticking them off one by one.

Glasses and cutlery – polished.
Flowers – everywhere in the flat, but especially on the dinner table, where they form a 'focal centrepiece'. I think the idea must be that, so long as you stare at the flowers, you won't think to turn on the telly and watch Casualty from over your shoulder.
Music – cued at a 'suitably unobtrusive' volume on the iPod, our carefully selected mood-matching playlist lies in wait.
Do food.

This is where I'm up to. Using one of Jools's cookery books as my guide, I'm turning wine, mustard, flour and lamb's fat into viscous Shrewsbury sauce. I chose the recipe next to the tastiest, steamiest-looking photo, in the book with the glossiest cover and the biggest writing. The thing I have to remember is that the recipe caters for eight and tonight there are only going to be four of us, so I must divide all measures by two.

Yuk-yuk-yuk. There he goes again. Jools is laughing too. Really laughing. Or laughing loudly, at least. I'm dying to know what's so important they couldn't talk about it in the office. I couldn't help but giggle when Lester arrived. I was expecting someone Bartlett-sized. He barely comes up to my cheekbones. When Lester went to his car to get something, I said to Jools, 'Quick, do me a Lester!' But he's being all grown-up and pretended not to have heard me.

I open the oven door. The smell of rosemary and the heat of my first-ever lamb blast out. I'm at the point of measuring the wine for the Shrewsbury sauce when the doorbell rings. I put down the jug and buzz the communal door open. I check my list: wine, serviettes, 'suitably unob—', yeah, yeah... food... just one more after that.

Relax!

I draw two quick, deep, therapeutic breaths and, heart pounding so I can almost hear it above the extractor fan, tick the final box. I wipe my hands on a tea towel and sprint through the hall to meet her at the top of the stairs. *Normal people*, I tell myself. *Just like normal people. Only cleverer.*

I open up. An impish face peers at me from under a wide-brimmed hat. 'Ruby?'

I nod at my name and say hers. I manage not to curtsy.

'I heard you were a beauty,' Tommy says and stands amazed, 'but I wasn't expecting this!'

I stretch out my hand and get ready to say that I'm delighted to make her acquaintance. She steps into the flat, puts down her suitcase, and takes me into her arms.

'*Sooo* pleased for you both. He's a wonderful man... And who's this?!'

The dog lumbers through and dabs her thighs with his nose.

'Grande. *Grand-ay*. It's Italian, I think. Means "big".'

'How old is he?'

'Not sure exactly. Six, we think. He was a stray.'

'*Che carino!* She falls to her knees in the hallway and rubs her face against his. '*Ciao, bellino. Come stai?*

Jools appears from the study and makes his way past me to where Tommy is by the door. They say nothing, only embrace. I stand and grin and wait for the embrace to end so that I can take her coat. I have long enough to notice a grain of sleep in Grande's eye, which I pry with my thumbnail.

'You'll have to forgive the dress-down,' she says, when finally I take her stuff. 'Been wearing this frock for three weeks. Literally, it's the only one I possess.' It's ethnic and hand-printed. When she moves she rattles with bangles and beads. Her tan is deep but patchy; unmanaged, like she got it just from working in the sun.

Jools introduces Lester, who's joined us.

'Legarde of the eponymous firm?'

'Call me Lester.'

This time she takes the outstretched hand.

'We've finished our business,' Lester assures her. 'We won't be talking shop.'

'Talk as much shop as you like. The law fascinates me.'

Jools leads them through to the lounge. I take their orders for drinks. Jools warned me this morning that Lester doesn't like alcohol so I've bought him ginger beer. He says that'll be 'wandafoo'. Tommy says she'll have anything. I don't want to spend my evening facing a panel of non-drinkers, so I decide she'll be getting as much of my white wine as I can force down her. I catch Jools's eye as I go to the kitchen, hoping he'll tell me what's up. But he's still not giving anything away.

I return to the guests holding a tray. Tommy's eyes are everywhere as she leads Lester around the lounge, hunting for clues about us among our books and pictures and ornaments.

'Ah!' She picks up a book the size of a shoebox that Jools bought the other week. 'Have you seen this yet? *Sapiens*. Finally, they've translated it from the Hebrew. I read it at the airport on my way out.'

I catch Lester's hand as it goes for the book and fill it with his tumbler of ginger beer.

'Ooh, wine. Lovely!' Tommy says as she takes the glass I offer her. She has the most perfect teeth I've ever seen.

'Cheers,' says Jools.

We raise our glasses.

'You been somewhere nice, then?' Lester nods at Tommy's tan.

'Mali.' She beams at him. '*So-oo* beautiful.'

'Mali, eh? Don't think I know anyone who takes their 'oliday there.'

'I've been working. Making a TV documentary about the women cotton workers.'

'Sounds like one not to miss.'

She laughs. 'Yeah. Making it was the easy part. Now I've got to find a company who'll buy it!' The humble touch does nothing to dim her aura of having a cool-sounding job. 'So,' she asks, turning to Jools and me. 'When's the big day?'

I smile at my fiancé and wait for him to speak. 'Tomorrow,' I say, giving up. 'If I had my way.'

Her mouth falls open. 'Lester and I could be your witnesses.' She looks at us one by one. 'We can go to church in the morning! You can be on your honeymoon by the afternoon!'

''Aneymoon?' Lester laughs. ''E's got too much on his plate for any 'aneymoon.'

I shake my head and use an assertive-sounding sentence I've said before. 'What I've got in mind is gonna take a *lot* of arranging.'

'Full coach-and-horses production, yeah?'

I show Tommy my resolute face.

'Wearing white?'

What great questions she asks. I could give her a documentary on each of them. But is it polite to talk about what interests only me? And how long have I got? 'Gotta be white. I'm having a really long train and, yeah, I dunno, I just think trains only suit a white dress.'

She's maintaining eye contact. I still have her attention.

'Sarah Jessica Parker wore black and always says she regrets it. Kate Middleton, Jelena Djokovic, Victoria Beckham, they all married in white. I'd really like something by Sarah Burton. Her designs are lush. Not that I can afford—'

Tommy touches my arm. 'You'll look *so-ooo* gorgeous.'

That's probably how the younger royalty shut you up when you've babbled long enough. *Ouch!* I shouldn't have named those celebrities. I've just pretty much proved to this Italian-speaking reader of textbooks that I've a subscription with *Hello!*

''Ere,' says Lester, 'I don't want you takin' 'is mind off 'is work with these weddin' preparations.'

'Have you decided on your vows?' Tommy touches my arm again, this time to plead, 'Please don't say you're going to love, honour and obey him.'

'You can't promise to love someone,' I say, and, for a painful moment, watch as Connor's broken face flutters through my mind. 'It's not within your control.'

'What about "obey"?'

Jools's turn to speak on the subject is becoming overdue. It's starting to look like I'm hogging the conversation. But it seems, right now, he has more important things than marriage on his mind.

'I think I'll do a Lady Di,' I say, citing yet another celebrity, 'and leave that one out.'

'Honour?'

'I'm never sure I know what "honour" means,' says Jools, at last. Unlike me, he can get away with his ignorance without seeming thick.

Tommy thinks about it. 'Putting the other first?'

'Yes,' I say. 'I'll promise that.'

'What, like, giving him your last crust? Your last penny?'

'Yes.'

'Die for him?'

Again I look at Jools. 'I thought that was the whole point.'

He starts to nod. Whether this means he agrees with me, or if he's just caught up by the beat of the suitably unobtrusive music, I can't tell.

Tommy turns her beam onto our other guest. 'Are you married, Lester?'

'Twen'y-eight years next month. I was nineteen, she was seventeen. Four children, all grown up and flown the nest. Esther was the girl next door. Literally, the next terrace along. Little backstreet in Tottenham. Never thought *not* to marry 'er, really. Never thought not to go to school or get a job, come to that. Just something you do, where I come from.'

Exactly as she did when I was talking, Tommy looks like her mind has never been so blown. 'What's the recipe for a long and happy partnership?'

'Er, I dunno…' His mind goes blank. As our friends at The Jolly Thatcher found, the fact of being married is easy to confirm; its meaning is harder to articulate. Perhaps Tommy's word 'recipe' has knocked him off course. Maybe he can't think of marriage as being a thing of measures and timings and fresh ingredients. Or maybe, now the boot's on the other foot, the lawyer in him remembers that questions can lead you to where you might not want to be. 'We're chalk and cheese in some ways, me and my better 'alf. She's always been a contented soul, whilst I've been ambitious. She's 'appy with her TV programmes an' 'er chats on the phone with her mum. I can't *stand* stayin' in.' He pouts. 'Never seemed to bother 'er, lookin' after the kids by 'erself while I studied for my exams and whatnot. Feel like a criminal sayin' it nowadays, I 'ardly saw my family all the time I was buildin' up my practice. It's bought us a nice 'ouse in Stamford 'Ill. None of 'em complained. Me 'n' my missus rub along very well,' he concludes. 'I talk to 'er. I provide for 'er.

I'm there for the family occasions. Unlike some blokes, I never lose my temper—'

'Excuse me?' says Jools.

Yuk-yuk-yuk. 'Not at home, I don't, though I may do in the office. I've never raised my voice to my wife, still less my hand; nor 'as she done it to me. No, Esther doesn't arsk for much but she does insist that she be made to feel appreciated, an' I take care to show that I do appreciate her.' With a look that's full of *mwah-ha-ha*, he meets Tommy's gaze. 'And, in return, she knows not to enquire too closely into what I've been doin' or where I've been.'

'You're a rogue,' says Tommy, wearing what I imagine is the only expression a woman can have on her face when telling a man he's a rogue.

'There's yer recipe. "Don't arsk too many questions."'

In the kitchen, I stare into the baking tray at my Shrewsbury sauce. I should have googled 'viscous'. I can see from the picture that it probably means more 'looks like jam' than it does 'so that the fat floats in globules on the wine'.

Jools walks in. 'You okay?' He can see that I'm not.

'The recipe's for eight and there's only four of us, so I had to halve all the amounts of stuff and I got mixed up and did double instead and poured two pints of red wine into the Shrewsbury sauce when I should have put in half.'

He goes to inspect the baking tray. 'Oh, God. I thought you said you could do this?' He dabs with his finger and grimaces at the taste.

My ears are ringing. He's never spoken to me like this before. 'I'm very sorry.'

He lets out his breath. 'No, *I'm* sorry. That was an arsehole's thing to say.'

'It was going all right, then the doorbell rang and I—'

He shakes his head. 'Don't worry about it. They'll just have to wait whilst we make some more.'

I move away from the work surface so he can see the recipe, but he seems to know it by heart. 'Is there anything I can do to—?'

'Guess what?' he says, and hurries about, grabbing pan handles and dipping into packets and pots. 'Lester's looking for an equity partner. Wonders if I'd be interested.'

'I thought you said there was no chance of getting a partnership at Legarde's?'

He nods. 'He always said he needed full control. Now he wants to concentrate on his Crown Court advocacy. Looking for someone to run the business side.'

'Would you be okay with that?'

'Definitely.' He presses more juice from the lamb. 'I told him I'd need an assistant with my caseload, but I'd be able to keep the big clients. The business itself is straightforward.'

'Wouldn't he normally go for someone older?'

'Hayley, Conrad, Giles. They've all got more seniority but he says I'm the only one he can trust to put in the hours.'

'Omigod, that's fantastic. But why did he need to come here to talk about it? Why couldn't you discuss it at work?'

'I think he wanted to be sure I'm the respectable, dependable sort I appear to be, not some liability with a dodgy double life. He probably also wanted to see that I'm good for the money.'

'We haven't got any money.'

'Hmm. Yeah, we'll have to cross that bridge when we come to it. Anyway, it's not a definite offer. He's just sounding me out. But do you know what the really exciting news is? You remember I asked you if you knew the name Mark Wells? The gangster-stroke-businessman my mate Steve was representing on a murder charge? Well, he got convicted and now he wants to appeal. He's sacked his solicitors and he wants to instruct us.'

'Is that good?'

'It is if we get him off. If *I* get him off. Lester wants me to visit him in Belmarsh.' Jools whisks in new wine with the flour and mustard powder. 'I think Lester's giving me Wells as a test. Get the firm a good name with big fish like Mark Wells and, you never know, this time next year I might be a partner in one of London's leading criminal law firms.'

'And then can we set a date for the wedding?'

He's sensitive enough for this to touch a nerve. 'Ah, darling, we're not going to wait that long. Back there,' he nods to the room where he left me to drown in my own marriage conversation, 'I just didn't want to give Lester the impression that I'll not be a hundred per cent focused on the job. I mean, he jokes about it but he really does expect a huge commitment.' He brightens up and takes me by the waist. 'We'll be married before you know it.' He starts to kiss me.

'Shouldn't you be with the guests?'

'They're getting on fine by themselves.' He licks my bottom lip. 'Anyway, who's gonna guard my sauce? Its safety can't be guaranteed so long as you're loitering in the vicinity.'

'Lordy,' says Lester to Tommy as I stand baked Camembert before him at the table. 'You don't want a job at my place, do you?!'

'Why?'

'You do a bloody good line in cross-examination. You should be a lawyer!'

She claps her palms together. Her fingertips squeeze her bottom lip. 'I'm asking too many questions. I'm sorry. I'm always doing this.'

He laughs and claps her on the back. 'You arsk your questions. I'm only pullin' your leg.' Lester's hand, having stamped its reassurance, now grips the back of Tommy's chair.

'So, then. I pay your wages?' She turns to him, eyes wide, perching on the edge of her seat. 'Me, the taxpayer?'

'Partly, yeah.'

'So what do I get for my money? Payback time, I get arrested. I call for Lester Legarde, top solicitor. How does he help me?'

Lester chuckles. She's giving him the third degree. 'The police are going to arsk you questions. If you get a brief, then he'll tell you in advance of the interview the questions they're likely to arsk. It's a bit like preparin' for an exam.'

'What, so if I go it alone they won't give me the examination topics?'

'No.'

'So having a solicitor is like preparing to cheat in this exam.'

'Well, not really. 'Istorically, your right to silence, your right not to say anythin' that might get you in trouble, is protected. It is in this country, at least. That's why everyone's entitled to free and independent legal advice at a police station. And the most important advice I can give usually is whether my client should answer the officers' questions. Obviously, as the police tend to accept, that advice can only be meaningful if they tell me their case.'

'What if they don't?'

'Then I advise my client not to answer their questions and I announce the reason on tape.'

'Okay. So I'm in my cell. You arrive. What happens then?'

'We go into a consultation room and you give me your instructions.'

'My instructions?'

'You tell me your side of the story.'

'Can I trust you? I mean, this is the first time we've met. Won't you just tell the police?'

'No. It's all in the strictest confidence. I'm not going to tell a soul.'

'Let me get this straight… mm, *delicious* Camembert,' Tommy says in between nibbles. 'You know what I know and you know what the police know and you know what questions they'll ask. And now you're going to tell me if I should answer them.'

'Advise you. You don't have to follow my advice.'

'But what I don't understand is, why wouldn't I answer questions if I've got nothing to hide?'

'How do you mean?'

'Well, I won't have done anything wrong.'

'That's what they all say.'

'But I don't break the law. And if I did, I'd want to do the right thing and own up to it. So why don't I just tell the police the truth, same as I do to you?'

'Do, by all means. Just remember, doin' nothing wrong is not always the same as not breaking the law. But you're right. I'm really there for people who aren't as law-abidin' as you. Fortunately for me and Julian, our clients don't have to *deserve* legal aid.'

'You mean your clients are criminals?'

'Well, yes. Many of them.' Lester looks to Jools, who is sitting opposite, grinning into his cheese. 'I'm a *criminal* defence lawyer.'

Tommy laughs and turns to me. 'What do you think of that, Ruby? We hard-working taxpayers have to cough up so the likes of Jools and Lester can help criminals get away with what they've done?'

Great fun for a copper, that, looking on whilst one of our dear legal brethren totters against the ropes. I'm getting to like Tommy, and any other time I'd probably gang up with her and stick the boot into both lawyers present. She's at least as smart as they are. I could nip out from behind her and chuck a few bricks of my own. But I've just learned that my fiancé's job might soon be bringing in all kinds of nice things, so I'm pretty much forced to be loyal. 'Keeps bread on our table...' I say it with a sad smile and a nervous laugh and I hope she'll leave it at that.

But Lester and Tommy are still looking at me. They want more. Lester wants to see that I'm staunch. Tommy wants to know if I'm capable of generating my own thought. She wants proof that her friend hasn't picked one of those wives who believe that thinking, like DIY or the household finances or other scary tasks too big for them, is the man's department.

'Yeah. I do have a problem with the situation, actually. The caution. Telling suspects about their right to silence. "You do not have to say anything." I agree with you, Tommy. It's like telling someone they don't have to tell the truth.'

Lester asks, 'Do you think people should be made to speak to police officers?'

'I don't think they should be *made* to do anything. It's just that I can't understand why, if you've not done something wrong, you wouldn't say so.'

'So what should happen if a suspect doesn't answer your questions?'

'I should be able to relax and put away my papers, knowing that a jury will treat that the same as a confession.'

Lester takes another glance at Jools, then chops up more of his food. 'Nowadays, that's pretty much what you've got,' he says. 'When I started out in practice there was no "it may harm your defence" stuff. The right to silence was the same as what was written on the tin.'

The main course is divided up and steams on four plates by the hob. The green beans are al dente, the meat is pleasingly pink, the rebranded Shrewsbury sauce crawls and clings and makes threads. Viscous. I crown each little pile of lamb slices with a sprig of rosemary. 'I cooked a proper meal!' I write under the photograph I've taken for Lorna. 'It's got vitamins, nutrients, everything!'

At the point of pinging it over, the phone goes off in my hand.

'Lorna?'

She sounds serious. 'Have you checked your Facebook account?'

'No.' I do it. '"Simon Marocco wants to be my friend." Is that what he's said to you?'

'Yeah.'

'Does Mum know?'

'I can't tell her, can I?'

'But it's been sixteen years. We can't *not* tell her.'

'We promised, though, didn't we? She made us promise.'

'Omigod… You haven't accepted him, have you? Don't, whatever you do.'

'Not going to. Not unless you do.'

'What do you think he wants?'

'No idea.'

'I feel sick.'

'So do I.'

''Ow d'you know these two lovebirds, then?'

'Jools and I knew each other at university,' Tommy says.

'University, eh?'

'Mostly the journeys to and from,' says Jools. 'We're both from the East Midlands. Tommy had a "car". We used to go halves on the petrol.'

'And on replacement tyres and windscreen wipers and exhaust pipes,' says Tommy. 'It was during those long hours waiting in lay-bys for Green Flag that we laid our plans for world domination. Happy days.' She sighs.

'Not for me, they weren't,' says Lester. ''Ard slog. Library and lectures was all it was for me. An' in the evenin', a wife and screamin' kids at 'ome. I bet you did the 'ole sex 'n' drugs 'n' rock 'n' roll thing.'

Tommy and Jools smile at each other for about two seconds before she speaks.

'I think at London we were encouraged to make a grab for all the opportunities. Recreational and intellectual.'

Conversation gives way to munches and grunts and praise for the perfect hostess, which I am too distracted by this Facebook thing to pooh-pooh. It must be a wind-up. Does Lorna know a joker so warped; do I have an enemy so cruel? Or, now that we're grown and don't need him, has our father decided at last that he wants us in his life after all?

Suddenly, it's a sunny morning and Lorna and I sit cross-legged on the floor. It's near the end of the school holidays and our dad has been 'working away'. All summer long we have failed to wonder, even for the briefest moment, why a window cleaner would need to 'work away'.

The unheard of is about to happen. Without warning, without it being bedtime, the telly is about to be turned off. Mum doesn't even use the switch. She just pulls the plug out of the wall. All these years later, Lorna still swears it was *Scooby-Doo* we lost that day. I think it was *Garfield and Friends*.

'Do you know what a promise is, girls?'

All we can think of is the television. In our home, the first out of bed puts it on, and whoever turns it off at night does it long after we've been washed and sent to bed with hot milk, to drift off to its strains and mumbles through the wall. In between, it's never-ending. At mealtimes we talk over it. When guests come, they usually give up on us eventually and watch whatever's on.

'Your father has left us. He's never coming back. And, now that this has happened, I want you to promise me that neither of you will ever mention his name to me again. Do you understand? Never in my presence. Ruby, do you promise me? Lorna?'

She tells us what it is to break a promise, but already her point has been amply made. Our father's gone. The morning's TV has just been assassinated. Words wrung out of us when a catastrophe like this is in progress are sacred. Clearly.

And it's months before one of us makes a slip. When that happens, Mum gathers us close. 'In the summer you both made me a promise. You both know what it was. I'm beginning to wonder if I made it clear what it means to break a promise. So, let me remind you…'

But, once more, all that she needs to do is done. She's brought back to our minds the dreadful solemnity of the day the screen went black. This time the awe and the terror stay with us. From that day to this, whilst in our mother's presence, neither I nor Lorna has spoken of our father again.

9.10pm

'Does that present a problem for you? In your relationship?' Tommy nods across the table, first at me, then at Jools. 'I mean, with you rounding 'em up, and you setting 'em loose again. Don't you stand for opposite things?'

I turn to Jools, who I hope has been listening.

'We wouldn't be together,' he says, 'if it weren't for our jobs.'

And no sooner am I back in the present than I'm yanked back in time once more. September 1999 a minute ago; now it's the 4th August 2012. The opening chapter of *The Story of Our Love*, as narrated by Jools. It's not the best version I've heard, technically. With the different perspectives of his listeners to take into account, he's having to bend it about a bit, dock it in parts. He was much less businesslike than he's having Lester believe. And, probably for Tommy's sake, he's really paring down the mush. I'm not going to correct him or fill the story out. We've learned from other couples, who talk over each other and quibble about details and thieve the other's punchlines, how not to do it. In fact, for my part, I'm pleased that he's telling the story at all, and seemingly with pleasure. It's his way of saying sorry to me for stowing himself away the whole evening, deep up his boss's backside.

'Sonny Bryant, eh?' says Lester. 'Can't be many as feel a debt of gratitude to 'im.'

'But now that you're together?' Tommy persists. 'You wouldn't be able to work in opposition on the same case?'

'It's interesting that you ask,' Jools says. 'Why don't you think that would work?'

'You've promised that you'll each put the other first. And, I'm supposing, your client or your chief constable would say they expect you to put them first, too. So, if one of you is trying to build a case and the other is tearing it down...?'

I've sometimes wondered what the expression 'the elephant in the room' means. Now I think I see. Jools and I haven't spoken of Freya Maskell since the day of our engagement. Not directly. He knew I was working for the MCT but I didn't tell him how that ended up: that Freya had been charged. Nor has he ever asked. And now the subject has become taboo, Tommy has it by the trunk and is coaxing it here to the dinner table. I fix my attention on the blade of my knife as it saws off a sliver of lamb.

'It's not a problem for us, so far as I know,' Jools says, after a prolonged chew. Out of the corner of my eye I see him looking at me, checking if I agree. 'We're professionals. We keep an emotional detachment. We have our different roles within the same system. I think we respect each other's position.' Now he stoops his face, rooting mine from my plate. 'Don't we, Ru?'

'Yes.'

The table grazes in silence.

'In fact,' he continues, 'it's rather topical. I didn't tell you, Ru. You remember that interview we did together in June? At Cattlegreen nick? That woman's new solicitors have been in touch. I don't think I told you, Lester...'

He tells our guests, in general terms, about the evening of Friday 13th June and the detail, the one I didn't think he knew, that we charged the suspect with Tony Gibson's murder.

'Why did you not carry on representing the woman?' Tommy asks.

'Yes, I'd like to know that,' says Lester, who's probably thinking that his firm's coffers are never too full to accommodate uplifted legal aid payments on another murder case.

'Seeing as you and Ruby are professionals and can handle being in opposing camps?' Tommy adds.

'Mm… I work in London. I live here. You could walk the dog from here to where the suspect lives.' Jools twists his mouth and looks around. 'All a bit close to home.'

I clear my throat and ask, 'What do her solicitors want?'

'They want me to give them a statement.'

This elephant, I see, isn't just with us in the room. It's been squatting in the flat for the past three months.

6

'It takes a good two hours to decorate a Christmas tree,' my father used to say. 'Do it in less an' you ain't done it properly.'

And it was true. It did take Mum that long to dress the tree. 'How you gettin' on?' she'd ask, dusting her hands as she came through from the kitchen.

In the time that she'd left him in charge, maybe an angel had been removed from a box, a chocolate coin hung to twist on a branch. There'd be an electric drill left on the carpet after a demonstration of the quickest way to peel an apple (you stick the bit through the core and hold the peeler to it as it spins). We'd been taught how to rub circles on our stomachs while our other hand patted up and down on our heads. Since Mum last saw us, Lorna and I could now say a whole sentence in burp.

'What's this all over the wall?'

The three of us simmered with giggles.

'Quick apple peel.'

One Christmas, Dad was in trouble for desecrating Lorna's Advent calendar. He'd written 'Lorna is a yinky!' in one of the little windows and somehow sealed the door so she didn't know he'd been tampering. Mum thought this was going too far. What made it so bad was that the words were in a bubble coming from Jesus's mouth.

'Oh, *Si-mon!*'

He stopped untangling a string of lights, which he'd stored in a hurry eleven months earlier and which now looked like what people draw when they scribble. Mum insisted he apologise.

'Sorry, Lorna,' he muttered to the floor.

Baubles were tied on in silence; tinsel was miserably unfurled. When Mum lit a candle, no one said, 'Ooh' or 'Aah'. Dad pulled Scroogy faces behind her back but neither Lorna nor I dared laugh. Then, quietly, Lorna said, 'I don't mind.' After that she began to sing, '*Lorna is a yinky! Lorna is a yinky!*'

Eventually, helped by the spectacle of our father, who, without meaning to, had tied his hands together with the lights, Mum saw the funny side. She freed him and put Slade on the CD player. He got up onto the dinner table in time for the scream. '*It's Chriiiiiiissstmaaaaasssss!*' We nearly jumped out of our skins.

What is a yinky? Apart from my father, the Lord only knows.

The tree I'm decorating seems smaller than the ones we had then. It was the last one in the store and it bends at the top. I hope I have children one day. It's not much fun doing this on my own.

Someone is pushing at the flap of our letter box. Post bounces against the floor. I stand up, leaving shapes in the fallen pine needles where my knees have been. On the doormat, the mail is in a bundle inside this week's *Cattlegreen Messenger.* A headline catches my eye.

Man Dies in Station Tragedy

Police are still trying to identify a man who was struck by a high-speed train on Thursday night. It appears that the man, who was in a wheelchair, may have propelled himself from the platform at Fountainford railway station into the path of the late-night Portsmouth-bound express train. A source from the British Transport Police said, 'We believe the gentleman was able to conceal his presence on the platform before the station closed. This was a tragic and desperate act and we would ask anyone who may have information as to the identity of the deceased to make themselves known.'

I go through the cards and letters. Amateur Athletics Association… Basil and Ali next door… What's this? Tiny, tiny card, massive capital letters. Addressed to Jools. *P… P…* I turn it ninety degrees. *Peckham.* That's where it was posted. Who does he know who lives there? Quietly, ceaselessly, I prepare to unravel the mystery but my eye is caught by a letter. This spoils my fun. It's also for Jools, although I know what's inside it. I got one like this yesterday.

I bring Jools's post to the study door. I shouldn't need to knock on any door inside my home, but I do.

'Just a mo…'

I wait for him to hide whatever it is he doesn't want the resident police officer to see.

'Okay.'

I go in. 'You making progress?' I ask.

He groans and leaves it at that. He's been racking his brains for six weeks now in the service of his client, Mark Wells. Still he can't see a single thing wrong with his conviction.

'You've got a summons.'

He opens the envelope and unfolds the paper inside. Over his shoulder I read:

IN THE SOUTH CENTRAL CROWN COURT... REGINA V FREYA MASKELL... MONDAY 5TH JANUARY 2015.

'Ages since I was in the Crown Court,' he says. 'I've forgotten how you address the judge. Your Honour? My Lord?'

'Don't ask me. I've hardly ever done it myself.'

'Well,' he says, putting the summons down and getting back to his work, 'nothing to worry about, I'm sure.'

'I *am* worried, actually,' I say, ignoring the cue to leave. 'Why has she pleaded not guilty? I don't understand what they want us to say. We were both there when she came into the police station and confessed. We both heard—'

'Careful,' he says. 'Mustn't discuss the evidence.'

'How do you mean?'

'Well, we can't, can we? We're witnesses.'

'But we live together. Obviously we're gonna talk about what we've—'

'Shouldn't really,' he says. 'Might end up collaborating over our testimony. Inadvertently, of course.'

This gets so much on my nerves that I have to beat away the urge to repeat it in a silly voice. If I had my way there'd be a house rule about using stuck-up words like 'collaborating' and 'inadvertently'. There'd be one about door-knocking, too.

'Aren't you going to open your card?'

'What? Yeah, I'll just finish this. Hey,' he turns to me, 'you making breakfast?'

Dutifully, I go to the kitchen. When I call out, he comes in all smiles, rubbing his hands and showing signs of a healthy appetite.

'Looks good,' he says, and kisses me on the cheek. 'What time are you going in?' He's forgotten that we've had this conversation once already.

'I'm on lates. Driving up to Hereford?'

He nods and speaks to Grande. 'This protruding nose-mouth combo thing.' He runs his fingertip down the dog's snout. 'Any practical use? Can you do water-divining with it? Clear hoover tubes? Or is it in case of infestation, when there are no anteaters available?'

Grande looks at him soulfully. *Oh, master!* he wails inside. *Oh, maaa-ster! You ridicule so. Show mercy!* Then he snaps round vengefully, bitten on the ribs by an imaginary fly.

Just as I'm laughing, Jools asks, 'You got any objection if I spend a couple of days with Tommy?'

'Is that who your card was from?'

He nods again. 'She's got tickets to see The Nephews. And then she thinks we could pay a visit to a couple of old university mates up in the north.'

'No. I don't mind. When... when are you going?'

'The gig's on the 28th.'

'You're coming back for New Year's Eve?'

'Course, yeah.'

After which I talk as much and as cheerfully as I can about whatever unconnected matters come to mind.

There are two routes you can take from where we live to join the M4 and, now I'm on the motorway, I can't remember which one I took. It was five minutes ago.

'Got a problem?' I growl, and give the evils to the guy behind, who's had to brake and, taken in by the mufti and my unmarked car, has given me a blast on his horn. Not sure if I did indicate when I overtook him back there. Still, he can have a blast in return. One, two, three… four seconds it goes on for. Our eyes meet through glass until he looks away. This is the assertiveness that deserted me an hour ago when Jools made his airy request. I just want to check it's come back.

I tell myself it's no biggie. I remember that I'm down to do earlies anyway from the 22nd to the 26th and that Christmas was always going to be a washout this year. But I didn't think that… I try laughing. I lower the bucket down into the humour well and haul up an image of Lee giving my sister a peck on the cheek and asking if it's okay if he has time out with a hottie he probably shared willies with in the not-so-distant past. *To do what, exactly?* my fantasy Lorna asks, as she grips the edge of a work surface in a bid to control her breathing. *Oh, y'know. Bit of inadvertent collaboration.* Still my gloom fails to lift. I change tack and count blessings. I think of Tony Gibson and the man I read about in today's paper. I think of the Christmas dinner tables and the two empty chairs.

I park by the 'For Sale' sign that has been planted in Hannah's garden. Taking a swig from my water bottle, I see she's waiting for me at the window. I've had a week's intensive family liaison training since my epic overshare back in June. This time I'm going to have more self-control. Really, I am. For all I know, throwing herself out of an upstairs window may still be on Hannah's to-do list.

She comes and hugs me on the garden path. I ignore my week's training and hug her back. Neither wants to be the first to let go.

'I'm glad it's you,' she says. 'I asked them to send you.'

We hold each other at arm's length. I smile and try to hide my shock. She's aged twenty years. She's become an old woman.

'You're moving,' I say as we go into the house.

'Trying to. Not had any firm offers.'

'Where will you go?'

'I'd like a flat. Modern. Small, so I don't rattle about.'

She leads me to the kitchen and makes tea. She doesn't bin used teabags any more, just leaves them to dry with the other dozens on the worktop. We take our mugs and sit at the kitchen table.

'To be honest, I don't care. I just want to be out of here.' She looks about the room. 'I feel like a stranger. It's like it's been someone else's home all along.'

'How are Phoebe and Ryan?'

'I told you they fell out before the funeral?'

I nod.

'Course I did, sorry. Can't remember what I've said to who. Yeah. Their partners have got involved and they've fell out too. So now the two families aren't going to have anything to do with each other over Christmas.'

'What are *you* going to do?'

'Me? Going on a cruise. By myself. I'm rich now, don't forget.'

'Tony provided well for you.'

The surface of her tea trembles as she lifts it to her lips. 'Turn my back on the lot of 'em. Not even gonna see my grandchildren. Doesn't bother me, if you want to know the truth.'

'Have you given any thought to the trial?'

'I don't have to give evidence, do I?' She looks at me quickly.

'No. But do you know what to expect? I mean, you're clear what our case is?'

She shrugs. 'I suppose that someone will say my husband was found dead. You'll say that the prostitute told you she'd murdered someone. Then they'll show the CCTV of them together, the night before she made her confession. The other hotel guest will say what he heard... And they'll tell the court what you found on Tony's computer.'

I nod. 'You'll be okay with that?'

She stares into the air. 'One thing I'm not clear about. When did she make her confession?'

'On the Friday night. A couple of days before they found Tony.'

'I mean when on Friday? What time?'

'6.17pm. I can tell you that precisely.'

She draws a deep breath. Claire Luthwood told me about this phenomenon, this fixating on seemingly irrelevant detail. A common feature of the grieving process, apparently. Facts, signs, statistics – anything that might hold a grain of significance. All things to comb for in the rubble; things that might be used to build a shelter. Always worth a try.

'So,' I say. 'Shall we make a start on the family impact statement?' I unzip my laptop and stand it on the table. 'There's always a chance that the defendant will change her plea. If she pleads guilty there won't be a trial and the judge will consider the sentence. It's not likely that they'll do that on the first day, but we need to be prepared. One of the things the court takes into account is how the crime has affected the bereaved family, so what would we like the judge to know? Remember, you don't have to read it yourself but the whole court will hear what you have to say.'

Over the course of the next two hours, I write down her reply.

In the two days that followed the news of my husband's death, I was completely unaffected. I spent the time comforting my children, making tea for police officers, and generally living my life as normal. Then I made three suicide attempts. First, I tried to swallow a large amount of paracetamol. Then I ran a bath and tried to hold my breath under the water. Then I tried to jump out of the bedroom window. My actions were not thought out and my children had little difficulty keeping me safe. However, I have no history of self-harm, or even of unhappiness, and the events caused my family much upset.

Unfortunately, because my husband had been murdered, the police were unable to return his body for a considerable time and the funeral had to be delayed for several weeks. In that time my family came to learn of things concerning my

husband's private life that we never suspected or
thought possible. Mainly, these had to do with his
relationship with the prostitute Freya Maskell. I
believe that what we have learned has affected us in
different ways.

My son's reaction caught me by surprise.
We've always thought of ourselves as a close family
and Ryan and his dad were especially close. After
the police told us about the circumstances of
Tony's death, however, and what had been found
on his computer, Ryan began to have all kinds of
suspicions and negative thoughts about his father.
In fact, since June hardly a day has gone by when
Ryan hasn't told me of some new theory he's had
about other things my husband may have done
behind our backs. The police had to get quite firm
with him because he kept demanding that they give
us back the computer. It was as though, because
Tony had had his thing with the prostitute, he was
capable of any kind of wickedness. Last week Ryan
told me he thought Tony had been planning to kill
me.

In the end, Ryan refused to come to Tony's
funeral. This really upset my daughter, Phoebe,
who has always been quite a religious person and
since her father's death has become fanatical. She
thought Ryan's staying away meant Tony would
not have a proper burial and so would not find
peace. She and Ryan fell out about it and, so far as
I know, have not spoken for months. Phoebe has
also been quite angry with me. Whenever Ryan's

not here she will come to the house and interrogate
me. Sometimes it's hard to get her to leave. She
demands to know what I did to drive her dad away.
'Into the arms of another woman' is how she puts it.
She keeps on at me about the sanctity of marriage
and a wife's duties to her husband. Tony and I never
punished our children physically, but one night
Phoebe said that if I'd gone to the doctor about my
frigidity then her father might still be alive. I slapped
her on the face.

As for me, these days, I do a lot of thinking. I
don't sleep properly any more or go to work. I lie
awake or I sit in a chair and I think. But I don't work
anything out. I don't reach conclusions or make up
my mind on any point. My head just whirrs away
without making anything. Ask me one day what
I'm thinking and I'll tell you that I agree with Ryan.
I'll say that this family was only ever a part of my
husband's life, not even the most important part
for all we know, and that what we had and I thought
valuable – things like our home and our plans and
our memories and the things we saved our money
for – meant nothing to Tony and so really had no
value at all. At times like this, I end up believing that
Tony was a stranger to me all my married life and
that I just got used to never knowing him. It's really
frightening. Another day it will seem to me that
Phoebe is right. I suppose I must have been a less
passionate person than Tony would have wanted. I
never minded the physical side of our marriage but
I felt that, once we had our children, the need for

it fell away. I knew that Tony wanted it more than I did but he was always the perfect gentleman. He never sulked about it or anything. And so I must have overlooked what Phoebe thinks is obvious: that 'all men have needs'. When I look at it that way, it makes me think it wasn't Tony who messed everything up for all of us; it was me. I think that I've been too lazy and selfish to be a proper woman, and that I've not been an adequate wife. So on 'Phoebe days' I think I've failed.

I wish the prostitute, Freya Maskell, had never been born.

7

'The phone rang in the CID office. You picked it up.' The defence barrister is going to keep on staring at me until I admit it.

'Yes.'

Freya is sitting across the courtroom, behind a Perspex screen. Six months of prison food have filled her out. She's looking well.

'What did the caller say?'

'It was Zuzanna, the receptionist.' Zuzanna, who went home to Poland and is now untraceable, leaving me the only one on the goodies' side to believe. 'She said that a MOP had just said—'

'A MOP?'

Willing my hand not to shake, I reach out yet again for my plastic cup of water. 'Sorry. A member of the public… had come to the police station and said that she wanted to report a crime.'

'"A crime"?' With every sentence I outrage him more.

'Yeah. A serious crime. Something like that.'

Suddenly he forgets about me and writes a note on his pad. Then he turns a page of his law book. Before I was called to give evidence, the judge sent the jury away. I'm glad they're not here to see this. I'm being made to feel that I'm the one on trial. Still, there's no shortage of spectators. The extended Gibson family have a section of the public gallery dedicated to them. Team Mum occupy two rows, Team Dad the other two. Hannah has a seat on her own. In the well of the court, DS Bibby sits with ants in his pants behind the prosecution counsel, bobbing back and forth to whisper into her ear. Alone on the third row, DI McQuade, who has a million more important things to do in the office, is here to support me, a member of his team.

The barrister stands up again. He looks at me for three or four seconds, then casts his eyes downwards and puts his hand to his mouth. '"A serious crime" is what you said in your evidence in chief. Which was the phrase Zuzanna used?'

'Yes. A serious crime… And that the MO… the member of the public said she was responsible for that crime.'

'What did you do then?'

'I went downstairs and spoke to the woman… the defendant.'

I nod in Freya's direction. As usual, she avoids eye contact. Has she ever actually *seen* me? Would she recognise me if I passed her in the street?

'I confirmed with her that she was the person who wanted to make the report. I introduced myself and asked her her name. Then I asked her which crime she had committed.'

'What did she say?'

'"Murder."'

'What did you do then?'

'I arrested her.'

'Did you caution her?'

'Yes.'

'What words did you use to caution her?'

'You want me to say them?'

'Yes.' It would make his day if I got this wrong.

'"You do not have to say anything but it may harm your defence if you do not mention when questioned something which you later rely on in court. Anything you do say may be given in evidence."'

'And then you took her away?'

'Yes.'

'And what you have told us just now was the whole of your conversation?'

'Yes.'

'You're sure about that, are you?'

'Yes.'

'But it wasn't the whole of your conversation, was it?'

'It was.'

'The first thing you said upon hearing the defendant mention the word "murder" was, "You look much too nice to do that." Isn't that correct?'

'No.'

'And that was indicative of the lack of professionalism with which you dealt with Freya Maskell throughout.'

'Pardon?'

'You thought the whole thing was a bit of a laugh.'

'Absolutely not.'

DI McQuade recommended that I wear my uniform to

show respect for the court. But after a year in civvies, my tunic feels like a straitjacket. It's hot and it rubs and it gets in the way. Breaking the silence which, serenely, the barrister pours over what I've just said, as though to preserve it in liquid cement, my stomach gives a prolonged rumble.

'Officer, are you aware of the provisions of Code C of the PACE Codes of Practice?'

'Er, Code C deals with detention and questioning.'

'And, specifically, are you aware of Paragraph 10.1? Just to help you, it's the paragraph that deals with cautioning of suspects. It says, "A person whom there are grounds to suspect of an offence must be cautioned before any questions about an offence, or further questions if the answers provide the grounds for suspicion, are put to them if either the suspect's answers or silence (i.e. failure or refusal to answer or answer satisfactorily) may be given in evidence to a court in a prosecution."'

Is he asking me or telling me?

'Okay.'

He does some more note-taking and a little more legal research. Anyone would think he was alone in his study, not under the gaze of strangers impatient for justice to be done. 'At what point during that Friday evening did you first have grounds to suspect that Freya Maskell had committed an offence?'

'I suppose when Zuzanna told me that that was what she'd come to the police station to report.'

'Whilst you were upstairs in the CID office?'

'Yes.'

'Before you'd even met the defendant?'

'Yes.'

'So it would be true to say, wouldn't it, that, according to the provisions of Code C, the first thing you should have done upon meeting Freya Maskell would have been to caution her?'

'Er, if—'

'Not ask her what crime she had come to report?'

'Well, hang on—'

'Or make any facetious comment upon how pretty or how "nice" she looked?'

'I did not say that.'

'No further questions, Your Honour.'

The judge says I'm free to go. I stare at her until I understand that she is not going to let me catch her eye. Shoulders back, chin up, as the DI advised, I step from the box and make my way to the back of the courtroom. I see Ryan Gibson, who looks away. In fact, everyone seems to stare at me until the point I look at them. Everyone, I notice, except the person in the dock.

I want to get out of here but I can't. The defence barrister landed punches. He's given the impression that I've something to apologise for and if I leave it'll look like I'm running away. I push at the little swing door that hives off the public gallery and stand at the end of a row. The man sitting closest to me looks up once or twice but doesn't move. He's willing the dodgy copper to go away. When I don't, he budges up, allowing me space. I sit and I take stock.

It surprises people when I tell them how rarely the average police officer enters a courtroom. We're summonsed often enough, but all we normally do is hang around in other parts of the building, drinking coffee and playing with our phones. We seldom give evidence. I've hardly done it at all. And this might be why it has taken me until today to appreciate what lawyers are allowed to do here.

That was truly horrible. It was dishonest. The judge let the lawyer make out that real, unrehearsed life is different from what it is. She did nothing whilst he scowled and sniffed and made me out to be some second-rate actor who hadn't learned her lines. That thing he did, repeating what I said in a slow, deliberate way, so that what was normal and proper began to sound wrong and misjudged. It was a trick, a game, the one where you pick a word randomly and repeat it until, by a process of overthinking, it starts to sound strange. And that mountain-sized molehill he made over Code C. Oh, come *on*! So, what, a completely unthreatening woman throws herself down at the mercy of the authorities and before I'm even allowed to smile, or offer her a seat or build up any rapport, I'm supposed to caution her? We're human beings, for God's sake. I'm not fitted with a computer-generated warning that what people tell me may be recorded for quality and training purposes.

And then, after the barrister had roamed free, branding me as incompetent, as unprofessional, as a liar, and the judge had looked on blandly whilst he pretended to be scandalised about things he really couldn't care less about, except insofar as he could use them to make me seem like a fool, after all that, when it was time for me to explain myself, to add a bit of context, to remind the people listening of how life is actually lived, *he just stopped and sat down!* I couldn't believe the judge didn't tell him to get back on his feet right then and stop being so damn rude.

Just how much talking around the point was she going to let him get away with? No one's claiming that Freya didn't confess to a murder. The judge and the barrister know that she did. And still she gave him licence to ignore this, what I would call, basic and important fact, so that he could angle the spotlight onto something much more by the by and make it seem a huge deal. Where's she going to stop? Where is she going to draw the line? Will she, at the end of this, let him say to the jury, in his calm and experienced and self-assured voice, 'Well, the defendant may be a murderer but at least she doesn't give the caution *in the wrong second!*', so that they all think, *Crikey, I see what he means!*? After all my years of innocence, I see finally what a very dangerous place a courtroom is and why the guilty sometimes go free.

The usher calls the next witness. 'Julian Main.'

Jools enters the courtroom and is led to the witness box, where he says he would like to affirm. He smiles and points out to the usher that she has given him the wrong card. She couldn't be more apologetic. They have a little giggle. He's so well turned out he looks glossy. I imagine him as an *X Factor* judge who's viewed my testimony via live-link from an adjoining room and will now evaluate my performance.

'Why were you at Cattlegreen Police Station that evening?' the defence barrister asks.

'My fiancée is based there.'

'Who is your fiancée?'

'Ruby.'

'Learner Detective Marocco? Who we've just heard from? You're going to be married?'

'Yes. Well, I proposed that same weekend.'

I didn't mention my relationship with Jools. I did what witnesses are supposed to do and only answered the lawyer's questions. If I'd been asked about it, I'd have said. The defence barrister pauses so that the court can have a moment to stare at me.

'I'd come to meet her,' says Jools, who I think is filling the silence. 'We were going to go out.'

'Who was in reception when you got there?'

'Apart from the receptionist it was empty.'

'What happened?'

'I took a seat; texted Ruby to let her know I'd arrived. I got my tablet out to do some work. Then the defendant came in.'

'Was there anything about the defendant that caught your attention?'

'Not at first. I heard her say at the counter, "I want to report a crime." The receptionist obviously thought, as I did, that she meant she'd been the victim of a crime. It was only then, when the receptionist gave her a form to fill in, that I looked up.'

'Why was that?'

'Because the defendant said, "No. A crime that I committed."'

'And were those the words she used?'

'Yes. It was at that point that I began to record everything I heard on my tablet.'

'Why did you do that?'

'I could see that, potentially, I might be needed as a witness. As it turned out.'

The defence barrister nods and holds Jools's gaze. In conversation with an equal he seems less angry. Jools says that after Zuzanna phoned up to the CID office, Freya took the next seat but one from his.

'Did you observe her during that time?'

'Yes. Naturally I was curious, because of what I'd just heard. Obviously, from a professional standpoint I was alerted.'

'How did she seem?'

'Quiet. Nervous.'

'What happened next?'

'Ruby – Learner Detective Marocco – came into reception. She asked the defendant if she wanted to speak with a detective.'

'How did the conversation go from there?'

Jools asks if he can read from his tablet. The judge smiles and, at the same time as she glances at the prosecutor, says, 'I'm sure Miss Hargreaves will have no objection.' The prosecutor says she won't. I have the feeling that if Jools had asked, 'Okay if I smoke?' he'd have had the same response.

'Ruby: "Can I ask what it's about?"'

'The defendant: "A murder."'

'Ruby: "Are you sure? You look much too nice to do that." Then Ruby said, "Would you like to come this way? There's an interview room free."'

'It was at that point that I introduced myself to the defendant and asked if she wanted a solicitor. Then Ruby arrested the defendant and cautioned her.'

'Did you record the whole of the conversation between Ruby and the defendant?'

'Yes.'

'As it happened?'

'Yes.'

'And did Ruby caution the defendant at any time prior to the arrest?'

For the first time since he's been in the witness box, Jools appears less than completely happy. 'No.'

The courtroom falls quiet. Some look about to catch another's eye. Others, embarrassed, look down at their knees and toes. One or two frankly stare straight at me. The judge asks the prosecutor if she has questions, but seems to know the answer in advance. Jools is free to go. The judge beams after him as he walks to where I am sitting.

'Budge along,' he whispers.

'Aren't we going home?'

'Don't you want to see what happens?'

'Here,' I say, and stand up. 'Have my place.'

The DI said, after giving my evidence I should bow to the judge before I leave the courtroom. But I'm through the doors and marching down the concourse before I remember it. I grab my coat from the police room.

'Hi, Ruby!' Frederick Warne, sociable burglar, calls as I step back onto the concourse. He must be here on that going equipped I charged him with. I push at the revolving door.

After I have crossed the length of the car park I glance over my shoulder and see that the door is still turning from the force. I unlock the car and sit in the driver's seat. Jools and I came here together and if I go he'll have to take the train. *Good*. On board he can get his tablet out and do some work on his priorities. I switch on the engine.

Connor would never have *dared* do what Jools did back there. It wouldn't even have *occurred* to him.

I manoeuvre out of the space and, directing the car towards the exit, think ahead to meeting Jools at home. I'm too angry to be frightened. In fact, I'm looking forward to it. He's going to hear some home truths. We're going to clear the air. He's going to learn what my shout sounds like when my mouth is pointing at him. He may even have to dodge a cup or a plate. I press my lips together. For the rest of this day, my fiancé and I are through with being reasonable and grown-up. We're going to be childish, like the healthy, normal couples where I come from. We're going to have a fight.

Sounds from the gearbox are turning people's heads. Then, somehow, I hear a gentle, coaxing voice above the noise. *Che carino. Come stai, bellino?* Tommy. In my imagination. Almost as though she's smiling down at me from the rear-view mirror.

I take my foot off the gas. This may give Jools the excuse he's been waiting for. Maybe he won't take the train if I leave him here; could be he just won't come home. Maybe he *has* reflected on his priorities, did it on his minibreak with Tommy and his old uni crowd, and now he understands what London's newest superbrief actually wants and deserves from life: friends who see the bigger picture, who talk about higher things; a home close to his workplace in the Smoke, free of cops and dog hairs, where he'll have chance to grab *all* life's opportunities; a wife who will borrow the odd sentence from Italian and not forget herself from time to time and say, 'dor-er' instead of 'door'.

I glance in the mirror. The space I have left is still vacant. I drive round the car park and park in it again.

Yes, I think I'm beginning to see. All the things Jools did to reassure me – the texting and calling when he was with her after Christmas, the photos I didn't ask for but which showed he was sticking to the itinerary, and, when he was back with me, the right amount of talking about the trip, midway between secretive and gushing, so that I was genuinely interested and didn't suspect a thing – all of it may have been a trick. He's probably been plotting his exit ever since, making sure it's quiet and discreet and orderly, keeping me in the dark until the appropriate time. He might seize on today as a golden opportunity. I'm not sure I can put it past him. He's a lawyer, after all. He may be leading me like Chicken Licken to his Foxy Loxy earth, like his cross-examining buddy did just now. All the more reason to drive off without him. Let him end it, if that's how he feels.

End it? Is that really the word that I thought? No, no. I don't want him to end it. I really don't want it to *end*.

Over by the courthouse entrance, a haze hangs above a crowd of smokers. There's a PCSO, whose name I can't remember. If I could, I'd ask him for a fag. I don't know why, but I want one. The not having one becomes important; a problem to tackle head-on. I get out of the car and walk across the street to a newsagent's, where I buy ten Mayfair and a box of matches. I don't want to do this in front of people. I expect I'll cough and feel sick. I can't very well smoke in the car. I wander about and end up behind the courthouse, where I unwrap the packet and spark up. I hold a mouthful of smoke in place and dare myself to inhale.

'I didn't know you smoke.'

It's Jools. He must have seen me through the concourse window. My nerves in shreds, his sudden appearance makes me draw breath and, for the next thirty seconds, I sound like I'm drowning, having jumped into an icy river, out of a burning flat.

'Ah, I see that you don't.'

He pats and rubs and encourages. From the corner of my dripping eye, I see his changing expressions as he tries to gauge the mood.

'Er, yeah. Sorry, Ru, you wanted to go. I thought I'd stick around for a while…'

He keeps looking at my cigarette. I'd put it out but the vileness of smoking is more than made up for by the pleasure of alienating him.

'Wanted to listen to the legal argument, see if I could get inspired.'

'How do you mean?' I rasp.

'This Mark Wells case I'm doing? I dunno, I just thought it might give me some ideas.'

I'd stare at him if I could bring myself to make eye contact. Does he really think that's my beef: that he wouldn't come instantly when I wanted him? Or is he just hoping it really hard, so that it might start being true? 'Did you get any?'

'Not really. It's a different sort of case.'

We've already established that, so far as fagging it is concerned, I'm sitting wrong way round on the horse. So I've no idea why I'm now attempting to blow smoke rings. 'You didn't have to give evidence today, y'know,' I say, as the last of my rings wobbles off, as packed as a mint imperial, not like a Polo at all. 'I googled it. When Freya Maskell's solicitors phoned you up and asked you to make a statement, you didn't have to say yes. You weren't under any legal obligation.'

He looks at me. 'Is that what this is about?'

Still I can't meet his eye.

'It was the truth.'

'Yeah, but… what you said in there made me look… really stupid.'

'It was what happened. Maskell's solicitors needed to know. The court needed to know.' He sighs. 'This has been gnawing away at us for months. I'm not blind, I'm not stupid. Look. Why wouldn't I agree to give a statement? The only reason would be that it would make things easier for you.

My fiancée. A police officer. And, yeah, why should I mind doing that? But then, if I went down that road, then I'd have to believe that Freya Maskell didn't deserve to have the truth told on her behalf. But everyone does. Come on, Ruby. You know it. You're an honest person. Extremely honest—'

'That's not what you were saying in court.'

'What are you talking about?'

'"Are you sure? You look much too nice to do that." Or whatever it was. I did not say that.'

'You did.'

Memory stirs, like the first faint rustle of leaves when a gale is on its way. Now I think about it, I might have… no, he's doing what the defence barrister did. He's drawing us away from the main point. Maybe I did say that; I'm not sure. But, if I'm guilty, it's of uttering a throwaway line. Not of the murder that, from his forty-three minutes of private consultation with the perpetrator, I think Jools knows a great deal more about than he ever lets on. Isn't that the precious truth? Isn't *that* what all should have a right to hear – what his client told him about why and when and where and how, and with what red thing, she killed Tony Gibson? Don't the rest of us have this right to the truth, or is it just his client? Why is it only the things that come out of my mouth that are put under the microscope? What's so special about hers?

'I loved working with MCT,' I say, unrelatedly. 'The stuff they deal with, it's not the same as usual police work. It's, like, important? The people there… they're really good. Seriously, not everyone is up to it; I mean, hardly anyone is. To be in MCT, you have to have more dedication and commitment than the average copper. Total focus, twenty-four-seven. You've got to be super resilient and never show you're scared.

Of anyone. You're up against the very worst. And, I suppose, yeah, you've got to be clever in a funny sort of way. But mainly you've got to have belief. Y'know, like a true, cast-iron belief in what you're doing, and, well, yeah, I was only doing it a week, if you don't count the family liaison stuff, but I began to think – actually, I knew, because I've been quite near the top of the athletics world and you get exactly the same kind of people there – that I'm capable of having that belief. In fact, I knew I could do all of it, that I could be part of MCT, that I'd fit in very well. And, if I did that, if they recruited me, that would make up for a lot because I sort of bottled it with athletics. When I had the chance to go for the big events, when the right kind of opportunities were starting to come my way, I… I dunno, I suppose my confidence took a dip and I didn't bother. That's always felt like such a mistake. But the noises they were making at MCT were, well, really encouraging. They were saying that when a place comes up—'

I'm interrupted by the scrape of a metal gate which swings outwards from the wall we're standing by. A woman leaves the building carrying a large polythene bag. She is unattended.

'Hey!'

It's Freya Maskell. She's escaping. Jools holds me by my arm.

'Hey!'

'No,' says Jools. 'Leave it. They've let her go.'

I stop pulling. I look into his face.

'The trial's over,' he says. 'The judge has excluded the confession.'

'What does that mean?'

'She wasn't going to allow the jury to hear what Maskell said.'

'About committing murder? But… but that hardly left us with anything. Apart from that there wasn't…'

He nods. 'The prosecutor offered no evidence.'

'Finished?'

He nods again. 'It's over.'

PART TWO

8

'Hello?'

'Legarde's Solicitors, how may I help you?'

I tell her my business and overhear the office banter before I'm put on hold. I hear the word 'eponymous'.

I'm on the Little Cattlegreen Bridge, which spans the London-to-Portsmouth railway line. I've had to come up here to get a signal. I can see the gasometers at Mintsley. And there are the old army barracks. I can even see Mintsley Heights, the tower block where I was born and raised. Every year the council used to promise to repaint it. It never happened. Last I heard, they were going to pull the place down.

They do wheelspins in their cars, where I was brought up, and shout out of upstairs windows. They plant themselves in doorways whilst they smoke and scowl at the street. The council tax band is in the oxygen-depleted outer regions of the alphabet. I know from a colleague that I wouldn't be allowed to patrol there unaccompanied, amongst the abandoned cars and the bobbing, hunched youths in hoods. There's no way I'd want to move back. But I'd rather work there than here. The Cattlegreen Heath estate is crimeless. I've been patrolling these little, neat, pavement-patch lawns all morning and I've not uncovered so much as the litter of a single spent scratch card. In Mintsley, even with a buddy to protect me, I'd have more to keep me on my toes than the thought of a lunch break. Which – I check again – is ninety-eight minutes away.

'Ms Marocco?' a friendly man asks very suddenly. 'Stirling Bann, probate department. You'd like us to draw up your wills?'

'Yeah.'

'You're Mr Main's partner, aren't you?'

'Yeah.'

'I understand Jools has popped the question. Congratulations!'

'Oh, we've been engaged for months.'

'Really? I got the impression he'd proposed quite recently.'

'Ah, yeah. No, it was back in June. He's just given me a better ring.'

'Right. Old proposal. New ring.'

The new one's so expensive I've had to insure it separately. I have my mum to thank for it, really. I went into a bit of a downward spiral after Freya Maskell's trial collapsed. It ended up with me leaving a note on the kitchen table and roaring off to Thames Frockley, pretty much in second gear all the way. Mum put me up in the spare bedroom and left me to cry for three days. After that she made me tell her everything. 'He was only doing his job,' she said at the end of it. 'Ru, he's done nothing wrong.' So I went home, and then Jools bought me the new ring. It's the one he gave me on Leith Hill that I'm wearing, though. It holds happy memories. Also, I'm not so scared of scratching it or losing it in a fight.

'Have you fixed a date for the wedding?' Mr Bann asks.

'Not yet.' Jools was glad to kiss and make up, but not to that extent.

'Okay. Shall we leave it until then? It sounds like it won't be long, and you'll only have to make new wills once you're married.'

And that's the way we leave it. Well, it was only an idea. Another from *Berkshire Brides*.

Best go and reassure someone, I tell myself. That's why I'm walking around the Cattlegreen Heath estate. Reassurance patrol. On the subject of which, I'd like a little reassurance myself. Can't shake the thought from my head that that was Tommy I heard in the background just now when I phoned Legarde's.

'Hello, little lady!' I squat to be on equal terms with a Bedlington terrier cross. 'Just taking a look at her tax disc,' I say.

Her mum looks guarded whilst I fiddle with the tag on the collar.

'And I'd better check the tread on her paws.' I bend up the ankles and examine the dog's pads. 'All seems to be in order.'

The owner's really not sure about this.

'I'm joking.'

It takes a moment for this to process. She lets out a big, loud laugh.

'What's her name?'

'Groover.'

'How old is she?'

'Seven.'

Same eyes as Grande's. One full of hope, the other in doubt. No say at all in the human's next decision.

'My ex got her when she was a puppy.'

'You walk your ex's dog?'

'Wednesdays I get access. And every other weekend. It's part of the court order.'

I didn't consider *that* when I did my flounce on Jools. I stoop to ruffle the dog's chin. 'Hello, little Groover!'

She honours me with a wag. Dogs aren't like us. They only smile when they mean it. A tail, unlike a mouth, can't lie.

'And I'm allowed to send emails and birthday cards.'

I look up. Now she's smiling. She's as mad as me.

'When me and Paul broke up we said we didn't want to set eyes on each other again. Could have done it if it hadn't been for Groover. Now, with just the dog to argue about, we get on a lot, lot better.'

She tells me about Groover's type and I weigh up the pros and cons. I'm coming close to admitting to myself, as I sift the information, that I'm considering Grande's successor. I don't even feel bad about it. Dogs don't live forever. It's a fact we owners have to face. You love the one you have with all your heart, but also with half an eye out for the next.

'I've just read a really interesting book,' she says. 'It's set in the future. The idea is that women suddenly lose their attraction to men and it leads to a fall in the birth rate. It gets so bad that the government develops this policy of making the male half of the national population more appealing by transforming them almost into dogs. There's this special aerosol and every day participating men are sprayed, and gradually they complain less and become more faithful. Their egos dry up and they start to be satisfied with their lot. They lose their memory, so they forget how great they are and they don't bear grudges. And they don't have the ability to look ahead any more, and, because they can only live in the moment, they lose the faculty to be unhappy so they're always eager and in a permanent good mood. Next, they lose the ability to speak altogether, and they can't say stupid things all the time.'

'What happens in the end?'

'They grow lovely felty ears and glossy coats. The population soars.'

I wish them a nice day. *Damn.* I forgot to ask the title of that book. By the time I remember, they've gone too far to call out.

'Good morning!'

A lady on Canberra Avenue is aiming the ferrules of her walking frame, wary of uneven flagstones. When she looks at me I see the same mild anxiety as Groover's mum had. I don't know why they call these tours reassuring. Cattlegreen Heath residents have saved up long and hard to live in an area where the police don't need to be. So they're not reassured when they see us. If anything, it gives them the creeps.

'Is everything all right, Officer?'

'Yes. Just routine patrol.'

'Only we don't usually see police… people… round here.'

'It's for reassurance. We don't want anyone in the borough feeling they've been forgotten about.'

Again, the lady stares at the pavement. Now she's calculating. I'm an opportunity she doesn't want to let slip by. 'Seeing as you're here…' She turns and raises an arm. 'You see where those tall trees are?' She indicates a row of leylandii that divide an oblong of lawn. 'My house is behind those trees. My neighbours won't cut them down. They were no higher than this walking frame a few years ago. Look at them now. They're interfering with my ancient lights.' She cranes her head towards me, taking me into her confidence. 'I think they're doing it out of spite. They moved here from Manchester. They seemed perfectly nice to begin with. I thought that they might start parking ugly vans on the driveway or storing things on the lawn. Coming from the north. But no. I was pleasantly surprised. Then after a few months...'

My mind's going to wander during this, I can tell. To hide it, I stand up straight and lean forward. Clasping my hands behind me, I narrow my eyes and meet hers.

The world seems different without the DI. It's like he's died. I imagine this is what it'll feel like when the Queen finally gets away. *Back in a hat, eh, Ru?* I can hear him, I'm sure, somewhere up in the clouds, chuckling at my pressed uniform and my shiny shoes. *It's a knock-back. Temporary. You'll be back in the blink of an eye.* It's only wishful thinking. More likely, he wants to forget us all. He may even hold me to blame. Twice I've phoned and left messages. He hasn't called me back.

He's taken early retirement. Forced into it, more likely. Fallout from 'the Tony Gibson fiasco', as the *Cattlegreen Messenger* are still calling it, or 'the post-Maskell shitstorm', to give it its gossip-name back at the nick. Relatively, I suppose, I came through the whole thing unscathed. At least with my job. Or *a* job. Lucky, really, seeing as I was the one who messed up the case. The thing was, letting a murderer get away with it came at a bad time so far as my final CID assessment was concerned. And it didn't help that, with the DI gone, my first line manager, DS Teague, was acting in his place.

'This room big enough for you?' she asked. We were sitting in the DI's office. He'd been gone two days and already she had pictures of her kids on the desk. ''S just that Rashid says he's gonna need a wall to give his presentation.' She giggled. 'What is he like?'

I'd seriously thought he was joking when he showed me the eight-minute film he'd made of himself kneeling by a MOP's wheelchair, understanding her concerns, and talking the viewer through the fail-safe seven-point plan he's devised to ensure his files unerringly meet the national casework standards. 'They'll think you're taking the mick,' I warned.

He'd grinned and said, 'Watch this space.'

'I was told that I just need my case diary.'

'Oh, is that how they do it here? In the Met you've got to show evidence of your competencies.'

She tapped on her keyboard whilst I checked my texts. I knew where this was going. Superintendent Bartlett had passed me on the stairs the day before. 'Very, very disappointed,' was all he said. He gave me his ultra-warm smile, confirming I was out in the cold.

'So then…' She looked up at me. 'What do you think have been your main achievements during your CID probationary period?'

As far as I'd prepared at all for my final assessment interview, it had been on the assumption that I'd be here with DI McQuade, who'd been keeping a close eye on me throughout my probation. He wouldn't have needed a promo video celebrating my achievements. There was nothing I could tell the DI about myself that he didn't know already.

'Erm… qualifying as an ABE interviewer, I think, is one of them. And I, erm, I got a lot out of my family liaison training. And I, erm…'

'Erm', roughly translated from the original Dumboslavian, would be something along the lines of, 'My attendance record was a hundred per cent. I was punctual (mostly), and I never rushed to finish a job. With the public, I was unfailingly patient and polite. When the brass needed a volunteer for a dirty job, I stuck my hand up, always. At the rare times when there was danger, I jostled my way to the front. I never used my personal life as an excuse to bunk off early; never used my gender to claim special treatment. I never boasted or lost my temper; I never sulked or took offence. Not once did I complain.' All things that the DI would have noted across the months. And, yeah. On the odd occasion I might have punched a scrote's front tooth out, or sobbed snot onto a bereaved's nice coat. Might even have pleasured myself on an injured party's lavatory. But what do you expect? On my wage, you're not going to get Inspector Lewis, are you?

DS Teague stuck out her hand. 'Show me your case diary? Hmm,' she said as she read. 'Quite light on DV.'

This remark actually warmed me to her. I hadn't known she could laugh at herself.

'Er, you allocate the cases?' I smiled at her, willing her to keep up the banter. 'You give Rashid the ones he wants? Mainly DV and hate crime?'

'That young man can be so-o persuasive.' Her smile gave way to a very cold stare. 'We can't hold your hand twenty-four-seven. You can't expect supervisors to keep a tally of who gets which case, or to worry about who needs experience in which area.'

She saw that my eyebrow had slanted.

'Managers chop and change. Here today, gone tomorrow. Not being neg but the reality is, we have 1,001 things to do apart from getting to know the troops, still less get involved with their career development. It'd be nice but we don't have the time.'

All of a sudden I was being encouraged by thirty-two of the most yes-can-do teeth I'd ever seen.

'Sharpen your elbows, eh? It's a man's world out there. Don't sit meekly in the background, waiting for your boat to come in. Grab the buzz cases. Hunt 'em out. Steal 'em off the next guy if you have to. Get yourself noticed by the people that matter!'

She clattered away on her keyboard. *Objectives for Next Twelve Months*, as I was to learn later, when I was emailed a copy of my review. 'Ruby and I discussed the need to use her initiative and take ownership of her caseload.'

Her fingers stopped and she looked at me. Dainty curls appeared at the corners of her mouth. 'And what do you consider to have been your major learning points? Where would you have done things differently?'

'What? Better?'

Her smile had decided the coast was clear and finally broke cover. 'The Freya Maskell case?' I asked.

She nodded like it was our little secret and, for the five hundredth time, made me relive the mistakes of the 13th June.

'Cool,' she said more than once whilst I narrated. There were lots of non-judgemental 'yeah's and 'okay's. 'So you didn't tell the DI the brief was your boyfriend? Okay.' She nodded; she understood. 'At no time did you think there might be a conflict of interests? Right. Aha. I see.' More teeth; a chuckle. She knew how hard it can be. 'It's easily done. Friday night, knocking-off time. Mind on other things.' She twisted her mouth in a mime of fear and squeaked, 'You didn't caution her! And it all went tits up! And the DI had to carry the can!'

She took a deep breath and concluded. 'Like I said, we've all been there. You're keen, you want to make a good impression. You take a punt on a case – why not? You know, deep down, maybe you should leave this to more experienced colleagues but, hey, if you weren't a risk-taker, you wouldn't have joined the cops! Thing is, the Tony Gibson murder put Cattlegreen police solidly under the media spotlight. And the one thing Joe Public knows about us now, because of the failed investigation, is that a hooker killed a man and the crime has gone unpunished. Because of us. As far as Joe Public's concerned, it's hooker one, Cattlegreen CID nil.'

Seven more minutes in private contemplation of my phone whilst DS Teague tapped and ticked. Nice text from Lee:

Q: Why do women have fannies?
A: So men will talk to them.

Then DS Teague shut her laptop and looked me in the eye. 'Ruby, I'm not going to recommend you for a permanent CID placement.'

And so now I'm back in a hat.

'...and it's not as if they've not noticed. I see them trowelling on fertiliser and trimming the branches. And all the time it gets darker and darker in my home. I'm losing my ancient lights!'

I find that I'm caring so much about the leylandii problem that I've crooked my finger against my chin. 'Have you spoken with them?'

'Pardon?'

'I mean, have you asked them if they could cut off a few feet from the tops?'

She is offended. 'Well, I don't know them. I mean, they're my neighbours, but, you know, you're the police officer. I think you should, well... Can't you give them a knock?'

I shake my head. My career is in enough trouble without arresting citizens for growing trees. 'I think the people you need when you have a problem like this are the council. Have you...?' I break off and get my phone out. It's contrary to the teachings of the unconscious bias course DS Teague sent us on, and I know you shouldn't make assumptions about people just because of the way they look, but sometimes you just know, don't you? The lady has not googled this. 'Let's see...'

I move to her side so she can see the screen. We discuss what we find and decide on a plan of action. The thought of helping herself begins to quite excite her. I jot down a telephone number on a note, which she folds – exactly corner to corner, with sharp, sharp creases – and puts in her purse.

'Thank you, Officer,' she says, and looks at me meaningfully. 'Thank you very much.'

'Good luck,' I call after her as, girding herself for war, she pecks back to her side of the road.

Fifty-two minutes till lunch.

Eponymous. There can't be *two* people I know who'd drop that word into conversation. Who, apart from Tommy, would even know what it means?

'Excuse me.' A man is walking towards me from his driveway. 'Excuse me... I'd like to report a crime.'

He's pulling my leg; he's got to be. But no, he's not in the mood for japes. I can tell from the stern, fleshy chevrons on his forehead. And he's fat and bald and, if he's about to confess to having *committed* this crime, I shall be in no temptation to say he looks too nice.

'They've broken into my shed. It's a burglary.'

I accompany him to the end of the road, where he opens a gate and leads me round his house to the back garden. His shed stands next to a metal fence, which separates his land from the railway embankment. As he begins to explain what has happened, the train to London dashes by twenty feet above us and drowns out what he says.

'I'm sorry,' I say when it has passed. 'I didn't catch that.'

'I said, I don't think they took anything.'

He opens the door and stands back, allowing me to go in. But I can see from where I am that, if a burglar's been here, he's done what we might call a very tidy search. Nothing has been damaged or disturbed. The man's seed boxes are stacked neatly. The spades and forks, which he has coded on the handles with different-coloured paint, and which are either new or else he actually cleans them after use, still stand in descending order of size, each steadied by a little clamp he's screwed to the wall. I've had worse houseguests. It's so clean there probably aren't even any spiders. But I'm not going to take the risk.

'Have they broken the lock?'

He makes way so I can inspect. 'It wasn't actually locked.' He now seems a little sheepish. 'I've been meaning to put one on but, well, this sort of thing doesn't really happen round here.'

I can't think what to do, so I nod gravely, and say, 'Mmmm.'

'Why do I think there's been a burglary?' he asks, helpfully reading my mind. 'Because if you look here...'

I let him go in first.

'...one of them's dropped his phone.'

I pick it up. It's quite a good one. 'You don't recognise it?'

'It's definitely not one of ours.'

I press the power button. It's dead.

'Are you going to send SOCO round?'

'I'll file a report and see what they recommend. If you can, avoid the shed for a day or two, and don't touch the glass or metal surfaces.' I write out a receipt for the phone. 'I'll be in touch,' I say, and offer him my pad to sign. 'In the meantime...' I glance down at the signature. '...Mr Kelsey, I'll charge up the phone and see if it leads anywhere.'

12.15pm

Still a quarter of an hour to go. It wouldn't look *that* unmotivated if I called in now and got someone to come and pick me up. It'll probably take until lunchtime before they get here. No, I decide. I'll stick it out. I've only lived in Cattlegreen since I moved in with Jools and I still don't know the place that well. It won't hurt to do a bit more exploring, although here on High Trees Lane, where the houses have grounds and remotely operated gates, there's no one around for me to reassure. Likely there's no need. They'll have private security firms to do that.

A nameplate at the next junction reads 'Athelstan Way'. The words give me the sort of jolt I expect a pregnant woman has when she feels the first stir of a limb. For, it occurs to me, the street I've been google-earthing a fair bit recently – or 'stalking like a drone', as Jools puts it – connects to Athelstan Way. I walk on. Yes. Here it is. My baby is breakdancing. Southwell Road. *My God.* I wonder if there's a chance I can grab a sandwich here.

If I think about this, then I shan't do it. But that's no problem. *Hey*, if I weren't a risk-taker I wouldn't have joined the cops! Round this bend there'll be a windmill. Here it is. Well, a house that someone has designed to look like a windmill. And next to this is a house… with a yellow door! Which means that the next house… I stand on the opposite pavement and I stare.

Well, I never did.

No security gates or Grecian columns at the doorway. It's not so far from being what you would call grand, for all that. The garden is beautiful. And no one's postponed the painting on the front. Obviously, the windows are sparkling. I inhale and think the word *Charge!* I cross the road and stride up the driveway to the door. After I've knocked it takes almost a minute before anything happens, by which time I've turned to go.

'Hello?'

I stop in my tracks and look round. This is not the man I've been trailing on Facebook. This looks like his elderly dad.

'Oh, it's you!' he says.

I stand motionless, waiting for instinct to kick in. That's what happens. I know from watching *Holby* and *EastEnders*. In a moment, me and the MOP in front of me will throw ourselves into an embrace and we'll wail the decades away.

'Can I come in?'

We stare.

'Eh?'

It dawns on me. He won't have seen me in uniform before. May even not know what I do.

'Course you can.' He stands to one side to make way. 'The lars' time I 'ad the Ow' Bill at me door,' he says, 'was when they tol' me I was a widower.'

I smile politely and wipe my feet on the doormat. Moving past him, my gaze closes in on a photograph in which a happily dazed groom with my nose hugs a bride who is not my mother. I think about offering condolences but can't remember when it was that she died, or even if I'm supposed to care.

'Is this a social visit or are you 'ere in your, er, professional capacity?'

Welfare check, I almost quip. I'm glad I don't. He looks like he could actually do with one. 'Just passing,' I say.

'Well, this is a surprise.'

We freeze again. Then he lurches into life.

'Cam on in, then. Make yourself at 'ome! I was just about to 'eat up sam soup. You wan' sam?'

'Yes, please.'

Ushering me through to the kitchen, he struggles to keep up as I lead.

'You all right…?' Saying 'Dad' will take time to get used to.

'Nah, not so good, as it goes, Ru. I'll tell you about it in a minute. But, 'ere…' He wafts me urgently to where the food is. 'Let's get you sammin' to eat.'

The carpet is sumptuous. Underfoot, it feels like a marsh. The home is so light you can see that it's properly clean. I recognise some of the furniture from window-shopping, which is when I have my wildest dreams. Everywhere there are photos.

'Nice place you've got.'

'Yeah, 's awright, innit? Millie's, really. Well, mine now. We bought it wiv 'er money, though. An' she decorated an' designed an' that.'

'How long have you lived here?'

'Ooh, mas' be five year, now. Yeah, four or five.'

'Can't believe I've not seen you around.'

'We was 'ardly 'ere. Used to spend 'arf the year in Spain. Most o' the rest o' the time on cruise boats an' such. Sounds fancy, I know.'

The kitchen is straight out of a showroom. Granite work surface. Copper handles on the units. He's even got one of those boiling-water taps so that there's no ugly kettle to spoil the view. It's a funny old world. A couple of hours ago I was reminiscing about Mintsley Heights. Now I'm here in my old man's new place, on the other side of the tracks. I don't know why, but I'm having to fight back a smile.

'I can't imagine you standing on *this* table and bellowing, "*It's Christ-maaaaas!*"'

'Cor.' He chuckles. 'Millie'd 'ave freaked if I 'ad.'

Same as in the lounge, photos hang everywhere. Dad and Millie at work. Dad and Millie at play. At home. Abroad. Always just the two of them. I'm surprised he hasn't got a plaque outside: 'The Museum of Marital Bliss'. The theme is so pronounced it feels false not to mention it.

'Ah,' he says when I do. 'Nah, that's me. I put most of them up. Since she passed away.'

This shape of island is in the shops now. Either Millie died quite recently or she was well ahead of the curve. I'm teasing out this theory when I'm distracted by the sounds of exertion. He's trying to open a can.

'Here. Let me do that.'

I take it off him. He's out of breath, and sits down. I clench inside. His head is like a skull.

'Gotta fend for meself today. Normally I 'ave a carer cam in but 'er boy's fell dahn in the playground an' she's 'ad to go an' take 'im 'ome.'

'Why have you got a carer?'

'It's my pancreas. Got a cancer. It's the treatment more than the cancer, though. Knocks you for a six.'

I feel I should have been wearing a seat belt. That word, twice in quick succession. Initial impact with whiplash to follow. I grunt sympathy at him which he testily bats away. He's done a lot of research. He seems more interested in the disease than frightened by it. After he's said the little he wants said about it he turns the conversation my way.

'Not seen so much on Facebook about yer weddin' plans of late. Still goin' ahead?'

'Yeah,' I say immediately, but with a tone that maybe doesn't altogether hide the possibility of delay. As in, *Yeah, when Jools has won his appeal case and got his partnership and starts to notice me again.* Or, *Yeah, once 2015 has stopped dumping on me and I can pull myself free of the pile.* Or, *Yeah, just as soon as Jools has finished his affair.*

'So when's the 'appy occasion?'

'We're still saving. Not fixed the date yet.'

He nods and meets my eye. 'You gettin' cold feet?'

'No.' I say it quickly, guessing that the sooner I say it, the truer it will be.

''Cause you gotta back out if you are. You don't wanna go

through what me an' yer mum 'ad to.' He keeps on studying my face. 'You know what 'appened, don't you? With me an' yer mum?'

'I know… Aunty Rita told me… Didn't you and Millie have a relationship before you met Mum?'

He nods. 'We was engaged an' she broke it off. Met another fella. Pretty soon after that I met Cath an' married 'er instead. An' I did with Cath all what me 'n' Millie was gonna do together. Rent a 'ouse, 'ave kids, play 'appy families. An' then Millie got back in touch. Said she'd made a mistake.'

'What did you do?'

'Dropped everything and ran back to 'er, didn't I? Left you all in the lurch. Didn't think twice about it.'

'Didn't you mind not having Lorna and me in your life?'

He shrugs. 'I wanted to see you. But yer mum didn't make it easy. I didn't 'ave much money to contribute at first. An' by the time I did, Cath refused to take it. Said you didn't need me or my money any more. I should 'ave fought it but, oh, she can be a very determined lady, can Cath. An' then Millie 'ad 'er medical problems an' couldn't conceive. Dunno, it somehow seemed, like, disloyal, me 'avin' kids in me life an' her not.'

'Did you do the right thing, do you think?'

He brings his fist to his lips, like he's going to answer by way of a tiny microphone he has hidden in there. 'Yes and no,' he says at last. I don't remember this reflective side to my dad at all. 'Right to be wiv Millie, of course. We was, y'know…' he looks almost apologetic, afraid that by saying something so obvious he will insult me, '…meant to be. I was wrong to marry yer mum. Considerin' the mess I caused. But then, if I 'adn't, there'd be no you 'n' Lorna… Didn't know me own 'eart.' He looks at his wall of photos and nods. 'You gotta know your 'eart.'

Through all this, the microwave has been humming, and now finally it gives a *ting*.

'You're a yinky.'

'You're not wrong there, Woob. If there's one thing life 'as taught me, it's that I'm yer genuine, God's honest, original yinky.'

I take his bowl from the draining stand and another from the back of a cupboard.

''Ow is yer mum, anyway? An' little Lorny?'

'Yeah.' I nod as I pour out the soup. 'Both good. Lorna's with Lee. He's a plumber. She's training to be an estate agent. Mum's doing really well at the vet's.'

'Still at the vet's? After all these years?'

'General office manager of four practices.'

'Good for 'er. Always was a grafter, Cath. Did she remarry?'

I have a feeling I'm being led onto dangerous territory. It reminds me of when my friends at junior school dared me and I pushed open the door to the boys' toilets to have a peek.

'Long-term partner.' I trot out an old family joke. 'He came as our lodger and we never let him leave.' There's another story, supposedly true and which Rita, at least, finds funny. Having grown close swapping horror stories about their exes, and making themselves laugh with their theories about marriage and its suitability only for divs, Mum finally got it together with Ian on the day his decree absolute arrived and he showed her on the home computer how to get her own online divorce. But I'm not going to tell it to Dad.

'Is she 'appy?'

'Expect so,' I say, and hear the clank of the boys' bogs door as it slams and is locked behind me. 'She loves her job. Got a great house. She and Ian are always doing stuff. In the garden, walking the dogs…'

There's a photo exactly at head height, just to the right of the stove. Probably, whilst Dad boils an egg or warms some milk, or whatever it is he can manage, he spends more time looking at this picture than at any of the others, which is why he hangs it there. And yet it's been bothering me. It looks like he's hugging Millie so hard he's actually hurting her. On closer inspection, though, I see that his hands, in fact, rest lightly on her hips and that he's applying no pressure at all. It's not pain in Millie's face, I realise, but something of what Jess Ennis went through on the greatest night of all. The climax of years of training. Love training, in the case of these two world-beaters. Dad's face is equally intense. Yinky, weak, window-cleaning Dad. And Millie. The Mo and Jess of love's Olympics. And in – what? – a few weeks, they, and their photos, and all they achieved will be gone and forgotten forever.

'When I get married, will you give me away?'

He looks like he must have misheard me.

'No, I'm being serious. I'd like it if you'd do that.'

Now he thinks I'm out of my mind. 'Would I be welcome at your weddin'?'

'It's *my* wedding. You'll be welcomed by me.'

We sit and eat in silence.

'Well, if you're sure you do wanna marry,' he says, 'the answer to your question is, "Yes. I'd be honoured to give you away. 'Onestly can't think of anythin' I'd rather do."'

'That's brilliant.'

'Only if it don't cause no problem, mind.' He lowers his spoon from his mouth. 'Yeah? It's a special day and the last thing I wanna do is spoil it.'

He is seized by a fit of coughing. Suddenly, the table is spattered with soup. I slap him between his shoulders but it does no good. He keeps on coughing. He's going to suffocate if this doesn't stop. There's no point calling for assistance. It'll be over by the time anyone comes. There's nothing more I can do. I rock him, like he's a baby. I soothe him and whisper in his ear. Finally, the coughing stops. He looks up at me through his tears and he chuckles.

'Better not leave it too long, though, eh?'

9

'*Hell-ooo*, my dear!'

Candida Swaffham. Back in 2012, on the day I arrested her for obstructing the highway, I researched her first name on my phone before booking her in. I thought in all the excitement I must have written it down wrong in my notes. It wouldn't have been right to make my prisoner feel foolish in front of Sergeant Jenner. And highly embarrassing for me if he thought it was one of those psychological slips where you say what's on your mind, not what you're supposed to be talking about. But no. Candida. In 1940, if there wasn't a name of a queen or a Hollywood star that you liked, you christened your daughter in honour of an itch between the legs.

I'm barging my way through the magistrates' courthouse entrance, exhibit bag in each hand. Candida approaches, arms outstretched. I'm glad of the bags because they will prevent me from hugging her back. Not that I dislike her. I admire people who are prepared to fight for their principles. And I never usually mind hugging anyone who's got a soft spot for me. But these days it's a worry, having impulses at the same time as being at work. Especially on a day like today, with Trunky's people everywhere, with their human rights, and their watchdog lawyers prowling, pens poised, straining at the leash to enforce them. Hug someone else's witness round here and they'll probably tell the court. I'll be bringing my profession into disrepute one way or another, or treating some institution with contempt. And then I'm in for the sack. Prison, for all I know.

'This has been going on *soooo* long!' Candida speaks into my ear, then holds me at arm's length to examine me. 'Three adjournments. Two and a half years since the demonstration. So long ago, it's hard to remember what happened!' She draws close again. 'I know that feeling still runs high with some of my associates. But, to tell you the truth, to me it's water under the bridge. I've moved on.'

We're here for the trial of *R v Trunky*. It's the last of six trials spawned in a single afternoon when, after months of rubbing along good-naturedly outside a plant where fracking tests were due to take place, cops and protesters began seriously to get on each other's nerves. Under the spotlight today is the alleged assault of my colleague, PC Tom Barnard. Other arrests we made that day were for obstructing police, obstructing the highway, common assault, criminal damage, acts of public disorder, and minor road traffic offences. So far, thirty-two days of court time have been spent untangling the momentary feuds and the split-second decisions of that afternoon. Three of the trials have resulted in acquittals. The two convictions earned the offenders, respectively, a conditional discharge and forty hours' unpaid work. Estimated cost to the public purse – £180,000 (my stats are courtesy of a Vanguard group chat thing that my former colleagues seem not to have noticed I'm still party to, in spite of my two years' silence). Unlike the rest of them in the van, this is the first of the trials I've been summonsed to.

'I do remember how tiresome I was, sitting there in the middle of the road, refusing to budge. I remember how patient you were, and how kind. I didn't tell the others but I'd never been arrested before that afternoon. I was scared, though I tried not to show it. But at the police station, well… you couldn't have made me feel more welcome!'

Two dishevelled men push past us, looking like they have better things to do than be here. They scowl at the cop and the posh, loud biddy who are holding up the queue. Candida and I slowly move out of the way.

'Sket's up there,' she says, nodding up the stairs to the concourse. 'So's Trunky.' She looks concerned. 'Shall we walk together? I wouldn't want them to… show disrespect.'

'Sweet of you.' I beam at her. 'I'll be okay.' I don't want Candida to think I'm biased, so I don't say that the disrespect of her fellow campaigners is definitely something I can live with. The number of convictions Sket and Trunky have notched up for violence, intimidation and dishonesty I would guess matches even that of their noble causes and enlightened ideals. Also, I need desperately to go to the toilet.

'See you up there. Bye. Lovely to see you… you, too!' With a clank of jewellery and a rustle of her plaits, Candida turns to greet the security guards, who switch off the metal detector when they see her. There's laughter, and I gather her metal hip has set it off before. Candida wouldn't miss one of these trials for the world.

I feel sick. As sick as I decided, at about four this morning, to pretend to be when it was time to get up. I changed my mind about that in the end. After the generally unfavourable reviews of my last performance in the witness box, Jools might have thought that I'd lost my bottle. The truth is, I couldn't care less about giving my evidence today. Still, wish I'd phoned in now and given it the croaky voice.

In the toilet cubicle I check my phone. Maybe he's messaged me with a joke or a love-wish or a simple word of encouragement, like old times. Nothing. Maybe I should have told him what was bothering me. Maybe he should have known.

Please, God. Don't let them reject me.

I breathe in and, staring at the lock on the door, think about who will be here. Tom Barnard. Of course. And I shan't be flaunting my new ring at him, now that he's not on his own. Eric Foley, I think he was there on the day. Russ Rogers, maybe… hopefully. Noel Creme. Sarah Dix (oh God, Sarah Dix!). Connor's face appears in my mind. Not crumpling with grief this time. Alarming in a totally different way.

I remember, years ago, we got a three-nines call to The Queen's Head; a pretty place out in the country. A travelling family had come for Sunday lunch. At the bar, one of the men had demanded change for a fifty, although he'd paid with only a twenty. It may have been a genuine mistake on the man's part and the manager tried to appease him, giving him the cash. But this only encouraged everyone, and next the beer was sour and the food was no good, although they'd drunk and eaten the lot. By the time we got there, the whole clan was blockading the bar. Grannies were pulling at our shirts, screaming about discrimination. Toddlers were throwing forks at other customers. Frankly, I was scared. Connor stepped behind the bar exactly at the point when the manager, in his despair, was handing over to the mob the till tray and all its contents. He stayed the manager's hand, shook his head, and the tray was put back in the till. With the face that I'm seeing now – bored, haughty, sickened; literally, about to be ill with contempt – he pointed to the man who'd started it all. 'Why don't you and me go to a private place and talk this over?' No idea what he said, and he never told us. But by that time it didn't matter. The game was up; the show was over. All – and I have no doubt about this – because of that look on Connor's face. It just took the wind out of sails. Twenty minutes later, we and the travellers were gone.

Please, Connor, please. Don't look at me like that today. I give the bowl a deceitful flush. In front of the washbasin mirror, I fix an expression that I hope reads, *This'll be great!* Then I stride out of the toilets and, as easily as if they were weightless, carry my exhibit bags up the stairs.

Coming down the other way is Sket. There's no one else about. I don't know if this area of the court is covered by CCTV. He's trotting towards me, rolling a cigarette. He sees me and hesitates, then raises his upper lip. The gap in his teeth is still there. Brightening my expression still more, I walk past him.

On the concourse, the ushers are all smiles. A lady from the witness care service is kneeling, making much of an earth mother-type my age, who's sitting on the floor with her baby and musical instruments and what I think are picnic things. It's always like this on alternative-lifestyle days. I've read about it on the group chat. Court staff make out the place is a pop festival and go about being so full of friendliness it looks like they're holding their breath. Like me, they don't want to seem judgemental.

'Morning, Officer.'

I don't recognise Trunky to begin with. He's grown a beard; a real nipple-tickler. He's with a group of supporters who exchange glances upon my approach. Someone whistles the theme from *Laurel and Hardy*.

'You givin' evidence against me?' The accused winks. 'You can if you like.'

'Oh, Trunky,' Candida Swaffham says. 'Grow up, for goodness' sake.'

I find the CPS room. I knock and a voice calls, 'Come!'

Inside, a short, bothered-looking lady sits at a desk.

'Are you prosecuting in Courtroom 3?'

She faces me with a smile. 'I do indeed have that honour. You here for the anti-frackers?'

'Yes. PC Marocco. I've brought the exhibits.'

I do as she asks and put them down on the floor. Her attention is on very short loan, I can see, so I grab my chance whilst I can.

'Am I actually needed?'

'Heaven knows,' she says. 'I haven't had a chance to read the file yet.' The trial is due to start in twenty minutes. 'Let's see…' She scrolls down her screen to the MG5. '"The Crown will say that the defendant, who wishes to be known only as 'Trunky', is guilty of assaulting PC Tom Barnard. On the afternoon of…" dahdidahdidah… Oh, I see… So you were arresting the old woman and Trunky tried to stop you—'

'I didn't even know he was there. Tom intercepted him before he got anywhere close.'

'Ah. "Whilst being restrained, the defendant swung his

elbow into PC Barnard's chest, causing immediate discomfort but no injury." Just let me check the case management form…' She scrolls back up. 'Well, the defence have called everyone who made a statement. Do you want to be away?'

I shrug. 'If I've got nothing to say that can help.'

She scans my statement. It takes no more than five seconds to read both pages. 'OK, I'll speak with the defence and see if they can let you go. You'll have to stick around in the meantime.'

My heart skips a beat. There's nothing for it; I'm going to have to brave the police room. I exit the CPS office and step back onto the concourse.

'Cuff me to the tea bar an' spank me with your truncheon, Ruby!'

I can't see who says this but his New Age friends find it funny.

'Careful,' I hear someone else call out. 'She can pack a punch.'

If I'm cast out of the police room, these are the people I shall spend my day with.

I reach my destination and push the door open a crack. A story is being told. Craning my head round, I see who's here. The dog handler, Noel Creme. There's one man I don't know. He's telling the story. Connor is speaking on the phone. I see that he's got his stripes. Russ 'Raise You' Rogers has not arrived. The story withers to a standstill.

Is this the fascist oppressors' enclosure? I thought up that opening gambit about six hours ago. It was too ballsy for me ever to dare say it, I decided, so I opted to pull a sickie instead. After I gave up on *that* idea, I forgot to think up a replacement.

Sarah Dix, who I've not seen for more than a year, glances up, holds my gaze for a moment, then looks back to the screen of her phone. Eric Foley raises his eyebrows in acknowledgement but stops short of hoisting a smile. Tom Barnard, studiously reading his statement, pretends not to have seen me. Noel and Amanda Dee cast their eyes towards Connor, in need of a clue what to do. The face of the man I don't know lights up in welcome. The seat next to Tom is unoccupied but he's put his cap and his notebook on it. I enter and prop myself on the edge of a table, which people are using for their mugs. The whole of the room is willing Connor to end his call. Then we'll know how to be.

From the concourse we can hear a chant. '...*one Mr Trunky, there's only one Mr Trunky. One Mr Trun-ky...*'

'Hmm,' I muse. 'Cramped like sardines with just a thin wall to protect us from the jeering mob. Where do I know this from?'

Amanda Dee laughs but then looks to Tom, who she sees is still blanking me, so she checks herself. The friendly man isn't Vanguard and doesn't know what I mean. Eric Foley gives a quick-dying grin to the floor.

'Do we know if it's going ahead?' I ask.

Connor's voice is saving the room from complete silence but there are long gaps whilst he listens and looks at me as the person on the other end of his line speaks. One of the gaps is longer than Eric can bear.

'Think so,' he says. 'She hasn't said there's any delay.'

I nod and we listen to Connor. 'Yeah, all right, babe... See you there... Nah, I shan't. Yeah, gotta go. Bye... Bye.' He snaps the phone shut and stands up. ''Ere you are. Park your arse here.'

'Nah, I'm good.'

'Really. Wanna stretch my legs anyway.'

''S okay,' says Tom. He gathers his things off the next seat. 'There's a seat here, Con.'

There's room for one more in the lifeboat. I'm not going to be cast to the seas.

'Congratulations,' I say, after a moment suppressing a smile. With my fingertip I draw chevrons on my shoulder.

'Ah, yeah,' Connor mutters. 'I'm glad someone's noticed. Don't think these wankers have.'

'Might be sergeant,' says Eric. 'Still gotta fetch the fucking tea.'

They used to put their hands over their mouths after swearing, to acknowledge that I was around. No one remembers the joke. The atmosphere is awkward but polite. They all still keep glancing at Connor, even though he's shown it's okay. To disarm them further, I try and fail to think of some other sassy quip that no social pariah would ever make.

'Your old mate's out there,' Tom says at last.

'Who, Sket? Yeah, seen him. Still hasn't had his tooth fixed.'

'Been dining out on that gap,' Tom says. 'Shows the magistrates, every trial.' He draws up his lip. '"A poleeth offither punthed me in the faith."'

'He doesn't say I did it, does he?'

'Nah. Stops short of admitting he got thrashed by a woman.'

'He had the last laugh, though, didn't he? I was on light duties for two months after that.'

Stupid thing to say. It was during those light duties that I met Jools. The room falls quiet again and my mind slips back to those dark moments when Sket dragged me to the bushes where men who weren't protesters were waiting.

'Back in a hat, then, Ruby?' says Amanda Dee, leading another of my elephants into the room.

I rouse myself and nod.

'Scandal,' says Noel Creme. 'What happened to Len McQuade. Bloody witch-hunt.'

Amanda sits up and makes eye contact. 'So what *did* happen? I only know what I read in the papers.'

I consider, quite quickly, what percentage of the truth my old mates are entitled to and what they are likely to do with it when they have it. I estimate the amount of pride I still have to protect, and with what measure of loyalty I should guard the good name of my fiancé in their minds. Then, partly because I realise I still hate Jools for what he did in court last month and the sermon he gave me afterwards whilst Freya Maskell walked off with her polythene bag, scot-free, but mainly because I'm so damn grateful that these guys have let me stay and haven't cast me outside to the wolves, I think, *Sod it*, and tell it all as it was. The love-struck bungling of the 13th June. The story behind the body that Tom watched over by the Thames. The struggle I had to have my CCTV ident believed. The trial that never was. The face-to-face with DS Teague that put me back in a hat.

Sarah Dix looks up from *Angry Birds* on her phone. 'You still with him?' She glances at Connor, whose face has turned into the one I was praying not to see. She thinks, because she's just referred to Jools, that Connor's aiming his contempt at him, and so at me. A sneer begins to form on her face.

'Is she that one who stands about this close to you when she speaks to you?' Connor places his palm vertical by his nose. 'Always touches you?'

'If you're male,' I say.

His expression blisters and withers, just as it did at The Queen's Head. With neither Jools nor me in his mind as he pulls it, but DS Teague, I could sit here and watch it all day.

'This DS Teague,' says the guy I don't know. 'Not Katie Teague, is it?'

'Yeah,' I say. 'Katie.'

'From the Met?'

I nod.

'So this is where she ended up.' He chuckles to himself. 'Has she told you why she transferred?'

'She said she wants a better life for her kids.'

He smiles. 'I knew her; we were on the same relief. She loved the Met. If she hadn't been caught showing bonding behaviour with her DI, I expect she'd still be there. It would have been all right but the DI's missus found out and complained direct to the divisional commander. So the brass made a thing of it. The DI got demoted and Katie got run out of town. *That's* why you've got her.'

'GSS,' Amanda Dee whispers to Sarah, who's been frowning since hearing the phrase 'bonding behaviour'.

Sarah nods; all is now clear. 'Sharin' willies,' she mutters to Noel Creme, who's understood neither term.

'You know what'll happen?' Tom Barnard says. 'She'll go for Len McQuade's job.'

'She's only been a DS five minutes.'

Tom nods. He knows force politics inside out. 'Bet you fifty quid. She'll draw on her recent "murder investigation experience", say she dealt decisively with the fallout, she'll evidence her involvement with whatever bees the Home Office has in its bonnet this week, and in two months she'll be sitting in the DI's chair. I can guarantee it.'

To my right, there is giggling. Eric touches my arm. 'These disclosure issues, yeah? Reason it's taken so long to hear this trial?'

He nods my attention to Sarah, who passes me a statement. 'Read what he wrote,' she says, and points to Noel.

Noel gives me a grin. I look at Connor. We all know we shouldn't be reading each other's statements.

'It's okay. Noel's been stood down. He's just staying here to keep warm.'

I read that on the day of the demonstration, a man 'who I now know to be Haydyn Carver but who told me that his name was "Sket"' was seen by officers to wrestle with PC Marocco, who was attempting to effect an arrest. Carver appeared to be dragging PC Marocco away from her prisoner and towards the bushes that lined the perimeter fence. 'Using reasonable self-defence', PC Marocco freed herself from Carver, who, upon seeing officers approaching, ran away from the scene. PC Creme and PD Snow were called to assist, and an hour later Carver was seized and detained in a ditch where he was hiding.

'Trunky's side wouldn't agree on a trial date,' Eric says. 'They said it was impossible to prepare his defence without a statement from PD Snow. The district judge said, "The issue is whether Trunky assaulted PC Barnard. What's Haydyn Carver got to do with that?" But the defence insisted and the judge backed down. Ordered that PD Snow's statement be disclosed.'

'What?' I say. 'No one realised?'

All shake their heads. Sarah passes a second sheet of paper. 'So Noel had no choice but to oblige.'

This is a proper s.9 statement. Typed, dated, with the declaration printed at the top. 'This statement is true to the best of my knowledge and belief and I make it…' and so on. With due dignity, the name of the witness is prefaced with his title: PD 98 Snow. In the main body of the page is a single exclamation: 'Woof!' The rest of the paper is obliterated by the signature: a giant, inky paw print.

'They actually sent this to the court and the defence.'

It's the first belly laugh I've had this year, and of all people, I'm sharing it with Sarah Dix. We're rocking forwards in our seats, looking at each other through teary eyes. Sarah is the van sheep. She'd sell her soul to fit in. And she's brought me in on a joke. So, as much as the joke is funny, I'm laughing because I've been forgiven. If truth and reconciliation have seeped *this* far down the social order, I'm well and truly back in the fold.

The prosecutor enters and looks along the faces until she finds mine. 'You're free to go.'

'Oh.'

'The defence say they wrote to CPS months ago. Said they didn't need you to attend. I take it no one told you.'

'Er, no.'

She looks like she's going to stand there until I do something. I'd actually like to stick around. It's odd. Last night I binged on an entire box set of worries, all acted out and shot inside this very room. Now that I'm in it, I've not been so happy for months. But the prosecutor has gone to some trouble on my behalf and I feel I've got to go. I put on my coat and sense Connor looking at me. I wave a general farewell and manage not to meet his eye.

On the concourse, the earth mother's children have been provided with bats and are playing a game of rounders. One of the ushers is fielding. A tennis ball is whacked at her from two yards and she manages both to make a joke and, at the same time, shrink with terror as she fumbles the catch. Serenely, the earth-mother sits mid-pitch, changing her baby's nappy.

I'm negotiating a possible safe route to the exit when I feel a hand on my shoulder. 'Ru.' It's Connor.

'Hi!'

The tennis ball ricochets against the wall, six inches from his face. Indifferently, the earth mother glances our way. Gently rocking her baby, she begins to sing a lullaby. '*We shall over-cuh-uhum, we shall over-come...*'

That look is beginning to re-form on Connor's face. 'Can I walk you to your car?'

'Sure.'

His stripes give him a grown-up appearance. Even I feel an urge to mind my Ps and Qs. I can see why kids look like he's hit them when all he's asked is that they cycle off the pavement.

'I want to say I'm sorry,' he says when we're out of harm's way.

'What for?'

'Y'know. All that in the van. The cold-shoulder stuff. Freezing you out.'

'You took no part in that.'

'I could have done more to stop it.'

We begin to walk down the stairs.

'You'd done nothing wrong and I left you, right out of the blue. The van was a tight-knit community. I expected what I got and I deserved it. Now it looks like it's over. All behind us.'

The words sound more sensible and to the point than any that would normally come out of my mouth. But they sort of say it all. At least, we're on the ground floor before he can think of anything to add, and then it's only, 'Cheers, Ru.'

We smile. It's quite funny. All this time, we both thought that we were the guilty party.

'Do you want to come back to the van?'

'What?'

'Nah, it's just… Seems you're not very happy where you are. There are places. I could probably swing it, if you're interested.' He pouts and flicks his chin in the direction of his sergeant's chevrons.

Such momentum as there has been, pushing me gently through this comfortable stroll, now collapses altogether. Behind me, as I face Connor, the security guys bleep and pat. Close up, he looks different from what I remember. He *knows* he's good-looking now. It shows, and somehow it only improves him. He's looking at me in a way that 'babe', I think, could only disapprove of. And maybe I'm being hysterical, but I wonder if he and I and all the van could just pretend the last thirty months never happened; if we could pick up from where we left off.

A voice sounds over the Tannoy. 'Would all parties in the trial of *Crown versus Trunky* please go to Courtroom 3? All parties in *Crown and Trunky*, Courtroom 3.'

'Anyway. Think about it. It'd be great to have you back.' Connor keeps my eye and, holding an imaginary phone to his face, takes a step backwards. 'Give me a call sometime.'

Back at the flat, the dog is waiting for me at the door. He stamps and sneezes and rattles his ears, then, narrowing his almond, eyelined eyes, snuffles among the new smells on my clothes.

'Can you smell Connor? He was your old daddy. Do you remember Connor? He used to teach you tricks.'

Grande's gaze meets mine, and for a moment I think that he knows. I pin him down and we wrestle. Stupid thing to do in my newly dry-cleaned uniform but I'm trying to chase away the thought of how much better my dog's opportunities would have been if I hadn't broken up his home.

We're rolling on the carpet growling at each other when I hear the lock turn in the front door. *Jools*, I decide. *And Tommy. They won't expect me to be here.* I scramble to my feet. Humiliating enough that they use my home as a love nest. Much worse if, to get to the bedroom, they have to step over me mid-growl. I tear open the door.

'Oh.' On the landing, a young woman stands with a key. 'I've come for Grand.' She gapes, as though caught in the act by a searchlight.

'It's Grande. As in Emeli Sandé.'

'Gran-Day.'

I shouldn't, but I stare at her. She has acne, a squint and an overbite.

'Becky couldn't make it? I said I'd stand in?' I've never seen eyes so wide. 'I'm Alice. The dog walker?'

Forgotten all about her. I deflate and let her in.

'Sorry I'm not the normal one. I mean, I *am* normal. It's just—'

'My fault. I finished work early.'

'No. No. No. I should have knocked. Well, no, not knocked; you're not supposed to be here. I mean, I'm not saying you shouldn't be here; it's your...'

Grande comes to the rescue.

'…And who's this? Is this Gran-Day? But I like Grand. Because you *are* grand.' She falls to her knees on my carpet. I am entirely out of her mind. 'Very, very grand. Ooh, you are a handsome boy. Although you shoulda barked when you heard me. Yes, you shoulda. Woof. Woof. Woof.' She chops between the words with her finger. 'I might have been a burglar. You gotta give it some woofety when a stranger comes to the door.' She gruffs up her voice and, in pure *Emmerdale*, commands, 'Gi' it some woof-eteh!' She and my dog look up at me. It's hard to say whose eyes are the less calculating. 'He's beautiful.'

'Thank you, I…' The force of her sincerity has dazed me. I've gone simple. I can only blush and grin.

'We're goin' walkies, Gran-Day. I bet you like walkies. Ah coos 'e das.' Now she's auditioning for *EastEnders*. She's good; she'd probably get the part. 'Look a' dat flaffy tile!' Back to Yorkshire farmer. 'Gi' it some wagget-eh, Grand-Eh!' Her eyes implore me. 'Can I give him a treat?'

She pulls out a dog choc. 'Sit!' Grande does as he's told. Alice rests the dog choc on her palm. 'Wait!' His eyes go to hers, then to the dog choc, then back. He looks like he's going to cry, but Alice is silent and firm. Grande licks his lips; the treat is inches from his nose. I can be quite a strict mistress, but even I wouldn't stretch it out this long. With the tips of her finger and thumb, Alice clamps the dog choc and suspends it next to his lips. 'Gently,' she whispers. Bit by bit, she relaxes her grip on the dog choc. Delicately, as more of it is exposed, Grande nibbles away. 'Good boy.'

I've never met anyone like Alice. To be truthful, I'm a bit anxious to leave my dog with her. I ask if she minds if I come along. 'Could do with the exercise. Been shut up in court all morning.'

She looks at my uniform in wonder. 'Ah, yeah. You're a police officer! I'd love to have an interesting job like yours.'

I get changed and we drive up to Fountainford Common. On the way, she tells me she's worried about Sydney, the golden Lab she takes out twice on a Tuesday. 'I said ta-ta in the morning and posted his biscuits through, y'know, the letter slot in the door? Well…' Mastering her emotions, she takes a deep breath. 'I came back in the afternoon and there they were, still on the carpet. He hadn't touched a single one!'

On the common she picks up a stick and throws it into the distance.

'He doesn't retrieve,' I warn her. 'We've tried but…'

Grande sprints off, bites hold of the stick and, at the same pace as he went, returns to show Alice his work. Meanwhile, she tells me about her Friday dachshund, Sybil.

'I dreamed about her last night. So. We're having our walk on Cattlegreen Heath. We get lost and end up in France. You know how dreams go. Anyway, I'm trying to speak to people and I can't make myself understood. It's really frustrating. Sybil, on the other hand, is barking away with the local dogs and quickly making friends. And when I ask her how she does it she says, "Ah, *c'est naturelle*, ah speak ze language."'

And she thinks *my* job is interesting.

On the way back to the car, Grande's collar snaps as I try to put him back on the lead. It was only cheap. Alice knows a shop near the station where they sell proper greyhound collars. We drive and park up close to the parade. As we walk under the viaduct, Alice stops dead in her tracks.

'Oh my God.' She draws breath to call out. I follow her gaze to the opposite pavement. 'That's Freya Maskell. I know her.'

I wonder if Alice is being odd. But no, there she is, gorgeous as a film star, carrying a big bunch of flowers.

'She was in my year at school.'

Freya turns into the station entrance. Alice wants to go after her but there's traffic. She decides the moment is lost.

'What? Were you friends?'

'Not really.' She's struggling to gather her thoughts. 'I didn't know her that well.'

For the first time in the two hours that I've known Alice, she's not talking. And now we are in the pet shop I suspect she's not even thinking about dogs. I thought she'd go mad in here, weighing up tonics for Sydney, seeking a tricoloured coat for Sybil. But when I hold up a greyhound collar for her inspection she just shrugs and says it'll do.

'She was "the new girl",' she continues when we're back on the pavement. 'She didn't start school after the summer holidays, when everyone's new, but after Christmas or Easter. Only kids who'd had something happen to them did that. There was a new boy as well, from Kosovo. His village got bombed. But he wasn't as exotic as Freya. She was from London. Everyone thought she'd have seen things even he hadn't.'

'What was she like?'

Ignored, Grande has started to bark. He's discovered a new word. *Unsatisfactory!* he says. In his own tongue, of course, but his meaning is clear. *Unsatisfactory! Unsatisfactory!* If he expects me to make a fuss about his new collar, though, he's going to be disappointed. To say that Alice has my full attention is an understatement.

'Like a woman. A fourteen-year-old woman. She had a chest and wore make-up. Yeah, I don't know how she got away with that. And she used to stub her fag out right at the school gates. It was like different rules applied to her.'

I'm quite sure that Alice doesn't know of Freya's connection to me. In fact, I'm beginning to think she hasn't even been reading the papers; nor that she knows about Tony Gibson.

'There were always lots of rumours about Freya. Someone said she'd seen a child being crushed to death under a lorry and that ever since she'd been physically unable to smile. There was a story that a social worker had had to end a contact visit in McDonald's when she saw Freya's father French-kissing her. At the time, she was fourteen months old. She was supposed to have been the first girl ever to bring a phone into class. A teacher confiscated it. They said that Freya got so furious she had an epileptic fit.'

'Was any of it true?'

'Dunno. Doubt it. We did find out she'd been placed in foster care out here, or put into a children's home, or something. And I think she might have seen something bad happen on a road.'

I'm trying not to ask too many questions, but she keeps stopping and staring into space. It makes me want to grab her by the collar and shake the information out of her. 'Why do you think that?' I ask, as patiently, as quietly as I can.

'She wrote a play about it.' Alice's eyes light up. 'She was amazing.'

Grande crouches and crooks his tail. Absent-mindedly, Alice peels a bag off a little roll she has. I worry she might lose her concentration, so I snatch it from her and duck to scoop up.

'I was in her drama group. We weren't in the same class but drama was a sort of cross-year subject. Most of us only did it because if you didn't do drama you had to do games. It was a bit of a divvy's subject, really, for people who couldn't do anything else. People like me, I suppose.' She winces as the memories return. 'The first time we had to perform in front of the group, we had to be an animal. Someone had to go first.'

She pulls the dog to a halt and bends to give him some fuss. She's hiding the tears in her eyes.

'There was a girl in our group called Honor Duggan. She lived on a farm. She had quite severe behavioural problems. We were sitting on this mat and she said to me, "You go first." I was paralysed. "Oi." She jabbed me with her finger. "Go up and be an animal." I couldn't even look at her. Honor shuffled over on her knees and said in my ear, "Go up there and be an animal or I will hurt you." I was so scared I actually thought I was going to wet myself. I mean, I couldn't act to save my life.

'Then out of nowhere, Freya said, "I'll go first."

'Honor said, "You? Bet you ain't never seen a fuckin' animal."' Alice's own word startles her. 'Sorry about the language. That's what she said.'

'What happened next?'

'Anyway, Freya stood up and went to this space which they'd cleared for our presentations and, like, to start with she didn't do anything. Just stood there until people started to giggle. You could see that any minute the teacher was going to say something. But then there was this little lamb noise. Then she did it again. I mean, it *was* a lamb. Then she got on all fours and jumped and somehow kicked her knees to her hands in the middle of the air. We couldn't take our eyes off her. Literally, she'd turned into a lamb.'

'Then what did she do?'

'She went, "*Mooo. Mooooooo.*" That loud. And she stamped about like a cow and, like, we were laughing. It was funny. And after that she did a duck and a horse and all the other farm animals. At the end, we all cheered. She did a curtsy.'

'What about the play?'

'Erm.' Alice stares at her toes as she walks. 'Well, yeah.' She grins. 'It's coming back to me now. *Daddy, Don't Open the Door*. That's what it was called. I played "the Little Girl". It was the part that Honor Duggan wanted. We were all well into drama now. She said, "I'm the Little Girl. Freya, tell 'er!" Freya said… I shouldn't repeat things like this to a police officer…'

I see her blush in the twilight. I tell her it's okay.

'"I'm not 'avin' no retard farm girl oikin' ap my play."'

'I couldn't believe it. Honor went to hit her, but Freya didn't move. Honor stopped dead in her tracks, then started roaming about the room, punching herself in the face till she began to bleed and the teachers took her away. Never saw her in any drama class after that.'

'What happened in the play?'

'I can't remember exactly. I was in the back seat of a car at one point. My dad was in the front, at the wheel. Can't remember who played my dad – some boy, I think. We were waiting at some traffic lights. Something had happened before we stopped. Some road-rage thing with another bloke who didn't like my dad's driving. Freya played the other bloke. She did this funny "angry" mime by our car. My line was, "Daddy, don't open the door." But he did, and the other guy had a knife and he stabbed up my dad.' She giggles. 'Sounds stupid but it was a really good play. She was fantastic at drama. Wasted it all, though. I think she got expelled in the end. She stopped coming to school anyway. Didn't sit any exams, so far as I know. I think this is the first time I've seen her since the play.'

Alice looks frustrated, as though her story has run its course before she's come to her point. 'The thing is, she was a real inspiration. Really, I was rubbish at acting to begin with. But I got quite good in the end, and it was because of her. She took a chance on me, giving me a part in her play. She seemed to see that I had it in me, and I don't think the teachers did. She encouraged me… and, yeah, I guess just now I wanted to say thank you.'

I can see where my car is parked. Alice says she wants to nip into the newsagent to buy a lottery ticket. I wait outside with Grande under the viaduct. Across the road I see Freya Maskell again. She's coming down the same station ramp she walked up ten minutes ago. She's not holding her bouquet any more.

10

60 hours unpaid work. Try it n he might like it. Ya
never know. Next fing he might wanna get a job wv
PAID work for 1st time in his life!

Trunky's been convicted. The group app is buzzing. The Vanguard are meeting up at the boozer to celebrate the end of the fracking trials. 'Maybe St Joan of Arc would care to join us?' Eric Foley has written. Yes, I might pop by in a bit. Not much going on here at the flat. Jools isn't due back from Yorkshire until late. It's either The Grapes or tackling the catch-up in-tray.

I change into my onesie and microwave what's left of the curry Jools made on Sunday. Tray on lap, I prop myself in front of the box and scroll down the modules of what he calls my 'Open University degree in rocket science': *Britain's Next Top Model. A Question of Sport. Hollyoaks. The Only Way Is Essex.* There's a weekend's work here.

199

In *A Question of Sport* Sue Barker presents the name of a British athlete in the form of an anagram:

IS HER DIN ASTHMA

The teams can't work it out, but I can. Of course I can; she's practically my next-door neighbour. Dina Asher-Smith. Not yet twenty and already a household name. In the European Junior Championships, not only did she run two hundred metres in 23.6 seconds, from what I've heard she did it into a strong headwind. In case Grande won't believe I know it, I say the answer out loud.

It's making me envious. I try *TOWIE* instead but there's a guy on it who reminds me of Sket. I flick through the live channels and end up watching a documentary about a murder investigation in Manchester. A woman DC, my age, describes her theories and feelings. She reminds me of my colleagues in MCT: ordinary in appearance, except for that look in her eye. Quiet. Ceaseless. Is this week's TV actually on a *What Ru Marocco Could Have Done With Her Life* theme? Now there's an ad break and, as I watch a baby toddle in its nappy, I feel an urge to wobble my mouth and call out, *Looka da liddoo fa-ace!* Soppy div.

Mum phones. I've got a new ringtone. I let my lion roar three times before I pause the toddling.

'Lorna's shown me your dad's Facebook page.'

This was another reason why I didn't sleep last night.

'Does Jools know what you've done?'

'What I've *done*?'

'I can't believe Jools would agree to this. Your father giving you away and paying for the whole shebang? You haven't told him, have you?'

'No.'

'Does he even know you've made contact?'

'He hasn't been around.'

'Were you thinking of telling *me* at any point? I mean, I've been around. Or was it supposed to be a nice surprise for me, bumping into your dad at your wedding?'

'Literally, Mum, I've not had a moment. Course I was going to tell you.'

'A slap in the face. That's what this is. Me and Ian, we've been asking ourselves, "What have we done to deserve this?"'

Silence. 'I don't know what you want me to say.'

'We're the ones who raised you, Ru. Si abandoned you. We were the ones who cared for you. It's one of us should be with you at the altar, not your father.'

'But he *is* my father. It's what you do at a wedding. And, Mum, he's not well. He's dying.'

'Lorna told me.' She sighs. 'But that seems to be something else you've not thought about. I'm not being funny, but pancreatic cancer is... quick. These plans for a celebrity-style wedding, I mean, you're not serious, are you? That's going to take months to organise.'

'His doctors think that having the wedding to look forward to might extend the time he's got.'

'"Extend the time he's...!" You know what this looks like, don't you? From where I'm standing it looks like you've been bribed. Seriously, it looks to me like your father is buying your forgiveness. And for the sake of a posh reception and a honeymoon abroad you've agreed to go along with it.'

'That's not how it went. I asked him to give me away. He offered all this after.'

'But look at the position it's put me and Ian in. I can't see how you can expect us to come to your wedding in these circumstances. I mean it, Ru. How can we? I'm not saying it to be spiteful, but really…'

She expects I'll back down, like I do when people I'm close to confront me. But I've thought about this, about having and not having the nice things, and I've decided which I prefer. 'Well,' I say, 'we've agreed it now.'

Mum ends the call.

I run a bath. A foot deep. I pour in oils and scents. The water's so hot I have to lower myself in inch by inch. Now my chin is submerged and my nostrils breathe little dents into the surface.

What did Freya Maskell do with that bouquet?

I reach for my phone and take another look at the group app. This morning's taste of rehabilitation has left me hungry for more. No one's joined in with Eric's invite. I thought there might be something from Connor: *Yeah. Get your arse down here, PC Marocco, and that's an order!* Something like that. Then, maybe I'd go. I could gaze at him over our drinks, the way he gazed at me this morning. We could start an affair. I could play him and Jools off against each other and make them compete for my favour. And I'd give myself to the one who knocks me up the quickest, gets me out of my stupid job.

My eyes close. The day's catching up on me. I yawn. Can't believe it. Freya Maskell. The victims' champion, actress extraordinaire. Walking the streets like nothing happened.

She wrote three plays with Tony Gibson. At least, that's how many Russ and I found on their computers. At the Travelodge she was this black-widow-spider type who killed her men after mating. Before that he'd been a schoolboy in detention. Another time he was a rock climber, injured at the foot of a cliff. Freya was a passer-by who turned out to be a doctor and, as luck would have it, a rapist. No idea where they put on that production. I couldn't help but laugh when Russ imagined Tony, in his car between work appointments, driving whilst rehearsing his lines: 'Really, I should complain about the room service... This pen smells of chloroform, miss... *This* isn't CPR!'

And he was hardly exaggerating. Some of the dialogue was like that. Really corny. But Tony took great care directing it. In the classroom, when his miniskirted teacher summoned him to her desk, having dropped a pen by her feet, she was required not merely to say, 'Would you pick that up for me?' but to say it 'slow and sleepy, with a stare'. His doctor, as she straddled his supposedly broken pelvis, explained 'a bit sarcastically', 'We have to cover the wound.' On their last night, as he lay stripped and bound and she held a knife-substitute to his throat, she was directed to nod 'at my todger' and command 'in a businesslike voice', 'Make that so I can use it.' We read all this in the week that followed the night of my engagement, when I confessed to Jools about the toilet incident and discovered what happens when, at the perfectly judged moment, you utter your obscene surprise. So it made an impression.

The heat is pooling in different areas of the bath. I raise my hips, part my knees and feel the water swirl.

I open my eyes. There were some things Freya said no to. Tony wanted her to drug him with Rohypnol at the Travelodge. She vetoed that on health and safety grounds, which seems a bit rich, seeing that she saw no health and safety issues with murdering him. Another occurred when she played the doctor. The cliff was her idea. He wanted to be the survivor of a car crash. She said that, for personal reasons, she couldn't go along with that. Does this connect with *Daddy, Don't Open the Door*?

My hair spreads and floats. The skin on my thighs is slimy with the oils. *Oh God.* It's been two weeks and I still haven't charged up Mr Kelsey's phone. I try to imagine Freya, slow and sleepy. Just her and me in an interview room. *Would you pick that up for me?* I should phone Mum and say sorry. And Dad. My phone buzzes. The group chat, I expect. I'll look at it later. And now a vision of Dr Maskell, jockeying up and down, stethoscope jiggling on her chest. Was that really the last of the curry? I should message the guys at The Grapes. Did Tony ever get to make his todger so that Freya could use it? Did I feed the dog?

'Where's the bag?'

Not sure if this is an interview room. Looks more like a dungeon.

'No comment.' Freya hangs in manacles from a dripping ceiling. In the glare of a bright light, sweat sparkles on her skin.

'Where's the red bag you used to kill Tony?' Yes, I remember. I did feed the dog.

'No comment.'

The DI twiddles a pen and consults a sheet of paper. 'Eyebrows.'

I glance at him. He squints again at the sheet.

''S what it says.'

I expect Jools will object. Instead, he turns in his seat and watches. Hands clasped behind my uniformed back, I step forward into his client's personal space. 'You heard the DI,' I whisper. No, I say it in a businesslike voice. 'Where's the bag?' My face is so close to Freya's we can feel each other's breath.

I remind myself that this is my duty; that I get paid to do it, I have no choice.

'No comment.'

I study the pencilled arc that runs through the length of her right eyebrow. I trace it with the tip of my tongue.

'Eyebrows,' the DI prompts. '*Zuh.*'

Freya lowers her chin to resist me. I'm an inch or two taller than she is. Her head now bowed, I note her pure and mushless scalp and the fine hairs that seem to have been planted one by one. I crook a finger under her jaw and make her look at me. Breath shoots from my nostrils down her face. I open my mouth. My chin brushes her nose. I lick her other eyebrow.

'Did you throw the bag in the river?' I speak into her neat, pink-scrubbed ear.

Her eyes are closed; she licks her lips. 'No comment.'

Behind me, the DI sighs and chunters. 'Who thinks up these modern interrogation techniques? Nothing like this in my day.' He tilts his flow chart, as though its meaning is contained within a marble that might roll off and land in his palm. '"If suspect declines to comment... go to 'Eyebrows'. If suspect continues to withhold evidence, go to..."' Frowning, he turns the chart through ninety degrees. '"Go to... 'Teeth'."'

The word fills the room like a gas. Freya opens her mouth to protest, then thinks and closes it again. Our noses are nearly touching. I glower and try to look cruel but, really, I'm the one who is scared. This is dangerous. If a stranger got this close to Grande he might bite her face. And my suspect is much worse than a dog. I look down into the gap that divides us, at our rising, falling chests, mine behind its stiff tunic, hers sweating in rags.

I slip my tongue between her lips. This time she doesn't flinch, but she doesn't encourage me, either. I lose my nerve and pull back. My mouth has pooled with saliva and I feel the urge to swallow. I check myself. That would look weak. I dip into her again and, at the same time as I rest the point of my tongue against the porcelain of Freya's front teeth, dribble brims over my bottom lip and drains into her mouth. She shows no revulsion. A thrill of shame runs through me as I think of my unrefreshed, cells-stained breath wafting into this murderess's nostrils. In millimetres, in nags and nibbles, I rub my tongue up and down.

I wake up. The water's gone cold.

Guilty Secrets is part of Southern Escorts. It's where you find the girls who offer role play. The other, non-GS girls are, I suppose, normal escorts whose services you don't have to wait or prepare for. They're all very attractive. Some, like Sabrina, specify that they're bi. Back on the couch in my onesie, I scroll down to study her spec.

> *Bubbly South African, passionate about all sport and travel. She describes herself as 'a big-hearted country girl, up for all adventures'.*

A scene develops in my mind. Me and a smiling, suntanned Sabrina, enjoying a drink in the bar of the Thames Frockley Travelodge. There's something about a handkerchief, then, suddenly, it all ends as I fast-forward to the river's edge and glimpse my body in a blue rubber bag. Unaroused, I remind myself that not all prostitution has to take place in the Thames Frockley Travelodge. I move the action onto safer ground, to a restaurant with a comfortable room upstairs. By candlelight, she's charming. I learn about sunlit life in the open. We talk about athletics, then move the conversation on to our bodies.

But, again, that's as far as it gets. Screw my face up, squeeze every thought-muscle, I can't get her up those stairs. In desperation, I invent a home for her, where I ring a bell and wait for the door to open. The curtain in the next window twitches. Inside Sabrina's house there are bills and washing, and children to feed. I'm her chore, and her neighbour's reason to call the antisocial behaviour hotline. The tale ends in slapstick, when my colleagues raid and I wind up face to face with Sergeant Jenner, turning out my pockets at the custody desk.

I take another look at Sabrina's photo. She's gorgeous. But she's unimaginable. It's those bubbles and that big heart. I just can't square those with having to *pay* for this. Antoinette, the opposite of Sabrina, is 'urban through and through'. She'll drop her aitches for me 'and so much more!' Which, to judge from her scowl, is about the only laugh I'd be likely to get from her. Sabrina's face says, *Come aboard! Always room in my life for one more.* Antoinette wants you to know the drawbridge is firmly up. No confusion about the money here. I'd probably have to pay up front. For her, this is strictly business and she's not going to pretend that it's not. I like this better. I shan't have to get to know her. I won't even have to stand her a meal. I'm going to use her like a household appliance. Ah, this is much easier to imagine.

We're up the stairs in no time. I lead her into the room and tell her to stand there and strip. Her face tells me she doesn't like being told what to do but here, where the customer is king (I can imagine this really clearly), I'm the dominant partner and what I say will go. She looks at her watch. She's reluctant but starts to do as she's told. 'You're doing really well,' I tell her, using my mum's bossy voice. 'Now take it all off.'

She's down to her bikini. Borrowing from my dungeon, I moisten her chest with a sheen of Freya's sweat. I monitor my pulse and my glands. Still nothing has stirred. Trudging on with my vision, I stroll around Antoinette like she's a museum piece. She's got a six-pack. There's a cluster of tiny hairs on her coccyx. She's perfect, but my confidence drains; I don't know what to do next. I'm losing control of the situation.

Then there's a knock on the door. 'Room service!'

In comes Jools, dressed as a waiter, pushing a trolley. Antoinette looks relieved. She almost smiles, and I have to remind her not to move. Jools and I circle her, observing the artwork of her body. Now we're getting somewhere. This is more like it. I'm beginning to really like what I see. But when he faces her she turns all saucy and they share a private grin. She puts her arms around his neck; he…

Ah, *what*?! I've just gone and hit her! Punched her straight in the mouth. She's cursing, but she's too alarmed to do anything. So's Jools. I give her my meanest look. She scurries back into her clothes and is gone. Goodness. I wasn't expecting that. That bit was majorly real. I'd have to be careful if I ever actually did this. I wouldn't, obviously. I can see that now. But if I did, I mean, would Guilty Secrets shop me to the police?

I sigh. Am I even bi-*curious*?

I click into the Guilty Secrets section of the Southern Escorts website where, for some reason, the first thing I look for is a tribute to Tony Gibson. *Our valued customer, sorely missed.* That would have been nice. Maybe Phoebe could have loaned them the snow-to-Eskimos photo. I pull myself together and browse the girls, or actresses as they're called here. No mention of aitch-dropping or adventuring by these fine ladies. They list *their* vital statistics in terms of their academic achievements, which include teaching degrees, diplomas in counselling and therapy, and qualifications from drama school. I note from the picture galleries, though, that, like their less sophisticated non-role-playing sisters, they've shed their caps and gowns and are all dancing in stilettos, lounging in lace, standing side-on in basques. All of them except my girl – there she is – back in business, trading once again as 'Vixen'. I don't know if these are her usual portraits. Maybe she marketed herself more seductively in an earlier portfolio that was taken down whilst she was on remand. But none of these show her pretending to sulk, or trying to look unlawfully young, or have-ably stupefied, or viciously oversexed. They show her listening with close attention, caught by a great idea, being taken completely by a nice surprise, and in one – can you believe it? – laughing like she'd better clamp her knees. The photos show only her face.

It's starting to come back to me now. £50 to register. Yeah, I remember thinking that was a bit steep. Payment details are 'entirely confidential and your true identity will never be disclosed to any actress unless you expressly wish it'. Once you've registered, you type a message in a box, naming your choice of actress and explaining approximately where you live and whatever unholy thing it is you have in mind. Your actress is then supposed to reply within twenty-four hours. She'll tell you if your fantasy is up her street, and if it is, and just so long as it's not illegal, degrading or a health threat – 'The safety of our actresses is our paramount concern' – she'll advise you on setting, dialogue and direction. You have to keep an eye on cost, of course (which they say they bear in mind), and regular payments on account are required, particularly if your actress has to source props or travel to find a location. Every email you get will cost you £30.

I navigate back to the registration. I type out my debit card details and confirm that I've read the T&Cs. I stare. On the screen I see a girl in soft focus and a ship that will take me to a foreign land. I twiddle a boarding card between my fingers. I click the mouse.

Elsewhere in the flat there is movement. A rattle of ears. A sneeze. A slow and stately drum of paws. I go to the dialogue box on Freya's page. *'Vixen', for goodness' sake, not Freya. She mustn't know we're acquainted.*

I type.

Do you do girl on girl?

'Nah then, lass.' Jools enters the room with a Jaeger carrier bag, puts it down, and leans over the couch to kiss me. He smells of cold clothes.

'You're back early.'

'Took an afternoon's compassionate shopping leave. How was court?'

'Didn't have to give evidence in the end.'

'Stand up,' he says. He reaches into his bag and pulls out an item of clothing. 'Don't look so worried. I've kept the receipt.'

It's a jacket, short with a wide-ended belt. A cross between a cardigan and a judo top. Not what I'd have chosen, but it fits. I look at myself in the mirror. 'Mmm.'

'Let me see you.'

I cross my karate hands and crouch. 'Hah!' I'm ready to spring.

'Sex on a stick, if you ask me. But, like I say, we can change it.'

'No, I like it.'

He goes to put on the kettle. I twist some more in the mirror. It's growing on me.

'Mr Wells and I have had a bit of a falling-out,' he calls from the kitchen.

'Nothing serious, I hope.'

'I expect it'll blow over. He wanted me to pass on a message to his girlfriend. I told him to get one of his men to do it.'

'What was the message? Oh, you can't say, can you?'

'It sounded harmless but you never know what it might have led to. And, anyway, it's the principle. He knew it was out of bounds. He was just trying to make me break the rules; see if he could.'

'What did you say?'

'I told him I'm perfectly happy to act for him as his solicitor, but I am a solicitor, not a member of his staff, and I shan't be pressurised into doing anything I shouldn't. Actually, it was high time he and I talked about this. I saw Steve Ridealgh the other day – you know, his last solicitor? The SRA have suspended him from practising. They've accused him of colluding with Wells. He won't have. At least, not knowingly, not dishonestly. It's just the way Mark Wells operates. He winds you in so that, before you know it, you're his associate, his "personal friend". And then you owe him loyalty.'

'Was Wells okay with what you said?'

'Not really. He paced about the conference room at one point. The guards began to hover outside. I called time on it; said I'd see him next week. He just muttered. Dunno. I think I had to draw a line in the sand. He might sack me. We'll see.'

The fridge door closes. The microwave hums.

'Ten years in practice, I thought I understood criminals pretty well. I've just been scratching the surface. The types who usually instruct me, the ones you guys catch, are the amateurs. Hotheads, addicts, the mentally ill. The Mark Wellses of the world take their vocation seriously. They're dedicated to their craft.'

I'm still preening and saying the word 'Jaeger' to myself when Jools's face appears at the serving hatch. He looks like a newscaster.

'Mark Wells is a phenomenally horrible man. But he is persuasive. And although his trial was carried out to the letter and the evidence seems watertight, after half an hour with him you end up believing that, so far as murdering Femi Yar'Adua is concerned, he didn't do it. I know they all say that but in his case…'

'What can you do to help him? It doesn't sound like you've got an appeal.'

'I've got to find fresh evidence. Wells says he's been stitched up. His car was dented an hour before the murder took place. He thinks it was done on purpose and that someone will have witnessed it. There was a cigarette butt found at the scene. It had his DNA. He says it was planted there. I'm trying to find out who by. I write letters enquiring about CCTV, or demanding the police have another search of their unused material. I've got a team of private detectives, some of them villains themselves. I spend whole afternoons waiting in pubs, seeing if some rival gangster will keep their appointment to tell me what they know. These people make your blood run… Bloody hell, what's this?' He's back. Tea mugs steam in his hands. He's looking at my laptop. '"One teatime when she was eight…"'

I look over my shoulder. It turns out I snuffed Guilty Secrets only to land on Dad's Facebook page.

One teatime when she was eight or nine, my firstborn munched her grub in silence. Hang on a mo, I thought. More rabbit than Sainsbury's normally, my Ruby. This definitely wasn't right. 'Penny for 'em, Woob?' I asked.

'I'm deciding who I'm going to invite to my wedding,' she replied.

'We didn't know you was getting married,' I said, exchanging a look with her mum. 'When's the happy day?'

'Oh, I've got to find a gentleman first. And a gentleman of the very highest quality, so it's likely to take some time.'

Well, it did take some time and, the way things turned out, I've not been there for my girl for most of it. But I'm privileged and proud to announce that the gentleman of the very highest quality has now been run to ground and the happy couple are soon to be wed. And I've had the honour bestowed on me of giving my Wooby away!

This is just to let you know, sweetheart, that whatever it is you're wishing for, on the day itself and beyond – a coach and horses, a flourish of trumpets, a holiday in the Maldives – it's on me. Money will be no object. This will be your special time.

I haven't been the best of dads, Woob. But fate has given me this final chance to make amends and to prove to you that childhood dreams can come true.

Jools looks at me. 'I didn't know you'd traced your dad.'

I tell him the story, from the night of the dinner party to Mum's call today. He can't understand it. Every new detail makes him shake his head.

'So, he ignored you for all those years… and now he wants to send you to the Maldives? Hang on, after all he did… you've forgiven him? Wait a minute, he wants you in his life… but only at the point he's found out he's dying?'

Jools once said that a client of his had let out a 'mirthless chuckle' from the dock. Only now that he lets one out himself do I see what the action involves.

'I can't believe you've not told me before. We used to talk about your father all the time.'

'I didn't think you were interested any more.'

'Not interested?' He looks offended. 'I thought, when you came back from Cath's, that we'd said all our home truths. You've not got any more surprises for me, have you?'

I smile at him blandly.

'You've not won the rollover jackpot? You're not carrying another man's child that I'm going to have to raise as my own? You've not found God?'

'No.'

'Sure? There's nothing else on your mind?'

I think and then shake my head. 'No. I thought I'd found God, but I checked the misper register yesterday and it turned out to be someone else.'

'I'm being serious.' He says it gently as he smooths out a crease in my jacket, then holds me at arm's length to pronounce on the final effect. He frowns. 'Do you think you could try it on *without* the onesie underneath?'

'I will.'

He holds my gaze. 'When did we last go out?'

'Tuesday, two weeks ago. We went to watch *Fifty Shades of Grey*.'

'When did we last make love?'

'The Saturday before last.'

He smiles, a little bitterly, I think, although from what I can remember the session was quite nice. Then he takes another look at my laptop. '"A gentleman of the very highest quality." Is that how you described me to your dad?'

I nod.

'And – be honest – is that what you think I am?'

I nod again.

'Explain.' He looks like he's going to be hard to convince.

'You do good impersonations. You'd take a bullet for my dog. You're excellent during a Shrewsbury sauce crisis.'

'Be sensible.'

'I mean it. It's true.'

He's determined not to smile.

'You listen. You remember. You're kind. You know how to pay a compliment. You stick up for me. You're patient. You're encouraging. You never sulk. You don't shout. You're well informed. You say interesting things. You're free with your money. You've got a cheeky smile. You've got a nice bottom. You make an effort with my friends. You get on with my family. You make me proud to be seen with you. You like the things I like. You can compromise. You've got a future. You're doing something with your life. You know how to have a good time.'

'Really?'

'No. Not the last one.'

'Oh, yeah. Used to, though.' He turns serious again. 'I'm not the highest anything. A well-meaning bungler, at best.

Even when you left me… I mean, God, if it hadn't been for your mother… Do you still want to marry me?'

'Yes.'

'I've *beyond* taken my eye off the ball.' His face drops low, then bounces back up with a plan. 'Can you take some time off?'

'Probably.'

'I'm owed that much leave, if I don't take it soon I'll lose it altogether.' He reaches for his phone and begins to tap on the screen.

'What are you doing?'

'Texting Lester. I'm telling him I'm taking a break.'

I look at him. He winks.

'You're sure you still want to marry me?'

'Yes.'

'Well, this wedding's not going to arrange itself, is it?'

11

'She's not known to us,' says Sergeant Tan, reading from his screen. 'Why don't you caution her?'

'Her brief advised her to go "no comment".'

He bites his lip. 'If she'd coughed it we could have cautioned her,' he says.

'And her mum could have got to work on time.'

'What do you propose?'

It's been announced, with appropriate solemnity, on the force Facebook page that police car sirens officially go *nee-nah*, not *woo-woo*. Pupils at one of our primary schools voted on it and the *nee-nah*s won by sixty votes to twenty-six. The actual new V8 Mustang used in this public enquiry stands in the pound and my skipper says I can sit in it as soon as I'm free. I want to know if I'm a *nee-nah*er or a *woo-woo*er.

'Sticks in my craw, to be honest, Sarge, that we don't do the "victim", too. Fancy complaining to the police that you've had your cannabis stolen.'

'How old's the victim?'

'She's fourteen, too. It was her parents who reported it. They said they were disgusted that the school weren't taking action, and so they came to us! I think if we're going to prosecute Skye for robbery then it's only fair we do Leah for having cannabis in the first place.'

'Why didn't the school deal with it?'

'Took place outside the school gates. Not their remit. I mean, can't I tell Leah's mum and dad that we'll have to arrest her? They'll drop the charges pretty quick then, won't they?'

Sergeant Jenner might have gone with this. He's never afraid to use a bit of common sense. But Sergeant Tan is nervy. They say, in the heart of any city, you live in the knowledge that you're never more than six feet from a rat. Sergeant Tan feels the same way behind his custody desk. Except in his case it's not rats, it's complaints. I fear that the vision I'm offering, of loud-mouthed parents, a procedural sleight of hand, and not just one youth in custody but two, with all the codes-of-practice complexities that's going to bring, is unlikely to make his mouth water.

He shudders and shakes his head. 'Take it to CPS.'

With which my Mustang dreams are over. CPS. Can't Play with Sirens.

Getting through to the Crown Prosecution Service on the telephone takes time. We have a callback facility at Cattlegreen, but no one knows how to use it, so I've just got to stay within earshot and be reminded every thirty seconds how important my call is. I take the opportunity to charge up the mobile I took from Mr Kelsey's shed.

'Good morning, CPSD.'

I switch on the power point and run to the phone. 'Hello!

Hello! Hi, I'm looking for charging advice on a youth we have with us.' I tell the prosecutor about Leah's allegation.

'You don't need to come to CPS,' he tells me. 'Theft's a police decision.'

'It's robbery.'

'How come?'

'Allegedly, Skye said to Leah, "Give it here or I'll dash you."'

'"Dash"?'

'Must be a local expression. Refers to the employment of force.'

'Right.' In whichever part of the country it is where schoolchildren don't routinely 'dash' each other, the lawyer scrolls down through the documents I've scanned and sent him.

'I was wondering, though. Is it legally possible to steal something which it's illegal to have anyway?'

'Yeah. Drugs are still "property". It's settled law.'

I'd better remember that. Means if I catch Jools with something of Tommy's – her underwear, for instance, under his car seat – I'd better hand it straight back.

'What about the victim here? Do you think she should be prosecuted for possessing cannabis?'

'Have you got the cannabis?'

'What? No, it's gone.'

'Then we'll never know for sure if it was cannabis. The girls might have thought it was cannabis when it wasn't.'

Wow. They think of everything, these lawyers. Seems such a waste. I reckon if I had the brains to get a law degree I'd use them on something less daft.

'So we charge Skye with robbing... what?'

'"A substance". If we do charge her. But first you'll need to send me the completed ten-point youth checklist.'

'The what?'

'It's a Q&A. I see that Skye hasn't been in trouble before. I need the checklist in case she's suitable for a caution.'

'But she hasn't admitted the offence, so she can't be cautioned.'

'I know. But I'm not allowed to authorise charge without it. I'll email you a copy and you can phone us back.'

'But—'

He's gone.

Half a minute later, the ten-point checklist plops into my inbox. *Ah, seriously?* Do I really have to ask scowly Mrs Fordred all this personal stuff?

Is Skye subject to any notification requirement pursuant to s.80 Sexual Offences Act 2003?

I've no idea what that is but the question doesn't sound like one you'd put to someone you suspect of being a *good* parent. Oh well. Better get it over with. I print off the checklist and march to reception, clipboard under arm.

In the conference room, mother and daughter focus silently on their phones.

'Hi. The guy from the Crown Prosecution Service has a few questions about Skye. Is it all right if I take a seat?' I take one and read from my script. 'Is Skye a looked-after child? Is she a carer for anyone else? Has she mental health difficulties?'

We get to the sexual offences question. Both shake their heads. Straight away, without looking at each other. Maybe as in 'not any more'?

'How is Skye's behaviour at home?'

'All right, really,' says Mrs Fordred. 'We fell out over this but we've patched things up.'

'That's good,' I say, and smile, Teague-like, at Skye.

'Yeah,' she says. 'Mum had to pay Leah's mum for the green but I paid you back, innit?'

Mum says nothing.

'Pardon?' I've got a feeling I shouldn't go here but I want to be sure that I'm not going mad.

'Leah's dad only heard about what happened 'cause I sold the skunk to Leah's mum. I never knew she *was* Leah's mum. I always supply her.'

'Don't tell her that,' hisses Mrs Fordred.

'Anyway…' Skye glances at her mum, who glances at me. Mum's expression softens. She's afraid I'll think she might have been too severe just now. Skye deems it safe to go on. 'Her dad saw his wife with *his* skunk and thought she'd chawed it. He started to dash her, so Leah had to own up and tell him she'd nicked his stash and I'd nicked it off her.'

Mrs Fordred looks at me. Her mouth twitches at the corners. She's beginning to see the funny side of it and is willing me to join in. 'So I had to pay Leah's mum what she'd paid Skye.'

The child is now beaming. 'And I've had it docked from my pocket money.'

I head back to the office. Along the corridor I glance through the window. It's crisp and sunny outside. As soon as I'm out of here I'm going for a very fast eight-mile run. I'm going to sweat this day out of me, soak up the stink of it in my kit, then make it disappear without trace in the washing machine. I do a double take. For a moment, I think I see a javelin, thrown high against the cold, blue sky.

Back at my desk, I email the completed ten-point checklist back to CPS and join the phone queue once more. A few days ago, in the aftermath of this 'robbery', I took a family impact statement from Luke Stanlow, Leah's dad. I pick it out of the file and remind myself of what it says:

> *This crime has blown our world apart. I just hope that Skye will one day come to realise what she has done, just as we hope that, one day, we can find it in our hearts to forgive her.*

The randomness of evil had left the poor man so bewildered, I remember, I volunteered to help him find the words. Bravo, Woob.

'Hello! Hello!'

It's a different prosecutor this time. The one I want is working on another case. I can wait or, as I decide, take it from the top with this lady.

'Have you sent the ten-point—'

'Ye-es.'

'Ah, here it is.' She reads down her screen. 'We used to call this bullying,' she says, after I've filled her in. 'Except in my day we only stole each other's sweets.'

As the budding lawyers amongst you may have noticed, this is the second time that a member of the public has tried to dob themselves in to me in the environs of the reception conference room, and, again, at no stage did I caution Skye with the 'You do not have to say anything…' announcement. To be honest, I still don't think I've completely got the hang of it. So awks, somehow, just to drop it into a conversation. Anyway, I probably should have said it and so there's no way I'm going to let the prosecutor in on the truth of what's really happening here.

'I mean…' She sighs. It's her way of saying, *This is so not what I signed up for.* I know because I've been doing the same sigh for two months. 'Is there really a public interest in prosecuting this?'

'Mmm.'

She tuts. 'I'm just reading the family impact statement. The victim's dad sounds really put out about what's happened… Sod it. Just charge her. "Robbery of a substance". There'll only be a victim right of review complaint and I can't afford another of those on my monthly stats.'

I phone custody, where, in the background, I hear signs of what might turn out to be a negative Tripadvisor rating. 'Dinlow feds. Mushmalt pigs. Gavver melts.' I can barely hear Sergeant Tan's voice above it. I try to work out who the disappointed visitor to Cattlegreen nick might be. Dunno. Don't think I've had the pleasure. Sergeant Tan informs me that there'll be a short wait before Skye can be charged. I bring her the news and, just in case she calls to mind an urgent prior commitment, escort her into the care of the detention officer who will keep her under lock and key.

Mr Kelsey's phone lights up. Most likely it'll be locked, in which case I'll pass it on to the techies. If not, I'll assume it's lost property and call round the owner's favourites to see who's lost his mobile. And I'd better just flip through the texts. It's forbidden, but there might be some good jokes. And if the owner has taken a selfie, and has shared it with his friends, all recognised nominals, and has written a caption – 'Let's rob the shed!' – complete with a devil emoji, well, I'd be gutted if that job went to anyone else.

I prod at some of the buttons. It's not locked. 'Oh.'

I've mentioned before that, generally, my response to shock or the entirely unexpected does not involve the deployment of vulgarity. I don't know why I've turned out this way. I never met anyone else in Mintsley Heights who did. But, for me, a 'Heavens!' or a 'Never!' or a 'Flip!' is usually enough to vent the feeling. 'God' might get a mention, if I'm tired or if the provocation is extreme. In this particular moment, though, as I stare at the screen saver and the unmistakable image of Freya Maskell, I feel very close to expressing myself more in the vein of a proper, normal, healthy police officer. Or anyone else, come to that.

'Crikey.' I step back from the brink. This is the third time I've seen her face in twenty-four hours. I'm so excited that, if I breathe any quicker, I'll be panting. And yet, strange coincidence as it is, I'm not all that surprised. One of us seems to be following the other.

In the shot she's cheek to cheek with a fella. He's got stubble and olive skin. He'd be handsome, except he has a birthmark over his eye, which makes him distinguished instead. They're a good-looking pair. Until a month ago Jools and I posed in the same way on my phone. I've got Grande now, taking a bath in a puddle.

I glance over my shoulder. I'm not sure why, but I'm certain: no one must know I have this phone. There are strict rules about coppers sticking their noses into people's lives by way of their mobile phones. But, in the case of Ms Maskell – there's a fifty per cent chance that this phone is hers – well,

I'm sorry. Her human rights have been getting in my way long enough.

I go straight to the photo gallery, which I expect will show who she associates with and the clubs she goes to. Where she holidays, what her parents look like. In a moment, I'll know if she plays sport and what car she... But this isn't a normal gallery. These are not random happy moments, captured on a whim. It's a photographer's portfolio. Every shot is staged. Make-up, costumes, poses. Freya's in a lot of them – clad like an empress; painted up like a cat. Impersonating a police officer, or a 'WPC' from the era when we usually wore skirts. But I don't think this is her phone. At least, there are a lot more shots of her boyfriend, or her client, or whoever he is.

It seems to me, as I scroll through, that there's something odd about these photos. Not odd. Characteristic. But I can't think what it is. If this guy is just one of Freya's role-playing clients, he seems to take his acting responsibilities at least as seriously as Tony Gibson did; probably more. Look at these two! What did they get up to toga'd up as Romans, I wonder? What service was she paid to provide for Nelson, or Napoleon, or whichever half-limbed empire-builder this is, squashed between his throne and a giant Cornish pasty hat? Is there a history theme going on here? Is that what these shots have in common?

I'm caught by a glimpse of some wallpaper. It's in the background of what looks like a Halloween group shot. Lorna and I had the same wallpaper in our bedroom. You don't see it any more. A true '80s pattern: rows of half-shaded circles, like columns of moons, the dark sides olive green, the empty halves outlined in blue. I used to stare at those circles from my bed. They made me think of lottery balls, ready to spill down tubes, roll over the carpet and make us all rich.

But what *is* it with these photos? In front of the wallpaper, underneath an Amy Winehouse beehive, from behind a coating of chalk and bright red lipstick, Freya bares her teeth. She dangles a wrist from the far shoulder of a black man who has a dagger handle sprouting from his chest and drips with theatrical blood but otherwise, with fag in one hand and glass in the other, appears to be having a fairly chilled evening. He hangs his arms around Freya and her boyfriend who, beaming in his skeleton catsuit, wields a triumphant thumbs-up. As usual, he is sitting. *Sitting.* I riffle again through the pictures. The lens has been aimed carefully, always to hide a handgrip or a wheel, but that's the common factor; that's what these shots all suggest. Freya's bloke doesn't walk.

I stare into space, overwhelmed by a sense that, in years to come, I shall look back on this moment, in this dingy office in Cattlegreen nick, and pick out a seam in my life, the point at which the first part joined to the rest.

I snap open my work mobile and tap on Mr Kelsey's name. 'Hello?'

'Mr Kelsey? PC Marocco here. From Cattlegreen police? About your shed—'

'Ah, yes. Scenes of crime still haven't come, you know. They'd better hurry up because I'm going to need to go in there. The growing season's about to start, and my lawnmower—'

'Just a couple of questions, if you don't mind. When had you last been inside the shed?'

'Before the day I saw you? Er, well… That might have been the first time this year. Yes, it's not like me. I'm out in the garden quite a lot normally. But it's been so wet this winter.'

'And… and…' I have to compose myself. So much hangs on what he'll say. 'The little window that was open. On the side by the railway embankment? Would that have been open when you were last in there?'

'Yes. I use it as a sort of air vent. But,' Mr Kelsey chuckles, 'there's no reason the burglar would have needed to make use of that. I told you, the door was unlocked anyway.'

The cloud-slicing javelin I imagined an hour ago, reappears in my mind. It is starting to fall from the sky.

'You still there?' I hear him ask. 'Hello?'

'Thanks, Mr Kelsey. I'll be in touch.'

I snap my phone shut and reach for the one he gave me. I remove the SIM and fill out a subscriber's check. Back on my work phone, I scroll through the directory for a contact I hope I still have in the British Transport Police. Gez Tattler, there he is. Hmm. I wonder if I dare. He and I met on a drink-drive course, where they plied us with regulated amounts of booze and made us blow periodically into the machine. Surprising how much you can drink and stay legal. But we were all drunk at the end. He came on to me and I can't quite remember how it ended. I know he didn't get what he wanted, but did we part as friends? What the heck. He's had about two years to get over it.

'Hello? Gez?'

'Who's calling?'

'Ru Marocco. From Cattlegreen?'

A moment's silence. '*Aaallo*, Ruby! 'Ow ya diddlin'?'

No hard feelings, then. We do the usual copper banter. I make out he's a slacker; he makes out I'm a div.

'Reason I'm phoning – I was involved in a CID job a few months back and there's a couple of loose ends. Long shot, but I think there might be a connection with that fatality you had just before Christmas. At Fountainford station?'

'Stephen Hawking? It was mine, that.'

'Was that his name? Ste—?'

'What? No, it's just what we called him. You talking about the guy in the wheelchair?'

'That's the one.'

'Yeah, my case, that. Still don't know who he was.' Gez sounds excited. 'You think you might be able to find out?'

'It's possible. Thing is, what I'm doing's covert, yeah?'

'Totally understand, Ru. Won't press you. You wanna come round? You free now?'

I find Skye and Mrs Fordred and escort them to the custody suite. Skye is charged with robbing her substance and is bailed to appear at Thames Frockley Youth Court on a Wednesday in two weeks' time.

'Yeah, whatever,' comments Mrs Fordred, and checks the texts on her phone.

Twenty minutes later it's my lunch break and, at the BTP offices in Fountainford, DC Gez Tattler is about to show me some more photographs.

''Ope you've eaten,' he warns, with his British Transport leer. 'They're in date order. This… is what we found on Day 1.'

They're very proud of their skin here at the BTP. It's a standard centimetre thick and made from a mixture of reinforced tyre rubber and powdered rhino scars. And they like nothing more than a demo to those of us who don't make our living hosing people off bridges or carrying them off in pails. Obviously, if it's a girl they're baiting, so much the better. But I'm not usually that queasy, so if Gez expects me to turn green and faint, he might find that I'm not putting out. On the other hand, I don't always know what I'm looking at when I'm presented with grisly pictures. Ankles can look like ears to me, and chins like the backs of knees. Depends which way round I'm holding the photo, and if it's a close-up. So if making me feel merely stupid is any consolation, seeing as he can't make me feel sick, then, if the first picture is anything to go by, he probably won't have to wait very long.

'Er. What is it?' I can see that it's long, but not if it's big or small. It could be a finger or a leg.

He points to the glove at one end.

'Oh. An arm.'

'Detective work, you say you're doing now?'

I have to smile at that.

'Fin Leech found it. Got us off the mark. We all had to buy him a drink... And this, yeah?' With the tip of his finger he drags another picture across the desk. 'This was recovered by dogs. Landed in a badger sett.'

I shake my head. 'Go on.'

'Liver. So I am reliably informed.'

'Ugh!' I exclaim dutifully. I don't know how Gez thinks this will help me identify his Stephen Hawking but I'd better play along.

'And on Day 2, finally, after ninety-seven man hours on the job, the Holy Grail...' He shows me half of what I think is Freya's fella's head. 'PC Havering climbed up a tree and seized this. Put her prize money, I understand, towards a minibreak in York.'

I draw my face close. It's him all right. Olive skin, a week's worth of stubble, birthmark over the eye.

'Instantaneousness. Absence of pain. Aesthetics.' Gez returns the photographs to their sheath. 'That's what the would-be suicide must consider. Unfortunately for Stephen, or those of us who survive him, maybe, a high-speed train ticks only two of the boxes.'

'He definitely killed himself?'

Gez sits me down in front of a laptop and presses a couple of keys. CCTV footage appears. Through the darkness I recognise the coast-bound platform of Fountainford railway station. It seems to be entirely deserted.

'Keep your eye… here.' He points to the bottom right of the screen. 'He must have been hiding out of view. Nobody knew he was there. Watch now…'

'*Whoaaaah!*'

From nowhere, a figure in a wheelchair propels himself out of the shadows and towards the platform edge. What happens next is hidden by the sudden passing of a very fast train.

'Never did find out if he had a ticket.'

'Cor.' Life. No life. All in the blink of an eye. I can confirm, from my occasional reruns of Diana's funeral, that this gentleman lived his life like a candle in the wind. 'So how far did Stephen… get?'

'Some of him made it all the way to Hazeldene. That's how far it takes to stop a train like this.' Gez looks sad now. The funnies are wearing thin. Even with his special skin he can't keep it up indefinitely.

The two of us stare into space.

'The thing is, Ru, we still have absolutely no idea who this guy was. No wallet, no phone. No one's reported him missing. We've reassembled nearly the whole of his wheelchair. We've put posters up everywhere, launched an appeal… I know you probably can't say anything yet, but if you've at least got a theory…'

I nod and remember that Gez is still probably wondering if I know who the real Stephen Hawking is. 'I've got a theory of everything.'

Back at the nick, I run into Rashid. I've heard from him only once since my departure from CID. A text to say he's got his permission to drive.

'Hey! *Brum-brum*.'

He smiles and we wait for the fog to clear. 'Ah, right. Yeah. Got my wheels. Finally.'

'Have they given you a motor?'

'Nah.'

This has come at a bad time for both of us. He's in a hurry and I've got a dead man's phone. I can almost feel its radioactivity glowing through the pocket of my tunic.

'So, what you working on?' I ask.

'This and that… like…' A moment too late, he remembers that we were close once. With his 'This and that', which sounds to us both like a friendly 'Mind your own business', he's let slip that I'm now an outsider. We sweat a little in our shirts whilst he digs himself out of his ditch. 'Rubbishy stuff, really. Just off to see a kid's mum. Possible grooming jobbie.'

'Ah.' I nod. Doesn't sound rubbishy. Sounds like what detectives do.

Mentally we hunt around for something more to say. The cupboard is bare.

'We must meet up for a coffee,' he says, already walking. 'Have a proper catch-up.'

'Yeah. See you later.'

This should hurt quite a lot but Sergeant Tan, whose face appears around the door frame I've just passed, gives me terror instead.

'Hey, Ruby!' He's seen the radioactive glow.

'Hey, Sarge.' I retrace my steps along the corridor to the custody area.

'Can you email me the MG3 for Skye Fordred?'

'Doing it right now.'

In fact, I don't do it right now. Back at my desk, I find that the result of my subscriber check has been emailed. Skye, and the terror of a moment ago, are both forgotten completely.

Brandon Anthony-James

DOB: 4.3.1986

127 Ephraim Close, Carshalton, Surrey

Carshalton. Up Croydon way. I've seen signs for it when we've been to IKEA. Thirty miles from Fountainford? Poor guy. What a way to go. It would have been his birthday yesterday. What would he have been? Twenty-nine? Maybe that explains why Freya had flowers. But what's odd is that there's a poster in the window of the BTP office at Fountainford station. It shows an artist's impression of Brandon, and there's a caption: 'Do You Know This Man?' Freya couldn't have missed it when she walked up the slope to the platform. It would have stared her right in the face. She just ignored it.

She hasn't told the authorities, so maybe she's not told anyone. Maybe Freya and I are the only ones who know that Brandon is dead. And in the meantime, the lives of friends and relatives dangle uselessly from a feeble thread of hope. I can't get my head round this. There's going to be a Mrs Anthony-James, I'm sure of it. A gentle mother, quietly withering away, or a feisty wife who bangs her fist each day on the Carshalton nick front counter. There must be a dad or brother out there missing Brandon; a friend or work colleague demanding news, writing to the local MP, threatening legal action because the Old Bill aren't doing enough to find him. Meanwhile Freya, who's known all along, has done nothing. I can't square this coldness with what Alice told me yesterday about what she was like as a girl, or with that warm and open face on the Guilty Secrets website. Then I think of why I know Freya Maskell and remember that she'll probably care as little for Brandon's survivors as she did about Tony Gibson's.

I drum my fingers against the computer keyboard. I should forward this email to Gez. He'll see it's from me; it won't need further explanation. He'll just tap the side of his nose if anyone asks about his source. There's no reason it should lead back to the phone.

What the hell's been going on? What *have* the police been doing these last three months? Carshalton's not the end of the earth. How, for a whole winter, can the misper unit at Carshalton and the Fountainford BTP have managed not to join hands on this one? Could someone have mistyped the data; missed out the hyphen in 'Anthony-James'? Or, because coppers think BTP are different, because they don't own a county like we do and everyone thinks they can't drive and have to ride on trains, might someone not have thought to check with them because they forgot the BTP are there? Hard to imagine, maybe. Unless you're a copper yourself and you know what really goes on.

But what am I *thinking*?! I need to be in touch with Paul Bibby. With someone, at least. *Of course* I can't keep hold of Brandon's phone! It stopped being a harmless item of lost property the moment I saw whose face is on the screen saver, at which point it became a potentially crucial exhibit in two violent death investigations. And I'm not involved in either of them. For as long as the phone stays in my tunic I'm hampering those investigations. Concealing evidence. Perverting the course of justice.

Suddenly I'm sad. But relieved, too. The excitement drained out of me, it's nice to feel this relaxed. I stretch back in my chair and yawn. Definitely out running tonight. And I'll try and make something nice for Jools's tea. I'll text him in a minute, see what he wants. Not that the thought of my magic in the kitchen will make him scurry home in a sweat. But I hope he'll appreciate the gesture. He was so sweet about my dad last night.

I email Sergeant Tan his MG3. Now I think I'll make a cup of tea. After that, I'll let Gez be the lucky one. I'll forward the result of the subscriber check and he can make a trip to Carshalton, break the news to the bereaved. Then I'll call Paul Bibby, tell him what I've found. Obviously, he'll be interested. He's as convinced of Freya's guilt as I am. Who knows? He might take me back on MCT.

I have a notification. There's an email on my personal phone.

> Hi, Lurcher!
> Yes, girl on girl is certainly part of my repertoire. Why don't you tell me a little bit about your tastes and the sort of role you see for yourself? Then perhaps we can work together on a script.
> Kind regards,
> Vixen x

9pm

Number 127 is a bungalow, amply spaced from its neighbours, on a wide, tree-lined road, like the sort you get in the Cattlegreen Heath estate. The front is paved and planted with the odd little bush. The lights are off. No one seems to be in. I knock on the front door anyway.

I'm Lily, I tell myself. *I used to see Brandon around. I was in Fountainford this morning and I saw a poster. I just thought…*

No, no one's at home. I've brought pen and paper but I can't really leave a note. This has to be done face to face. I'll wait for a bit, see if anyone comes. If not, I'll just keep coming back.

I return to my car and keep an eye on the driveway. At the same time I have my phone in my hand. This must be the fifth time I've reread Freya's email. It makes me smile. 'Kind regards.' How polite.

Sorry, Gez, I think to myself. *Sorry, Paul.* I know I should call them. But if I do, one way or another, I think it might turn out badly for Freya, and I don't want that. Not before we've had our date.

Whatever am I going to write back to her? *Am* I going to write back? *Really?* Thinking about it, I find I can't be serious.

Hi, Vixen!

Just outside Brandon's place at the mo. About to do your work and explain to his family what's happened. Deffo up for a rug-munch. LOL.

Lurcher x

Lurcher. I don't know why I called myself that. Why bring Grande into this? Maybe it's reassuring to know that, if Grande and a fox had a contest, probably my dog would come out on top.

Someone is coming. I compose myself. The pedestrian passes by. My hysteria comes back.

Hey, Vix!

Found Brandon's phone. Maybe there's stuff in there that will incriminate you. It's given me a great fantasy idea about you fighting to stay out of prison and trying to snatch it back off me. Reckon you'd look hot in wrestling gear!

Joking apart, teasing out my inner lesbian, and deciding what things I should pay a murderous sex worker to do with her, are going to take careful planning. Although I'd better do it before Jools's and my time off. Not going to have much chance during our week of intensive wedding preparations, when we talk to vicars and choose a church and I hunt for a pretty white dress.

Brandon's phone started to give me the willies back at the nick. I bottled it completely when I thought about reading the texts. I didn't even want to have it in the flat. So I've got it here in my bag. I could take a look now. I've got time to kill, and no one's going to look over my shoulder here. And if I'm not doing anything else with it, then…

I get it out and run my finger through the directory. I try 'F', then 'V'. I try 'ICE – In Case of Emergency'. Not much chance I'll find Freya here, I think. Too sensible, too conformist. But I'm wrong. These texts are clearly to and from her. Bingo! I reel straight down to the second week of June of last year.

Brandon: Butterflies.
Freya: Remember ur doin this for ur dad.
Brandon: Performance of a lifetime.

Those were all from the 11th. Nothing else until the 16th, the day Tony was hauled out of the river.

> Brandon: Buried him. It's over.

That's as much as there is. All that I can understand, at least. I scan back and forth but, if they mention Tony directly, they have a way of doing it that's safe from prying eyes. They're friends; they have their own code. And, at times, Freya's spelling's even worse than mine. I dig out Brandon's most recent messages, his emails as well as his texts. I want to see what made him throw himself under that train. There's something here to his doctor:

> Got the report. Obviously not what I was hoping for. Willing to pay for a second opinion. Who do you recommend?

There's also a conversation he had with social services. That goes a long way back. In 2013 he wrote:

> Not complaining about Femi. He's a good carer but talking of leaving UK. NEED TO INTERVIEW ANY PROSPECTIVE REPLACEMENT MYSELF. NO MORE NUMPTIES!!!!

Brandon had sex on the brain. The amount of pornography here is making my eyes water. It looks like he may have been a pimp.

> Yeah, mate, you're in funds. She's called Sonja. No boundaries. You'll love her. Told her to call you after work.

Ugh. What am I getting myself into?

I look at my watch. I've been here an hour and a half. I put the phone back in my bag. Still no lights on in the bungalow.

Based on the messages and the photos, I've a hunch that Brandon lived alone. If I'm right, and with news of his demise not having filtered back to Carshalton, apparently, it might be that no one's thought to make his place secure. There may yet be an open window or an unlocked door. I could take a look around. And if the bungalow is secure then maybe I could break in. There might be evidence here. You never know, I might find a red handbag.

The street is empty. I get out of my car and walk along the footpath to the driveway. No one is coming. I approach the front window and shine the torch from my phone through a gap in the curtains. I waggle the beam into the corners of the room. It's bare. No carpet, no pictures, no furniture. What's going on?

Feeling exposed, I go to the side of the bungalow, where there's a high fence to shield me from the neighbours. I point my torch into what I see is the kitchen. Again, no trace of habitation. No cups or jars of tea and sugar, no bottle of detergent by the sink.

Behind the bungalow the lawn is overgrown. I angle my light through some French windows into what may have been a lounge or a dining room. Everything has been taken away. I'm beginning to wonder if the subscriber check may be wrong; if this isn't where Brandon Anthony-James lived after all. But now my light arcs and stops on a wall. The wallpaper has a pattern of half-shaded circles, like rows and columns of moons. It's hard to see in this light but it looks like the dark sides of the circles may be olive green; the empty halves outlined in blue.

12

Mum glances down to her right. 'Remember to go into second when you take the roundabout.'

Ian's got his test next week. I never thought I'd live to see the day.

'Do you think they'll want me to start straight away?' Jools springs forward, closing the gap between his mouth and my mother's ear. 'I should have thought to bring a change of clothes.'

'We're not at that stage yet,' Mum says. 'This is to show you the sorts of things they need volunteers for. Introduce you to the dogs.'

Jools nods hard and fast. I think of a pneumatic drill. 'How long have Waifs 'n' Strays been your clients?'

'Oh, decades. All the time I've worked for the vet's.'

I give Jools a look. His chin is still drilling down on the air. Since January, when she persuaded me to go back to him, my mother has been his idol. But I don't think this is just

239

to say thank you, or to get her to come to the wedding. He genuinely wants to volunteer.

Ian drives us so slowly around the roundabout I wonder if he's about to park up.

'So, are you okay with open spaces nowadays, Ian?' I ask. 'You seem to be getting out and about quite a lot.'

He checks the gearstick and the speedo, glances in all three mirrors. It's safe. He gives me a carefully measured portion of his attention. 'Yes. It's getting easier. Noticed it after we moved out of Mintsley. I've been doing some online CBT, which has helped.'

Agoraphobia. Today I'm aware that it's a genuine and serious condition. When I was growing up it was a byword for staying off work and getting paid for it, and giving the dreaded outside world the impression, for all Mum's care to avoid it, that hers was a one-parent family.

'It was moving to Frockley that made the difference,' Mum says. 'Safer environment… It's all clear, you can start to pick up a bit of speed.'

'You can really smell those hyacinths,' I prompt. They cost Jools a fortune. Mum hardly even looked at them; just put them straight in the boot.

She turns her head towards us. 'You didn't buy them today, did you? You shouldn't have. They hike the price up on Mother's Day.'

'You're worth it.' Jools beams at me, gloating. Teacher's pet is on a roll. Mum sees it in the rear-view mirror and gives a little chuckle.

Waifs 'n' Strays, or 'the Centre' as we've always called it, is near the border with Wiltshire. Thankfully, the bays aren't marked in the car park. We have a table booked for one o'clock back in Fountainford and Ian would probably need until close to then to make sure that all four tyres were precisely twenty-five centimetres from the white lines.

'Mm,' says Mum, looking at her watch. 'Think I'd better drive us back.' Then we can use the M4. It's only The Hungry Harvester we're going to, but even the thought of arriving there a minute late is liable to spoil her mood. They're quite a pair, Mum and Ian. 'You did really well,' she tells him as, holding his arm until he finds his land legs, she steers him to the entrance.

1pm

What must be the day's largest and brightest bouquet ticktocks from side to side, looming ever larger as it approaches from Lee's car. Behind it, at all four points of the compass, parts of him flash in and out of view: his bobbing, blow-dried hair; his pencil-sharpened elbows; his brand-new trainers which kick out at ten to two.

'It looks like it's swaggering by itself,' Lorna says.

'D'you think it's going to ask one of us for a dance?' I ask her.

Beside us at The Hungry Harvester's door, Mum momentarily disappears from sight as Lee presses the flowers into her. Jools observes, 'Cath could get changed and emerge in a different outfit and we wouldn't have seen a thing.'

'*'Aaa-py Mather's Day, Mrs M!*'

'Thank you, Lee,' says Mum, looking like she thinks she's expected to stroke them, 'and Lorna. They're…' gingerly, she prods with her nose, '…nice.' She turns to Ian. 'Take them to the car, will you, dear; put them with the others?'

'Bruv.' Lee greets Jools. The two of them work through the stages of an urban handshake which I know Jools learned from one of his clients. Lee, I'm told by Lorna, practised his over several sessions in front of YouTube. 'Not heard tell of your stag yet, Joolsy.' He winks. 'Text me if you want a few pointers. Bit of a stag connoisseur, though I say it myself.'

I take hold of Lorna. '*Awwwwww.*'

'Good to see you two out together,' my sister purrs in my ear. It's the first family gathering since Jools and I had what everyone's calling our 'little bump in the road'.

Lee holds the door for Mum. Gallant, he bows as she passes.

'Aren't we waiting for Ian?' Jools asks.

'He'll catch us up,' says Lorna.

Inside, our table is long, not round. As the waitress draws out for her the end chair, Mum casts around for Ian. She wishes she'd waited for him now. She'd have put him at the head of the table. Mum has an even bigger problem with the limelight than she does with being seen to receive gifts.

'Sit there,' Lorna says, bagging a seat for Lee. 'Then you can…' She holds his eye and jerks her chin to her shoulder. On the TV that hangs behind her, pundits are debating the match to come. 'Boy, girl, boy, girl, boy…' she jabs her finger, allocating the rest of the chairs, '…girl.' She plonks herself opposite me.

From my right, Lee calls over to Jools. 'You 'eard they've cancelled flights into Heathrow?'

Mum looks up and senses, a fraction too late, the rumble of an oncoming joke. Before anyone can involve her, she's saved by the appearance of Ian. She catches his eye and pats the empty seat between herself and me.

'Yeah, 'uge mushroom cloud. The cleaner at the Emirates 'ad been told to dust the trophy cabinet.'

'Actually, we won yesterday,' Jools says, assuming his courtroom face. 'Much to Oxo's disappointment. They were going to jolly up their image and put Arsène's smiling face on the box. "Laughing Stock".'

That's old. They used to tell that one in the van.

'Was that Emma Fickling in the bar?' Lorna asks.

I nod and make my eyes wide. It was a struggle to identify Lorna's old classmate.

'She used to be an athlete.'

Lee sees that Emma's time on the track is behind her. 'Only 'urdle she 'as to overcome these days is getting to the pie shop before it closes.'

Our waitress, by contrast, is slim and pretty. She stands with a pad and pen. Aping the ad on the telly, Lee gets in first with her line. '"Have you ever been to a Harvester before?"' He's good. Only Lorna doesn't like that. Even Mum has to grin. But he's not the first to have said it. The waitress smiles and rolls her eyes.

Mum orders a large gin and tonic.

'Mother's Day. Mother's ruin,' says Jools. He and Lee are on lager. Me, wine. Ian, who'll chauffeur us home, asks for sparkling water.

'Pepsi, diet. Ice and a slice,' commands Lorna, who doesn't like our slutty waitress who's been flirted to.

Undeterred, the waitress makes a moment's eye contact with Lee before she goes off. He returns it with a leer that virtually wails, *If only* she *weren't here!* The party atmosphere always hangs from a thread at our family gatherings, so it's a good job Lorna doesn't see that.

Lee and I had a heart-to-heart the other week. He told me that my sister will jot down the readings on his van's odometer and compare them with his explanations of where he's been and what he's been up to. If he says he's been to the gym, she'll expect to see a photo of his receipt. What amazed me was that he doesn't seem to mind. He thinks this is what a normal couple do. It occurs to me, from what I've just seen, that he probably thinks he deserves it.

'Lorna,' Mum calls out, 'guess where Julian's been this morning?'

Lorna rolls her eyes at Jools. 'She hasn't got you to volunteer at Waifs 'n' Strays, has she?' A smile spreads over her face. 'Is that why you all came in the same car?'

'They want to start him off right away. Walks to begin with. Then he'll be in the kennels.'

'Jools, you yinky!' My sister puts her hand to her mouth.

I clench inside. *Yinky*. A Dad word. I hardly dare look at Mum.

'Lee,' my sister continues, interrupting a conversation he's holding with a ten-year-old at the next table who's wearing the new Man U shirt, 'make a run for it. Mum's press gang's on the prowl again. She's rounding 'em up for the Centre!'

I steal a glance at Mum, who chuckles into her G&T.

'How much are you doin'?' Lee calls over to Jools. Somehow Lee has always swerved Mum's appeals on behalf of Waifs 'n' Strays.

'Three half-days a month. I'll love it. A complete change from everything I do.'

Mum smiles into his eyes and pats – *caresses* – his fingers on the tablecloth.

'I'm glad you gave me the idea,' he tells her. 'Dogs, they're so… I dunno, they just ask for so little and they give so, so much.' As charm offensives go, this is offensive to the point that he's got Mum to touch him. I've never seen her do that before. I didn't think she even liked him. Jools is playing a blinder.

Over lunch the two of them talk politics. Lorna looks up from her phone to pull faces as phrases like 'single transferrable vote' and 'collective responsibility' float into her hearing. As kick-off approaches, Lee and his new friend grow animated. Making full use of their eight limbs and a rolled-up serviette, they demonstrate moves and tricks.

Left to our own devices, it's likely Ian and I will talk about dogs. Our three: Alfred, Piglet, Grande. Traditionally, that's the extent of our overlap. But today I'm daring to hope for a little more. He was kind when I stayed in January. He tapped on my door and brought coffee, watched a soap or two with me whilst Mum was at work. He stopped short of asking how I felt at any stage, but he didn't always look ready to run a mile in fear that I'd tell him anyway. I'm hoping he'll broach what seems to be today's forbidden subject and talk about my wedding. Now Mum knows I've turned down Dad's sponsorship offer after all – Jools quickly talked me out of that – I want to know how the land lies.

'Are you up to speed on anal glands?' Ian asks between mouthfuls of steak. 'Piglet's carrying her tail an inch away from her body.'

'Just going to the toilet,' I say, after I've told him what I know.

I've been saying, 'Just going to the toilet,' so much recently that Jools has asked more than once if I'm okay. The other day I interrupted negotiations with an ice-cream man, who we want to set up outside our reception venue and give out free ninety-nines. *Every child's dream*, I should have said when they asked my opinion. Instead I said, 'Have you got a toilet here?'

Here in the ladies' at The Hungry Harvester there are mums of every size, age, shape, creed and colour. One is waiting but, when a cubicle becomes free, someone greets her and, whilst her attention is diverted, I nip in and whip out Brandon's phone. Sorry, but I'm desperate, even after the countless comfort breaks I've taken. Desperate to solve the mysteries about Freya, and Tony, and why Brandon took his own life. Not that it's likely to happen. After ten straining days on the lavatory I've hardly found any clues at all.

I should start thinking of Brandon as 'Abran'. That's his real name. He emailed his birth certificate to the immigration authorities. Abran Fernandez, born in Cali, Colombia, on the 4th March 1986. He sent photos to prove who he was. There's one of his christening ceremony. A mud shack in the countryside, with happy rows of relatives dressed in what, I guess, must be hired clothes. Abran, somewhere inside what looks like a baby's wedding dress, complete with dangling train, is so heavy in his mother's arms she's having to flex her muscles. The opening page of his story. The story that ended with the Fountainford badgers. Makes me want to cry.

A sweet-looking child, but as an adult, as Brandon, he made enemies. He was obsessed with someone called 'Pozos'. Vengeful texts citing that name go back years. The slang makes it hard to make out but in one message I think there is reference to a gun. He also had it in for his carer who, for reasons I'm here to unearth, seriously got on the wrong side of him. I'm learning that, once Brandon took against you, you were never far from his mind.

I reckon a lot has been deleted, which makes this like trying to complete a jigsaw while knowing that pieces are missing. The abbreviations and the spelling make it still harder, as does the fact that he had nicknames for everyone, only some of whom appear by those names in his contacts. It's a struggle to know who's who. And it would help if I knew any Spanish. There's quite a lot of it here.

I've got as far as the Ss. I scroll down and tap the name 'Shark'. Randomly, I open a message. It's dated the 14th September 2013.

> *Our private dick has been watching the house. It seems you're paying for a man to sit on your roof and smoke cigarettes.*

The attached photo seems to prove the point, whatever that point may be. This sounds like it might link up with something Freya said, something about... I'm beginning to see that my method, of cross-referencing emails, letters, photographs and texts, is like that memory game we used to play – Pairs, or Apples and Pears or something – where the cards are face down on the carpet and you have to pick up two the same. You turn over, say, a nine and then you try to recall where it was in the grid that you last glimpsed another nine before it was laid again on its front. Here, I don't know what's significant until I match it with something else, by which time I can't remember where the first thing of interest is stored.

I go back to 'ICE' and sift down. What did Freya text him in September 2013?

That's not funny. Don't even think about it, Abran.
Go straight to the feds.

That wasn't what I was thinking of. No, that wasn't it.

Back at the table, Mum's tipping back what's left in her tumbler. Last time I looked she had a goldfish-bowl glass. That must be her third G&T. She had wine with her dinner as well. She doesn't normally drink this much. In her other hand, she's holding Lorna's phone. '"A gentleman of the very highest quality." Do you remember saying that?' She's reading what Dad wrote on Facebook.

'Dunno if I remember saying it or just being reminded of it every week for the next fifteen years.'

'You'll have got it from *Pride and Prejudice*. Some period drama or other. You used to watch anything with a wedding in it.'

'Omigod,' murmurs Lorna, recalling the wet, fancy people and their soppy, stiff ways. 'Ruby and her bloody weddings.'

Mum smiles. 'Do you remember the Charles and Di video? You had it from Aunty Rita on permanent loan.'

'Aunty Rita?' Jools asks. 'Whose divorce party we went to?'

I nod. Rita, who in the early days with Rico would think of her marriage and stare in absent-minded awe. 'It's perfect,' she would murmur, as though it were a newborn's ear or hand.

'You drew pictures.' If Mum's still trying to avoid the subject of my own wedding, then she should know she's skating on very thin ice.

'That's right!' Lorna says. 'You used to pause the video and lie on the floor with your sketchbook. Even after they'd divorced.'

'I think their divorce hit you more than mine did. Oh, my word. For years, it was...' Mum puts on my childhood face. '"But how can Charles have loved Princess Diana if he was already in love with Camilla? But the Archbishop of Canterbury said that they were joined!" When Dodi came along – *ooooh*. "But she's already given her heart away. I saw her do it!" You'd stare at me like you expected me to do something about it!'

Lee trots round. 'May I leave the table, please, Cath?' He nods towards the gathering in front of the TV.

'Of course, Lee.' She considers for a moment, then turns to her right. 'Ian, why don't you go and watch the match, keep Lee company?'

He blinks. 'Sure.'

'And, Lorna, you go too.' Mum reaches over to give Lorna her phone back. 'You don't mind a game of football, do you? And there's something I just want to say to Jools and Ruby.'

Lorna stands up. The look she gives me says, *Rather you than me.*

Mum waits until they have gone. 'Okay,' she says at last, straightening in her seat like she's chairing a meeting. 'The problem we're facing is this. With his usual impeccable timing, your dad's come back into your life just as you want to marry. You've asked him to come to the wedding and he's agreed. And I've said Ian and I shan't be there if your father is. You'd like us all to come – of course you would. And I'm assuming that, to some extent, all that you've been doing lately that's been so lovely – having us round for supper; you helping out at the Centre, Julian; you, Ruby, offering to supervise Ian before his test – has been to make me change my mind. If it has, I don't blame you. It's been great seeing so much of you guys. It's just that you're missing the point.'

She turns and stares at Jools. 'When I go off on one of my marriage rants, it's nothing personal against you. I worried after that silly party of Rita's last year that I might have given that impression. For what it's worth, I think you treat my daughter brilliantly and I like you very much. I don't even think there's anything particularly wrong with being married, if I'm honest. I say some spiteful things, I suppose, about how much a wedding can cost and how the religious side of it can seem a bit hypocritical, but I know plenty of married couples who are happy. Of course I do. Some marriages work out, some don't. That's the only true thing that can be said on the subject. I try to protect myself by pretending otherwise. But you shouldn't hold it against me.

'I think I may have been, er, a little hard to get to know. I'm sorry. It's no secret that I was very fond of Ruby's last partner, and when the two of them split up…' She turns to me. 'When you walked out on Connor, Ruby, I felt you'd made a mistake; one that you'd come to regret. But I was wrong. Something I saw when you came to stay in January made me understand that, dear and good man though Connor is, he was never the one. Julian, I want you to be aware of something.' She takes a meditative sip of her gin. 'We love differently in our family. We're not like other women. We make you our home, you fellas, when we've fallen for you. We move all that we have inside you. We leave our former selves behind like old addresses. We give you everything; we can hold back nothing. We are utterly devoted.'

'That's how everyone feels,' I blurt. 'That's just being in love.' I have no idea what I'm saying. I'm panicking. I'm talking just to stop my mother doing it.

'Okay, picture this,' she says. 'You've not got a baby yet, so it may be hard. Imagine any baby. There's a house fire. You can only rescue your man or the baby. Who would you save?'

She looks at me, awaiting a reply. I can only gape. It's what she's suggesting about me, as much as the flames, that makes the vision so awful. She smiles, triumphant.

'Utter devotion,' she says, holding my eye. 'No, we're peculiar.' She opens her handbag and takes out a tissue to blow her nose. 'Me and you are. Not sure about Lorna... I could see it in you from the start, with your Charles and Di, and your *Pride and Prejudice*, and what have you. We love absolutely.' She turns and looks Jools in the eye. 'But we can only do it once.'

He shakes his head. He's not sure that he's awake. 'How do you mean?'

'I mean you've got my daughter for good. Ruby and I can't fall out of love. We're incapable of it.' Dreamily, she looks at the table. 'I expect you and Lorna have always thought I hate your dad. I expect you think, because of what he was like, how he treated us... From the moment I wake in the morning, Si's face is in my mind. That's the point I start to think about him, worry about him. *Where is he? What's he doing? Is he okay?* So it goes on through the day. I'm wading through accounts: *He'd laugh his head off if he could see me looking so businesslike.* I'm discussing the animals with colleagues: *He'd give a home to this kitten, if only I knew where he lived.* In the evening, well, as you know, Ian and I sleep in separate bedrooms. At night I have a recurring dream. A room with no door and no windows. It's small. It's my life. And there he sits in the middle of it, filling out this giant throne... I've not seen or heard from him in nearly seventeen years and do you know the first thing I did, when Lorna told me he had pancreatic cancer?'

We shake our heads.

'I phoned in sick. First day off work due to illness in my career. It wasn't even a lie. I wouldn't have been able to function. Spent the whole day staring at his house online, fighting with myself, wanting to go to him, but at the same time knowing it would ruin everything. It would kill Ian, literally.'

There are shouts of 'Yes!' from the television area as one team scores a goal. I don't think Jools has even heard.

'Ru, when you were with us earlier this year, do you remember sitting for a whole day in bed, staring at a mark on the carpet? I kept coming and going and you just hadn't moved. You probably hadn't blinked. It was like you'd had your batteries taken out! Now, Connor could never have had that effect on you. I started to wonder if it was something in our bodies; a rare blood group or a genetic thing on the female side of the family. But do you know what the really funny thing is? It dawned on me. Si is exactly the same.'

Jools and I stare at each other.

'He's like us: he loves once and for all. He was a teenager and he met the girl who was his destiny, only neither of them knew it and it wasn't their time. When the time did come for them to be together, that's what they did. If I'm to be completely honest, if I'd been in his shoes – so young, with his life ahead of him – I have no doubt at all that I'd have done what he did.'

Ian appears. 'Are we staying?' he murmurs to Mum. 'Lee bought me a drink and now his glass is empty. I thought you'd want me to buy him one back but I wasn't sure if we were staying.'

'Buy him a drink, love.' Sadly, she smiles at him. 'Do you need any money?'

'I've got a tenner. I can buy Lee one. I can't get one for Lorna as well.'

Mum opens her purse and gives him a note. 'Get a round in, yeah?'

Ian goes off, clutching the note in both hands.

'So, yeah,' says my mum. 'Please don't think I'm being selfish. I'm not boycotting your wedding. I'm not trying to make a point. If it was all to do with my own feelings it'd be completely unreasonable to stay away. The thing is, I *can't* come. I can't help it. I absolutely mustn't see your father. I've no idea what it'd do to me. I owe it…' she looks across to Ian as he bobs behind heads at the bar, still holding his note, 'to others.'

In the car, Mum falls asleep. Jools and I try to smirk, but it feels false. We abandon the effort. She had a lot to drink back there but it was her, not the drink, that talked. And it won't be easy to forget what she said.

Ian drops us at our place. We wish him well with his test.

'Don't forget. Second gear on your roundabouts.'

Jools guides me, nurse-like, to our front door. Treating me like an invalid, he's still trying to make light of what's happened. Maybe it's the right thing to do. I feel like we're reeling home from the surgery after hearing of my diagnosis.

'Let's take these shoes off,' he coos when we're inside, helping me onto the sofa. 'You're L-U-V positive; you need to rest.'

'You'd better wear protection tonight,' I say, lending him a helping hand as he tries to make it all seem like fun. 'You might get infected and end up liking me forever.'

Chuckling, he goes off to the kitchen to make us some tea. On my own phone I have a notification.

> Hi, Lurcher,
>   Haven't heard from you for a while. Just wondered how your script is developing.
>   Kind regards,
>   Vixen x

I hope she hasn't charged me thirty quid for that.

'You know what this means?' Jools says, reappearing at the doorway.

'We're going to have to postpone the wedding until after my father has died.'

He droops his face in sad agreement.

We make love. Afterwards, as we rest and I can't bat them away any more with activity, Mum's words swarm. The poor, poor woman. What an existence. Loving someone, living with someone else. Being with one only to stop her thinking about the other, and the whole project not even working. And poor Ian, who Lorna and I have never felt the need to call 'Dad'; whose status, in our eyes, never rose above that of a lodger, and who, for all I know, is still paying my mum rent.

This could make me very unhappy, sifting through the wreckage from the day's raining bombshells. I'm not in the mood for that. I turn my mind to Mum's theory about our family and our knack for indestructible love; to my not-loving-Jools virginity being lost, forever beyond recall. Now that *was* the drink talking. Although, in this moment, as he faces me, his fun-wrinkled eyes half-closed, a tired, cheeky smile beginning to die on his lips…

I turn to charge up my phone. Fitting the USB, I take another look at Freya's email.

Hi, Lurcher,
    Haven't heard…

Whatever was I thinking? Sorry, Vixen. No, thank you, not any more. It was a nice thought – lots of nice thoughts. Just not me, not my world. You can keep what I've paid on account. Lurcher is leaving the building. Good luck. Over and out.

I delete her and turn again on my pillow to face my man. 'Night, my love,' I whisper.

'Night-night, Tommy.'

13

The alarm's gone off and he's up and about. Whilst I play dead, he plays the innocent, brushing his teeth, sliding drawers, pushing clothes hangers along the rail to find his Monday suit. Or maybe he doesn't realise. Was that a whistle? In the kitchen he is whistling a tune. No. I think he has no idea what he's done.

Why don't you go? My face screws into the pillow. The bed feels like it's crawling with maggots. But if I get up I'll have to speak to him. *Hurry up and go to work!*

And now, finally, gently, *clump*. Considerate of my sleep, my cheating fiancé carefully closes the front door behind him. The air is packed tight with silence.

I kick off the duvet and go to the toilet. I'm dizzy from lack of sleep. I flush and flounder into the spare bedroom.

'Grande.'

I only have to whisper. In the lounge, limbs strafe on the carpet. There's a sneeze and a rattle of ears. A trot of paws.

Blam – a weight tightens me in the cold new covers. A wet nose touches my eyelid.

What a world. Get your cannabis nicked, what do you do? You call a copper, tell her to sort it out. Have your man stolen? *All is fair in love and war*, the cop is bound to say. Car theft, mobile phone theft, identity theft. No love theft. Tommy is free to burgle my life. She can rob me of all that is in it and be reckoned to have committed no crime. So why should I pay my taxes for this level of service? And who makes these laws anyway? Why do I even vote?

Somewhere in the flat a telephone sounds. I feel about in the fur over Grande's muscles and work my way to his head. Between my knuckles, the tips of his ears lick like tiny tongues. The phone stops ringing. I open my eyes. That wasn't mine. That tone plays on Jools's phone. He must have left it at home.

I close my eyes again. What is *wrong* with me? I'm pathetic. Trusting, complacent, pathetic. Why did I cower in bed just then, pretending I was asleep? Why did I lie awake all night, speculating instead of demanding the truth? For God's sake, is it me Jools wants to be with or Tommy? (*Night-night, Tommy.* Oh my goodness. *Ugh!*) My sister wouldn't have done that. If it had been Lee, Lorna would have plated up her suspicions there and then, heaped up high and steaming. She would have stood over him and made him force them down, like a meal he hadn't been at home to eat. After what my mother said yesterday, would it not have been a reasonable line of enquiry to find out if Jools is, maybe, a Si; if Tommy is his Millie? With all we know about married couples – Mum and Dad, Rita and Rico, the Gibsons, the Carmichaels, Charles and Di – wouldn't, like, straight away have been the time to ask if this is really what Jools and I want? Why have I never pushed him into a seat, given him an ultimatum, made him tell me what he and Freya said in those forty-three minutes on the 13th June last year?

The ringing came from the study. I get up and walk to the door.

'Jools?'

He's not here; still I wait for a reply. Now, with the gung-ho I pretend to have on a drugs bust, I shoulder-barge the door. The bottom edge clicks against something metallic and shunts it along the carpet. It's his phone. Must have fallen out of his pocket. I pick it up and feel the weight of it in my palm. Lorna whispers, *Go on. Do it.* But I don't need her advice. My mind is mad with itching; my conscience doesn't even put up a fight. This phone will cut my itch to ribbons. Like a shard of pottery. They do. I know from handling Abran's.

Damn. He's changed his PIN. *Bloody hell.* I'm going to throw this thing at the wall. We've always had the same screen-lock PIN. 6285. The 6th February 1985. Sonny Bryant's birthday. Jools has written it on so many legal aid forms he knows it by heart. It's been our joke. And now he's changed it.

The word 'Ephraim' flashes through my mind.

6285. I try it again. Still it doesn't work. Why would he change it? Wasn't it secure? 6285 seems random enough. Whose eyes wasn't it safe from? Sonny Bryant's?

My eyes refocus on a legal document at the top of a pile that lies on Jools's desk.

Neutral citation number: [2014] EWCA Crim 1227
No: 201900879/A3
IN THE COURT OF APPEAL
CRIMINAL DIVISION

Royal Courts of Justice
Strand
London
WC2A 2LL
Tuesday 30ᵗʰ September 2014

Before:
LORD JUSTICE VILLETTE
MRS JUSTICE TROUGHTON DBE
MR JUSTICE WREN

Regina v Wells

Facts: In the evening of Thursday 31ˢᵗ October 2013 the Applicant (A) was in The Butcher's Arms in Purley, Surrey. Also in the pub was a man called Brandon Anthony-James, although the two were strangers to each other and had no interaction. A left the pub at around 10.15pm and went to his car in The Butcher's Arms' car park. He immediately noticed that there was a large dent in the front bumper of his car, a BMW, and that one of the headlight casings was broken. A handwritten note had been placed behind one of the windscreen wipers: 'A disabled man drove into your car. I know him. He lives in Carshalton, in the white bungalow in Ephraim Close. He was in a blue Mercedes. Just drove off.' The note was unsigned. The BMW was not parked in an area covered by the pub CCTV and it is not known who left the note. Nevertheless, using the information within it, A immediately drove to Ephraim Close and found a blue Mercedes parked outside a white bungalow.

What happened next remains in dispute. A's version was, and is, that he rang the front doorbell and, when nobody answered, he walked around the side of the bungalow and found the kitchen door ajar. He entered and passed through a small kitchen into a room at the back of the property, which was in disarray and where he was met by the sight of a man lying on his back on the floor. The handle of a knife was visible, protruding from the man's chest. There was a lot of blood. The man was clearly dead. A promptly left the bungalow and, by his own admission, reported what he had seen to no one. He did not call for an ambulance. He did not inform the police. At trial, he explained his omission as follows: 'I panicked, really. To be honest, I've always had a bit of a problem with authority and I'm not the sort who'd think to contact the police necessarily. It seemed like someone else's mess. I suppose at the time I thought I'd got off lightly with a dent in my bumper; thought I'd better cut and run.'

The Crown's case rested on the testimony of their prime witness, Mr Anthony-James. As noted, he, too, had been at The Butcher's Arms that evening. Mr Anthony-James said he had been in company with a female friend named Freya and his carer – later the deceased – a man named Femi Yar'Adua. It is of note that Mr Anthony-James suffers from illness that makes him incapable of entirely independent living, and relies upon a wheelchair to get about. CCTV from inside The Butcher's Arms confirms that a man in a wheelchair was present that evening, together with a black male and a person who appears to be female, although it was Halloween and all three were dressed for the occasion and their features were obscured. The identity of these persons, however, was never a matter in dispute. Mr

Anthony-James said that his party arrived and left in his blue Mercedes, although it was Mr Yar'Adua who drove the car both to and from the pub. He accepted that, upon reversing in the car park, Mr Yar'Adua collided with a BMW and then failed to stop. When Mr Anthony-James was questioned about this at trial, he admitted that Mr Yar'Adua had drunk alcohol in the pub and that all three in the car had agreed that he should simply drive off in case he was over the limit. Mr Yar'Adua then drove the car to Purley railway station, where Freya was dropped off, then Mr Anthony-James and Mr Yar'Adua returned to Mr Anthony-James' home at 127 Ephraim Close.

Some minutes after their arrival, whilst they were in the bathroom preparing Mr Anthony-James for bed, there was a banging, first on the front door, then on the door at the side of the bungalow. Mr Yar'Adua went to see who it was and immediately there was a loud altercation, during which Mr Anthony-James, who managed to lock himself in the bathroom, heard a man shouting, among other things, 'Don't they do the Highway Code in Monkeyland?' All soon fell quiet. Eventually, Mr Anthony-James felt it was safe to exit the bathroom. He entered the back room and found Mr Yar'Adua lying dead, just as A, in his testimony, described.

Mr Anthony-James saw nothing of how Mr Yar'Adua came to be killed and could only say what he heard from inside the bathroom. However, a cigarette butt was discovered on the pathway at the side of the bungalow which bore a full profile of A's DNA. This led to A's identification and arrest. For the sake of completeness, during his police station interview, A made no comment to all questions put to him. His defence, however, was stated in outline in the defence case statement submitted at the appropriate stage of the court proceedings.

On the first day of the trial, and out of the presence of the jury, the prosecution applied to adduce as evidence some of A's 'bad character', specifically a previous incident in which A had been involved in 1998; a matter in respect of which he had been both tried and acquitted and yet which, prosecuting counsel argued, bore sufficiently similar features to the present case to justify reference to it at the trial. Defence counsel opposed the application vehemently, reasoning that the evidence, which seemingly had not been accepted by the jurors who acquitted A, would unfairly influence the present jury and would make a fair trial impossible. The trial judge granted the application and, as the trial got under way, the jury were made aware of the details of the earlier matter.

The facts of that case, briefly, were that on a Saturday morning in June 1998 a man named Costa Fernandez was driving with his twelve-year-old son in Purley, Surrey. They drew up at some traffic lights and were stationary in a lane of traffic when Mark Wells, the Applicant in the present case, approached on foot from behind, walking between the lanes of traffic to their car. He knocked on the window of Mr Fernandez's car. It became apparent that something about the manner of Mr Fernandez's driving had displeased him. Mr Fernandez and his son got out of the car. A quarrel ensued which became heated and then violent, and both men produced knives, although it was unclear in evidence who drew his weapon first. The incident ended with both Mr Fernandez and his son receiving stab wounds. Sadly, Mr Fernandez later died of his. Of significance to the present case was that two of the witnesses heard remarks made by the Applicant during that dispute which bore striking similarity to words attributed to the Applicant in this matter. 'You're not in Monkeyland now, geezer,' was how one of the witnesses put it. The other witness reported, 'They'll be taking you back to Monkeyland in a fucking box.'

The essence of the Crown's argument to adduce this evidence was threefold. Firstly, the expression 'Monkeyland', if it can be said to exist at all, is not of common parlance and must feature in the vocabulary of very few. Prosecuting counsel said it 'is of almost DNA- or fingerprint-type uniqueness'. So, she reasoned, it is highly improbable that anyone other than A would have used the term. Secondly, the use of the expression overheard by Mr Anthony-James must have been addressed to Mr Yar'Adua, who was the only other person present and, therefore, must be supposed to have been alive when the Applicant set foot in 127 Ephraim Close. This would contradict the defence, which was to the effect that Mr Yar'Adua was already dead when A arrived. The third basis put forward by the Crown for admitting the 1998 incident as evidence was that it probed A's propensity to 'road rage', as it is commonly known; the suggestion being that, in instances when A perceives bad driving in others, he will massively overreact.

This appeal by the defence is made on the sole ground that it was wrong and unfair to admit the 1998 incident as evidence...

My lips hurt from mouthing the words. *Applicant? Adduce? Predu... Prejuci... Prejudic...?* I need a break. There's only so much I can take in. I've got the gist, though, and I know more or less what it means. It means that, legal or illegal, right or wrong, Ruby-ish or Lorna-ish, I'm going to spend as long as I've got reading every last thing on this desk.

First I walk the dog. I can't get this straight in my head. Every time I place one fact on top of another, the one underneath squishes out. Trying to build the facts into a thought that will stay upright is like playing Jenga when you've had one too many to drink. I give it another go. So: Jools is working on an appeal that has to do with a murder that took place at 127 Ephraim Close, Carshalton. Jools is. My fiancé. 127 Ephraim Close is where Brandon Anthony-James lived. His phone, which is in this flat, proves a link with confessed murderer Freya Maskell, who was present, at some stages at least, on the night of the murder of which Jools's client, Mark Wells, has been convicted. Which means…

I make a coffee. I sip and stare into a corner of the kitchen and have another go. Something occurs to me. I go back to the study and reread the bit in the court report about the road-rage incident in 1998. The victim's name was… yes, I thought so… Fernandez. As in Abran Fernandez. Father and son. Dad didn't make it, but son, a twelve-year-old boy at the time…

'So *Daddy, Don't Open the Door* happened to Abran, not Freya.' I think I actually say this out loud. I certainly give voice to what DI McQuade would tell me if he were here. 'Hang on a mo, Ru, not so fast.'

Yes, mustn't jump to conclusions. I mean, I know we're supposed to be equals in the relationship and all that but, well, Jools is the hotshot lawyer with the brainbox degree from London University. I'm Failed Detective Marocco with my 2:2 in sports science at the local tech for jocks. Realistically, if I can see that he has actually *met* the person who is his likely ground for appeal, that he actually *knows* her, then so can he.

But he can't. He doesn't. 'PML', next to a devil emoji, as the uncouth Ms Maskell is wont to write in her texts.

The closest I can get to describing how I feel is this. It's as though miniature people in tiny overalls have entered my head, deep-cleaned, decorated, and rearranged all the furniture. Light and space fill my mind. Houseplants. Interesting artwork. Tasteful soft furnishings. Suddenly it's a comfortable place to be.

I start at the top of the documents pile with the aim of working down. I soon discover that Mr Wells has more 'bad character' than his trial judge let on. Only, as Mr Ridealgh, Jools's friend and Wells' last solicitor, insists in his indignant letters to the CPS, it *isn't* 'bad character' because Mr Wells was never convicted. It's true. There's an MG16 here with the facts behind some of the allegations that have been made against him over the past twenty years. By a girlfriend who phoned 999 as she lay with broken legs on the ground below the third-floor window he'd pushed her from, but who was too scared to give a statement and refused to attend his trial. Not guilty. By a witness who alleged that Mr Wells was intimidating him, but who retracted his statement after his parents had petrol poured through their letter box. Not guilty. By a man Mr Wells thought owed him money, and who alleged that he was being harassed. Before the trial the man committed suicide and there was no case to answer. So the much-maligned Mr Wells is, in fact, every inch the model citizen. I can see why Mr Ridealgh was so put out on his behalf.

I quite like Jools's style of writing. There's no foam or bluster in his letters to the police and CPS; no threats or synthetic outrage. Steve Ridealgh and others, I see, used phrases like 'We shall have no alternative' or 'We peruse your comments with utter disbelief'. My fiancé, I'm pleased to note, is respectful and minds his Ps and Qs. Then again, he's not as candid as the solicitor Wells instructed before Steve Ridealgh. *She* wrote:

Your deficiencies as prosecuting authorities have reached a level where a defence argument of abuse of process may very well succeed, in which case a highly dangerous individual will escape justice and be free to kill again.

And then… *golly.*
 There's a photograph.
 Oh, gosh…
 And here's another.
 Oh, fuck me sideways with a broom.

14

I can see okay through these glasses. It's a sunny day. My reflection is clear against this shop window. Jools was harsh about my red, bobbed hair. Said I look like a matchstick. And I'm not sure my skipper will approve, either. He'd have a hernia if he saw me in this baseball cap. Set eyes on the goth-grade rouge and yellow eyeshadow, he'd be in hospital for a month. But these are just for today.

'Excuse me,' I say to myself. 'You dropped this.'

Couldn't be simpler. Harder for her, I'd have thought, to drop the thing in the first place. And yet I'm so *nervous*. It's like she's going to judge me. Am I the first punter in the history of the sex trade to crave the good opinion of the supplier?

Tic-tic-tic-tic.

Is that her? I mustn't look along the pavement. It'll ruin the whole thing if we make eye contact before we get inside. I scan the world behind me, mirrored at the margins of the window. It's not her. It might even be that builder, perched on scaffolding on the other side of the road, bashing away with a hammer.

'Excuse me. You…'

She takes it seriously. That's what unnerves me about Freya. If I don't reply to an email for more than forty-eight hours she'll send a reminder. Last month, when I stopped writing altogether, she sounded genuinely hurt. And she's strict. She won't have any larking around. In *Medical School Anatomy Lecture*, in which I cast myself as the specimen woman, with her as the professor, indicating my parts with a stick, I switched the dry, academic voice that was her idea for a silly German accent – 'Vot ve see here ven ve part ze mature female's legs…' She simply changed it all back without a word.

She was generally so encouraging I didn't pick up on it at first but, now I think about it, she was iffy about the anatomy lecture from the start. I can remember exactly what she said:

> Hi, Lurcher, how are you?
>
> Really enjoyed your fantasy. Nothing there that crosses my line; will be happy to go along with the script 100%. You say it's your first GOG experience so I can understand that you may want a passive role. Just wondered if you'd like to make some extra directions so that you have the option to initiate some GOG stuff yourself? You may find that you want to explore a bit as the scene plays out. I'd have to clear your proposals but if you'd let me know the sort of thing you'd like then maybe we can rework the script a bit so that you have the choice to take the lead, if that's the way the mood takes you…

She talked me out of it in the end. I agreed we needed a scenario in which I would be required, at least, to move. And, when my mood was low and I worried about being blackmailed, the vision of my anatomy going through the photocopier and being Blu-Tacked to the custody suite walls did zero to restore my confidence. What killed off *Medical School Anatomy Lecture*, though, was the pricing. Hiring just a handful of 'students' would have cost an additional £600.

Tic-tic-tic-tic.

She's here. A metre away, looking in the same window as me. 11.30 on the dot. She's wearing the Russian hat. I was particular about the sort. She asked if it mattered if she couldn't get the precise one and I said no, no biggie, whatever she could find. I think she knew I really wanted her to wear it, though. I think she may have gone to some trouble.

I walk away, puffing my cheeks as I go. I've had this feeling before, as a girl. At the pool, crouching, curling my toes around the end of the highest diving board, making a spear with my arms. *Tic-tic-tic-tic.* She follows in her stiletto heels. At the foot of the steps to John Lewis I turn. She waits at the pelican crossing, staring coldly ahead. I push through the revolving door.

The air in the department store is serene. Everywhere there is quiet grace. An assistant at the Benefit counter offers a free makeover. She gives me no hassle, just a sunny smile. She's sleek and immaculate. I'd have to get up an hour earlier to arrive at work looking like that. One stray dog hair behind that counter, and I bet they'd starburst in fright.

I glide up the escalator into Lingerie where, glancing in the direction I've come from, I sift through a rack of basques. I can't see her. Did I lose her? No, here she is again. She's tall in her heels. That fur coat comes from a much more expensive shop than any in this town. 'Old-fashioned, aristocratic elegance,' was my phrase, although, when I wrote it, I don't think I really knew quite what I meant. I do now. She looks both braced and disgusted, enlivened by her plunge into this great pool of vulgarity, like the well-bred of a hundred years ago, venturing onto land they didn't own. I mustn't stare. We're supposed to be strangers. But if I don't see her drop her item I'll miss my cue and my fantasy will remain just that.

We amble about in a circle, maintaining our distance and keeping to our separate displays, as we sort through knickers and bras, corsets and stockings. She's taking her time. She knows I'm her client, doesn't she? Not shown a flicker of recognition. No, she can't have missed me. Not unless she was expecting some other bespectacled punk rocker to be here shopping for underwear at exactly 11.30am. Belatedly, I remember to switch off my phone. In a mirror, I study her. Oh, she is regal! She looks like she's carved out of ice. Pretty soon she'll snap her fingers and issue a command, and within an hour or two items will be delivered to her country seat and charged to her account.

Seemingly by accident, a bra she's holding falls to the carpeted floor.

'Excuse me,' I call as she walks to another rail. My accent is pure Berkshire. 'You drarped this.'

My grin withers in the blast of her offended glare.

'Thank you,' she says remotely as she takes the bra from my hand.

I'm totally no actress. I just retreat to the nearest display, clunk clothes hangers to and fro and wait for my next cue.

'You don't know what the time is, do you?'

I look at my watch. 'Eleven forty-severn.'

'I've longer than I thought.' She sounds like the Queen. 'I'm terribly sorry to impose,' she says a minute later. 'But could you stand upright?'

I do as she asks.

'Now face me.' She smiles. 'Chin up. Shoulders back.' She nods. 'Exactly Penelope's shape.'

'Penelope' was my idea. After Lady Penelope in *Thunderbirds*. The first sniff I ever had of posh.

'You couldn't do me the most enormous favour, could you? I want to buy one of these for my sister but I don't know that it'll fit. You wouldn't model it for me, would you?'

I stare at her for a moment. 'Y'know, that's really ferny. I'm tryin' t'find a bra to fit my merm. You're 'er shape. Will you do the same for me?'

'Oh!' she exclaims. 'Well, I don't see why not. I suppose we should take a few.'

It was her recommendation that we ad lib this next bit and, except for the accents, be ourselves. We squabble politely over our choices. It almost feels like we're friends.

'Yes,' she says as we make our way to the changing rooms. 'She's a difficult person to buy for, Penelope. Pretty thing, but hasn't a clue how to make the best of herself. Of course, I'd bring her to the shops with me, if she'd come. Simply won't hear of it. A complete tomboy. She'd rather be out riding her horses or drinking with the boys at the rugby club. Shopping's her idea of hell.'

'Oi know what yer mean.' Hearing my old bumpkin voice, I understand why they laughed at me at training school and why I felt I had to change it. 'My merm'd really like to 'ave a boyfriend. But the way she turns 'erself out, 's no wonder she don't get no bites. I tell 'er, "Come sharpin' wi'me, Merm. Let's get y' some'in' sexy t'wear."

'"I ain't got no time fer tha'," she says. "Some of us 'ave ter work fer a livin' an' keep a roof owver our 'eads." So I thinks, *Right, Oi'll go an' buy it meself.*'

The girl at the changing rooms counts our items and gives us each a plastic disc. Mine has a '3' on it; Vixen's has a '5'. All the cubicles are empty; we can take whichever one we want. That's what we thought would happen. That's why we picked this time and day.

We take a cubicle at the far end of the corridor. She locks the door behind us and hangs her coat on a hook. Her dress is black and close-fitting, with the hem just over her knees. She drops her disc. As she crouches to pick it up, her thigh shows through a split, up to the band of her stocking.

'Take your things off,' she says.

I pull off my jumper, then my T-shirt. The light is brutally frank. From my throat down, my skin looks like it's been bleached. Above, I'm like a gaudy football scarf that someone's balled up and stuffed in a jar. The line she's about to deliver is the product of an entire full-comment interview I held with a boy who'd been driving whilst disqualified. An inspired split-moment to dream it up, five furtive seconds to write it down on a Post-it, the rest of the time smiling and nodding at the boy and daring myself ever to hear it spoken. Here it comes.

'Let's have a look at you.'

Bossy, not unfriendly, quite loud. I make a little squeak.

We face the wall-sized mirror. I feel and hear her breath. It's in the script that, at this point, I reach behind to unclip, but when I do she stays my hands. She undoes the catch herself and takes my bra off, so slowly that, if it was an old plaster, it would tug out every painful hair.

I'm beginning to worry. She shouldn't have done that. Definitely shouldn't have done it slowly. The whole point is that she's brisk. And now she's doing nothing, except breathing loudly and staring into the mirror. Has she recognised me? Keeping my eyes on hers in the mirror, I focus on the possibility of a fight. But she's not trying to look through my make-up, or imagine away the redness from my hair. It's just my bare chest that she's looking at.

Has she actually forgotten her words? She's supposed to say, *Try this one on first, would you?* But she just stares. And swallows. *Oh.* Is it *my* turn to say…? Now my worries disappear. Suddenly, I'm proud and shameless. I realise that this was her plan. She's made me want to show off. I lift my chin, pull back my shoulders and fill my lungs with air.

She turns and takes a bra from one of the hooks. 'Try this one on first.' Her voice is parched. 'Would you?'

Back in Lingerie, I chose this one myself. I just took it and stuck it in her hand. One of Jools's favourites. Close to it, at least. It's sheer to the point of being pointless, which I suppose is sort of the point.

'Mm.' She stoops in front of me and, with her back to the mirror, brings her face up close. Again, I feel her breath. 'Not sure,' she says finally. 'Try this one.'

The Wonderbra which she wants Penelope to wear down the club. 'She'll knock 'em dead,' she guffawed during the selection process. 'They'll be sticking out of her like a pair of rugger balls.'

She adjusts the straps whilst I wriggle around. 'Ye-es. Oh, yes. This is good.'

Am I supposed to believe it's her sister she's thinking about as, for long seconds, she appraises? Is this bit bad acting, or really good prostituting? She's making me vain and I like it. Love it.

Eventually she changes this for the next bra, which is a lacy peach number. In between, my nudity makes another brief, disorderly appearance. It's like a feral drunk who keeps barging in through the door.

'Just bend this way slightly,' she says as I model the last of her selections. 'Lean forward.'

She guides me through various poses. It's a bit tight, this one. She works her fingertips under the wire to where I'm sticking out. We're back to brisk at this point.

'I hope you don't mind my saying,' she says. 'You're very well proportioned.'

This, I wish to make perfectly plain, is *not* in the script. I'm not even sure who's saying it; whether it's Freya, or Vixen, or this toff in a Russian hat.

Now it's my turn. I've shown her mine and she's got to show me hers.

'If my merm 'ad a dress as nice as this, the men'd be round 'er like bees round a 'erny part.'

She turns round so I can unzip it. Revealing itself inch by inch on her shoulder as I do, as though uncoiling, is a tattoo of a snake. I shouldn't be judgemental of prostitutes and murderers, I expect, but quite frankly I'm a little appalled.

'Can I assist you out of this, ma'am?' 'Ma'am' comes out of nowhere, or probably because I've been saying, 'merm'. I've accidentally introduced a mistress/servant vibe to the proceedings. But I'm with a pro. She gets us back on course.

'Thanks, do. I'm a little stiff from the gym, to tell you the truth, and it's not that comfortable reaching round.'

Heat rises from the vent I've made. The strap of her bra's a bit damp. At last I feel, as I remove it, I'm finding out some of Freya Maskell's secrets. She's bigger than me. Her nipples are brown and wider and more sticky-out. I'm impressed. But what makes the difference between a professional sex object like her and an enthusiastic amateur like me is the face. Defiant when she most should look vulnerable. Proud when she should look ashamed. In charge of her feelings when the situation is beyond her control. A lot like the aristocrat she's pretending to be. She's bewitching. So much so that I don't even feel bad for cheating. No man could resist her, not even Jools. I wouldn't even blame him.

We do it twice more and that's my lot. Now we're supposed to thank each other and agree we'll try elsewhere.

'The peach is sensational,' she says. 'These, I think, are a match.' She has a pair of knickers in her hand. 'I know it's really unusual. But you're so exactly like Penelope. Would you mind desperately…?'

She sees that I'm paralysed.

'Here, let me help you.' She stands behind me, topless still. Her hands go round my waist.

'This isn't in the script,' I murmur.

Her fingers press and rummage. She unbuttons the top of my jeans. 'Go with it,' she breathes in my ear.

I try to do as she says. I tell myself I trust her, that she's my therapist, that she knows exactly what to do. My buttons are pinging open. I imagine her reaching in and dragging out, kicking and screaming into the daylight, my sexual true north. Then I look in the mirror at her hands – the left one

resting on my hip, the right one burrowing between my legs –
and at my eyes, as wide as the lenses of my spectacles.

'No,' I say. I push her hand away. 'No!'

Raising her palms in surrender, she backs away. 'Okay.'

'I'm really sorry.'

'No, no, no.' She shakes her head slowly. 'Don't be sorry.'

We get dressed. I see she's about to put my bra on by
mistake.

'Sorry,' I say to draw it to her attention.

'Oh,' she says, and hands it to me. 'Sorry.'

Neither of us smiles. We shuffle about in silence for what
seems like a long time. The cubicle feels like it's shrunk. I don't
know about her, but I'm taking great care not to accidentally
steal anything. Finally, her Russian hat back in place, her five
garments on their hangers, she looks at me.

'You paid me nearly a thousand quid. Clients normally
expect a lot more for their money than this.'

'I know.'

I stare at my feet, guilty of having wasted her time. When
I raise my eyes, she meets them.

'There's a restaurant on the fifth floor,' she says. 'Shall we
go for a coffee?'

The girl at the changing rooms entrance counts the
garments back in. She smiles and says goodbye. She has no
idea that her role as temporary brothel-keeper is at an end.

Unhurriedly, in a silence that ought to be awkward but
isn't, we make our way to the escalator. Freya surprises me by
linking herself to my arm. In the restaurant, she pushes our
tray along the runner to where an assistant stands in front of
the coffee machine.

'What do you want?' Freya asks me.

'Er, O'll 'ave a flat white.'

'You don't have to speak like that any more,' she tells me before turning her attention to the assistant. 'A flat white and a skinny latte.'

The woman turns to the machine, where a plastic bottle with a green top stands by an aluminium jug.

'Wait. That's semi-skimmed. I want skimmed.'

'I don't think we've got skimmed.'

'When will you know?'

They look at each other.

'We might have some in the kitchen.'

'Go and look.'

The assistant doesn't move. She's holding out for a 'please'. She gives up and walks off, then returns with a half-litre of red top. Nothing more is said until the coffees are made and she asks for £4.90.

'*Please*,' says Freya, withholding the fiver she has in her hand.

They stare at each other again.

'*Ple-ease*,' mimics the assistant.

Freya drops the money onto the counter.

We take a seat by the window. Freya sips her non-fattening coffee and takes in the panorama over Thames Frockley.

'You're Learner Detective Marocco, aren't you?'

I just nod.

'Are you wired up?'

'No. Is that what you were trying to find out when you started to go down my jeans?'

She shakes her head and blows froth. 'Professional pride.' Her glance warns me not to smile. 'You'd paid for a service. Or the police authority had. I wanted you to have your money's worth. Reputation's everything in my trade.'

'I'm not here on duty.'

She scoffs.

'Honest, I'm not.'

'Well, you're not here for fun, are you? You haven't got a gay nerve in your body.'

'You made me feel gay a few minutes ago.'

Her face lights up. 'You still with my solicit-ah?' I nod. 'Does he know you're here?'

I shake my head and wonder if the cockney hard case who's suddenly appeared in front of me is the real Freya Maskell, or whether she's an act, like Penelope's stuck-up sister.

'Ah, man. I can't believe this.' She's chuckling and scratching her head. 'I've been role-playin' with the police officer who sent me to jail for six months. This is totally... This is doin' my head in.'

'When did you know it was me?'

'In the changing room!' It comes out loud, and a woman at the next table looks up from her book. 'It's that stare of yours!' She draws her face close to whisper, 'We was lookin' in the mirror an' I thought, *I know her. She's the police officer who stared at me all the time she was interviewing me!* She turns solemn. 'You do know you can't be tried for the same thing twice? I was acquitted. End of.'

'I think they've changed the rules on that. Anyway, that was about Tony Gibson. It's the Femi Yar'Adua thing you might have to worry about.'

'Femi...?' She tries on an innocent person's frown.

'I've got Abran's phone. I've got the picture.'

'What picture?'

'Your trophy photo. Halloween. You and Brandon? Abran? Whatever you want to call him. You're holding Femi between you, propping his body up. I thought it was a costume handle sticking out of his chest. Then I saw police photos of him lying on Abran's floor.'

Her changing face reminds me of the woman on my satnav when I don't take the route she's advised, whose silence sounds like a gulp. You know she wants to yell at you but all she can do is recalibrate. 'So… Are you going to arrest me?'

The thought makes me laugh. 'I doubt they'd let us into the custody suite.' I mimic Sergeant Jenner's gruff dismay. '"Not you two again!"'

Freya, after her ten minutes in his company last June, takes him off much better. '"You don't give up, do you, Learner Detective Marocco?!"'

Our eyes meet and our smiles subside.

'No, I'm not going to arrest you. But I'll be breaking the law if I don't hand over the phone.'

Freya twists her mouth. 'So what does your picture prove? That I don't pay due respect to dead people?'

'You told me that you murdered someone.'

She laughs. 'You're not seriously going through all that confession stuff again, are you? Nah. You fucked that one up, girl. You didn't caution me. What I told you don't count for nothin'. They proved that one in court. Nah. The three people in that photo are the only ones who know who murdered Femi and I'm the one still alive. You've no witnesses, no confession. You've got nothin' on me.' She takes out her phone and, with a smile of satisfaction, checks her emails.

'Do you know who Mark Wells is?'

Her eyes still on the screen, the victory drains from her lips. 'Pozos?'

'Is that who Pozos is? Mark Wells?'

Finally she nods. 'Spanish for "wells".'

'The photo makes it likely that Mark Wells didn't kill Femi. And, I'm guessing, it won't be long after I've handed the phone to his solicitor that Mr Wells will be a free man.'

'A free man, maybe, curious to find out who set him up.' She sniffs and taps out a message. 'And then it's only a matter of time before I'm fuckin' dead.' She stares down into the town. A teardrop builds on the rim of her eye. She looks more beautiful than I have ever seen her. 'Fucking Abran.'

'I thought you were close.'

'We were. We grew up having no one else.' She looks at me. 'You know why he was in a wheelchair?'

'Was it... from that thing with Mark Wells at the traffic lights in Purley?'

'You *have* been investigating.' She raises her eyebrows. 'Pozos thought Costa had cut him up so he murdered him. Just for that. Nearly murdered Abran, too. Knifed him straight through the gut.'

'I thought... didn't his dad use a knife on Wells?'

She sneers. 'Costa was a carpenter. He had his tools in the car. It was only when Pozos started coming at his boy with a knife that he thought he'd better tool up himself, too. And then Pozos got off at trial, saying it was self-defence. Self-defence against a twelve-year-old child. And then...' She breaks off to reproach herself. 'What you doin', girl, sayin' all this to the feds?' She sips her coffee. Her teeth chatter against the rim of the cup. 'Why are you 'n' me actually here?' Disbelieving, she looks around. 'John Lewis's? Why

John Lewis's? I was thinking when we were dreaming all this up, *Does she think she'll be safer in a public place? Or does she actually want to be caught?*

'Safety. Partly. Mainly it was based on a dream I used to get. There had to be a Russian hat and a big public building.'

She draws breath. 'I thought I'd seen it all. Never 'ad a 'at-'n'-public-building fan before.' She looks me in the eye. 'So why me? You're not doing police work; you think you might be bi. Why not some other girl?'

'I thought about it but… it only seemed right with you. I thought we'd made a connection.'

'A connection?'

Even through my ton of make-up, I know she can see my blush.

'Yeah. I was the one you nearly confessed to. I don't know why but I felt that somehow meant I'd gained your trust. And, well, after I'd read all that on your website about it being bad to bottle things up, I reckoned, if you still felt there was something you wanted to get off your chest—'

'*No-ooh* way.'

'Oh, it wasn't on today's agenda. This was when I only knew about Tony Gibson. This was when the body count stood at only one. I didn't come here hoping for an off-the-record confession.'

'Pleased to hear it.' She laughs. 'I am so over the conscience stuff. Done my bit of stir. Slate's clean, so far as I'm concerned. I sleep easy.'

'Okay. I get that. Although there was something else I hoped you could tell me. Something that wouldn't get you into any trouble.'

'What?'

'Well, since that day you walked into the nick, it's been really bothering me what was said during your legal consultation with my boyfriend.'

'Why's it been bothering you?'

'You'd said you wanted to confess to a murder. You holed up with Jools; then all of a sudden you didn't want to confess any more. When I interviewed you, when I stared at you,' I go cross-eyed to remind her, 'you refused to answer my questions, I expect because he told you to. And what happened after that was, I humiliated myself in court, I lost my career as a detective, the Gibson family didn't get the justice I'd promised them, and...'

'A killer walked free?'

'Well, yeah. Anyway, I'd like to know what he knew all along whilst this was going on. When all these bad things were happening, I'd like to know what he could have done to stop it. I'm supposed to be marrying the guy. I want to know where I stand in his priorities.'

'Why don't you ask him what we said?'

'I did. He won't tell me.'

Freya looks out of the window. 'I didn't see this in any of the draft scripts.'

'I didn't write any of it down. I realised it wouldn't work.'

'But you still came here today.'

'By that time I was too... curious to pull out.'

'You fancied me.'

I nod.

'And when your chance comes, when you have me, all you do is try a few bras on.' She twists her mouth and wriggles in her seat. 'In a way,' she says, 'it was quite exciting. Different, at least. But, gaw, is that it now for you? You've done gay now, have you?'

'I suppose so.'

Her eyes go wide. 'I wish you gave up this easy when you're trying to get me for a murder. There's so much you could learn. So much I could teach you.'

Frowning, the woman at the next table hurriedly turns a page of her book, chasing the words with her eyes. Freya's so loud, I wonder if she's reading at all.

'Do you want another coffee?' I ask.

She takes a long time deciding, then flicks up a 'yes' with her eyebrows. I go to the till, where the woman takes my order and reaches first for the milk bottle with the green top; then, as she remembers, the one with the red top instead. I say a very distinct 'Thank you' and drop my 10p change in the tips tray.

Back in my seat, I clear my throat and wait for the words to form. 'I know how Abran died.'

'Yeah,' Freya says indifferently. 'Chucked 'imself under a train.'

We sip for some moments in silence.

'Why do you think he did it?'

She does her 'urban girl' shrug. 'Dunno. Maybe he didn't like what he'd become.'

Silently, I will her to continue.

'He hardly spoke a word of English when he came to Greymoors. That was the home they sent us to. I wasn't much better. We learned to read together. We read books. Plays. We started to act. Abran could still walk in those days; his injuries didn't seem so bad. He wrote a pantomime for the kids once. The staff got involved. Those were the good days.

'But his mobility started to get worse. An operation went wrong and he had to use crutches. We were teenagers by this time and he got frustrated, not being able to do things. He really liked girls and he was scared he wouldn't be able to have one. And he really missed his father. His mind grew very dark and he began to fixate on Mark Wells. Pozos. Said that one day he was going to get even. He wrote plays about it: how it was going to happen, where... They made us do our rehearsals away from the home. The screams were disturbing people. I lost my virginity in one of those plays.' She looks at me and nods. 'My first time. Scripted. I was Pozos's victim. Abran played Pozos. We made an effigy out of straw and old clothes. After he'd raped me we burned him alive.'

I start to say something but the words don't reach full term.

'I didn't mind,' she says. 'Helped him write the script, so far as I can remember. No, I'd have done anything for Abran. Didn't matter how weird it was. The weirder the better. I loved him.'

'How long were you together at Greymoors?'

'Two, three years. More and more, they sent him to special hospitals, until in the end they gave his room to someone else. Didn't see him again until we were in our twenties.'

'What did you do after you left care?'

'Got a job. Went to assisted living. Then went to live with an older gentleman.' She smirks. 'My sugar daddy. He was the one who gave me a taste for fine things. Then, when I'd had enough of that, I tracked down Abran in Carshalton – or Brandon, as he was calling himself by then. He'd changed a hundred per cent. Completely chair-bound by now, but very confident. Outwardly, at least. Talked like an English gent; dressed like, I don't know, Laurence Llewelyn-Bowen or someone. Seemed to know everyone. Said he had this business idea and asked if I wanted in. Escort agency thing. He wanted to call it "Guilty Secrets".'

'Did you... go out together?'

'Sort of. Well, yeah, he became, like, my boyfriend again. But by now he couldn't really do anything and I'd started seeing girls. Which he kind of enjoyed, to begin with. In the end, we got more like brother and sister, I suppose... Sorry, do you mind if we talk about something else?'

'Course.' Her morning's work over, the money in the bag, I can't see why she wanted to talk in the first place.

We fall back into our easy silence and watch the world go by.

'I wanna get one of those bras,' she announces, and reaches round for her bag. 'Comin' back to Lingerie?'

I process this and drain what's left of my coffee. We start to make our way towards the exit.

'I've read that one,' she says as we pass the next table, to the woman who is still reading her book. 'She dies in the end. Of curiosity.'

On the escalator she turns her attention back to me. 'What we done in the changin' rooms, yeah? So, that's what you dream of at nights?'

'It's the bit that takes place once I'm through the doors of the public building. The bit I could never get myself to dream.'

'Is that all you could come up with? I mean, after all these years, aren't you disappointed?'

'No.'

'What? You liked it? You got your money's worth?'

'Mostly it was just... too new. But there were moments – one? Two? Three separate moments? – when I was so excited

I thought I was going to faint.'

'Which three moments?'

Freya, I see, is a workaholic. She wants feedback. She's demanding a performance review.

'Yeah,' she says, as we break it down and go through it. 'Yeah, I liked that, too. Nah, that was when I saw it was you and I thought, *She's gonna arrest me*.' She's becoming so animated I'm worried she'll trip on the metal stairs. 'Ah, yeah, that was wicked. Like, suddenly, there was your tits!' This is so loud the girl from the changing rooms looks up. Freya waves and calls out, 'Hello, again!'

We return to the lingerie department where I, the bumpkin, and she, the fine lady, first met. Already, it seems like a lifetime ago.

'Where is it?' she mutters as she riffles through a display. 'Where's it gone?' She stops what she's doing and turns to me. 'Don't wanna freak you out. I've got a proposal.' She waits for me to react. Only then will she find her courage.

'What is it?'

'I, er…' My reaction hasn't quite done the trick. Her eyes slide from mine. 'I've taken a lot of your money and I don't think I've given you very much in return. That troubles me.' At every attempt to restore eye contact, her glance swerves off to the side. It's as though there's a groove that's worn out, so that the catch won't hold. 'Also, I'm afraid what's 'appened today is not going to leave you with a very clear impression of what Guilty Secrets can achieve. I expect you think we're just a bunch of slags, but I'm very proud of the work we do and I actually believe that it helps people. I think that, if you an' me carry on, it might help us both.' At last, she gets there with the eye contact. 'Wanna be my actress?'

'Excuse me?'

'I'll give you back your grand.'

'I'm not with you.'

'We won't script it. Just a few basic directions. We'll do it like it's real.'

'Do what?'

'Interrogation. What you want to know? Maybe I'll tell you some of it. All of it. But you've got to get it out of me. It'll be strong stuff, though. It's gonna be more torture chamber than John Lewis changing room.'

'Torture?!'

'Well, I'll provide your instruments. Use them for pleasure or pain. Your decision. You'll have to find out what I respond to. You'll be calling the shots. But you know me. I don't give away my secrets easy.'

'But… now that you know I've got Abran's phone, I mean… Aren't you just going to disappear?'

She considers this as she continues her search for her bra. She stops, shuffles back a couple of hangers, then produces a version of the lacy peach one she posed me in. 'I suppose I should. Probably, I will. But you don't wanna grass me up just yet, do you? Before you've found out a little more about… what's going on?'

'"Going on"?'

'Y'know? Who murdered who? Who it is you're marrying? What it's like to truly go with a girl, not just prat around in a changing room?'

'But why would you ever want to see me again?'

'Professional pride, like I said. And, yeah, maybe I don't sleep so easy after all. In spite of what I said. Maybe I do have some guilty secrets festering inside. And maybe I think that you're the person who may be able to help me. Hold this.' She passes me the bra she has selected and writes what appears to be her personal phone number on a card. 'Also.' She gives me the card and takes back her bra. 'What you started back there.' She nods across the floor to the changing rooms. 'You can't leave it at that. You can't take me half the way. You just can't do that to a girl.'

'Oh.' I nod at the bra in her hands. 'Are you going to try that on?'

'Nah.'

'You haven't even checked it's your size.'

'I'm not gonna wear it. It's in case you don't call me an' I never see you again. It's a souvenir. I've had an educational morning. I've enjoyed it.'

'I'm glad.' In fact, I'm elated.

'But do call, yeah? Let's end this, once and for all.'

'You are, er, gonna pay for that?' I nod at the bra. 'I mean, you're not gonna just stuff it in your bag?'

'Yes, Officer. I promise. I don't want you to tie me up just yet.' She's whispering, wickedly, humorously. 'Wear your uniform and bring your cuffs.'

She turns in the direction of the tills, then stops for her parting shot. 'There's gonna be no solicitor to hold you back. There'll be no one to protect me. I'll be stripped of my human rights. Don't mess about this time; do it properly. Remember, you're being paid for this.'

15

Femi Yar'Adua
DOB: 17.4.1975
No convictions. No cautions.

Damn. Though I don't know why I'm disappointed. Social services were hardly going to employ him if he'd done time for rape or murder. I suppose it'd just make things easier if I could hate him a little.

I come out of the screen before anyone can see what I'm doing. My burner phone, purchased for colluding secretly with my partner in crime (an idea inspired by the drug-dealing fraternity), gives a *ting*.

You not speakn to me any more?

And before that:

Call me when ur 3.

And before that:

I feel reborn.

Reborn after a very difficult rebirth. She was black and blue when I left her this morning.

I scroll up to the first text she sent me. Still makes me smile.

Can you call me Freya?

So I called her. When she answered we both waited for the other to speak. Turned out she hadn't wanted to talk to me; she'd wanted me to stop calling her 'Vixen' and start to use her real name. Sweet.

I snap the phone shut. Sweet, my backside. I had another look at the photos in Jools's study when I got home. *Ugh!* To think, last night she and I…

The skipper's appeared out of nowhere. 'What's happened to your hand?'

'Caught it in the car door.'

'Ouch. Can you move it?'

I waggle my red-and-mauve fingers.

'You should put a bandage round that. People'll think you've been brutal. What you doing here, anyway? You're on leave. I thought you were going to… where was it?'

'We're going to Wales for the week. Just come in for Katie Teague's thing.'

'Oh, that's tonight, is it?' He looks sceptical. 'You a fan?'

'Of Katie Teague? Not particularly. It's more the pips that I'm applauding.'

'Can't make it myself, I've…' He abandons the search for a reason. 'What I wanted to say: I had a call from a Mr Kelsey. You seized a phone from his shed? Got quite shirty, actually. Said if you're not going to investigate the matter he'd like the phone returned. Said it's his legal right.'

'Is it?'

'Apparently. He read me a citation from the *Reader's Digest* law reports.'

'Right. Better get my finger out.'

'Yeah, do. Oh, and as you're here, this pigeonhole of yours…'

I stand up. It's the third time he's had to ask. 'I'm on it.'

'Would you mind? Only, it's a disgrace, and it'd be a shame if I had to have you extradited back from Wales just to clear out your shit.'

I go to the part of the office where the mail is delivered. I see what he means. There are so many unopened issues of *POLICE* magazine I can barely get my uninjured fingers around the edges to prise them out. They come slowly, together with some flyers for training courses, pension updates, and a notice of a widows and orphans charity run. A thick white envelope slips from the pile and cartwheels onto the floor. It's addressed to me. It looks like it might have been here some time.

Inside there are two letters.

Dear Ruby,

I hope this finds its way to you. To be honest, I don't know if you're still stationed at Cattlegreen.

*I think you may have been moved elsewhere.
Anyway, here's hoping.*

*Superintendent Bartlett paid me a visit this
week. It was very kind of him to come all the way
up to Hereford and explain to me personally what
went wrong with the trial and why Freya Maskell has
been released. However, I was rather alarmed when
he told me that you have been 'let go' by the CID
and are now 'back in uniform' (isn't that what they
say on the television?). He didn't put it in so many
words but, I'm afraid to say, I think he thought this
was good news and that I'd be pleased to hear it. His
gist was that, now you are no longer a detective, the
mistakes that were made during the investigation of
my husband's case are unlikely to be repeated.*

*I'm writing this because I VERY CLEARLY asked
Superintendent Bartlett to let you know that there
is no one in my family who feels disappointed
by you or who holds you to blame in any way for
anything that he may have thought was not done
properly. I remember that I asked him SEVERAL
TIMES to do this. Since his visit, though, I'm
struggling to remember if he gave me an assurance
that he would do what I asked him to do, and I'm
beginning to doubt that he did. It's been bothering
me quite a lot.*

*To set the record straight, I told Superintendent
Bartlett that, in my view, for what it's worth, you were
a BRILLIANT detective and a TOTAL ASSET to West
Thames Police. You are clever and reliable, you listen
to what people say, and YOU REALLY SEEM TO CARE.*

As you know, life has quite simply been unbearable since my husband's death but – again, as I told the superintendent – it would have been a lot, lot worse if anyone else except you had been our supporter during that time. (Just to let you know, things go from bad to terrible here. I shan't go on, though. One good thing about not being in CID any more is that you won't have to hear any more of my woes!)

What I really want you to know, Ruby, is this: YOU HAVE NOT DENIED US JUSTICE. YOUR CONSCIENCE SHOULD BE ABSOLUTELY CLEAN.

Yours sincerely,
Hannah Gibson

PS: The enclosed letter was for Tony. It's from a friend of his mother's, who he kept in touch with across the years. I never met her and I only knew her first name: Bryony. Her details weren't in his address book and I'm afraid I didn't think to tell her what happened. Anyway, I'm aware you will have built up a very negative picture of what Tony was like and I just wanted you to have this as it shows a different side of him; one more like the person (I thought) I knew.

There is a slight tear in the next letter and I can't see when it was dated. This has also been handwritten, with the same scratchy sort of thing Sergeant Jenner still uses, by the look of it, and which I think he calls a fountain pen. The Ls stoop and the Ts wilt and the Hs bend as they go, like it's been a long race and they're struggling to the end of the line.

My dear Anthony,

It was wonderful to see you again after so many months. And to be taken out on my birthday, well, what a treat! You have always been extremely thoughtful and kind. Thank you so much for a truly special day.

The Frockley Flower Show has always been a great favourite of mine and, as you know, I go most years, health and weather permitting. But to be there on the opening day, 'hobnobbing' with royalty, so to speak, well, that was a first. I thought the Duchess did a very good job, formally opening the proceedings. I know it probably doesn't seem very much to cut a ribbon but, to me, what made it special was that she looked genuinely happy to be there, and I thought it marvellous that she took time to speak to members of the crowd, some of whom had made a big effort to see her. Whether she knows the difference between a geranium and a jocasta, I can't tell you!

And thank you so much for the kind offer of a lift home to Watlington. I had to say no because it's such a long way and entirely the other direction from where you said you were going, and on a Friday evening you certainly wouldn't want to get caught up in the traffic. As it turned out, of course, I almost had to ask you to go and fetch your car after all, didn't I? The train you put me on at Thames Frockley was the last one of the day and I made it with just a minute to spare!

*Thank you again for your kindness. As they say,
you made an old lady very happy.*

With much love,

Bryony

I fold the letters carefully and press them back into the envelope. The skipper's right; I should bandage up these fingers.

Even Freya says she has no idea where we were taken to last night. In the countryside somewhere. When we were led from the car, there was no distant buzz of traffic. The air was damp and smelt of fields, and there was mud underfoot. When the guy took our blindfolds off it looked like we were in a recording studio. Somewhere soundproofed, at least. My first thought was, *No one will hear the screams.*

Obviously, Freya's fantasy of truth-extraction by force had been on my mind all week. But imagining myself free of the things that keep me honest during a police station interview – which, basically, I suppose, are the law, my pension, the solicitor sitting opposite, and my not much caring either way whether or not my suspect talks – was no preparation for the reality. And it turned out to be no help to have given myself lectures on how restrained I should be, how responsibly I should act, when placed within easy reach of instruments that would make me a very efficient interviewer indeed. In the event, what happens is the instruments take over. They decide what you do, just by being seen. You use them, you justify it. What I told myself, amid the groans and the sighs, the whimpering and the screams, was that I was acting in the name of the truth; that, by removing her festering secrets, I was healing Freya. I was being cruel to be kind. I was more a nurse than a Nazi. That's how you get through it. Terrifying how easy it is.

Ping.

Ah, really?! My mate, Caz, has dropped out. I'm going to have to go to Katie's thing on my own.

The staff social club is behind the nick on the far side of the car park. It's packed. No measure of Katie Teague's popularity. It's always packed on a Friday night. I stand in the doorway and look for a group to attach to.

'Ruby! Over here!' It's Sarah Dix. Can't see Connor but quite a few of the Vanguard are here.

'Golly gosh, it's St Joan again,' says Noel Creme as I approach their table.

'Well, bless my soul,' says Eric Foley, making space. 'Twice in so many months.'

'And here's me thinking this was an exclusive occasion,' I tell him. 'Turns out they'll let anyone in.'

He goes to get me a drink.

'You set a date yet?' Amanda Dee asks, nodding at my ring.

'Nah. We've got illness in the family. We're having to put it off.'

'Then you gonna retire and make babies?' Sarah asks. 'Live off your rich solicitor?'

'Oh, I'd love that,' I tell her. 'Actually, I get paid more than he does.'

No one remarks on this, although I know they've taken it in. All coppers are money mad.

'When's the hen?' Sarah asks.

My eyes go wide. It sort of feels like I've had my hen. Handcuffs, sex toys, dressed up like a strippergram. Tearful, frank confessions. A panic-buy snatch of illicit last-fuel-for-a-hundred-miles sex. Still got my hangover. (The only guy there, Vin, our driver/tie-er-upper/paramedic, advised that I'd save time conquering my better feelings if I drank some of his Blue Label vodka. Advice that I took to heart.) Not sure I want to go through all that again any time soon.

'Is that the new DI?' Eric asks, freeing me from Sarah's stare.

Katie is doing the rounds, going from table to table. Baring teeth from every angle, she looks like, if the price is right, she might be prepared to sell one or two.

'She's only been at Cattlegreen five minutes,' Amanda says.

'McQuade has left her some very big boots to fill,' says Eric.

'DS for less than a year,' Sarah says. 'I reckon they sent her from London to shake us yokels up.'

'Bartlett's doing, I've heard,' says Amanda. 'Taken her under his wing.'

Now she's here at our table. '*Ru-uuby!*' She comes for me, arms wide, so quickly I don't have the option to stand. '*So-ooo* great to see you!' She clasps my head to her midriff. 'How *are* you?' She turns to my companions. 'I don't think we've been introduced. Katie Teague. Here from the Met. Thanks so much for coming.'

'Congratulations, ma'am.'

'Ah, guys, yeah. I can't believe it. "Chuffed" doesn't start to describe it. Tell you what, though.' She adopts a 'joking apart' face. 'If I can earn just half the respect that Len McQuade got, I'll have to think I'm doing something right.'

Her phone goes.

'DI Teague.' *DI Teague.* With some who are newly promoted, I've noticed, a new title takes a while to bed in.

They announce themselves with a lot of *ers* and *I means*. Katie, though, has hit the ground running and gets it word-perfect. And it looks like she's hearing good news. Even her most stay-at-home teeth have ventured forth. But now her smile straightens. Danger. The teeth scuttle back to the nest. 'Something's come up,' she tells us. 'Have to love you and leave you. Really nice meeting you guys. Hope to catch you later.'

The talk at our table turns to the subject of new Vanguard member PC Ronnie Hyde, who they don't think has much between the ears.

'Had to review one of his statements the other day,' says Noel. 'His witness said, "He kicked me in the colder sack." Colder, yeah? Opposite of warmer.

'I said to Ronnie, "Is he talking about his ball bag?"

'He looked blank and said, "No, it's where it happened."

'I said, "Eh?"

'He said, "Ain't that what you call 'em? Little roads of houses with wide bits at the end?"'

Ronnie replaced the fella who replaced me. I've forgotten that guy's name. It's starting to feel a long time since I was in the van; since I knew these people.

'What a wazzock!' Sarah says, ungratefully. It's only Ronnie's novel dimness that stands between her own shortcomings and the Vanguard's cheerful disdain. She should thank him.

Noel's doubling over in his chair. Amanda's mascara has started to run. The laughter is infectious. I join in. Sarah repeats the punchline, squeezing the last of the juice. I laugh all the harder.

Now I stop. Something has occurred to me about those letters in my pigeonhole. I get out my phone and google under the table. The buffer spins like a roulette wheel. I wait to be rich or poor.

Well, I'll be. So Freya *was* telling the truth. This was the thing I thought she was holding back. Jesus. Is *no one* what they seem? Here's someone else I've cuddled who I should have had jailed instead. It hardly seems possible. This is one dark, dark horse. Hannah Gibson.

A text from Jools. Mr Wells has had him holed up in a hotel in Yorkshire all week, making up for the precious time he keeps having off work. His train gets into Fountainford in ten minutes. I bet he's exhausted. I bet, when I get back, I'll find him with his feet up, switching off with a glass of wine, savouring the peaceful week to come, free of testy people and their angry assaults on his mind. At which point I shall let him have it: is it me or Mark Wells he wants to make happy? Is it me he wants for a partner, or is it Lester Legarde?

Face shown, excuses made, I wish the Vanguard a fun weekend.

In the car park is Superintendent Bartlett's Jag. He wasn't at the drinks. He'll probably come along in a bit. I'd like to have a word with him. Perhaps I can catch him in his office. I'd like him to explain why, over the three months since she asked him, and in spite of the dozens of opportunities he's had, he's never bothered to pass on Hannah Gibson's message of reassurance. I'm developing quite a taste for explanations. And I'm becoming quite good at getting them.

I skip up the two flights of stairs to his office. There's no answer when I knock, so I turn to go. Then I remember that he has something that belongs to me. I go in.

Superintendent Bartlett is standing by his filing cabinet.

'Get out,' says Katie Teague, who is in his arms.

It's a lawful command, I suppose, and reasonable in the circumstances. But, with their clothing not arranged in such a way as to maximise ease of movement, neither of them seems in a strong position to enforce it.

'You don't change, do you, ma'am?'

They stand frozen as my skipping-rope smile hangs dreamily between my ears. Katie's teeth, by contrast, are not to be seen. Maybe she's latched on to my subtle reference to our days in training school and the night in the bathroom in the old accommodation block. The time I heard sobbing in the cubicle next to mine.

'Why are you crying?' I'd picked my moment to emerge at the same time as my neighbour. I recognised her. A needy, toothy girl from the intake before mine. She stood trembling at the basin, alternately wailing and sucking her thumb. 'Is it to do with Sergeant O'Kill?' He was one of the tutors. I'd seen them together so often I'd assumed they were an item.

'I really thought he liked me!'

'Ah, there, there.'

Stranger to her though I was, pretty much, she threw herself into me, holding on like I was something buoyant that could save her from going under the waves. Through the sobs I worked out that she'd tried something on with him but had read the signals all wrong. Sergeant O'Kill had only been trying to help her with her insecurities and with a little private tuition (I knew, from her reputation, that Katie found the academic side of the training especially hard). Now she was terrified word would get back to her home force and her career would be over before it had begun.

'It won't 'appern,' I told her (this was before I'd de-bumpkinned my accent). 'People'll ernderstand. I bet yer've not been away from 'ome before?'

I felt the cool of the wetness as she shook her face on my chest.

'There yer go. 'Ow are you ter know what's fer the best? They bring us 'ere because they wanna change us. Turn us inter 'oo they wan' us ter be. 'S their fault, not ours, if we make mistakes on the way.'

How nice was I?! What she didn't say was that she was married and had two children.

Superintendent Bartlett hoists up his trousers and begins to march my way. 'You've just been told to get out.' He looks very angry. Anyone would have thought it was *my* conduct that warranted such a stern face.

My body spasms into a Lara Croft stance. 'One more step and you'll be on the floor.'

My pitch is assertive and, in the gathering silence as the office block empties for the weekend, very noticeable, I would have thought. He stops and, for a moment as I circle them, looks unsure what to do.

'PAA Sports Day 2011. Final of the mixed football. Hampshire versus West Thames Police. You were the referee. Remember?'

I say, 'remember' even louder than my threat, and I take a step towards him as I say it. This surprises him. Now I continue to behind the desk where his medals are on display. I help myself to the one with the blue-and-green ribbon. 2011 Winning Force.

'You stood right next to the Hampshire guy as he pushed the ball over our line with his hand. He didn't even try to hide it. He was actually having a joke. And you gave them the goal so that West Thames didn't get the points and Wiltshire, your force, won the day.'

I advance deep into his personal space, aware that I still have my silly smile. I think it's this, as much as my intimidating behaviour, that makes them both completely unable to react to anything I do or say. It's the sign of someone who doesn't care about anything any more. Must be disturbing to be in the presence of such a person.

I hold the medal up to his nose. 'Mine.' I swing it round a couple of times and try to think of a way of turning the conversation round to what I came here for in the first place. I can't; not without giving them time to gather their wits. I decide to quit whilst I'm ahead. I think they've both got my gist. With a lift of my eyebrows, I silently bid them a pleasant evening.

In the doorway I stop and turn for a quick girly chat. 'Oh, and not being neg but, before you tell me, ma'am, I know. You used to do this in the Met.'

The FME is in the house and bandages my hand. I get a text from Lorna. Can I call by the hospital pharmacy, pick up Dad's prescription?

The drive takes me past Fountainford industrial estate. I see a factory sign: 'A. Carmichael – Industrial Glazier'. The knife-and-golf-club man. His wife has her trial at the Crown Court soon. The magistrates acquitted him. Perhaps they grew up near where I did. Maybe they thought he did what any man would.

Jools will be home now, digging out maps, choosing his books, relacing his walking boots. How will Freya spend her

Friday evening? Probably won't want to show herself outside. Will she have enough food for the weekend? I'm sure she'll think of something, if not. What if she keeps on texting? I don't think she will. Something about her face as she slept made me think of closure. Even her little snores gave off an air of 'job done'. She won't pester me; she's not going to cling. Too dignified for that, I'd have thought. Anyway, I'm not taking the burner phone to Wales. I'll keep it in my drawer until I have news for her – whether she walks or should run; whether she lives or dies. Then I'll throw it away.

I can still taste Horlicks, mixed in with the vodka. Not had that since my childhood stays with Aunty Rita. It seemed quaint that Freya should have something so homely in her cupboard. Reminded me of the night I first met her, when she was being booked in for murder at the custody desk and she produced, of all things, a library card. Funny, how comforting a simple, hot drink can be. It was the first thing she went for after Vin dropped us off and we stuffed our blindfolds in our pockets and I helped her into her flat. We slurped away mutely, perched on the side of her bed. Afterwards, she rested her head on my shoulder and began to cry – shyly at first, then, as we watched the dawn lighten through the bedroom window, without restraint. In bed, she filled in the details of the confessions she'd had a first stab at on her rack, and told me of her sad and brutal life. The sobs, loud and long, came in bundles, each with a name attached; dismal dedications to the ones she had loved, hurt or lost. Femi. Abran. Her mother. Many besides. Moved by her frail need not to live except by way of the truth – a weakness, I'd noticed, the successful (the Teagues, the Bartletts, the Wellses) seem often not to have – I tended her wounds and soothed her with 'aah's and 'there, there's.

And in the end we made love. Can I call it that? Love? It's not what I felt for her, though, God, there were moments I came close. Tender moments when, with a force no greater than breath, I stroked where she was sore, and lay on her, light as gauze, so that she could bear to be touched. Not love. Maybe it was respect. Yes, that's what we engaged in. An act of mutual respect. The handshake of two lusting girls, acknowledging a deal that had been highly beneficial to both sides. She certainly got her money's worth out of me. 'I feel reborn,' was what she said in her text. 'I feel properly grown-up,' would have nailed it better for me.

If you love someone, set them free. That's the saying. And if I loved Freya that's what I'd do. I'd drive right now to the river, chuck in Abran's phone and, for her, this would all be over. But it's not Freya I love, it's someone else. And I need the phone because the person I love wants to marry me and I need to know if that's what I want, too.

The hospital is quiet. I get a parking space and Dad's medication is waiting for me, stapled in large paper bags. I'm in and out in no time. Leaving Fountainford on the dual carriageway, a gaudy sunset glows over Cattlegreen Heath.

Lorna answers the door. She's laughing, so much her cheeks are streaked with tears. Dad is behind her in the lounge, feet up, chuckling in front of the telly.

'What's going on?' I ask.

'We've just been talking in burp. Remember when the three of us used to do that?'

On the TV, a weather forecaster mentions 'light showers with sunny spells'. Dad repeats the phrase whilst he belches. It sets the two of them off again.

'Can *you* still do it?' Lorna asks.

I try but seem to have lost the knack.

'I've not had so much fun in years,' she says. 'Literally, this man is a yinky.'

Weeks back, when I said we should help look after Dad, Lorna wasn't enthusiastic. 'Mum'll go ballistic… He'll just think we're after his money… And anyway, why should we?' When I told her we'd never forgive ourselves, she only liked the idea less. 'Ugh!' she whispered. 'What about "personal care"?' So, remembering the extremely helpful reality check she administered when I split up with Jools, I got Mum involved.

It worked like a dream. 'Grow up!' she instructed my sister. Lorna came round to Dad's the same day. I relayed to her all that I'd learned from the district nurses. What meds and when. What food. How to operate his special bed. Only had to tell her once. Soon, she'd pretty much elbowed me out. Now she stays over and has her own allocated clothes space in the wardrobe.

'Snowdonia? Tha's where you goin' tomorrow, innit? North, innit? 'S not lookin' too clever, Woob.' Dad points to the screen and at the clouds that cover my holiday destination. 'Will yer be able to call when you've got there, let me know you're all right?'

'Not sure I'll be able to, Dad. No Wi-Fi and intermittent phone signal. That's what the website says.'

'So what you gonna do all week?' Lorna asks.

'Got three Danielle Steels to read. And I'm going to run up and down hills.'

'Christ almighty,' Dad says. 'Reckon I'll 'ave more fun wi' my bloody pancreas.'

At home there is music playing. Grande rests his jaw on the settee cushion and angles his eyebrows whilst my fiancé waggles his hips and throws his arms about.

Despairing, Jools shakes his head. 'The theory is so sound.' He's making one of his attempts to train the dog to tap his paw in time with the beat.

'You said that when you were trying to get him to wave back when you said, "Bye-bye." And when you wanted him to eat politely with his mouth closed when we have visitors.'

'Maybe I should try him on some grunge.'

'Maybe you should accept we don't call them dumb for nothing.'

He shrugs. 'You guys get them to sniff out drugs and burglars. I'm sure they're capable of mastering some of the basic social graces.'

'Have you had a good week?'

'Not bad.' He takes a seat next to Grande and rhythmically bounces his paw up and down. 'Oh, guess who I spoke to this afternoon? Finally. Mrs Chadwick!'

'The owner of the Centre?'

'Mrs Waifs 'n' Strays herself. I phoned when I was on the train to rearrange my days and she just happened to be passing through reception. Had a very interesting chat. I was able to tell her that the disused barn in the field next to the main kennels is not, as everyone there thinks, Crown property, but in fact is privately owned and, therefore, possibly buyable. I checked with the Land Registry. She thanked me. Said, "When there's funds, we could make an offer."'

'Mum's always saying they need more space.'

'Yes, they do. The dogs are virtually standing on top of each other.'

'And how's Mr Wells?'

He gives up on Grande and comes and takes me in his arms. 'Quite cheerful, actually. His prime suspect has just been sent down for seven years. The guy he's convinced set him up. Now he's in the prison system, he thinks his contacts can find him and maybe get him to confess. What that will achieve in terms of admissible evidence, I'm not sure. The courts can get quite sniffy about methods of extracting confessions. As we know. Wasn't going to say that to Mr Wells, of course. Didn't want to spoil his good mood. Said he hopes I have a good time in Wales… What's up?'

'Nothing.'

'You look weird. Got this weird smile. God!' He holds my bandaged hand in his fingers. 'You haven't been punching protesters again, have you?'

'No, I…' I look up at him. 'Why did you change the PIN on your phone?'

He ponders. '6285? Sonny's birthday?' He brightens. 'It's back. At least whilst we're on our holidays.' He shows me. The screen opens and there I am, smiling a less weird smile. 'The sort of person I've been rubbing shoulders with these last months, I wouldn't want them to know a single thing about me. Kicked myself today for telling the client we're off to Wales. Even that seemed a bit specific. Wouldn't occur to any of that crowd not to watch and remember if they see you unlock your phone; see who's precious to you. So I've been changing my personal data.' He frowns. 'Why did you need to get into my phone?'

'You called me "Tommy". I thought you were having an affair.'

'Why? Because of that? She was probably just in my mind at the time. You always call me "Connor".'

'I know. I only remembered that later.'

'But you still think I'm having an affair?'

'Yeah, I dunno. Like… then your screen was locked. And before that I phoned up your work and I thought I heard her voice. You'd been so distant. Especially after Christmas when… you spent those few days with her.'

'I thought we'd put this behind us.'

'Yeah. I figured maybe it was over between you two. It's just… I need to know.'

He holds me at arm's length and looks into my eyes. I stifle an idiotic impulse to caution him.

'I've done it again,' he says. 'I've been keeping other people's secrets for them. After what happened in January I told myself not to do that, not where you're concerned.' He holds me close. 'I'm sorry, hon.' Squeezing me, he kisses the top of my head. 'Lester. He's the one who's having an affair with Tommy.'

I push him away from me. 'Lester?!'

'As for my little trip away with her after Christmas, you're not the only one who didn't like that. Lester was furious when he found out.'

I can feel that my strange smile, which seems to be so disturbing everyone this evening, is finally disappearing.

'That letter she sent me before Christmas? She said she needed to talk to someone she could trust. I thought, as a friend, I should go.'

'What was wrong?'

'She was losing faith in herself as a journalist. Couldn't find a buyer for her documentary. She was broke. And I think she was lonely, although she didn't admit it. Lester had offered her a job in the office (he hadn't mentioned it to me) and she couldn't decide whether she should take it.'

'*Did* she take it?'

'Yeah. Against my advice.'

'So I *did* hear her voice on the phone.'

'She's training up to be the office manager. Making a good job of it. Making a good job of wrecking the Legardes' marriage, too.'

'So you're not...'

'I haven't slept with Tommy since we were at university. Even then it was only once or twice. We were never, like, an item.'

My emotions seem to be competing in a race to seize my voice. Anger wins. 'And you thought, as a true friend, and as a loyal servant to Legarde's, and as a lawyer worthy of the name, the right thing would be to—'

As though they're a couple of bombs he has to defuse, he focuses his eyes sternly on his feet. 'I thought I should try to be discreet.'

'—the right thing would be to tell me nothing.'

He looks up. 'If I'd had any idea that you suspected...' His courage fails him.

I remove his hands from my shoulders. 'Wait there.' I go to our bedroom, where I rummage in my scarves-and-hats drawer. 'That fresh evidence you've been looking for?' I say when I return to the lounge. 'The key to your appeal?'

Trying to be playful, I twiddle Abran's phone in my hand. In fact, I feel like the blindfolded recruit in that old police training method where they stand you on a table and order you to fall backwards. That your comrades are there to catch you, you have to take on trust. I press the buttons and call up the Halloween selfie. I turn the screen to Jools, who gives no immediate sign of what he thinks. I take his hand

and lead him into the study. He offers no resistance whilst I shuffle through his pile of papers to the police photos of Femi Yar'Adua. I pull them out and place them in his free hand.

'Same costume. Same knife. Same blood.'

'Is that... is that...?' He's finally registering who the woman is.

'Your former client. Freya Maskell. She killed Femi. She stabbed him in the heart. And then, together with this guy,' I point to Abran in his wheelchair, 'she pulled off an unbelievable stunt so that Mark Wells got the blame. This is what you're looking for. This proves that Mark Wells is innocent of the crime.'

'Whose phone is it?' Jools is almost gasping. 'How... how do you know all this?'

'I'd love to be able to tell you, my darling. But I'm afraid...' I tense every last sarcastic sinew I have, '...it's confidential.'

His smile lasts only a second. 'But can I take the phone?' He's holding it so close to his chest I wonder if he'll actually stuff it down his shirt.

'It looks like you wouldn't give it back if I asked.'

He realises and relaxes, and holds it out to me.

'No. Keep it,' I say. 'It's yours. Do with it what you think's for the best. But before you do anything, will you let me tell you about Freya Maskell?'

16

The man in Max Spielmann trots from his machine. 'I think they've come out really well.'

With care, arranging them out of the bright sunlight, at an angle most convenient for me, he lays out his efforts on the counter. As I look at them, I can feel his eyes on my face. He's waiting to see my reaction.

'Ah, yeah. They're great.'

The three of us went to Hampshire for the weekend. I've had photo blocks made up. In Lorna's, we're gathered around the New Forest pony which crept up behind her and made her jump, so that she effed and Mum shrieked, 'Lorna!' For which the pony earned its place in family history. Mum's having the view from the Spinnaker Tower. At least, a view of her daughters' goofed-up faces getting in the way of it. The one I'm keeping is the shot a waiter took in the hotel restaurant, around the moment we stopped worrying about the price of everything and how underdressed we were, and raised a glass to the future. Mum is leading the cheer.

'We used to go camping down there when we were children. We…' I lose my train of thought. It's hard to remember how to be with even the easiest of people nowadays. Deciding he's young enough probably still to have parents, I give him a piece of advice. 'Be with them. Talk with them. Really, just do it. You don't know how long you've got.'

Back on Frockley high street, we make our way to Venters. I have to collect a teacup, to replace one that Jools broke when we were in Wales. Just a normal cup, so far as I could see, not the sort they'd expect us to replace. But you know what Jools is like. 'I broke it, they get a new one.' Jools 'the Rules', I call him now, or just 'Rules'. John Lewis is over there; they sell this sort of cup. But John Lewis has associations for me. Besides, in a way, it was John Lewis's fault the cup was broken in the first place.

I can see the moment I walk in that the unsmiling assistant in Venters wouldn't get a job at Max Spielmann. Nor is she going to get any free advice from me that she should spend more time with her parents.

'Can I help you?' she asks, eyeing Grande.

I tell her about my order and she goes into the back. A yard away, dangling from a hanger, is a pair of baby socks. I take a step closer and stretch out my hand to touch.

'Is it already paid for?' the woman asks, suddenly reappearing behind her counter.

I drop my hand and tell her no. Uncaring if I like my new teacup, she asks for £3.75.

Telling the *whole* whole truth, on the night I offered up to Jools Abran's phone, turned out to be too much of a stretch.

I hadn't factored in that my fiancé might be innocent. It was disorienting, not being wronged. In fact, with my happiness unexpectedly returned, I lost all appetite for clean slates and swept cupboards and, having psyched myself up to perhaps being magnanimous, wasn't in any mood for admitting that *I* was the one who'd been sharing willies with someone else and should beg for forgiveness. In the end, the story that came out sort of implied that Freya and I had just bumped into each other in town and that, when I told her I had the phone, she'd simply crumbled and confessed to all her crimes. Not mega plausible, I would have thought, but Jools was on the back foot at the time and didn't think to question it.

The next morning, refreshed after a calm sleep in a maggot-free bed, I weighed up our holiday options. As I saw it, Jools and I could spend a solemn week in Wales continuing with our forensic inspection of our dirty linen, or we could be friends and have fun and maybe make that linen still dirtier. I hit on an idea.

'What do you say?' I asked him, propping myself up on my elbow. 'From the moment we get in the car to the moment we step back into this flat, we don't breathe one word about work?'

Jools stared at the ceiling. 'What do you mean by "work"?' The lawyer in him smelled a contract. Written or not, he was going to pull it apart and put it back together again before he put his name to it.

'Okay,' I said. 'Lester, Tommy, Katie, Ollie, Mark, Freya, Abran, Hannah, Tony. And, of course, the phone.'

Frowning, he got up and went to make the tea. Ten minutes later he came back into the bedroom and handed me my mug. 'Okay,' he said.

Later in the day, when we were on the M54, I remembered I hadn't told him about Hannah Gibson's letters. 'Oh, must just say before the ban—'

He lifted a palm from the steering wheel and stopped me dead in my tracks. 'No. We've made a rule.' Which was when he got his new name.

The first 235 miles of our journey we covered in under five hours; the last three took forty-five minutes. We crawled round hairpins, reversed to passing places, braked for sheep, juddered on cattle grids, dragged iron gates that blocked the road, swallowed as we went up mountains to equalise the pressure in our ears, bounced on potholes and squabbled over where we were and whose idea this had been in the first place and why, instead, we hadn't taken Si up on his offer to loan us his place in Marbella. The cottage, when we found it, was half a mile from our nearest neighbour and a mile from the last strip of tarmac. Another fertile terrain for some futile female screaming.

Which I nearly did the next afternoon. By then we'd read the guestbook and the flyers for the regional attractions, worked out what we were allowed to flush down the toilet and what not, and made our list of things we'd forgotten and which we'd get when we went into town. We'd woken up to the Welsh dawn chorus – hootier, less tweety than the Berkshire one – and over breakfast, with nothing to scroll through on our phones, discovered a whole new mealtime in which it is possible to talk. During our exploration of the locality, Grande had introduced me to field waterskiing as, the two of us linked by his lead, he powered his way towards the sheep.

At lunchtime it began to rain. Jools's self-discipline had been impressive, but it was starting to get on my nerves. I found myself looking at him every few seconds to check if anything was stirring. Nothing was. Sitting there by the fire, with his tea and his book with a dragon on it, full of tales of ancient lore, he looked thoroughly contented, like he hadn't a care in the world. If anything, I'd been flattered that he was observing his vow of shop-talk silence so strictly. It had been my idea, after all. But was he actually even *thinking* about Abran's phone?

I couldn't keep still on my sofa. I read the same Danielle Steel line over and over again: 'I clung to him just like a limpet... I clung to him just like a limpet.' In between, I kept on looking at Jools. Unable to get beyond the limpet sentence, I stood up and gave the fire a prod. Then I left the room and clattered about the cottage, examining the supply of wet-day board games and the items of domestic hardware kept under the stairs. I wanted him to take time over his decision, sure. It was important; it had to be fully considered. But exactly how much time did he need? Wasn't it obvious what he should do with Abran's phone? Why didn't he just say it?! As for the small matter of my confession, well, of course, I wasn't particularly looking forward to being in the middle of nowhere and with only Grande to protect me, at the moment Jools would come to learn that his blushing Berkshire bride-to-be had paid for sex with a prostitute, was herself a prostitute (quite a good one, according to the feedback), and – if this didn't kill off the wedding plans, nothing would – only three days previously had conducted an interview that was so spectacularly uncompliant with the Police and Criminal Evidence Act that, not only had the questioning been degrading and oppressive, the suspect hadn't been cautioned *again*! No, I wasn't looking forward to that. But keeping it bottled up was making me want to scream.

And then he welshed on our deal.

'Here,' he said, as I came back into the lounge bearing an armful of logs. By his chair lay the dragon book. In his outstretched hand was the phone.

'I didn't know you'd even brought it with you.'

'Didn't think we should let it out of our sight. Take it.'

I stacked the logs on the hearth and did as he asked.

'Don't want you getting into trouble with Mr Kelsey, or whatever his name is.'

'Seriously? Don't worry about Mr Kelsey. I'll buy him a phone out of my own money if I have to.'

'No, no, I'm not worried about that.'

'Do you not think it'll be helpful to your appeal?'

He spluttered. 'Oh, I do. And it's not just the photo. The texts, the emails… There's enough there to release Mark Wells three times over.'

I stared at the phone and I stared at the fire and I dared myself to act before he could change his mind. 'So?' I asked, trying to keep my head. 'You think it'll put Freya Maskell in danger from Mark Wells?' Although Freya's involvement in setting Wells up wasn't totally clear from the phone, I'd made a point of telling Jools all about it. I'd thought this would place him under an obligation to pass the information on to his client.

'I don't think it would. Not necessarily. I'd have to box a bit clever about how I came by the phone – I mean, I'd have to do that anyway, to keep you out of it, and, obviously, I wouldn't tell him what Maskell said to you…'

Oh, so I was wrong.

'…but he'd probably not take it personally that one stranger killed another. I should think it happens quite a lot, in his world. And, anyway, won't Maskell have disappeared, now that she's grassed him up?'

'Yeah, probably,' I said. 'But, what, you feel sorry for her? Is that it? Is that why you don't want to take Abran's phone? After what I told you about the life she's had and everything…'

'You're joking?' He looked at me like he really thought I was. 'She stabbed a man in the heart, that's what you told me. When he was asleep. A man who'd done her absolutely no wrong. Do I feel *sorry* for her? I don't. I mean, I'm sorry she's had a shit life, but I still think she ought to be punished. So would the family of Femi Yar'Adua. Flippin' heck, d'you think Mark Wells' life hasn't been shit?'

'Then why are you doing this?'

'Because I don't think you'll marry me if I don't.'

'What?'

He screwed his face up. I thought he was going to snarl. He was being taken on an epically uncomfortable mind-journey here, and was holding me to blame. 'You're testing me. It occurred to me whilst I was reading this book. I couldn't figure out why you'd shown me the phone in the first place.' He stood up and faced me. 'It's obvious what you want me to do with it. Give it to Kelsey. You want Maskell to get away with her crime and Wells to take the flack for it. The fact that we could do rather well for ourselves out of a successful appeal doesn't interest you half so much. So I didn't understand why you didn't just take the SIM and put the phone out of harm's way; never breathe a word to me about it.'

He sounded pretty convinced by his theory. Still, he looked at me to see if I was going to deny it.

'You are, you're testing me!' he exclaimed when I didn't. 'You're still on your hunt for your "gentleman of the highest quality"! You want proof you've got him. Well, here it is. I'm rising to the occasion. I'm there; I hit the mark. If colluding in crime and miscarrying justice is your idea of quality.'

'I don't want you to do that.' And now I felt ashamed. 'I just want to get things right. I don't want us to be like my mum and dad.'

'Sure, you don't want us to be Cath and Ian. The heart's also-rans. You want us to be Millie and Si. "Love's Olympians", as you called them.'

Did I? The thought of saying something so pompous, even to him, I could feel was making me blush. I must have had too much to drink.

The rug on the old red tiles had tilted. Thoughtfully, with his toe, Jools nudged it squarely in line with the hearth. 'But what have Wells and Maskell got to do with us?' he asked. 'They're strangers. Live in a different world. Why risk what we have because of them?'

'They became important. Him to you, her to me. I gave you the phone because I wanted to prove that, when it comes to what matters to us, I'll put your choice first.'

'And, in return, you expect the same from me.'

I looked down at the rug. He'd not got it quite right. I pressed down with my foot and tugged it an inch towards me.

'God, you're extreme,' he said.

I looked up. To judge from his expression, I was transforming before his very eyes.

'I remember thinking that, the first day I met you, when you told me you'd punched someone in the mouth. Who'd do that? And who would admit it, like it was the most natural thing in the world, to someone she'd only just met? And you haven't changed. Friday night, instead of leaving your superintendent's office, when it was obvious to anyone that that was your sensible option, what did you do? You stood and laughed at him and your inspector, and then you stole his medal. And now this…'

I should have struck whilst the iron was hot; whilst we were on the subject. Again, though, I couldn't bring myself to do it. If he thought *that* was extreme…

But on the Tuesday I could stand it no longer. We'd just had our tea and he was doing the drying-up.

'Before you make any final decision about Abran's phone, there's a bit more you should know…'

Jools froze. The lumped-up tea towel he was using to knead inside a cup stopped turning. What gruesome new truth was I going to confide now? I drew breath and limped off down the home straight, the full-disclosure touch-tape clear in view. I staggered and I stuttered. Southern Escorts. Guilty Secrets. The emails to and from Freya. I squeezed out those agonising last ten yards. It was when I mentioned John Lewis that he dropped and broke the cup. He didn't even register what he'd done. He just stared at me. Still I drove on. The eye masks. The smell of fields. The first aid kit. The screams and the sighs. The delicate, tender act of mutual respect.

It was all too much for him. He didn't believe a word of it. This was off the scale. He woke from his spell and started jabbing away on his phone, trying to bring up Guilty Secrets. Obviously, there was no signal, so he couldn't. 'Evidence!' he said. 'I want evidence!'

He bundled us into the car and whizzed off towards Harlech and civilisation. On the way, our phones sprang into life and our inboxes began to refill.

And there, on both our phones, was Lorna's text about Dad.

Outside Co-op Funeralcare, I tie Grande's lead to the railings. I've taken him into Venters and Max Spielmann but, extreme as I am, even I wouldn't feel right bringing him in here. In here, it doesn't even feel right speaking at a normal pitch.

'Hello,' I almost whisper. 'I phoned yesterday. I've come to take Simon Marocco's cremated remains?'

The lady smiles, remembering my call. She leaves me and reappears with a bag. Inside is a heavy plastic urn and a white plastic rose. 'If I could just get you to sign a release form,' she says, and invites me to sit at a table. 'How did the ceremony go?'

'It was really nice, yeah.'

By the time they finally descended on Harlech, Lorna's texts were already two days old. Dad had gone to bed on Saturday night feeling no worse than on any other night. There'd been no warning signs in the evening and nothing that woke Lorna when it happened, in spite of her being next to him on a camp bed on the bedroom floor. On the phone Lorna consoled us with the thought of how lucky we'd been, knowing him again for however short a time. She said there was no need for us to come back that evening, but that we should come round to hers the next day.

All the way home, Jools couldn't have been more caring. 'You okay, love?' He looked at me across the gearstick. 'You okay, hon?' He smiled and squeezed my knee. The prospect of marrying a freak was entirely gone from his mind. 'It's going to be okay, Ru.' He got so imploring I had to tell him to keep his eyes on the road.

On the Thursday, Jools, still on leave, went into the office to speak with Lester. He told him that the travelling and the long hours were having a bad effect on his home life and that he wanted to pass on Mark Wells to someone else. That someone else, both knew, would have to be Lester himself. The boss was cold and left him in no doubt that he'd blown it, not that Jools seemed to mind. At least, he reported the meeting back to me cheerily enough, acting out Lester's lines with the full cockney kazoo treatment. Assured that my fiancé was content with his decision, I paid a visit to Mr Kelsey and handed him the phone, with all its data wiped. I said the police wouldn't be investigating a possible burglary because there was a chance the phone had been thrown from a train. He didn't agree but had the grace to say that his wife had raised that possibility, too.

That same day, I received a text on my burner phone.

> *Sorry to bother you. Can you tell me what's happening? F x*

I replied along the lines of:

> *Abran's phone is gone. Cut up the SIM this aft. You're safe and free. Going for a run tonight. Will chuck this phone in lake. Have a good life. R x*

It had been Lee who'd had the sense to ask, whilst there was still time, what kind of funeral Dad wanted. Humanist, he'd said. A respectable turnout, not huge. A couple of his carers. His solicitor. Rita and Rico. Millie's sister and her husband. Two families flew over from Marbella, one of them a Spanish family. The biggest contingent was from the Cattlegreen Birdwatching Association, which surprised everyone else, who'd never known of his interest. Jools and Rita gave the readings. The celebrant was a laugh a minute, the eulogy more like a best man's speech. That seemed fitting, somehow. Unlike the summertime musical tribute, 'Merry Xmas Everybody'.

At the end the solicitor introduced himself to Lorna and me. I'd already asked who he was because I'd seen him whispering to people in the congregation and they'd turned and pointed our way. He told us we'd been named as the sole beneficiaries of the will, the entire estate to be divided equally between us. Based just on the forecast selling price of Dad's place in Cattlegreen – so, leaving his Marbella property out of the calculations, along with all his other stuff, the value of which still has to be worked out – we're looking at receiving £730,000. Each.

Mum was also at the funeral. She took the afternoon off work and had come in her business clothes. She held it together during the service but when I went to find her afterwards, to tell her I'll soon have a lot of money and to ask if she wanted some of it, she was nowhere to be found. We'd agreed we'd go together to the reception at The Bird. I found her in the crematorium car park, lying on the back seat of her car. Her sobbing was so loud I heard it from ten yards off, before I could even see she was there.

1.10pm

A couple of tables away there's a girl. No more than eighteen, at a guess. She's by herself except that on the chair next to her is a cot. The baby is smiling and doing that baby-wriggle, like she's trying to make herself comfortable inside an invisible suit. Mum is too busy texting to notice. And when her baby gurgles and giggles, she doesn't hear because she's got her earbuds in. She should be careful. The baby is hard to resist. Someone could help herself to that baby. Maybe I should…

Jools is standing in the doorway, looking round. He's smart in his courtroom suit. I wave and his face lights up. He winds his way to our table.

'Did you get them?' he asks. The weather is hot and his jacket clings to him as he tries to take it off.

'The ashes? Yeah. Cor, you get quite a lot for your money. I thought I'd get, like, a sachet.'

'Where are they?'

'I put everything in the car. We're still going for a walk, aren't we? Yeah, wasn't sure that Dad would want to come along.'

Jools jolts out his tongue and winces. 'That was probably the last time I'll ever go to Thames Frockley Magistrates' Court,' he says, changing the morbid topic of conversation.

'Why did they send you out here?'

'This was the money launderer's first hearing. Adjourned from two weeks ago. You know? The case that led to my downfall?' He stoops to kiss me and takes the seat next to mine.

'Ah, that one.' Things just don't stick to my mind since Dad died. Jools has to remind me about everything.

'All a formality. Forty miles from town. Five-minute hearing. Rather than get an agent to cover it, Tommy had me traipse out here. I'm getting all the rubbish now I'm leaving.'

Yes, I remember. Whilst we were away, Lester put Tommy in charge of the lawyers' diaries, so that she decides who goes to which court and who stays in the office to catch up on work. This is the case Jools and Tommy fell out over during his first week back. Lester took her side and it ended with Jools handing in his notice.

The waitress takes our order for orange juice and salad.

'And was the client nice? Was he a nice money launderer to pass a morning with?'

'I suppose he was all right.' Jools pulls his sniffy face. 'It was his "things" I took exception to. His Savile Row suit. His Porsche. I kept thinking, *But where does the money come from? Whose money do you use to buy all this?* I've got a downer on my clients generally, actually. I was with Sonny in Camberwell yesterday—'

'Sonny Bryant?' My face lights up. 'You didn't tell me.'

'Yeah.' To judge from his expression, the memory Jools has in mind is not our joint happy one. 'We were waiting at a pelican crossing. There was this street-cleaner next to us. He was really working hard, really taking pride in making the pavement nice. Then the lights change, and what does Sonny do? He drops his fag end and crushes it into the pavement, exactly where the man had been cleaning, with his brand-new stolen trainer. I just stared at him and thought, *You bastard.*'

'Ah, don't say that. You'll spoil our story.'

'*The Story of Our Love*?'

We put on our soppy faces. He bills it. I coo it.

'I wouldn't mind if there weren't so many of his type in *The Story of Our Love* from now on. In fact, I don't know why I ever thought criminals so interesting and rugged and colourful. Maybe I'm getting old. Nowadays I just can't see what's so hard about *not* stealing, or selling drugs, or hurting or sexually assaulting people.'

'Maybe you need a change of direction.'

'Funny you should say that. I ran into an old acquaintance this morning; someone from law school. She's in a practice out Newbury way and they're looking for someone to work part-time to cover for the conveyancer, who'll soon be off on maternity leave.'

'Buying and selling houses? But that's not what you do.'

'The work won't be particularly taxing. Won't be well paid, either. But she said they'd train me up. And if I do that, I can spend half my time at the Centre.'

Dogs, dogs, dogs. It's all he thinks about nowadays.

Our lunch arrives.

'I brought this for you,' I say, and pull from my bag a copy of this week's *Cattlegreen Messenger*.

'*One Year On.*' Jools reads the headline. Then he studies the photograph beneath. 'Who are these two?'

'That's…' I contort my mouth into a familiar impersonation.

'She looks different from what I imagined. Katie Teague, eh? And who's this Mulder to her Scully? "Superintendent Oliver Bartlett". Oh, your other great pal.'

His expressions change as he goes through the article. His eyebrows rise at the passing of time – it's been twelve months since Tony Gibson died. He pouts in awe at the superintendent's ambition to reopen the investigation and bring closure to the bereaved. He grins at the proof that what I've said is true: that Katie Teague will do whatever it takes to get on.

'"'I'll stake my career on this,' says Superintendent Bartlett." That's bold. "'My colleague, Inspector Katherine Teague, has both a wealth of relevant experience from her time with the Metropolitan Police and a deep knowledge of this case from her work with the MCT... together we shall work tirelessly, finally to bring Mr Gibson's killer to justice."' Hm. Best of luck with that. Do you think they'll get to the bottom of it?'

'Dunno. Maybe they're keeping something up their sleeves. If not, they'll need to rethink the theory that Freya killed him and start again from scratch. Otherwise, they'll be wasting their time.'

'But we don't know that Maskell didn't kill Tony Gibson. I mean, just because she swore blind to you—'

'She didn't kill him. Oh, God. I'm sorry, Jools. I didn't tell you.' Bless him, he's been so kind, knowing not to bombard me with questions whilst my mind has been all over the place. But it means there's still so much he needs to know. 'At the point you and Freya were sitting in the police station reception that Friday night, Tony Gibson was still alive. In fact, after a lovely afternoon at the Flower Show, he was at Thames Frockley railway station helping an old friend onto the last train to Watlington.' I tell him about my pigeonhole discovery. 'Hannah had sensibly torn the date off the top but it was a thank-you letter, so presumably it'd arrived pretty soon after the event. I remember now that, once, when I went to Hannah's, she questioned me quite closely about the precise time that Freya came to the nick to confess. Like I say, she took steps to make sure nothing can be proved against her, but it's a dead cert she knew, within days of his death, that Freya hadn't killed Tony.'

'Why didn't she say anything at the time?'

I shrug. 'Because she held Freya to blame for everything else that happened, even though she knew she wasn't responsible for Tony's death.'

'Why *did* she admit it in the end?'

'I'm not sure. She'd say she admitted nothing. In her letter to me she said Bryony's words proved only that Tony had a nicer side than the one we all learned about from his computer, which was why she sent what she wrote. But I think she was, very subtly, telling me not to worry too much about justice not having been served. She made it clear enough that, far from wrongly being freed, Freya should never have been in jail in the first place.'

'And yet she let her rot there anyway. Jesus Christ.'

'And, if I had thought to caution Freya that Friday night, instead of saying how "nice" she looked, that's probably where she'd still be.'

Jools considers this whilst he chews on his salad. He also considers – I know this because there's a smile threatening to break out over his mouth and he can't quite stamp it dead – saying something that I might or might not find funny, depending on my mood and the way he says it.

'Out with it,' I say, and he finally dares to grin.

'So, that nasty barrister who gave you a hard time over the caution, and that silly judge who ruled out Maskell's confession, and the whole idiotic system, were, well... right?'

'Hmmm.' This is a suitable point in the conversation to look over to the next table and check on that baby. I see she is safe and being attentively entertained by Mum.

'By the way,' Jools says. 'Seeing as you mention that Friday night. I never told you what Freya Maskell and I talked about when we had our consultation.'

'It's still confidential, isn't it?'

'Yes, although that issue has become, shall we say, er, rather theoretical, in light of everything that's happened.' Still he lowers his tone. 'Anyway, she's unlikely to complain if I tell you. You of all people. And she owes me. She's got away with murder because of me. She didn't even have to pay.'

'Why do you want to tell me now?'

'It's the last secret I can think of.' He glances at me, suspicious that the final day of the amnesty might have passed. 'We're still being open and honest?'

'Definitely.'

'Right, well, the truth is that she never told me anything that could have helped your investigation or would have altered anything that happened to you or anyone else.'

'What *did* she say?'

'So, yeah.' He begins to stroke his neck. 'As soon as we got inside the conference room I could see we were going "no comment". She was a bag of nerves. I thought she might be on drugs.'

'She may have been, I think, around that time.'

'Yeah, so.' He sniffs and takes a mouthful of orange juice. Breaching even Freya Maskell's confidentiality is dragging him through hell. 'When I did finally get her to string two sentences together, her precise words were, "I've done something dreadful. If I don't tell them about it before Monday, things'll get much worse." Monday was when Abran was called to give his "evidence" in the Mark Wells trial. That was when he "buried" him.

'At the time, she wouldn't say any more about it. I had to try and gain her confidence; that's what took so much time. And then, just as I thought we were getting somewhere and she was going to give me some proper instructions, she asked where she'd be staying that night. I told her that, if she confessed to the police that she'd murdered someone, then she wouldn't be going home, if that was what she was hoping for. She seemed to think she'd be released, that it'd all be done by appointment, that she could get her affairs in order and face the music maybe in a few weeks when she felt ready. Anyway, once she knew she wasn't getting her fix that night, or whatever pressing reason it was she had for getting out of there, she entirely changed the subject.'

'Onto what?'

'Well, onto…' He sighs. 'Onto you. She said, "She's very beautiful, isn't she, Learner Detective Marocco? How do you know her?" And I told her. In fact, I quite forgot myself. I was totally indiscreet. Told her about Sonny Bryant, Sergeant Jenner, Jess Ennis, the lot. She sort of…'

'Gets you to tell her your secrets?'

'Exactly. Anyway, it was when I told her that I was going to take you to San Gimignano's after the interview was over and ask you to marry me that I got the first real sign of life out of her. She was cross; said she couldn't believe I'd changed my plan for the sake of securing a client. And yeah, so, basically, she told me off. After which I explained the caution, advised her to give a "no comment" interview, tutored her through the tricks you'd pull to make her comment anyway, and that was that.'

'She didn't say anything else?'

'Mm, no. Not that I recall.'

'Nothing more about your marriage plans and where you should pop the question, seeing as it'd probably be too late after the interview to take me to San Gimignano's and, in any case, I might not by then be in a very receptive mood?'

'Erm…' He squints at the ceiling, appearing to try to recall. 'You know, don't you?' he says, dropping the pretence.

'Yes. Although I really had to beat the hell out of her before she'd tell me. Of all her secrets, that was the one she clung on to the hardest. But I want to hear your version.'

'Okay, so.' In his anguish, he undoes his top button and loosens his tie slightly. 'She said that when she was little she'd been placed in emergency care and her foster parents had taken her to the Surrey Hills. To Leith Tower, in fact. And they'd said that that was where they'd got engaged. And, well, Maskell thought it was lovely. And she'd always hoped that, if someone ever asked to marry her, that's where they'd do it. Which, looking back, may have been where I got the idea from to—'

I shake my head. 'All my dreams about my engagement day… all the time and money I spent on *Berkshire Brides*…'

He nods sadly. 'And it was all the brainchild of your murder suspect.'

3pm

Strolling along the Frockley stretch of the Thames towpath, I remember, as I do every few hours, that quite soon I'm going to be rich. Normally, the thought disappears as suddenly as it comes and then the same old faces resurface in my mind. Femi, Freya, Abran and – leading the pack, of course – my dad. So far, beyond having had my offer of a share in my legacy politely and firmly declined by my mum, I've not given any thought at all to what I'm going to do with it. This time, though, I think I may have a plan.

'So,' I ask Jools, 'are you going to go for this Newbury job?'

'I dunno. It's all come a bit out of the left field. But it'd be handy for Waifs 'n' Strays. I definitely want to get more involved there. Get on the payroll if I can, eventually.'

'How would you feel about moving out there?'

He looks at me. 'Yeah, I'd like to. It's rural, pretty. And it's not much further from Cath and Lorna, just from the opposite direction. What are you thinking?'

'I wouldn't mind putting some distance between me and… certain people. Make a new start at a different nick, a different force, maybe. Or even take time out. You still want to start a family?'

He squeezes my hand. 'Yes. I do. As soon as you're ready.'

I try to smile at him but end up biting my lip. The joy I feel is the sort that makes me want to cry. 'Shouldn't we get married first?'

'Again, as soon as you're ready. Coach-and-horses production? Honeymoon in the Maldives?'

'If that's what you want. Register office would do me, and a pint down The Grapes. Back to Wales for the honeymoon. I want to run up and down those hills.'

'Bloody hell, Ru. You've changed your tune.'

'I've learned that it doesn't matter where you make your vows, or who sees, or which holy book you swear on, or what you wear at the time, or what you do afterwards, or how much you spend on the whole shebang. It only matters that you've found the right person. And, as far as that goes, I think I've done my preparations. What? Don't you agree?'

He shakes his head dizzily. 'I couldn't agree more.'

'You don't think I'm… too extreme?'

In the aftershock of recent revelations, he snorts. 'You're sometimes… very extreme. But you're elite. I imagine top performers are all prone to taking things to the extreme. It'll make my life exciting. I just hope I'm not too dull for you.'

He knows this is a stupid remark and doesn't really expect me to answer. Anyway, I'm not going to.

'Something else I was wondering. Has Mrs Chadwick still got her sights on that barn?'

'She's been talking of little else. I made contact with the owners, who've said they're open to offers. Mrs C's discussed it with the fundraising people and there's talk of a massive drive.'

'If I bought it for the Centre do you think they'd agree to name it after my father?'

'"The Si Marocco Annex"?'

'Yeah, something like that.'

'I'm sure they would.'

We pause whilst Grande lopes down off a sandy rim and laps up some mouthfuls from the Thames. Meanwhile, Jools smiles to himself, digesting my proposals.

'I'm glad you said we should meet up after my court hearing,' he declares. 'I'm enjoying this walk.'

The river winds its way under the motorway and gradually back into town. The working day is ending. Above us is the sound of traffic. Here on the towpath, people head for the station or, like us, walk their dogs. Now we enter a quieter stretch; one that is suddenly familiar.

'Omigod,' I say. 'Look where we are.'

'The famous Thames Frockley Travelodge!'

There it is ahead of us, backing onto the river. I hadn't realised we were this close.

'You know,' I say, 'I've never actually been here before.'

A flight of stone stairs leads from the station approach down to the towpath. It occurs to me, as we come back into the sunshine from under the station bridge, that these are probably the steps that Tony came down after he'd kissed Bryony's cheek and she'd waved goodbye from the train.

'Did Maskell tell you why she came to the police station that night?'

We're walking more slowly now. I'm struggling to focus on Jools's question. For some reason, the closeness of the Travelodge is making me nervous. I'm starting to imagine Tony's corpse, ill-tempered and decayed, emerging from the water, staggering blindly to join us on the bank.

'She'd cracked under the strain. She and Abran had been plotting for years to get even with Wells, and now that his trial was about to start and it all looked like it might happen, she realised that she'd never thought it'd come this far.'

'Why did she have doubts?'

'She'd always thought the scheme was too elaborate to succeed. It depended on too many things. She'd had to steal one of Wells' cigarette butts from his ashtray at The Butcher's Arms. A little thing but, at a packed Halloween party, quite hard to do without being seen. And then, after Abran had dented the BMW – he said in court it had been Femi at the wheel, but Femi was so off his face he wouldn't have been capable of even drunk-driving – after that happened and they'd left the note on his windscreen, they had to get home and kill Femi before Wells turned up. If he turned up. Amazingly, it all went according to plan.'

'So where did Maskell kill Femi?'

'In Abran's bungalow. As soon as they got home. By this time Femi was sound asleep. And that was another reason why this all worked out for Abran and Freya. She told me there's no way she could have done it if he'd been able to defend himself. Anyway, yeah. They brought him into the bungalow, he fell back to sleep and she stabbed him.'

'It says in the court report that Abran dropped off Maskell at the station and she didn't go back to his house.'

'That was to throw people off the scent. No one would think Abran did it. So if Freya wasn't there, why wouldn't it have been Wells?'

'God.' Jools can't believe it. 'You know, it's funny. The one person Mark Wells never suspected of framing him was Abran. Or Brandon, as the Crown will have named their witness.'

'That's another reason why Freya was so scared of Wells' trial starting. Abran had really upped the stakes there. When Wells killed his father back in '98 he racially abused him. It appealed to Abran's sense of poetic justice that the words Wells used should come back to haunt him. So he wove the same words into the script, knowing that anyone investigating would see the similarity. The danger was, though, that drawing attention to that earlier crime might arouse suspicion, especially at court when, all these years later, Wells would finally see Abran again. Freya thought Wells might recognise him. But he didn't.'

Jools ponders. 'Maybe the name change foxed him. Or maybe Wells has given so many people a reason to want revenge, he can't remember them all. But why did Femi have to die? What had *he* done wrong?'

'He was the lowest of the low, in Abran's eyes. A traitor. He'd been Abran's carer. Abran had really relied on Femi, and liked him a lot. It was hard to gain Abran's trust, but once you were in, you were in. But if you let him down... *whooah*.'

'What did Femi do?'

'Fleeced him. Systematically stole from his account. Abran had made himself pretty rich but, from what Freya says, he didn't keep as close an eye on his finances as he should have. Let Femi deal with everything. And Femi might have got away with it. But then he got his brother in as a builder, supposedly to do work on the bungalow roof. Did no work and demanded thousands of pounds. Abran was on to him by this time, though, and got a private investigator in. Femi was rumbled.'

'It was all so incredibly complex, though. Why didn't they just get guns and shoot them?'

'They talked about using a gun. They actually fell out over it. Abran wanted to do all the killing himself. Femi first, then Wells. But Freya was scared he'd then turn the gun on himself.'

'Why would he want to kill himself?'

'His disability was getting worse, for one thing. It wasn't terminal but there was less and less he could do. And there wasn't much in his life apart from his schemes for revenge. The thought of getting even was what kept him going. I think, most of all, Freya knew the guilt would be too much for him. Turned out she was right. She said it was all he could talk about in the weeks before he threw himself under the train.'

The doors of the Travelodge bar are open and people are taking their drinks out onto a concrete patio. There is no sign that this is Tony Gibson's anniversary; no acknowledgement that he was once a guest.

I nod at the spot, not twenty yards away, where Freya dropped her handkerchief on the floor. 'That's where Freya and Tony met, just before he died.'

'And you've still no idea how that happened?'

I shake my head. 'We're going to have to leave that one to Mulder and Scully.'

Bryony's letter implied that, after he'd left her at the station, Tony was going to fetch his car and drive somewhere. Home to his wife, I expect. So if he *had* come down those steps, he'd have had no obvious reason to go back into the hotel. He'd paid his bill and his suitcase was in the boot of his car. In fact, now I think about it, if the doors to the bar had been open as they are tonight, he'd have entered the hotel that way and I'd have seen it on the bar CCTV. He must have continued along this path to the car park, a couple of hundred yards ahead. Except he never got there.

Our walk brings us level with the cricket field. I remember watching film of the boys playing as I kept CCTV sentry duty on Tony's stationary car.

'So,' says Jools. He blows out his cheeks. 'An innocent man languishes behind bars. A murderer stays at large. And you and I are the cause. Partners in crime until the day we die.'

'Good. That means you can never leave me. If you do, I'll tell.'

There is a loud cracking sound. From the pitch, a red comet flashes across my field of vision.

'One thing I've never... Eurgh!' There is a splash in the water. Jools stands dabbing his head, looking from left to right.

A panicked boy in whites hurries to speak to us at the mesh fence. 'Are you okay?'

Jools is badly shocked, but I can see that he hasn't been hit. 'What the hell was that?!'

'The batsman whacked a six and,' the boy points to a foot-wide hole in the fence, 'it must have gone through here.'

Jools can only open and close his mouth. 'A foot closer and it would have killed me!' he says at last.

'I'm so, so sorry. We reported it last year at the start of the season. It looks like no one got round to fixing it.'